BETWEEN TWO SHORES

BETWEEN TWO SHORES

Donald Bray

WILLIAM KIMBER · LONDON

First published in 1983 by
WILLIAM KIMBER & CO. LIMITED
100 Jermyn Street, London SW1Y 6EE

© Donald Bray, 1983
ISBN 0—7183—0502—7

Typeset by Scarborough Typesetting Services
and printed in Great Britain by
Biddles Limited, Guildford and King's Lynn

Setting the Scene

Two hundred years ago the British were engaged in almost interminable warfare with the French, and somehow had to pay for it. Income tax being then not even a glint in the taxman's eye, import levies paid most of the bills. Eighty-one pages of '*The Shipmaster's Assistant and Owner's Manual*', a handbook published at the close of the 1700s, list heavy custom duties on the commonest as well as on the most exceptional of daily needs; a tax on just about everything and therefore affecting everyone.

To collect all this revenue required a force which competed for manpower with the overstretched armed services. Thus it is hardly surprising that more escaped the net than found its way into the coffers of the State, tax evasion being as respectable then, however deplorable, as it is now. Indeed, poorer families would have lived even nearer the knuckle were it not for the 'free trading' of the smugglers. Strange as it may seem, you could legally buy smuggled goods; only the organisers and their agents were at risk. And while smuggling was condemned by and large throughout the kingdom, there were some, notably that great economist and apostle of Free Trade Adam Smith, who considered the imposition of import duties the greater evil.

Smuggling, not merely though mainly in liquor − brandy, rum, gin and Irish whiskey − yes, and in tea too, was widespread all along those coasts of England which confronted the European Empire of France. Where the Channel was narrowest and the barrels and bales could be embarked and landed in a night, violence was at its worst. In Cornwall 'the Trade' flourished in part because, although the whole operation took at best twenty-four hours, the naval patrols were too thinly spread at the Channel approaches. But more importantly there was an affinity between the two opposing shores − hence the title of the book. Bretons and Cornish are of one racial stock. Their native tongues are almost identical, the pure bred among them look alike, their place-names and traditions are similar. And until Napoleon's re-organisation half of Brittany was the French province of Cornouaille; Cornishmen and Bretons had more in common with one another than with London and Paris. The history of both peoples is of independence and insurrection, the Bretons not getting rebellion out of their system until the early nineteenth century. Smuggling was big, even friendly business conducted in trust to mutual advantage.

Nevertheless there was a war on. Cornish fishermen, all experienced seamen and many of them smugglers, were valued members of any Royal Navy ship's company, where they sang 'Rule Britannia' as loudly as the rest, and probably more melodiously. They also signed articles as privateersmen. The private warships in which they served were licensed to make war on the King's enemies by letters of marque, without which they were classed as pirates, with all men's hands against them. But licensed though they were, with the strictest penalties against abusing their privileges, many Cornish captains and their crews missed no opportunity to trade with their cousins across the Channel.

In the few months covered by *Between Two Shores* England was at war with King Louis XVI of France and his allies the rebellious British colonies in America. Cornish rivalry between two smuggling and privateering enterprises has been assumed to have reached a crisis, the protagonists being John Knill Esquire, Collector of Customs and past Mayor of St. Ives, and the Carter brothers based at Prussia Cove in Mounts Bay on the opposite side of the Penwith peninsula.

While the Carters are renowned as smugglers, Captain Harry Carter having recorded, at length, his experiences as both smuggler and privateer, there is no direct evidence that John Knill was. However it is common belief that the great man, at no cost to his reputation, and some of the local gentry with him, operated a smuggling ring in West Cornwall. Knill and the Carters certainly owned profitable privateering fleets. Bessie Bussow is a historical figure too, though it is unlikely that her involvement in the goings-on at Prussia Cove ever reached the climax detailed in the story. John Harvey did indeed establish a famous foundry and shipyard at Hayle; but whereas his furnaces were in full blast the yard was yet to be, so has been antedated. The places mentioned are on the map, except for Cobben Cove, conjured up to make a sizeable little bay east of Godrevy, and for Jarnac in Brittany (not to be confused with Jarnac in Charente).

But of course the whole story is fiction and none the worse, I hope you will allow, for that.

Donald Bray

1

The lone watcher took a step nearer the cliff edge, as if a foot or so closer would resolve the shadow he saw, or thought he saw, in the blackness of the bay. Staring intently for as long as a man might stay unblinking on a shivering night like this, he aimed seawards the dark lantern he carried, indiscernible save by the smell of hot metal and lamp oil. Opening the shutter emitted a glow which he shut off almost as soon as the eye could spot it. This he repeated twice, peering into the darkness with mounting impatience, and an unease which was manifest in his tilting back his shapeless hat and, chilly though the air was, drawing his sleeve across his brow.

'Not a flicker. Revenue brig, bad cess to 'un'! But mebbe not.'

He worked the shutter again — three double clicks, three flashes. And there it was, the answering signal from the shadow that was now assuming the substance of a ship in Cobben Cove.

'Long, short, long. *Roscoff* for sure, and half the pesky night adrift!' The watcher, whose name — or nickname, the two being practically synonymous in West Cornwall — was Smeecher, fumbled in the depths of his voluminous coverings and dexterously flipping the shutter with his thumb illumined an enamelled watch. 'Cripes, sun-up afore this night's work is over! Don't like it, not nohow I don't.'

Now there was nothing to do but wait. The breeze was light and an unaccustomed frost began to settle, driving him to pace up and down with swinging arms and growing ill-temper once he had exhausted the dregs of warmth from the expiring lantern. The moon broke through the cloud-wrack, magicking into ephemeral appearance the schooner *Roscoff*. A Breton prize of an earlier war, she rode at anchor with her three great sails draped apparently negligently over the booms, yet the more ready for instant hoisting.

Smeecher shook his head. Long practice had make old Captain Lemmo over-confident. He ought to be out and away, and come in to pick up his men later.

A cloaked apparition rose suddenly above the cliff edge. Then shuffle, clatter and oaths out-dinning the surf two hundred feet below, a serpentine of figures hove into murky view shouldering casks and bundles up the perilous zig-zag path, and on reaching the summit grunted past the leader to drop panting into the dark comfort of turf and heather. But he remained standing, and bunching his cloak about him glanced uncertainly around. Smeecher, who as look-out and link man had vanished until sure he would not have to demean himself by lifting and carrying, emerged to peer into his face with a 'You, is it, Mr Davy?'

The face, so far as it was visible in the moonlight beneath a tricorn which, jammed on the brow, bestowed upon its wearer a hawk-like silhouette, was that of a tall man. His hair in a no-nonsense seaman's queue hung stiffly astern. The mouth above the strong jaw curved into a grin.

'Jack-a-Lantern himself, or I'm a Dutchman! All clear? It had better be, we're a sitting duck.' A jerk of his chin indicated the schooner in the cove.

'I've waited till I friz,' growled Smeecher. 'What stopped 'ee? Foul weather?'

'Fair wind to France and back. Missed the tide t'other side. That bos'un and his damned stores! Never mind, we'll be away before eight bells. Off we go, lads.'

The bearers resumed their packs and filed a hundred yards inland to where, in a paddock blackly enclosed within wind-twisted hedgerows, a dozen mules and ponies were herded by a youngster who materialised like a spriggan and whistled. The casks and packages, which their handlers knew from long usage to contain brandy, geneva, wine, tea and silks from across the Channel, were transferred to panniers protruding on either flank of the patient beasts. These, hired or commandeered from nearby farms, were as knowledgeable about the job in hand as their temporary masters, and would move off nose to tail at a whisper. A few words of Cornish-English and most of the men disappeared into the night. The ten who remained, recognisable as seamen by their gait and by their flapping, ship-made canvas trousers, moved in on Davy.

'Never signed on for this we never, Mr Davy, sir,' grumbled one as big as a bear and as shaggy. 'Fighting seamen we be, sir. We does as we is told — you do know that — but there's a limit.'

'You'll be paid for it, Gurt Jan.'

'Tidn' what we belong to do—'

'Look 'e,' Davy explained, 'If you-all hadn't borne a hand up the cliff, half this stuff would still be down there in the cove, and dawn but a dog-watch away.'

'Ought to be in and out by now, not humping kegs and sich, prime seamen as we be.'

Ned Davy, mate of the privateer and occasional smuggler *Roscoff*, took a groat from his pocket and juggled it from hand to hand — a natural alternative, when his patience was tried, to counting up to ten. In navy days you did not argue with a rating. But where in the King's navy would you find a coxwain as useful and dependable as 'Gurt Jan' Stona? Equanimity restored, he reminded his longboat's crew that had they not been delayed across the Channel they would have landed the contraband in good time, with all hands lounging on the beach while the shore party shifted the haul. As it was, everyone had had to turn to.

'Bos'un bloody Jed Trainer — all his fault missing the tide in Brittany,' moaned the only Welshman among them. 'Thinks he runs the ship, he do.'

'Enough of that, Taffy Evans. Now lads, Pencobben's as safe a place for a'run' as any in Cornwall, and you'll be back home at St Ives for breakfast'.

Davy wished, as he ordered the Roscoffs back to the cove, that he could be as certain of their safety at Cobben as he had said. Lewin, newly appointed captain of the Revenue brig *Fox*, was reckoned to be a keen officer not to be turned from his duty by the rustle of bank notes. Moreover there was a growing unease among the privateersmen, not with Captain Lemmo's involvement in moonshining — most vessels operating under letters of marque from Bristol all round the coast to Deal were prepared to risk their licences for a good haul — but at the carelessness which continual success had bred. Davy knew, and the lads knew too, of the captain's preference of late for the hard liquor he supplied to 'The Trade', rather than for the cheap wine taken from their humble prizes. No red biddy had such a song in it! Old Lemmo, Davy decided, was due for a frank and sober confrontation and he, the mate, would do it.

A flood of moonlight, and being twenty-two, brought him respite from the problems of the hour. Davy saw, rising beyond the shadowy clumps of sea pinks and samphire at the verge of the cliff, the schooner's masts and the tracery of her rigging engraved on a silvered sea. All was well. He mounted the one remaining pony, held for him by the impatient urchin, and tailed the procession which was clip-clopping towards a building now distinguishable against stars in a clearing sky.

'That boat o' yourn—' the urchin observed. 'I hopes *The Fork and Grease* don't get her.' This remark not immediately registering, when it did evoked from Davy a guffaw which disturbed his pony's habitual tranquillity. *The Fork and Grease* – *Le Faucon Gris*, as it appeared more appropriately in the *Gazette!* There was no limit to the British aptitude, a fusion of ignorance and whimsy, for corrupting ship names. *The Grey Falcon* was the big French corvette that, ever since France entered the war on the side of the rebellious colonists in America, had been plaguing West Cornwall. 'Off Sennen yester-mornin' she was,' the boy continued. '*Roscoff* wouldn't stand no chance agin her, mister, would she?'

'Chance,' said Davy, 'is a fine thing.'

The building, a Basset farmhouse and as such held to be immune from the Revenue, was soon reached. A slate slab in the dairy floor had been raised, disclosing an excavation ample to contain the contraband pending distribution. Such hideaways existed by the hundred wherever the trade came in by moonshine. Few however were discovered by the excisemen, whose slender tally of successes was achieved mostly at the time of landing. So the young mate's worries were over – for the time.

Stowage was proceeding under the direction of the hastily dressed farmer's wife and her tousle-haired daughter Jess, who was enjoying the excitement and would have enjoyed it more had the young officer stayed. But Davy made for the parlour where Farmer Porris, night-capped and sporting over a grubby nightshirt a preposterous Turkey shawl – it could have come only from a wreck — huddled in a rocking chair as close to the greying embers as the hearth would allow.

'Spanish influenza,' he sniffed. 'Keep your distance, young Ned. Here!' He poured a bumper from the flask on the table, and another, demonstrably not the first, for himself. 'None o' your rot-gut. What do 'ee think to it?' He appraised the young man who sat himself thankfully at the hearth — dark Cornish stock, broad personable features, powerful, tall beyond average — and still liked what he saw. 'You're late tonight. How's that, ah?'

Davy explained the circumstances.

Porris stared into the ashes. 'Drop one o' they logs on the fire, do 'ee now.' The last of his glass fought with his breath for throat-way as it went down, and he at once refilled. 'You're wasted as Lemmo's mate, I been thinking, and not for the first time. Not for the first time I been thinking that. 'Ess, I know thee've got problems, but who 'aven't? How don't 'ee settle ashore?'

'I'm a seaman,' Davy said.

'Of country stock,' added the farmer. 'Born to the land.'

Davy drained his glass and refilled it. It gleamed ruby in the candle flame. In that angry glow he saw again his homecoming three years ago, after His Britannic Majesty's frigate *Heracles* had struck to the Yankee rebels. Early 1778 it was. That at the time of surrender he lay, when decks had been cleared for action, sick and delirious in the orlop from the fever that was the curse of the West Indies station — so sick indeed that the Yankees had sent him home — had been no alibi when he had haunted Admiralty House for another appointment. The taint of a dishonoured ship precluded him from employment or further promotion in the Royal Navy.

In Cornwall, doors where formerly he had found a welcome were shut in his face, and he did not care to imagine the tales that were spread about him. To avoid contaminating the family roof he had quit the Davy manor house at Boswyn to take service under the old privateer-smuggler Bart Lemmo, who was not particular.

Ned Davy had succeeded in living with his past and had hopes of living it down. Privateering retained in Cornwall the gloss won for it by the Grenvilles and their kind. As for the smuggling he found himself committed to as a sideline, one did as one must. Davy had no more scruples in pocketing the profits of 'The Trade' than had most of the gentry, many of the clergy and not a few of the new 'Methodies', for all that the Wesley brothers frowned on it. But the hole and corner aspect of the business was far from his liking.

Porris misinterpreted his silence. 'You're giving it a thought, then, this − how do you seamen call it − swallering the anchor?'

'I'm thinking it's time I were off, Mr Porris.' Davy nodded towards the grandfather clock that ticked and wheezed in the shadows. He fished a paper from his pocket. 'The receipt, and your signature, please.'

As the farmer scratched with the mangey quill from the inkstand under the lamp Davy could not for forbear to ask, 'What's it to you if I sink or swim? If I swallow the hook or if I don't?'

Porris replaced the quill, then as an afterthought retrieved it and tossed it into the revived flames, where it shrivelled pungently. 'I'll lay me cards on the table, young Davy, danged if I don't. See,' he sniffed, 'I've got the holding my family farmed when Squire only spoke French and Earl Richard ruled the duchy, and what with a bit on the side, like tonight, and proper husbandry, Bolitho's Bank has a pretty penny o' mine in the vaults.' He chuckled. 'I'll say they has! But' − and his bloodshot eyes filled as the claret wafted him into self-pity − 'I 'aven't got no son.'

As he spoke Jess Porris entered, the candle she carried illumining the flight of stairs against the wall. 'Mother's gone to bed, and your stuff is all packed safe below, Mr Davy, where 'twill never be found. Now mind you two gentlemen don't talk all night, or what's left of it, 'cause I'm that tired, and as I sleep in the talfet above, Mr Davy, every word you say do come through the planching.'

Coy? wondered Davy. But no, that face − it was handsome rather than pretty − expressed nothing but sleepiness.

'Night both,' she said, and ascended to the talfet, the loft which commonly half-covered the main room in ancient farmhouses, while the remaining portion of this older section of the building soared upwards to the rafters.

Davy rose as she left and remained standing, reaching for his hat and buttoning his cloak. The farmer checked him. 'Five minutes more. Nothing lost. I was saying, Ned Davy, I've got no son. But I've got a daughter.' He looked towards the creaking flooring overhead. 'Seventeen at Christmas. A harum-scarum comely maid. Comely, eh Mr Davy? A maid as won't look at none of the local lads 'cept to spit in 'is eye. And I don't say as I blame her. But Squire now — he've took to calling of late, and I'll wager a bullock to a bean it aren't my plum cider nor Mrs Porris's apple cheeks he's after. And help me God,' he added vehemently, 'if I has Squire's bastard as my only grandson! For there won't be none other if that old lecher do have 'is way.'

The conversation was taking a turn altogether too involving. Davy settled his hat on his head. 'A delicate situation, Mr Porris, which you must handle as only you, Jess and her mother can. And now I must bid you goodnight — or indeed, good-morning.'

The farmer heaved himself out of the rocking chair with an alacrity scarcely consistent with an invalid and grabbed Davy's sleeve. 'Maid do need a husband, me a son. What do 'ee say, Ned Davy?'

Davy tried to free his arm and failed. Matters were moving altogether too fast, though to be sure considering his mother's selection of likely and well bred maidens he felt he could do worse. But this was neither the time nor the place, and he said so.

'Take young Jess to wife. I know thee've little but debts to inherit, gentry though ye Davys be. But I been thinking about this for some time, if I've lacked the occasion to say it, and I counsel you to think on it too. I've took to you, young fellow, God's truth I have! Marry the girl — there'll be a wopping dowry — give us a hand with the farm, and when I'm gone it's all yours. Just change your name to mine—'

'You go too far, Porris.' Davy was affronted.

'Then keep your own name — damme, 'tis a good one! — but take my Jess. Here, come wi' me and see for yourself.' Picking up the candlestick he steered the sailor to the stairs.

'Good God no!' Davy protested, while from upstairs Jess called, 'Now don't you do no such thing, father, Ned Davy. I heard you.'

But Porris released his tow to fling open the door, and the

reluctant, half willing and wholly embarrassed young man saw eyes bright in the candle light peeping above the coverlet, and hair and rag curlers a-tumble on the pillow.

'Shame on you! Leave at once,' she said.

The farmer's next move startled them both. He clutched the bedclothes and with a single movement jerked them back in a heap over the bed rail. Her short nightdress was rumpled around her waist revealing the light and dark of her limbs. She squealed and turned over, plucking at her linen garment. 'Yours and one day the farm, for a wedding ring,' said the farmer, resoundingly thwacking the bottom there displayed. So, Davy realised, would he thump the rump of a mare just brought to market. The girl lay supine and sobbing.

'You − you disgust me.' He had heard of daughters so misused. But Jess—

She shuddered with a yet deeper sob, and he was at her side in an instant. 'No, not you, my dear!' She was desirable, soft and lovely, and pink where her father had slapped her. He pulled the coverlet back over her. 'He's a pig,' she wailed.

'Give it a thought, young Davy,' sniffed the farmer, summing up the situation and not at all nonplussed.

What was that?

Abruptly the sobbing stopped. Davy strode to the door. There was a tapping on the window pane downstairs. A voice. The boy's.

Mr Davy! Mr Davy, sor! Mr Smeecher says to come quick. The *Roscoff*. She've been took.'

*

What a night! And now − this. Davy stared down into the cove. There, side by side in the pallor of early morning, not one but two vessels rode at anchor − the schooner *Roscoff*, much the same as when Davy had left her in the middle watch, and a brig. A brig notorious along the coast. The Revenue brig *Fox*. A jolly boat bustled like a water beetle between them.

'Got 'er, Mr Davy,' said Smeecher, 'when you was up at Porris's. First light and there she were. Took. Never a shot. broke up, she'll be. Sawed into three pieces—'

'Stow your gab, damn you,' rasped Davy, feeling somehow responsible. 'What'll you do?'

'Me?' said Smeecher. 'I'm off.'

*

Back at Bethlehem Farm, the territorial progress of the moonshine venture soon pursued a parallel course. A furious knocking on the front door, a raucous bellow of 'Open up, open up in the King's name!' brought farmer Porris, snoring in his chair, to which he had retired to assess the profit and loss of the night's work both under the kitchen and over the parlour, to slippered feet in one instant and to the blunderbuss above the mantelpiece in the next. In that same instant a gap in the curtains revealed in the dawn light three dragoons at the porch and a fourth in the yard holding the horses.

Upstairs in the new wing Mrs Porris hurled herself from the four-poster in which, despite or because of her spouse's absence, she had slept so soundly this past hour although the hands had turned to and the milk was already swishing into the pails between the milkmaids' knees. She flung wide the casement and glared down upon a trio of helmets, one new and gleaming, the others dull and dented, at the farmhouse door. 'Well I never! Never in all my life!' She stuffed her hair into her mob cap, dressed in haste, and hurried down the wide and carpeted main stairs.

Miss Porris too was as swiftly out of the narrow bed she had occupied ever since infancy, and in which she had lately experienced so novel, so humiliating, so strangely gratifying an encounter. At the top of her humbler, bare stairs, in paper curlers and a wrap over her outgrown linen nightdress, with toes peeping and fluttering apprehension, she awaited what next would transpire in this extraordinary night.

'Open, I say, in the King's name! Open, or we'll break down the door!'

The manservant, muttering obscenely at such affront to his three-score and seven — he had been brought in from field and cot to big-house comfort in his old age and was not wont to rise until the family summoned him to the kitchen range — clumped down the ladder from the loft. Shirted and stockinged and ash stick in hand he stationed himself by the door, his skinny knees knocking.

'Leave 'em in, Jacob, blast 'em!' The farmer laid his gun on the table along with empty glasses and 'dead men', while old Jacob shot the bolts.

First came a sergeant, he of the raucous voice, then a trooper, both of them at the ready as if storming a breach. Last an ensign, immaculately accoutred, who thrust his way to the fore and sauntered into the parlour.

'Resisting entry, my man?' He fingered the ancient firearm.

The farmer reddened to his bald and wigless crown. 'Yeoman I am, and nobody's man, I'd have you know. And put the thing down, damme, or you'll blow your bloody head off and mine with it, I shouldn't wonder!'

'So that's your tone!' The ensign gingerly replaced the blunderbuss and gazed round the room. 'What have you done with it?'

'Done with what? And I'd have 'ee know you're trespassing.' The indignant Porris, in his oriental shawl more resembling a eunuch of the Sublime Porte than a Yeoman of England, took a step towards the young officer, who shrank back demanding, 'Why ain't you in bed?' Riper years and experience had yet to guide him along the tortuous paths of cross-examination.

'My wife snores,' retorted the farmer. 'I get up betimes; farmers do, you know. And what the hell's it got to do with you anyways, dammee?'

The sergeant came to the rescue. 'We has reason to believe as there's been a delivery of contraband to this here farmhouse from a schooner what's at present under arrest in Cobben Cove.'

A gasp at the stairhead diverted all eyes to Jess, who thereupon turned and fled to her room, slamming the door. With initiative and presence of mind the trooper rattled back the curtains, increasing the daylight from a slit to a pattern of diamond panes, grey-lit, but a few picking up the rosy tint of daybreak. The guttering flame of the surviving candle died in a last flash reflected in the ensign's helmet, which was now off his head and cradled in the crook of his arm. And Mrs Porris, clothes thrown on anyhow for the second time in the past two or three hours, descended to the parlour and took charge.

'You'll take your wicked eyes off my li'l maid—' she addressed herself to the officer '— and explain what you'm doing here at this time o' morning, rousing decent folk from their beds. Sir Francis shall know all 'bout this, that I do promise 'ee.'

'That 'e shall,' echoed the farmer.

'A pox on Sir Francis!' the ensign ventured.

'Really—' For such blasphemy mere words were not enough. But the sergeant moved in between the advancing termagant and the uniform he was drilled to respect. 'We has a warrant, duly signed by a magistrate—'

'Tell me his name. Who was 'e? 'E'm finished, finished, do you hear? when Sir Francis do learn o' this,' raved the lady of the house.

'—A warrant to search these here premises. Mr Jocelyn, my ensign here, will show it to you, if he'll be good enough.' It sounded more of a threat than a request, and the young man fumbled sheepishly in his skin-tight jacket for the document. 'And if you will apprise us,' the sergeant went on, 'where the stuff is, 'twill save a mort o' trouble and damage we shan't be responsible for.'

'There's nothing here,' snorted Mrs Porris, eyes ablaze and confronting the sergeant with her matronly breasts heaving. 'Get out, all of 'e!'

But a shove in that ample bosom sent Mrs Porris reeling into the chair occupied by the young sailor not so long before. There she cowered, her brief dominion ended. The trooper, carbine cocked, stood over the farmer who likewise shrank back in his chair, the spirit scared out of him and ruin beckoning. Whatever Sir Francis may have guessed — condoned, even — public confirmation of his tenant's clandestine activities was certain to terminate the tenancy.

'But one single son,' the farmer moaned, 'and never a lobster would have dared—' A dig in the stomach from the trooper's gun barrel, a gasp, and the soldiers went about their task without interruption. The ensign allocated to the sergeant the search of the kitchen, while he himself poked about the parlour swinging his bucket of a head-piece by its chin-strap. It was an aimless operation which suggested he had matters in mind of greater urgency. The grandfather clock struck eight on its cracked bell.

'Sir Francis shall hear all 'bout this. It aren't finished, not by a long chalk,' screeched Mrs Porris in a desperate reassertion of authority, as the querulous shrill of old Jacob, and the smash of crockery, provided an unwonted acccompaniment to the cockalorums of roosters in the yard. Meanwhile the officer, having prodded and fiddled with oddments of furniture, seemed to have come to a decision. He mounted the stairs. It was full daylight now.

'Jessie,' Mrs Porris mustered the pluck to scream, glancing apprehensively at the trooper's red knuckles about the breech of his firearm. 'Jessie, you keep your door locked. Keep 'un bolted and barred, do 'ee hear now?'

A staccato of raps upstairs. A boot to the lock and spurs jingling. A thud and a crash. A horrible cry. The sergeant rushed in from the kitchen, Jacob shambled after him, and the trooper span on his heels towards the stairs, down which reeled the ensign with hands to head and a trickle of blood between his fingers.

Again at the stairhead stood Jess, now in her shift and with a mob cap over the curlers. A splendid, blazing Jess. A Jael of a Jess. And in her grasp the handle of a shattered chamber-pot. Time trod a-tiptoe, holding its breath. The ensign ceased moaning and leaned against the wall.

Jess broke the spell. 'That'll learn 'ee, my cock robin,' she crowed.

'Od's wounds!' cried the sergeant, 'this is going to take some explaining away. A capital crime, Miss.'

'So is rape!' snapped her mother.

'Attempted rape,' her daughter assured her. 'Didn't get very far, he didn't. I got in first.'

'Struck me, she did, with that filthy—' The ensign was almost sobbing.

'Listen!' hissed the farmer.

It was not the wind in the chimney. Likelier it was a roll of thunder.

'Ssh!'

Gun thunder.

They stood regarding one another — the farmer and his wife out of their chairs and she clutching his arm; the two rankers; the ensign with the blood congealing on his scalp; Jess.

'Gunfire, by God!'

Hooves rang on the cobbles. Someone hailed the trooper

there. At the reply the door was flung wide to admit a corporal, who hastily saluted. 'Mr Jocelyn, sir. You all right, sir? Recall, sir. Something's up. Captin says to rejoin the troop at Pencobben Point, sir.'

The military lunged through the door for their steeds, the ensign last, shaky but recovering. Jess appeared at her parents' bedroom window and tossed the young man's helmet clanging down onto the flagstones. Without a glance upwards he retrieved it, dented and no less battle scarred now than those of his men. And the five horsemen wheeled through the farm gate and spurred to a gallop.

'God's truth, the Frogs, do you think? If 'tidn' one danged thing 'tis another!' cursed Porris.

'They French aren't going to hurt us nohow, don't you fret. Never bother 'bout 'en,' soothed his lady. 'Too out o' the way we are. Now you listen to me, Jethro. We've got rid o' they pigs, and now we must get rid o' this shipment under the dairy floor. Never ought to 'a' handled the stuff, we never, profitable though it 'ave been. Into your breeches, my lover. Load it onto a cart presently and shift 'un to they old workings up to Nancemellin before people are up and about on the downs.'

'You're sound, my girl, sound' declared the farmer, patting his wife's massive rump. 'Then I'm going to see Sir Francis at Tehidy, cussed if I aren't! Turning honest folk out o' their beds. Tidn' right, dammee! As for you, Jess lass, 'tis proper proud of 'ee I am, my handsome. But you pull off them rag curlers and make yourself vitty, because you must come with me and get in with your story first. They up-country dragoons is a passul'o liards, the whole danged shoot of em'. Lying foreigners!' he repeated, stamping off to dress.

Jacob shuffled into the parlour, buttoning up his trousers as he moved. 'Maister,' he quavered, 'I do 'ear cannon, the roar of the guns.'

2

'What the devil!' Commander Tom Lewin, captain of His Britannic Majesty's brig *Fox*, shifted his glass from the huddle of smugglers on the beach to a brace of newcomers who with arms waving were stumbling along a half-tide ridge to get as close as possible to the man-of-war. 'Stab me! where did those hobgoblins emanate?'

Lieutenant Hawley, Lewin's Number One, ducked under the cover that shielded a table bolted to the deck beside the binnacle, and in the glim of a candle-lamp swinging from a hook there scanned the chart of the coast. 'From Pencobben hamlet back of the cliff, I'd hazard, sir.' He emerged to focus his spy-glass, too, on the gesticulating pair. 'Trying to tell us something. Can't catch a word, though, for the hullabaloo that damned moonshiner's kicking up.'

The complaints of Mr Trainer, *Roscoff's* bosun, were reverberating from two decks down, where with brief intervals to renew breath and strength he roared and thumped on the storeroom door. Captain Lemmo's heavy breathing in the dark was his fellow prisoner's sole contribution to the uproar. Old Lemmo lay supine in the bibulous stupor in which, along with the senior officer then aboard the schooner, he had been bundled into the naval whaler when Lieutenant Canfield had seized his ship.

Lewin, a languid young man of portly and somewhat dishevelled bearing, winked at his executive officer. 'Methinks he doth protest too much,' he quoted.

'Meaning what, sir?'

'If you don't know, Number One, there's nothing I care to discuss further. Send someone to tell that Bull of Bashan to pipe down, or I'll clap him in irons.'

A hush fell upon the deck; there was no sound beyond the groaning of the brig's timbers in the swell, the creak of the rigging and the everlasting rumble of the surf. Early sunshine gilded the mastheads and sails furled neatly navy-wise to the topgallant yards, but all else gloomed in the shadow of the great cliffs. The faces of the shouting men on the rocks, however magnified, were featureless still, their lips unreadable.

Lewin raised his megaphone and hailed them. They pointed towards Godrevy headland, which separated Cobben and Fishing Cove from St. Ives Bay, then scrambling to higher ground vanished as suddenly as they had appeared. The captain leaned over the bulwarks, looking aft to where the jolly boat was secured astern. Anchor cable, ship and boat on its long painter lay in a line from shoreward to sea in the ebbing tide. 'Pipe the jolly boat's crew to investigate, Mr Hawley.'

'With respect, sir, the whaler's. The smugglers in Cobben Cove are getting restive. I submit we bring 'em in.'

Lewin smiled benignly at his lieutenant. 'And so we should have, an hour since, had not this been a specifically combined operation. Lobsters for the land, my lad, and us for the ocean wave. And there if I mistake not the lobsters are, brass cook pots and all, accoutred for war.'

Within the rim of his telescope the foreground on the day-lit summit resolved into patches of green interspersed with folds of heather purpled as though by innumerable sunrises. Stunted trees clustered forlornly. And over the Knavocks, the upland hump above Godrevy Point, bobbed the brass and scarlet of a mounted troop.

As if on cue a minor avalanche heralded a hasty descent of the cliff as a small figure passed out of the sunshine and skipped and crept and slithered down the steep path. The smugglers – Lewin could now discern that naval renegade Davy – gathered round the boy. A brief interlude in which their heads had closed together like mourners' at a graveside, then they ran their boat down the shingle and pushed off.

'They're coming out,' Lewin began. But routines must be observed. A nod from the officer of the watch, eight bells clanged – ting-ting, ting-ting, ting-ting, ting-ting. The watch mustered amidships. The drummer beat Colours and the blue ensign of Commander-in-Chief, Plymouth, fluttered up the jackstaff, captain and officers lifting their hats at the regulation angle above black-ribboned hair while the ship's company stood to attention. Lewin noted that everything was ship-shape in the prize. Canfield stood at the salute on the poop of the *Roscoff*. Surprisingly the smugglers were resting on their oars while Davy stood in the sternsheets of his longboat saluting too.

The rat-a-tat ceased. Davy was hailing. 'Speak up, damn you!' bawled Lewin through his speaking tube. 'Come aboard — as well now as later.'

Davy pointed towards the headland, then turned to his crew like a choirmaster conjuring up the final chord.

They shouted together. 'What the hell are they saying?' cried Hawley.

'Please sir,' shrilled the midshipman of the watch, 'they're saying 'French corvette off Godrevy head'.'

'Faucon Gris!' the officers exclaimed together. Of a sudden Captain Lewin was all action. 'Call to stations, Mr Hawley. Cut the cable—'

'Soft sandy bottom,' interposed Number One. 'I can get the hook up in a couple of minutes.'

'Look, damn your eyes!' exploded Lewin, flapping an arm towards the cliff top, 'and do what you're bloody well told.'

Dragoons were dismounting, to stand outlined against the sky. They too were pointing. Aboard the warship the drummer — he was thirteen — pelted back up the poop ladder with his drum banging against his knees and beat to quarters. There was a rush of seamen up the brig's shrouds. A signalman stood in the chains, semaphoring the prize. The anchor cable, its severed end lashed to a grating, splashed into the sea and the jolly boat was cast loose, both to be recovered when the emergency was over; and the *Fox*, coming about in a wide semi-circle that took her inshore of the longboat and set it rocking, filled her sails with the land breeze and flew to meet the foe.

The longboat continued to rock, from the laughter and nudges the eleven Roscoffs and the boy aboard strove to conceal in the unlikely event of anyone in the brig glancing astern. Led by Gurt Jan Stona, their huzzas sped her on her way. It was the sort of cheering St Ives fishermen reserved for the downfall of the pompous at the spring games.

'A proper job,' Davy commended, 'while you two who brought the news from Pencobben upalong would go far as Noah and Japhet in the Miracle Play at Perran!'

There was more laughter and chaffing as the *Roscoff* shore party bent to their oars. Their young Mr Ned had won the first battle of wits with the Revenue, and God knew what devilments he was planning to recapture the schooner and be off before the *Fox* returned from her wild goose chase. For Davy the laughter was soon over. The ruse which had sent *Fox* off to seek out French privateers had worked well, but its weakness was the speedy return of the brig to settle the affair in the only way the career prospects of her commander could allow, victory for the navy – unless Davy could find that fresh inspiration which at the moment was utterly eluding him.

'They redcoats top o' cliff likely to take a shot at we?' asked the boy. He was the urchin who had unwittingly suggested the *Faucon Gris* diversion on the way to Bethlehem farm a few hours – they seemed like days – ago, and who had skidded down the dizzy track to warn of the soldiers' approach.

'Well out of range,' Davy assured him. 'They couldn't hit a barn with those carbines at twenty paces.' But he cast a wary eye at the cliff top nevertheless, and was relieved to see that the dragoons, who had advanced so near to the edge as to be in view from sea level, were occupied with the navy's dash, all sail set, to battle.

Davy must now decide whether to spread the boat's skimpy canvas and scud for Portreath, or to make a desperate and perhaps fatal attempt to retake the schooner. Portreath was opposite to where the brig must set course to double the point, and he might with luck gain shoal water and get his lads up the cliffs there before the avenger caught up with him. But to leave the old *Roscoff* and twenty shipmates to trial, judgment and a sentence intended to deter these bold moonshine runs for years was not to be thought of. Besides, they would probably take Captain Lemmo to a London court, away from the people who had so often applauded his exploits – and Davy too, if they could catch him. Two shot rooks dangling in the cornfield as a warning to the rest of the flock. 'Edward Davy, late lieutenant of the ill-fated frigate *Heracles*, whose ignominious surrender. . .' He could picture the paragraph in the *Gazette*.

'This 'ere skiff any use to us, Mr Mate?' Rowing steadily seaward they were abreast the abandoned jolly boat.

'It is indeed,' Davy replied, his problem solved.

*

Lieutenant Canfield, the elderly officer in charge of the prize, cupped hands to mouth and bade Davy lay off or he'd blow him out of the water. Two of his half-dozen seamen manned swivel guns mounted on the bulwarks to repel boarders. Other than these seven the decks were as bare as when *Roscoff* had traded between Biscay and Chesapeake Bay in the days of peace. The score or so Roscoffs who had been herded below under the man-o'-war's guns were battened down in the hold, as was evident from the clamour which followed their captor's hail. The commotion gave Davy a chance to turn to the jolly boat, towing astern and with the longboat's lugsail heaped between the thwarts.

'After hold, Jan. Use that panel in the cabin bulkhead.'

The heap moved. 'Aye-aye, my cap'n. Tie 'er up at break of the poop, sir. That'll bring me under her counter like we said.' Stona's muffled tones rumbled from the depths of the sail.

''Twill bring you nowhere if you don't stay still.' Davy dropped his voice as the row in the ship subsided. He got to his feet. '*Roscoff* ahoy! We're giving ourselves up. *Fox's* jolly boat is in tow.'

'Come aboard and no tricks.' Canfield's anxious gaze was shifting from the boat to the mouth of the cove, where the brig was altering course to round Godrevy.

'The *Falcon's* off the Head,' called Davy as his men shipped oars, and bowman hooked on to a ring-bolt in the schooner's tarry hull.

'So I've been informed,' Canfield replied, his grey hair whipping across his shoulders in a gust that bespoke a blow later on. 'But it's no longer any concern of yours.' He had kept the gate in the bulwarks closed and a swivel gun trained on the point of entry, where the prisoners had to climb over the gunnel. 'Eleven' he counted as the boy came last up over the side. 'None of you adrift, it seems.'

'All present and correct, sir,' Davy assured him. One of the prize crew had secured the longboat alongside. Davy saved him further trouble, making the jolly boat fast himself by hitching its painter to a cleat. It drifted astern, to fetch up beside the rudder and underneath the overhang of the cabin. The navy would doubtless move it, but there would be the batch of new prisoners to deal with first. This process must be stretched to the limit.

Each man was searched and his name written down for checking later with the muster list. Canfield was a stickler for detail. 'And the time of the arrest?' he added to Davy. 'I see that you possess a watch, which for the present shall remain yours. But I'll trouble you to tell me the hour.'

'Twenty minutes past eight o'clock; ten minutes to one bell in the forenoon. But had you not best prepare the ship for action, sir?' Davy was genuinely amazed that the lieutenant seemed unperturbed by what he must assume to be the *Fox's* imminent engagement with a powerful foe. 'You cannot intend to deprive your captain of this privateer's fire-power,' he went on. 'Four nine-pounders and eight six-pounders — a considerable re-inforcement.'

'I have my orders,' rejoined the other,' and they are to bring you to trial and justice. Away with the lot of 'em,' he roared. 'Down in the hold with the rest.'

'I shall require accommodation with Captain Lemmo,' Davy persisted.

Canfield revealed yellow, broken teeth in a mirthless grin. 'The old sot's in *Fox*. So's his bos'un. What's good enough for your men is more than good enough for you, damn your eyes! You'll join your ship's company under hatches.'

Davy moved so that the lieutenant was between him and the manned swivel gun. 'I'd have you know I'm an officer—' said Davy, prolonging the interview and gratifyingly aware that every eye was upon him. The companion-way, he noticed, was opening inch by inch.

'I know you for a damned turncoat—'

Davy hit him, full in that yellow sneer. The man reeled backwards against the gun, bowling over the seaman there with the firing lanyard still in his hand and mercifully swivelling the muzzle outboard as it blasted forth its charge of nails and metal scraps with a flash and a crack and a flurry of smoke.

Never, Davy was wont to observe, harking back to that turning point in his career when he resolved to retake *Roscoff* from the navy — never had two or three minutes stretched so long. Canfield slithered to the deck, fist to mouth and blood oozing down his chin. His eyes held Davy's with a rattlesnake fixety.

'You poxy pirate, I'll see you swing!' The words bubbled in his throat.

Davy, deafened by the crash of the perrier, the swivel gun which, fired half a second sooner would have obliterated his face, heard them nevertheless and they nagged at him.

The seaman at the gun picking himself up was grabbed by the longboatmen, but his four mates, cutlasses flailing, scurried up the poop ladders to join the fifth. He, the leading hand of the party, had already unbolted the perrier he was manning, and cradling the bronze tube gingerly in his arms — it was loaded — pivoted it in a mounting on the poop rail to command an attack from the quarterdeck where his officer still sprawled and dabbed and spat. The unarmed Cornishmen were casting about for belaying pins and such makeshift weapons when with a roar the hatch erupted and a score of Roscoffs bounded cheering over the coaming.

Cox'n Stona had climbed aboard through the stern windows from the jolly boat, as Davy had planned. Keeping off the upper deck and by way of the smuggling panel in the cabin he had unbolted the orlop door to the hold, then led his shipmates up the companion, snatching cutlasses from the rack in the cabin flat. They rushed for the poop cheering and jostling, to stop dead before the gaping bellmouth of the swivel gun, in its maw the frightful charge that one jerk of the lanyard would spread among them with certain devastation. The cheers fell to a muttering. Below the hatchway someone was shouting. It was Caleb Williams, the gunner's mate. "Ow 'ave 'ee stopped, ah?'

'They got us covered, Billums. Bloody swivel.'

Then a hush. Clicks from the poop a man's height above their heads as pistols were cocked. Moments swelled into silence like a stoppage in time. Canfield lurched to his feet. 'Poxy pirates!' he howled again, and leapt for the ladder. Davy was quicker. Catching the grey tassel of hair that flapped beneath the bow at the lieutenant's nape he swung him round into the bear-hug of Gurt Jan, a yelp of pain bespattering the big man with blood.

'Hold him in front; they daren't shoot then.'

'Aye-aye! I'll squeeze the life out of 'un if he do say a word, Mr Davy.'

The other captive was also thrust struggling to the fore.

Stalemate. The rudder creaked as it answered the pressures of the tide, the hull lifted grumbling to a wave and tugged at the anchor cable. The naval party stood tense above them at the rail, fingers on triggers and the lanyard of the perrier. Thirty pair of eyes glared at them — and past them to the transom at the stern above which were materialising knuckles and then heads and hands. Canfield's lips opened to shout, but the shout was a sob as Stona's grip tightened about his neck. Some fool howled 'Billums!' and the prize crew span about as Williams and a handful of Roscoffs tumbled over the transom and in a couple of bounds were upon them. Blades rang like a cracked bell; a pistol thudded; someone screamed — sounds thin but clear above the renewed outburst as Davy sprang onto the gunnel and thence into the mizzen chains while his men swept up the ladders or swung up over the poop rail.

There would be killings, and this Davy would not tolerate, at least against erstwhile comrades of His Majesty's navy. Steadying himself against the mizzen shrouds he cupped his hand to his mouth but could not penetrate the uproar. It was well for one life that Stona looked up at him and caught the gist: flinging the choking Canfield to the deck he bounded up the ladder.

"Vast there; avast!' his voice was as big as himself.

'Belay, belay!' Davy was heard this time. 'Disarm your prisoners. And hark 'ee—'

But it was not to Davy that they harkened. Across the water came a boom and then a continuous rumble. And another. 'Gunfire, by God! Heavy gunfire.' Privateers, smugglers, navy, they froze where they stood, gaping seawards beyond the stern lantern.

Canfield had made the top of the ladder. 'Look!' he croaked, pointing.

Past Navax Point swept a ship, all sails drawing. A warship, trailing a brown fog and with the smoke of a broadside still writhing from her gunports.

'It's a bloody miracle!' gasped Gurt Jan.

Davy swallowed and stared. 'The *Grey Falcon!*' he said.

*

Smeecher, having despatched the horse-boy to warn Davy, collected his mount at Pencobben village and was jogging up the path which meandered across the headland and after a long haul would bring him round the Bay to St Ives. He rode slowly, bowed in thought. Lank black locks protruded unbound from a hat that had long since declined into greasy shapelessness, its brim pinned up in front to the crown. The pinhead was an opal. This incongruity was repeated in the China silk neckerchief on which his chin rested beneath the collar of an outsized and patched militiaman's coat of the fashion of the forties. The morning glittered in a solitary, thick gold earring which gave the man a piratical appearance, seaman though he was not.

Smeecher was debating how best to present the disasters of the night to his employers. Squire might indeed be ignorant of his favourite privateer's moonshining: but Mr Knill — not he! John Knill knew what side his bread was buttered. Collector of Customs old John might be, but half the 'trade' that came ashore between St Agnes Beacon and Land's End was reckoned to be his. It was as plain as the nose on your face that an informer was at large; a local man for sure. Some dirty son of a whore in cahoots with an Excise bastard who hadn't the sense to wear fog spectacles and bank note eyeshades when a run was pending.

'But hold hard!' Smeecher told himself, kicking his heels into Tom's fat flanks to no effect at all. 'They Carters to Prussia Cove, now. They'm extending their territory, driving the single free-traders to sign on along o' they or go under. Likes o' we, though, is too big to clunk so they'm aiming to force us out of business with a nod here and a wink there. They got their thieving hands in this corant, I'll flip my token.'

With this conclusion Smeecher, his journey barely begun, topped the rise which brought to view the sea beyond and on the other side of Godrevy — and had him reining the horse back on his haunches as abreast the point sailed a full-rigged man-o'-war, bow wave creaming at her forefoot, nine open gunports a black chequer along the grey of her side, and every gun run out. Not one of the infrequent Royal Naval fifth rates to visit these waters. A gust caught the ensign beneath her main to'gallant truck and extended it as flat as a plank. The lily flag of France! A great carved bird at the prow spread its wings as far aft as the catheads, as if to swoop. Smeecher knew her at once, as who along the coast did not. She was the French corvette, predator in two channels. *Le Faucon Gris.* Damn his eyes if that didn't cap it all! What a night! And now Johnny Crapaud! Well, the Frog 'ud give bel tink to that there Fitcher *Fox* of a Revenue brig once she'd catched up with 'un, which wouldn't be long, for God's sakes no!

Smeecher shook his steed into a gallop, down towards the islet which marked the beginning of the reef local people called The Stones. He swung out of the saddle, turning Tom loose to graze on the velvety turf there, and stood with his outsized coat ballooning. The wind had freshened, westering and calling up the white horses. A glance to the right showed nothing of Roscoff but upper masts and yards, the blue ensign of Plymouth command flapping above the privateer's regulation red. Out into the open bustled *Fox.* She and the *Falcon* were on collision course, and neither knew it; neither could see the other. Smeecher pored, as it were, over a chart of the immediate future. So, he supposed, did old Granny Wisdom, the Lelant witch, visualise the about-to-be. The Frenchman's readiness to fire was explained by a raider's need to intimidate the shore dwellers. But what crystal ball had warned *Fox's* captain to run out his cannon? Not that it would do him much good. The corvette was positioned to rake the Englishmen, who would have neither the time nor the sea-room to avoid or reply with an equal blow.

Smeecher watched the corvette reaching athwart the tide with her canvas bellying, the brig the lee of the land with hers hauled taut and flat. *Falcon's* broadside flashed and boomed, sending the gulls wheeling and screaming as Smeecher peered into the smoke close inshore and a hundred feet below. The *Fox,* beaten to the exchange, replied feebly. That broadside, Smeecher realised, smashing along the brig's decks from bowsprit to jackstaff, could have dismounted half her guns and destroyed their crews. He was aware, now he considered it, that although the French were as often a smuggler's friends as his foes while the Revenue were the eternal enemy, he wished no Frenchie the mastery of an Englishman. It was a confusing emotion.

Eyes fixed on the drama at sea, Smeecher fished in his pocket for the gypsy's stand-by — though whether or not he was a gypsy he had no cause to know — a groat, a knife and a length of cord.

The groat he spat on and put back; the cord he hitched around his middle, frustrating the attempts of his militia coat to bear him aloft like Elijah; with the knife he cut a plug of tobacco which he had conjured from an exquisite snuff box and chewed with relish. A second French broadside rippled and roared. *Fox's* foremast and then her main topmast dived into the battle fog.

Now *Roscoff's* hers for the taking, Smeecher decided. Davy and his party were off the hook if they could dodge the redcoats, but it would be a Johnny Crapaud prison for the prize crew and the Cornishmen aboard. It seemed, though, that she would make a run for it. Her upper masts, all Smeecher could see of the schooner, had started to move. Her foremast swung away into the morning sun, so that from the hill-top the masts appeared as one, then the spaces between fore, main and mizen opened out again as *Roscoff* nosed into the north. Three great sails jerked up the masts. Topmen spread out along the foot-ropes casting loose the gaskets, and two sails above the foretop beat free, urgent for the wind. The ship moved into sight dipping and heaving on the swell. Smeecher conjured a folding glass from the recesses of his queer jacket and through it watched a dinghy, towed astern, being hauled up to the waist. A figure was bundled into it, a figure clear within the spyglass's rim and shaking its fist before fumbling for the oars. It was a naval officer. Captain Lemmo must have retaken his ship, but where were the others of the prize crew?

The *Roscoff* was tilting to a soldier's wind, her wake white in the morning, and heading for the point. The *Falcon* had held her original course but was now coming up into the wind, a mile off Hodder Down. The *Gazette* had reported her captain to be a Leroux of Vannes, a family not unknown to the smuggling fraternity either side the Channel approaches. To capture the British warship would be a victory King Louis could compare with those Commodore John Paul Jones's Yankee squadron was winning with enviable and, it was said, unpalatable frequency against King George. Smeecher reckoned Leroux would let the schooner pass, short of a shot or two to speed her going, while he made sure of the *Fox*. It was an outcome hard to swallow, nonetheless.

The corvette was not unscathed. Her main topmast was shot through. Hands aloft were cutting loose the jaffle of sails and cordage and the spars which shivered in their midst like a spider in a web. The flying jibboom swung at her bows from the forestays and was being hauled inboard for refitting. That would cost her a knot or two meanwhile; if Leroux did intend after all to put the *Roscoff* into the bag he'd not catch up before old Lemmo put his helm alee and hugged the headland, to skirt the reef. Knew every rock and shallow of the Stones, Cap'n Lemmo did. The Frenchman would rip his bottom out if he tried to follow, while at the end of the reef the 48-pounders of St Ives battery then in range would daunt a three-decker.

Smeecher readjusted his telescope to the nearing schooner, scanning the deck. Most of the crew would be below at the guns. Of those in view he recognised everyone except a couple in naval dress. Great John Stona towered at the wheel, and beside him stood Ned Davy, megaphone in hand. When had he come aboard? And where was the captain?

A couple of shots from the brig set the seagulls screeching again. The navy weren't finished yet; but what a shambles! In Smeecher's lens a crimson trickle from a gunport caught the eastern light. The blue ensign was being nailed to the jagged relic of a mainmast. A clutter of gear and spars trailed alongside − a battering ram that threatened disaster. The hammering of axes hacking it away tapped distantly. Several hands were fishing a spare yard to the stump of the foremast. *Falcon's* third broadside roared and Smeecher saw no more of them.

The *Roscoff* was now within range of the Frenchman's guns, but it was obvious that to Leroux the schooner was of secondary consideration. He turned away, the smoke still wreathing from his gunports, to administer the *coup de grace*.

'Now's your chance, Mr Davy!' Smeecher yelled, hopping with excitement. 'Down with your hellum and away past the point, and you'm free.' Davy might almost have heard him; in a lull in the gusting breeze the hammering aboard *Fox* was desperately distinct, while a cheer rang from the *Roscoff*.

A couple of farm hands now stood beside Smeecher. 'What's up, cap'n, what do she think she'm about?'

Smeecher span round, knuckles whitened about his cudgel. Absorbed in the encounter off Godrevy he had not heard their coming. They could have been redcoats. That was what came of forgetting number one in concern for others.

'Somethin' up, iss fegs!' observed the other. 'Bloody cavalry and all! Yon's Squire's *Roscoff,* an' it?'

More people were hastening over the heather, tin miners among them up from the night shift. Soon the soldiers would be there too. Smeecher stared back at the ships. 'God Almighty! The young fool! He'm steering straight at the Frenchman. Them Davys,' he went on, not bothering to explain, 'are poor but proud. Glory for they and damn all the others.'

'Frog 'll scat 'um to rags,' said a farm hand.

The crash of the schooner's 6- and 9-pounders, sharper than the corvette's heavier armament, deafened the watchers on the Knavocks. They saw through the drifting smoke the Frenchman swing away from the brig, etching an S in the blue water as she surged towards the *Roscoff,* now making for the open sea. Both vessels were canting steeply in the reviving wind. Two flashes and smoke rings spat from the long-nines in the *Roscoff's* cabin as she hurled defiance at her mighty adversary. A ball ricocheted to the rocks at the cliff foot, bounding from crest to crest like a skimming stone. As an afterthought Davy was hauling down the blue ensign of his captor and flaunting the red jack of a privateersman at every masthead.

'I'd shake your hand if I could, young Mr Davy, damn your eyes!' Smeecher muttered almost in spite of himself.

'Troopers!' someone shouted. They were jogging up from Pencobben. Smeecher clambered on Tom's back and was away.

3

Now Ned Davy must decide. To run, or to stay? — a choice that had nagged ever since sending Canfield ashore. Whether, having as in a duel exchanged shots, honour was satisfied. Whether the need remained to expose his little ship and her crew, all personally known to him and many of them his friends, to the raider's overwhelming might. Whether as originally

planned to show his heels to the man-o'-war, former antagonist
and likely to be so again should she survive. Or should Britons
stand together against the common foe?

Other considerations intruded. The smuggling charge. The
townsfolk's expectation that *Roscoff* would fight. They still told
in chimney corners and the fishermen's lodges how, sixty-six
years before, a French warship had dared the guns on the Island
and bombarded the town. True, only a young woman was
killed: Mrs Polseth's great aunt, it were. But them Frenchies
mustn't never be allowed so close again. That there '*Fork 'n'
Grease*' had done enough harm as it was. So bad as in the old
days when the Spaniards and even they dirty Turks ravaged the
coast!

This would not be the owners' view. Not knowing who they
were, he could guess. He could also guess their attitude to one so
misguided as to cost them their investment, down to each
quarter part of every sixty-fourth share in the ship. Better lie
dead in the scuppers!

Davy shook himself out of a meditation that must be causing
comment. This was no way to steel the nerve or win a battle. He
had been in action before, though with no further responsibility
than to obey orders. Brave men and a swift and armed ship were
not then his command. That was the difference, a difference to
inspire rather than to depress. To run left too many problems,
not least that it would confirm the charge of cowardice under
which, however unjustified, he had lived since he was eighteen.
Davy squared his shoulders, all doubt set aside. And indeed,
had he known it the agonising of these past few minutes was of
no consequence. A bold heredity, a strong body, a clear mind,
British tenacity and Cornish pride — these were the ingredients
of the young man's choice, from the moment he had first
opened sticky eyes under the eaves at Boswyn. He was not bred
to run; and he knew the ship's company was with him.

Having as he imagined chased the schooner away, Captain
Leroux returned to complete his conquest. With greater
manoeuvrability Davy came about too but could not tempt him
to pursue. Davy wondered how Captain Lemmo and Bos'un
Trainer were faring in the very different conditions aboard the
Fox, and found that he did not care. But the thought brought
home to him that the *Roscoff* was short of officers, and that there

must be temporary promotions. He summoned Mr Berryman, who excluding Mr Nankervis, less of a seaman even than he was a doctor, was the only officer in the ship besides himself.

'Should I fall you must command the ship. Meanwhile appoint a good petty officer or killick as your deputy, to take charge below.'

Temporary promotions were quickly settled; Coxswain Stona to be second officer, Jenkins acting Boatswain, and a 'townie' of Berryman's, Gunner's Mate Osborne, to be deputy Gunner. They passed close to *Fox* and rendered passing honours, though without raising a cheer from the crippled brig. 'They thinks we'm leavin' 'em,' commented Gurt Jan, 'an' 'twouldn' be a bad idea at that.' Davy wore ship under the lee of Navax Point, rather, he mused, like a knight in the lists, wheeling at the pavilion to snatch up a fresh lance and charge anew.

Le Faucon was bearing down once more on the *Fox* which, with fore and aft sails rigged on the jury foremast and what remained of the mainmast, was able to present broadside to broadside. The corvette's discharge left the brig a helpless wreck again, with what punishment to the ship's company Davy shuddered to imagine. Telescope to his eye, he clung to the weather chains with the crook of his elbow. Her deck was strewn with bodies and streaked with their blood, but young Lewin was on his feet, and the activity of keeping the ship afloat was resumed.

Le Faucon was closing the brig again, clumsily and by the use of her sails alone, her steering obviously disordered. The loss of her maintopmast in the first clash with *Fox* gave her a gat-toothed appearance, an appearance none the less dangerous, however, as she bore down on her prey, 'She's going to board,' masthead yelled.

This was *Roscoff's* opportunity. She ran free with mainsail bellying to starboard and foresail to larboard, tossing the spray over her bland and bosomy figurehead. She had wings, and she flew. She crossed the Frenchman's stern little more than a cable distant, each gun firing as it bore — six well aimed shots that obliterated part of the cabin windows and the fine, ornamental gallery, upended a gun, as could be seen through the gap, cut a swathe through the men on the gundeck and — Davy was sure, though the result was not obvious — rocked the mizzenmast with a hit half way between deck and top. It was disappointing that the rudder, still on its pintles, hung no less steadily than before, though the hands who had been at work beneath the over-hanging stern were not to be seen. Killed, or more likely withdrawn as we came in, thought Davy.

The French captain now turned his back on the British man o' war, and for the remainder of the forenoon demonstrated his belief that before he could achieve the triumph of bringing a ship of His Britannic Majesty George III captive into Brest, he must first capture, cripple or sink this Cornish privateer which snapped at his heels and bit. It was a conflict of attrition, the 140-foot ship, essential repairs affected, seeking to bring her greater weight of metal to bear, the 80-foot schooner evading and harassing.

By eight bells the turning tide had swept the *Fox* back into Cobben Cove, Davy's last glimpse of her showing her at anchor and re-fitting. Corvette and schooner, meanwhile, were tacking back and forth off Godrevy island, each vessel seeking her own peculiar advantage. They could see St Ives at nearest a league to the sou'west, where Davy did not doubt that scores of spyglasses were trained on the warring ships, those of wives, lovers and parents in apprehension, of owners in disapproving anxiety, and of most in the breathless enjoyment of a good fight. Grey cottages backed a harbour bristling, under the considerable armament of the Island (as St Ives peninsula is called), with the masts of craft that had fled there from the raider. The freshly hewn granite of the pier John Smeaton had built, lighthouse and all, eleven years previously lay ashen under the pall of cloud which overcast the westward sky. Upon the headland both combatants saw artillerymen standing by the fifteen cannon mounted years ago behind an earth rampart to prevent such an attack as that of 1715. On the battery seaward of the little chapel of St Nicholas on the Island's summit stood one of the new 48-pounders in forbidding silhouette.

At the opposite extremity of the Bay on Godrevy Point, where shoals, rocks and low, crumbling cliffs are surmounted by grassland that rises to the heathered moors, spectators swarmed as at a gargantuan version of the summer games. Among them the tunics of the dragoons made a pattern of scarlet. Drab groups lined the sands and outcrops; Davy knew, and Leroux feared them to be, villagers and miners awaiting the opportunity to wreck. Further down the Bay field guns were being drawn by teams of oxen, doubtless commandeered from neighbouring farms, along Upton Towans from the Black Cliff battery. Soon they would cover the strip of deep water between Godrevy Point and Godrevy Island.

The battle of ships was reaching its climax. Surely the little schooner and the corvette − distance did nothing to diminish the contrast − were about to settle their dispute; and few among the onlookers doubted the outcome. Why didn't the *Roscoff* make a dash for the protection of the guns while her masts still stood? This was in fact what Davy had in mind to do. Glimpses of smoke from the schooner, followed more often than not by white spouts around *Le Faucon's* hull, were occasionally pursued to the reverberating hills by the double-thud of a hit, with what result it was impossible to determine. But should she venture too close to the corvette, as the raider had tempted her to do more than once, there awaited her a welcome she was ill-equipped to receive.

Davy surveyed his command. Two of his 6-pounders and one of the carronades were dismounted, the ball that had struck the latter also killing the two helmsmen. Three bodies lay side by side in the scuppers, decently covered to await committal to the sea. Five wounded endured in the orlop the ministrations of Mr Nankervis. Davy was pondering the advisibility of sending them ashore in the gig, but short-handed as he was he could not afford a boat's crew. Holes in the hull needed prompt repair, while one on the water line was keeping the pumps busy. The schooner's cordage had been spliced and knotted time and again; it and the ammunition were in short supply. Sails replaced and patched were now past patching.

Davy had one more trump card to play; the reef. St Ives Bay can be thought of as a bowl, the open end of it, from Godrevy Point to St Ives Head, being four miles across. Nor'west from Godrevy two miles of reef, the Stones, lie like a part-lifted lid. This leaves a gap through which vessels come and go − by courtesy of the heavy artillery on the Island.

The Stones are at most a third of a mile wide. Half a dozen crags, Hevah and Tide Rocks the only two named by the local people, rise clear at the ebb, smothered with mussels and weed and encrusted with tiny shells. The greater part of the reef is perpetually submerged, two channels across it negotiable only by the initiated and indicated by the named rocks. That very year Mr Knill had commenced building the obelisk that was to crown Worvas Hill as a landmark to his smuggling craft traversing the Stones.

Towards the reef dashed the *Roscoff* close-hauled, the wave crests rattling her closed gunports, rigging taut and humming, masts a-quiver, spray flickering above the weather gunnels. Three cables astern *Le Faucon* plunged in pursuit, Berryman and the crews of the stern-chasers crouching on the deck of the shattered cabin awaiting a nearer target.

Impudently close, the privateer had fired half a dozen shots into the Frenchman's bows during the forenoon encounter: an unplugged hole still revealed to Davy's glass a lantern swinging in the enemy's foc's'l. And yet again the corvette was charging her tormentor, this time cornered at last with the long barrier of the reef ahead and a vengeful antagonist astern.

'Sir, better get more sail off her.' A worried Gurt Jan, limping and with his trousers ripped from thigh to calf, watched the surf and the flooding tide surging across the Stones.

'Wait,' Davy replied with greater confidence than he felt, glancing from seething waters ahead to crowding canvas in chase. He swung himself up into the chains, staring across the heeling deck at a couple of peaks lifting above the reef. Shags perched on them drying their extended wings, like wet, black miniatures of the pursuing figurehead. 'Mr Stona, you may reduce to fore stays'l and mains'l. We shall turn between yonder rocks when I give the word.'

'The Hevah channel, sir? All right for a cutter or a lugger—'

'The Hevah channel, Mr Stona'.

The schooner, losing pace and heeling less steeply, approached the tall rocks. A ball wailed overhead, another under the lee counter raised a splash which ghosted above the bulwarks, but proved its substance by a downpour on the quarterdeck.

'Helm alee!' and round the schooner swung on her new course, under a scatter of chippings as a ball struck the rock.

Roscoff was riding the swell. Davy on the lee side and Stona to starboard had men with long sweeps to fend off the rocks, the seaweed from which was brushing the hull and waving like Medusa's hair as the rollers curved and creamed over the reef.

A squall had passed over St Ives and was hissing, a turmoil of wind and rain, towards the Stones. Another hazard. And the corvette — did she follow?

'God help us, she's heaving-to!'

Her larboard guns were run out, and this time there was no escape for the *Roscoff*. It was a scene her survivors, if such there should be, would not forget — *Le Faucon* beyond the rocks, the muzzles of her cannon about to erupt. *Roscoff*'s quartermaster at the helm, gaze aligned from the Hevah to the distant top of Worvas Hill above St Ives, the hull scraping a rock here, thudding against another there as the swell lifted the stern and surged forward to the bows, the larboard hands bearing on the sweeps, and the squall slashing along the reef.

Mr Berryman the gunner fired first; Davy saw the ball strike the Frenchman's mizzen mast, the mast he had thought to be hit earlier; men were falling amid a dusty haze of splinters. Then, gun by gun, the raider's broadside. What was left of *Roscoff*'s taffrail disintegrated. A ball gouged a groove along the poop deck, slivers of wood cutting down another quartermaster's mate and two of the hands at the sweeps. The gig that hung in davits over the stern disappeared and with it jackstaff and the ensign flaunted there. Lower down a ball, demolishing the relics of the cabin windows, struck number 12 gun with a bell-like clang that did not quite deaden the scream of a man crushed as cannon and carriage overturned. Hevah Rock foamed close a-starboard. Davy touched with surprise, and the first pang of pain, an inch of thick splinter protruding from his forearm, then glanced astern.

The corvette's mizzen mast was folding like a closing book onto the poop.

Then the squall struck, a few minutes of mad wind and blinding rain which swept past to leave a blue patch in the rack overhead, *Roscoff* clear of the Stones and with three fathoms between keel and sandy bottom, *Le Faucon* unmoving in the swirl of the sea, rigid among the rocks. They had got her! Berryman and the squall between them, they'd got her!

'Mr Stona, larboard about and hoist a new ensign.'

The horse-boy emerged, sooty and bleeding. 'It's Mr Berryman, cap'n. Been hit, 'e has.'

Davy ran down the companion into the wreck that had been his cabin. At the foot of the ladder he slid on a patch of blood.

There were more patches on the deck, vivid in the daylight that rayed through the shot holes. Both chasers had been dismounted. Beside one of them lay the gunner. Two of his lads were kneeling over him. 'He's gone,' they said.

Davy gazed down at him. Berryman had never been a likeable man, but his death was a high price to pay and his skill irreplaceable. 'His last shot saved the ship.'

'I helped.' The gunpowder smudges on the urchin's face emphasised an unnatural pallor.

'He done all right,' said one of the men. 'At it the whole action, he were.'

Davy pressed his shoulder and hastened back to the quarter-deck. The battle was not over yet. If the corvette could hold out and were not severely damaged, the tide would lift her off. Back across the reef, then, or call away all boats and carry her by boarding? She must be saved. The Roscoffs had fought like heroes and earned and paid for victory. Davy wanted nothing in the world but to take her. But there was competition. A lugger was moving out of St Ives harbour, one of the Carter brothers' smugglers, armed and like *Roscoff* holding letters of marque. An armada of small craft was putting to sea from the eastern beaches of the Bay; wreckers. Once they had fastened on a stranded vessel no force at man's use could dislodge them until they had stripped their prey. And round the point beyond them appeared what looked more like a raft than a ship. It was the *Fox*.

'Sir, sir,' yelled the look-out Stona had sent to the masthead, 'the Froggie's struck!' From her surviving mast Louis XVI's white ensign was briskly descending.

'Call away the longboat,' roared Davy. Mr Nankervis was fussing at his arm. 'No, get the damned thing out up here, and if you've not done this by the time the boat's in the water you can come along and do it there.' The splinter was jerked from his arm. The pain was red-hot, and Davy emerged from a dizzy haze with a bandage round his wound, a sling about his neck, the burn of rum in his throat, and Stona's voice becoming clearer '. . . boat's alongside.'

'Anchor. You are in command while I am out of the ship,' Davy managed to say.

He was almost himself again in the few minutes it took to reach the reef. Across the submerging shoals the corvette loomed ahead, pinkish-grey hull towering and formidable. It was hardly to be believed that at any moment those cannon would not blast forth. The French captain was leaning over the battered stern, watching the Cornish boat's struggle to breast the tide, which as each wave rolled over the Stones poured through the channel as if through flood gates. And the prize was swaying in the swell as inch by inch she lifted clear.

Where was the *Fox?* All Davy saw were rocks and the corvette, no more. He rose in the sternsheets, but still a little muzzy could not yet adjust himself to the motion as his men's short, powerful strokes gained a yard in every fathom against the surge. But for the coxswain's grip on his jacket he would have been over the side.

'What do you see, cox'n?'

'Billums' Williams had taken Stona's place. He stood retaining his hold on the tiller. '*Fox* is within range, sor. She'm lowerin' a boat, which I'm surprised she've got one left.' And to his crew, 'Pull, ye lubbers, or ye'll be sharin' wi' the navy yet.'

They would share in any case, thought Davy, particularly the *Roscoff's* owners, provided *Le Faucon* were safely brought in. It would be a good hand-out all round. But what mattered above all, to Davy at least, was that the Frenchman should yield to him as representative of the little ship which had fought so doggedly, and at the cost of fine seamen soon to be returned in sorrow to their families.

'We shan't make it, sor. *Fox's* cutter is there.'

The panting boat's crew eased on their oars to look over their shoulders, losing way and then, losing heart too, doing little to recover it. Davy's breath caught in his throat. Try as he would he could not appear indifferent. He sank his head onto his free hand, covering his eyes. The battle, the burden of command – all as nothing!

'Sor, sor!' Billums was clapping his shoulder. 'Lieutenant in the cutter's wavin' 'ee on. Seems he do want 'ee to go aboard first.'

'And so we shall!' cried Davy, marvellously restored to a world in which it was good to be alive and young. 'Pull, lads, pull'.

Lieutenant Hawley raised his hat as *Roscoff's* longboat tossed oars at the entry port. 'Commander Lewin's compliments, sir, and the honour is yours. By God, sir, you've earned it!'

Someone in the cutter called for three cheers, and the hurrahs echoed from a score of small craft already within earshot. These turned and began the pull back to shore, joined by others they met on the way; less, Davy considered, as a practical complement to those cheers, than as the more practical acknowledgement of the unlikelihood of gaining a footing on the stranded ship. The Roscoffs swarmed up the tumblehome. Davy decided, with a backward glance as he stepped onto the deck, that they looked as ferocious a gang of ruffians with their pistols and waving cutlasses as ever seized a prize.

Four bells in the afternoon watch; eight hours, or was it a lifetime? since he had been striding over the heather, with nothing of more consequence to mind than a watch below in his bunk and a run ashore in the uncertain future! Six hours since Jess Porris — but enough of that! Davy walked the captured quarterdeck, his red ensign lazing in the gentle breeze above King Louis' white from the surviving masthead. Captain Leroux had surrendered to him — 'I 'ad no choice, m'sieur. I am — *echoué* — here, and all Cornwall is coming out. *Les canots, les bateaux*, those terrible wreckers. 'O as not heard . . .?' The man was weeping, and in his place so, thought Davy, should I!

The victor returned his sword in token of a gallant fight, and Leroux was led below with the rest of the Frenchmen. Presently shore boats would fetch them away under guard. Half the cutter's crew had with their officer rejoined the *Fox*, the rest were guarding the prisoners.

With his own boat's crew Davy must now get his prize to port. Under jib and fore-topsails, and with the ensigns flapping to larboard, she was creeping towards Pednolver rocks, there to go about and sail in. Three feet of water were sounded in the well, but prisoners brought up protesting from below, where a broached cask had been about to provide the last good wine they would taste in years, were manning the pumps.

Since the last squall which had so dramatically settled the encounter the wind had dropped. Now but a whisper, and with cloud thickening again behind St Ives, it presaged an October blow which the *Fox* under makeshift rig was too slow to avoid and too damaged to endure. The *Roscoff*, to whose decks Captain Lemmo and the bos'un had been restored — Davy could see them there through his glass — was manoeuvring to take the Revenue brig in tow to Harvey's new yards in Hayle. Davy hoped that a double tot of rum had already been issued and that the galley was in full production. That would have been his first care; and despite the triumph of the moment it was with a pang he accepted that his temporary command was at an end.

The sails boomed at a puff of wind, herald of weather the corvette, too, was far from seaworthy enough to withstand. But no decision was called for. The pilot cutter bustled alongside, old Cap'n Hicks took over, respectful but firm and with a copy of port orders to hand; boats came out from St Ives manned by fishermen used to towing the great, tarry hulks that encircled the pilchard shoals, and made light work of a similar service to the French prize.

Invited to dine next day at Squire Stephen's battlemented manor house at Tregenna, Davy met Commander Lewin and Lieutenant Hawley dismounting on the terrace from their hired carriage. After the greeting and back-slapping in which young men express themselves when words fail, Davy drew Lewin aside.

'About that smuggling—' he began.

'What smuggling?' said Lewin.

4

First Officer Dawkins touched his hat to Davy, nodded to Second Officer Stona who had just relieved him for the afternoon watch, and turned to the companion-hatch of the privateer schooner *Roscoff,* of twelve carriage guns and, until prize crews had reduced it to bare adequacy, a complement of sixty. Arrived at the hatch Dawkins seemed to have recollected a prior commitment, for swinging round on his heels he strode for'ad. A tall, blond fellow surprisingly light on his feet, he trod the swaying deck in an unerring straight line, watched at every step by Stona and his captain, and dived into the foc's'l.

His disappearance eased the tension. Gurt Jan ambled over to Davy, who had shifted out of the glaring sunshine on the weather side of the poop — those three fathoms by one of planking sacred to him as captain — and stood in a strip of shadow cast by the spanker. He had taken a sight of Finisterre when briefly in view during the forenoon, and the Scillies lay six hundred miles dead ahead. Jan eased himself comfortably against the high taffrail. 'That there Jed Dawkins, Cap'n sir — I wouldn' trust he nohow, no more'n a dogfish among the herring.'

Davy raised his eyebrows. 'What's it this time?'

Jan made a further adjustment to his posture. 'Tell me, cap'n, where'd you go when you come off watch after four hours of clunkin' nawthin' but wind and spray? You'd go straight to your berth, wipe the brine off your chacks, and set down to a hot dinner; not go traipsin' among the hands.'

'Lieutenant Dawkins is ex-navy like me, Mr Stona, and the navy teaches that an officer's first care is to look to the needs of his men.'

'Well, my cap'n, I don't reckon as I'm adrift in that respect—'

Davy hastened to reassure him.

'And we aren't navy, however you do give fancy names like we was a King's ship, and the mate, begging 'is pardon First Officer Lieutenant Dawkins from Newcastle 'pon Tyne, don't give a pig's arse for the needs o' more'n his own crowd, rot 'im! Which what you was about signin' they lot on I shall never know.'

'Get to the point,' snapped Davy, only too often reminded that Celt and Saxon are no readier a mix than oil and water, and that communication between the two was almost nil since neither understood the accent of the other, nor tried to. He had been aware from the start of the voyage that Stona had been critical of his reorganisation of the *Roscoff* on naval lines, and that after six month' cruising between Ushant and the Canaries he still was.

'And watch your tongue, Jan Stona. Stand up, man. Stop lolling like a dead man's hammock in the netting.'

Gurt Jan stared at his captain, saw that he meant it, and heaved himself erect. 'Aye aye, sir! Well, this 'ere Dawkins, 'e'm brewing somethin' up. Half 'is watch below he do spend for'ad—'

'As do you.'

'Not wi' they Geordies as mess in the capstan flat, like he do.'

Davy grinned. In the casual days of old Captain Lemmo the bo'sun and the coxs'n, Chippie the carpenter and half a dozen other favoured souls had forgathered in a screened-off corner beneath the foredeck and beside the capstan, there to play that American import, euchre, while bottle and baccy went round. 'Well, it don't affect you now you've joined the after-guard, Jan. Besides, when you yourself go for'ad it ain't always to rouse the hands.'

Gurt Jan spread his hands wide. 'Sakes, Mr Davy, half o' they lads is cousins o' mine and a passul of 'em is yourn too! 'Tes the new hands you signed along o' Dawkins I'm jealous of.'

'Well, keep your suspicions to yourself − and me. And if that lubber at the helm don't steer smaller, Mr Stona, I'll want to know why.'

'His ears is flapping too wide, cap'n.' In half a dozen strides Stona was bellowing into the offending appendage while Davy pondered the unease which his right-hand man had expressed. It was an unease of which Davy himself was aware though could not put a finger on.

At the time Mr Knill had offered Ned Davy command of the *Roscoff*, a couple of dozen Tynesiders were at large in the numerous taverns of St Ives and seeking a berth either for home or for further adventuring. For their ship, a Newcastle barque, had been written off as a total loss on running aground at Clodgy. Her mate, Jediah Dawkins, had persuaded the privateer owner, John Knill, to give him a comparable berth aboard the schooner: a former master's mate in HMS *Thunderer*, he had traded on Mr Knill's newly aroused confidence in a naval background and got the job over the heads of several eligible Cornishmen who would gleefully have shipped with the local hero. Mr Knill had suggested − and who was the young skipper to refuse? − that he engage too as many of the shipwrecked crew as did not pine for the hearths and onion beer of the north; and after Dawkins had had a word with them only three or four decided against signing articles.

They were good seamen. Even Jan Stona, with disapproval of 'foreigners' in his blood, admitted as much. But they were deep-sea sailors, not the interrelated crew of a St Ives fishing-smack-cum-smuggler writ large. Moreover every man-jack of them, like the Cornish, was a shareholder in the cruise. You could not treat him as you would a victim of the press-gang. You had to allow for a measure of familiarity the navy would not stomach for an instant, Davy admitted, begrudging from the depth of his naval heart that you would never stop a privateer officer, whether you called him lieutenant or not, from hob-nobbing with his men. But Dawkins sought his companionship among his own people rather than with his fellows in the wardroom. You could hardly blame him, seeing their attitude towards him.

'Well,' Davy concluded, casting an eye alow and aloft before leaving the deck for a lonely dinner in his quarters aft, 'you'll never resolve those doubts of yours, Jan Stona, without you make some little effort to gain the man's confidence. Another week and you'll be shot of him and the lot of 'em, so hurrah for the homeward bound!'

'And for good pickings awaiting us! They Carters of Mount's Bay, with their great cutters, never sent in three ships all to once, like we done.'

Davy smiled. 'Not at once. It took us six months. Remember? The Company will be pleased, I don't doubt.'

'And so shall we,' said Jan. 'So shall we.'

The stern cabin, rebuilt after its battering on the Stones, was not at all as old Lemmo would have had it. Through curtained windows that ran the whole width of the stern the wake sent a thousand glints of light, which reflected from the white enamelled deckhead and danced on a damask tablecloth. This, with the silver, glass and china before which Davy sat in state that would have done credit to Drake himself, had graced the saloon of a French full-rigger conveying a great nobleman to the West Indies. All had been meticulously assessed against Davy's twelve shares of the venture due to him as captain, while his hapless lordship, by now no doubt in Cornwall, was probably parolled to Squire Stephens at Tregenna and awaiting ransom. These matters, such were Cornish contacts across the Channel, were arranged discreetly if somewhat leisurely. But what matter, since the expenses of board and lodging were included in the bargain?

The meal, served by a white-jacketed Tom Kernick — he who had held the horses at Pencobben — was nevertheless still the hard-tack to which Davy's digestion had become inured in the midshipman's berth aboard His Britannic Majesty's ships, even thought it was not stale water in a mug but claret in a crystal goblet that washed it down. All very proper; but it was no answer to the nagging doubt about Dawkins, the more difficult to resolve because 'Hang it'!' Davy exclaimed to nobody in particular, 'there's no doubt at all.' His first officer had been efficient and seemed loyal, and so had the rest of the Tynesiders. It was that confounded racial mistrust! And in future, Davy decided, no one, not even the great John Knill, was going to appoint either his officers or his ship's company for him.

As he packed his pipe, its clay burnt black and lovingly cherished, the thought of Mr Knill turned his attention to a bundle beneath the windows. It was the stars and stripes of the American brig *Joshua Clegg,* captured the day before yesterday and now bound for St Ives instead of Brest, nominally captained by Midshipman Pendarves but with Cox'n Caleb Williams to direct and advise, and with master and crew battened down under hatches. The cargo, mainly baled cotton, included a dozen barrels and three huge hogsheads of Virginian tobacco. It was amusing to consider Mr Knill having to levy excise duties, when the prize was brought into port in the eyes of the whole town, on a commodity his ships were more accustomed to sneak ashore by moonshine.

Yes, it had been a rewarding cruise, mused Davy, half filling his glass and gazing through a haze of tobacco smoke at the wake curdling astern upon a quiet sea. The traffic between France and her latest allies, the Yankee rebels, had built up; and whereas a year ago you could have patrolled for six months without bagging more than a lugger reeking of fish, he had already sent home the 500-tonner *Villon* bound for Martinique — this was the vessel that had carried the nobleman and the rich appurtenances of his entourage, and had been taken in a gale without a shot fired; next a barquentine, the *Marie Louise,* on the coastal run between Bordeaux and Bilbao, which he had snapped up under the nose of a *stationnaire* of the French navy; and last of all the *Joshua Clegg.* A fair tally! It had cost the lives of five Cornishmen and a Tynesider, good men all, the memory of whom clouded the satisfaction of the hour. A dozen more were recovering from wounds. Dawkins had sensibly, Davy thought, sent local lads home with the prizes.

Choosing a prize crew for the *Clegg* had been difficult. As in the engagement in St Ives Bay *Roscoff* was short of officers. The harmony of his ship would have been imperilled had he sent away either Stona or Dawkins, each with his distinctive following. Again the young captain, adjusting himself to the responsibilities of command, cursed the problems of a split ship's company and considered how he might otherwise have dealt with it from the start. He studied the revised watch-bill. Fewer than forty hands — half of them Cornishmen and half Northerners. With so depleted a crew he could hardly tackle anything larger than a coaster. Yes, it was time to go home! To Jess? Maybe. But home.

Davy looked round the cabin. For the first time in his twenty years he could live as he supposed his ancestors had lived, while his immediate care on the conclusion of the voyage would be to restore to his father and mother, in their genteel poverty at Boswyn, the comforts appropriate to a family which had for generations provided High Sheriffs, magistrates and the occasional member of parliament for the county of Cornwall.

These gratifying meditations were interrupted by a hail from the masthead. 'Deck-ho! Sail abaft the larboard beam.'

A messenger collided with Davy as he burst from his cabin. 'Mr Stona says, sir—'

'I know. I heard,' said Davy as he scrambled up the companion-way, with Gurt Jan's 'Aloft there, what do 'ee make of her?' thundering above his head.

'Large three-master, sir, sailing east. Could be a warship, sir.' The information filtered to the deck through a cacophony of ship sounds, the creak of the hull, the twanging of rigging and the thump of sails in the light breeze.

Dawkins materialised like the demon king in the pantomime. 'Shall I go aloft and take a look, sir?'

Davy, about to climb to the dizzy heights himself, nodded; it was seemly that Dawkins, and not he the captain, should go instead. 'If you please, Mr Dawkins,' he said.

'Deck! West Indiaman.' Dawkins sat astride the yard with an arm round the slender topmast and the truck, the wooden disk at the very summit, a few feet above his head. Davy caught glimpses of him through a mesh of rigging and canvas as the sails swelled and shivered in the light airs. With practised hand Dawkins levelled his spyglass at the stranger.

'Frenchman!' he yelled at length, and launching himself from his perch to slide down a backstay he ran aft. 'Do we take her, sir?'

Davy swung himself into the shrouds and steadied his own glass on the sails that were rising over the horizon like a summer cloud. The gunports were not yet in his lens, but there would be at least nine a side. 'We'd never afford a prize crew, but it's tempting.'

'She'll sheer off like a startled duck when she do see our ensign, cap'n,' Stona commented, 'and we'm too nigh the French coast for a long chase east'ards.'

'I was thinking as much myself,' Davy said, jumping to the deck. 'She shall rest easy while I'm making up my mind. The Yankee brig's ensign is in my cabin under the stern windows, Mr Dawkins. Be good enough to hoist it in place of our own. For the time being we'll hold our present course.'

'Nor' nor' west it is, sir, as afore,' growled the helmsman, 'so far as 'ee can hold a course at all with the wind shifting all ways like a whore's bum!'

Back in the great cabin Davy's forefinger checked at a line in the latest edition of Lloyd's List of Shipping. '*Ranger* — Salem — Topsail Schooner — Three masts — no figurehead,' he read. 'That'll do famously. Mr Stona!'

The big man's bewhiskered face beamed through the open skylight. 'Come down, Jan. But first of all send that gaggle of loafers on the poop about their business. Now look 'ee here,' Davy went on as Gurt Jan towered over the table, stooping low to avoid the deckhead beams, '*Ranger*, see? That'll be us.'

'Us?'

'We'll come about in half an hour — near enough three bells. While our stern is still towards the Frog you're to paint out *Roscoff* on both bows, and paint in the name *Ranger* instead. You can get it in between the stem and each cathead without cramping—'

'*Ranger!*' muttered Jan, scratching his head. '*Ranger?*' Ah, cap'n, now like the penitent at the meetin' house I do see the light!'

'*Ranger*,' Davy affirmed, jabbing his finger on the List. Set to it right away. And send the First Officer to me.'

'Aye aye, sir.' Jan paused at the door. 'What do 'ee know?' he persisted. 'I seen he just now in the chart 'ouse, and what was he doin'? He were studyin' a chart of how do 'ee say the word? – Malagasy. Now what would 'e want wi' that?'.

'Jan,' said Davy wearily, 'You've got twenty-five minutes.'

The cabin door clicked shut. Davy heard him shout across the poop to Dawkins, and for'ad to the bos'un and to Chippie the carpenter to roust out the key of the paint store.

Coming up into the wind with so little headway that a less skilful manoeuvre than Davy's would have fetched her in irons, the schooner settled onto a southerly tack. The Indiaman now stood on a slowly converging course, black and white checkered hull bold although in shadow, sails spilling and filling in the doubtful breeze, and rails and bulwarks surmounted by the heads and shoulders of passengers, eager for a break in the monotony of an Atlantic crossing.

La Reine de Cornouailles – Queen of the great Breton province to which Cornish emigrants gave their country's name when the Saxons invaded. A good augury! And as the Indiaman's name was clear in Davy's spyglass so, he presumed, was *Ranger* in the French captain's. He would now be thumbing his own shipping lists. Meanwhile Dawkins' squad, suspended on planks lowered from the taffrail as soon as the schooner came about, was hurriedly inscribing '*Ranger* – Salem' in place of '*Roscoff*' – St Ives' across the stern, the paint being so mixed as hopefully to prevent running and to sustain a close scrutiny.

Davy briefed his two officers, who then went for'ad to pass the orders to the seamen on watch, while he himself outlined the plan to the hands on deck.

'Now hear ye'?' It was the time-honoured prelude to a shipboard proclamation. 'We are making out we are the schooner *Ranger*, one of John Paul Jones's privateers which have been playing the devil with British shipping. Yes, the American commodore, Higgs; you've seen more of him on the East Coast than we have in the sou' west. We shall run alongside the Froggie with mail – no, Jem Harry, there won't be any! Also to warn her of a British squadron in the Bay of Biscay. The French captain will invite me below, and if he don't think of it for himself I'll require to see his papers. We'll get there somehow, Mr Dawkins and I with a couple from the capstan mess; they speak nearer Yankee than the lads this side of Tamar. Down there we'll grab the captain. Meanwhile our cross-tree swivel guns will have been manned and trained and Mr Stona will lead everyone else over the Frenchman's gunnels. Surprise attack; no problem. Cutlasses and pistols, but no shooting without orders. Bundle all the Frogs — crew, passengers, women — into the forehold, where Mr Dawkins will set guard on 'em. I'll be up on deck myself then.'

'Got it all worked out a mite too smooth, y'kna',' a northerner murmured.

Too true, Davy agreed, overhearing. But 'All you've got to do, leading seaman, is to obey orders,' he barked at the speaker. And of course, he meditated, tugging a fat Pierre le Roy watch from his pocket and passing it from hand to hand until, becoming aware of this lapse in a captain's proper imperturbability, he crammed it angrily back — of course, I can always outsail Johnny Crapaud if he bares his teeth, though with passengers at risk that's the last thing he'll do.

'Ah, Mr Dawkins,' he said as the First reported the painting aft finished, 'now I shall require you to hoist the signals — let me see! "Welcome home. Heave to, I am coming alongside. I have mail for you." Mr Stona, rig fenders to starboard if you please.'

'Sea's flat calm. Couldn't be better for the job,' Davy remarked as the flags fluttered up, brilliant in the white sunshine against white canvas. Dawkins was standing by the halyards at the foot of the foremast, looking across the swell at the West Indiaman. The expression on his face caught Davy's attention. It was that of a man who sees the harbour lights of home after an arduous voyage, the gleam of triumph when a goal is achieved. Odd fellow! Davy mused, adding for no reason at all, him and his Malagasy — Madagascar! What the devil did he want with that?

The French captain, who had hove-to as requested, plainly disliked Davy's threat to the paintwork of his ship's bulging sides. '*Ma foi!* How do you not send boat?' he hailed. But *Roscoff's* sails came down with a rush, leaving the Stars and Stripes alone and supreme a hundred feet above the deck, and she came round across *La Reine's* bows and up into the wind as gently as a dove.

'Give her a cheer, lads,' urged Davy; and to mutual waving and huzzahing and kisses blown by a pretty lady or two the schooner nudged alongside. Heaving lines whipped over bows and stern and the warps were secured, and according to plan Davy clambered up the tumblehome with Dawkins and a pair of burly Geordies at heel. From the corner of his eye he saw his guns' crews — two seamen to each swivel — standing by at the chains poised to climb aloft to their quarters.

'*Magnifique, m'sieur!*' The French captain had clearly expected worse ship handling from a privateer, and an American one at that. He introduced himself as Louis Charles de Vaucour, '*Le neveu,* the nephew, *m'sieurs,* of the Vicomte of that name and his heir should my cousin not survive an unfortunate riding accident' — an accident that singularly failed to depress him, however unfortunate, as de Vacour led his American guests below to toast their glorious revolution. They followed their voluble host — and how convenient it was, thought Davy, that his English was so fluent — through a score of passengers and knots of sailors with nothing to do but size up these wild Yankees who had erupted on the Gallic scene. They traversed a carpeted corridor between the numbered doors of passengers' cabins, Davy feeling at every step more and more a betrayer of the sacred trust of hospitality, yet more and more determined to fulfil his patriotic duty, and were bowed into the great cabin which spanned the entire width of the stern; at first glance a sober splendour of gilt and mahogany.

First glance, and for a while Davy's last! Swift blinding agony — falling, jostling, nothingness, dim awareness, excruciating cramp and an appalling headache warring for dominion of jangling nerves! And a shot. Two shots. Davy forced open his eyelids. He lay in a dim compartment close to an open door. A flickering pattern on the deckhead of an adjoining saloon seemed to have meaning for him; the pattern of wavelets reflecting sunshine through stern windows, as in his own cabin. But it was not his own? Then where the hell was he? Of course, it was the great cabin of the French West Indiaman, *La* — something or other.

Chairs came into focus, chairs on pedestals bolted to the deck around a polished table. In one of these a man sat, lashed to the chair with white hempen rope, a decorative sash knotted about his face.

And Davy, too, was gagged. Now why should that be? Something foul had been stuffed into his mouth, and he could not move his arms to shift it. He was sprawled on a bed, his wrists tied to the bedposts, and they ached. God, they ached! But it was an ache that was a welcome counterbalance to the otherwise intolerable acceptance of failure. He had been captured — a small thing compared to the loss of his ship. But perhaps Dawkins and Stona had got her away, and she was showing her heels to the prey he had misjudged so completely. He had blame only for himself. He jerked uselessly at his bonds, seeking in the agony of contorted muscles some mitigation of his burden of guilt.

The captive in the chair was glaring at him. Dawkins? Not he. Those eyes above the gag, that flamboyant uniform! The French captain de Vaucour, bound just as Davy had intended binding him though could not recall doing. Then where was Dawkins, who had been with Davy until whatever it was had happened? Dawkins — Malagasy — Madagascar. Of course! And what a fool Davy had been to ignore the clue to which even Jan Stona had given thought! It was still told in the seaports of Britain how ninety years ago a privateer's mate, Plymothian John Avery, had mutinied, seized his own ship the *Duke*, and turned pirate; the most notorious pirate of the age. He had talked over a few of his shipmates, and leadership and example had won him a crew. Avery had crowned his infamous career, so popular romance on stage and in story insisted, as a king in Madagascar with the Princess of India as his queen.

John Avery was Dawkins' model. No doubt he had long been planning to take the *Roscoff,* once her company was decimated by prize crews and losses, and when about to strike had seen *La Reine* as a better bargain. Once rid of encumbrances such as legitimate captains, obstinate seamen and civilians, he would round the Cape and clap on sail for the jungle-penetrating creeks of Africa's mighty, unexplored island. Thence the master of a powerful ship with a crew of desperadoes could prey on the rich traffic of the Indian Ocean and retire to his secret base when the hunt was on. An alluring argument for a sailor even with prize money a-plenty awaiting him at home!

As he struggled with both his bonds and his self reproach, Davy could hear crashes in the adjoining accommodation. Dawkins would have turned his lads loose on the passengers' valuables as a taste of plunder to come. The door of the great cabin was dashed open, and a couple of the Dawkins' gang dragged a terrified steward into it and beyond Davy's view, one of them returning to jerk open the trussed up captain's coat and pluck a key from a chain round his neck. They reappeared carrying between them a brassbound sea chest, hooking open the door to get it through.

As the echoes of their footsteps faded along the now empty accommodation, a small figure slipped into the great cabin and then, after flitting hither and thither, into the darkened sleeping berth where Davy lay. Kernick!

'Couldn't get in afore, Cap'n Davy,' whispered the urchin, glancing nervously over his shoulder. ''Orrible goings-on, sir. Till you seen what I seen you seen nothink.' Muffled noises from Davy stirred the shocked youngster to the purpose of his visit. He spoke with incredible speed. 'Mr Stona do say to leave 'ee like you is, sir, till 'e do give the word. 'E've joined the pirates, sir – the only thing he could do, 'e say, if he'm to get 'ee out o' this shimozzle, and they mustn't never suspect nothink not nohow they mustn't, not till the time's ripe.' Davy digested this torrent of negatives as well as impatience and curiosity would allow. 'Then'e'll deal wi' Mr Dawkins Mr Stona will, sir, and the rest is up to you. You'll think of somethink, he say, sir, like you always does. The rest of we 'ave took the oath too, all together like we was saying the credo in Gwithian church, sir, 'cause when we come up from battening down they Frenchies in the forehold, like you said, sir, Dawkins an' 'is mates got us covered wi' muskets and one o' they swivels and we couldn't do nothink else, sir. But Mr Wesley 'll put it right with God when we do get home. The brothers is due to St Ives 'bout now. Proper surprised them Frenchies was sir—' Davy could well imagine it '—when we come up yelling like bel tink over the bulwarks a-waving of our swords 'ere's mine, sir – and they didn't put up no fight at all when we drove 'em below. Some of they matelots 'ave joined the pirates, sir, and a sight more keen they was on it than we was, I can tell 'ee. Mr Dawkins 'ave shifted the passengers aboard the *Roscoff*, sir, and she'm adrift with 'er tiller lines cut. Not very far off, sir,' he added, answering the worry in his captain's eyes. 'And Mr Stona do reckon as he'll open the sea cocks or sink 'er by gunfire. 'E tell me to tell 'ee everythink, cap'n and I don't think I got anythink else to tell, so I best be off. I'll be back.'

But he was not. Davy was cut loose from the bed and prodded, gagged and with his hands bound behind him, along the corridor where broken doors disclosed tumbled drawers and smashed jewel cases and a scatter of female garments well picked over. He emerged into blinding sunlight at the break of the poop, and was shoved against the bulwarks near the larboard chains.

Accustoming his eyes to the glare he saw Dawkins, every inch the pirate chieftain, posturing before the ornate entrance to the cabin accommodation. The man had drawn on de Vaucour's wardrobe for the trappings of authority — full-dress coat of a captain of King Louis' mercantile marine, silk sash in which he had thrust three of four pistols, gem hilted sword swinging from a baldrick that was a masterpiece of gold lace and embroidery. Scorn rose in Davy's parched gullet like bile, obliterating for a moment the pain, the shame, the fear.

The latter-day Avery stood at a small table on which a scroll of parchment was held down at two corners by knives driven into the wood, at the third by an inkstand from which protruded an enormous quill, and at the fourth by a black book that must be a bible. A glance aloft showed Davy that the ship was still hove-to under topsails, with her courses shapeless bundles drooping from the yardarms. The sun was as high, almost, as when Davy came aboard. The whole affair had lasted a bare hour. Tyne-siders lined the broad rail overlooking the waist, each carrying a musket and with a pistol before him. They seemed sober; Dawkins had contrived to keep them from the Indiaman's wine store. Not so several French sailors who were at large, but unarmed. They clutched bottles of the rarest vintage, and were tossing it down their throats as though it were *vin ordinaire* in an *auberge* at Brest. But Dawkins was taking no chances with the Cornishmen. They were herded in the waist, abaft the great girth of the mainmast and before the wide, central steps which gave access to the quarter-deck and made a gap in the row of muskets above their heads. This gap was covered by the perrier on the poop rail, with two hands at the ready to fire on command. From where Davy was placed he could see little of his fellow townsfolk, but what he saw showed them dispirited and bewildered. And probably leaderless. Had Jan Stona been among them they would not be standing so listless, and there was nothing to expect from Mr Nankervis, the surgeon, whose sole aim seemed to be to stay as far from the firing line as he could and make himself small.

Dawkins watched Davy's assessment of the situation with amusement. 'Hark to yon banging for'ad, Ned Davy. That's the French crew, they as weren't wise enough to join the party, trying to get free. Your friends and relations dursn't let 'em out, they'd cut 'em to ribbons else. Wouldn't they, lads? Well, just you keep a weather eye open in case. Keeps 'em true to their oath, Davy; they need me more than I need them, God's truth they do! But now there are Articles to read. Not the Articles of War like at Divisions in the old days, but articles of brotherhood, with something for every man as signs, and the devil take them as don't.' It was infuriating to hear so much and say nothing.

Dawkins stalked to the head of the steps, a pistol in each fist. 'You'll have to chance those rowdy Froggies a while, lads, because you're going to drop your weapons on the deck and draw closer, here, beneath me. Drop 'em, you bloody Jacks! Move, damn your eyes!' A growl arouse. The Cornishmen stood looking at one another and at the tyrant on the steps. Some threw down their arms and shuffled forward, others held back. Davy saw an elderly fisherman – he was Tim Treloar – who had been unlucky in both fishing and smuggling, snatch a pistol from his belt and aim it at Dawkins. He was unlucky in that, too. Dawkins pulled both triggers at once. Old Tim sank to his knees while the man next to him, although he had dropped his weapons as ordered, howled and clapped a hand to his forearm.

'These are the articles to which you will affix your mark or sign, if there's a scholar among you.' Dawkins spoke through the smoke of the discharge as though there were not fresh blood on the deck beneath his feet. He moved aside to the rail, laid his smoking pistols there and two primed ones beside them, and producing a paper from his pocket read carefully, lest his northern accent should disguise the words, the Articles of the Brethren of the Coast. The *Gazette* had reported these articles from time to time in piracy trials. They had been drawn up over fifty years previously by the Topsham pirate Phillips, who had been so monstrous a villain that even his crew had enough of him, and put him to death a year later. But in the reading they were mild, seductive even, not to be compared with the Admiralty's schedule of 'if's' and 'death.'

'Article One.' This was a moment for which Dawkins had well prepared himself, and Davy, hating him from the depths of his being as he watched old Tim writhing in his blood, could not forbear admiring the rascal's confident leadership. 'Article One. Every man shall obey civil command; the captain shall have one full share and a half in all prizes, the master, carpenter, boatswain and gunner shall have one share and a quarter.

'Article two. If any man shall offer to run away . . .'

Davy, the wad in his mouth — he suspected it to be oakum — half choking him and an almost intolerable ache in head and arms, looked about him. The sails and the tracery of the rigging etched on the holy-stoned deck dark patterns which moved as the ship swayed. In the captain's chest, its lid thrown back for all to see, gold gleamed and dimmed as the patterns pendulumed hypnotically. A second, smaller chest displayed a tangle of jewellery now dull, now sparkling, and purses doubtless collected from the passengers' quarters, together with a heap of extravagant clothing: all this, and the reasonableness of the Articles, a bait for simple seamen. A lure towards a career of infamy they would regret all their shortened, brutish lives. But there was no hint of Tim Treloar dying unattended among his countrymen, no hint of two bodies, a civilian's and a French officer's, which lay in the scuppers and at every lurch of the hull stirred as if turning in sleep, as Dawkins continued:

'Article Eight. If any man shall lose a joint in time of an engagement, shall have 400 pieces of eight; if a limb, 800.

'Article Nine, and the last. If at any time you meet with a prudent woman, that man that offers to meddle with her, without her consent, shall suffer present death.'

The Indiaman was rolling more steeply. A gale would be blowing up before midnight, though the wind still puffed and faded. As the ship heaved the *Roscoff*, a few cables off to westward, rose and fell beyond the bulwarks. There was activity aboard. Figures were crawling up the ratlines, cautiously edging along the topsail yard. The spanker on the mizzen was rising jerkily, the peak of the gaff drooping and certain to jam the block. The landsmen aboard seemed determined to get her under way. And surely that was a woman standing by the binnacle, waving and pointing! You could imagine her directing the unco-ordinated efforts of the gentlemen. She stood in the shifting light and shade, a copper glow where the sunbeams caught her hair.

A rumble from the waist cut in on Davy's speculations, in the course of which he must have missed some provocative remark. No one could miss Dawkins's reply. 'Hark 'e, you stupid, jabbering clodhoppers' — so would a mate's voice reach the topmen in a storm — 'you're coming up one by one to sign articles, or I'll know the reason why, and so will you by God, ye snivelling troglodytes! First we'll see your young Ned Davy sign. I've plans for him when he do, and when he don't. Ah, Mr Davy, you heard?' He walked across and clapped him on the shoulder. 'I thought you were too taken up with your old lady. No, not the wench; you've spotted her as well, eh? I've plans for her also. Your old lady — the ship, man! Now don't you fret. She'll not get further than chasing her own tail, not with her rudder lines cut she won't. And when I've got me my full crew she'll not chase even that.'

He swaggered to the table. And my! how this quiet, secretive fellow has changed, meditated Davy. How Mr Frog grows! The pirate bent over the scroll, shook the surplus ink from the quill, and dashed his signature across the top. 'Jediah Dawkins, Captain,' he boomed, unfolding himself, as it were, while sustaining a still leaning posture on his spread finger tips. 'Jediah Dawkins, Captain. And don't anyone—' His angry glare traversed the deck and by coincidence even the knocking in the hold ceased, 'don't anyone doubt it.'

In another sudden change of mood he stepped back, thumbs stuck in his sash which, with the pistols still upon the quarterdeck rail, was a sagging mockery of earlier splendour. 'Jeremy Scrobbs, my old shipmate, you're elected bos'n, and you shall sign after me. Then Karl Ericson, elected gunner.

There'll be work for you before this day is done. And you, Mr Davy, ex-Cap'n Davy,' continued Dawkins as Scrobbs slowly lettered his name while Ericson stood impatiently awaiting his turn, 'you shall sign next. Cut him loose. No one shall say our former, I do not yet say late, master and commander was not free to choose whether to sink or swim.'

'Or hang,' bawled Ericson, jabbing the quill into the ink bottle.

'Or hang,' agreed Dawkins, pleasantly.

One of Davy's guards was fumbling with the knots about his wrists. 'I hope you don't hold this agin me, cap'n, I mean Mr Davy,' he mumbled. 'Tweren't none o' my doing, I can tell 'ee. All I wants is to get home to Sunderland. You'll remember me, won't 'ee, if you ever gets out o' this pickle?'

There was a morsel of comfort in the knowledge that someone gave him a dog's chance, that he had a friend among the opposition, even if only Ordinary Seaman Gamble of Sunderland. Davy's hands were free. He raised them to remove the gag, but reviving circulation left him agonised and helpless. Gamble snatched the scarf from his face and Davy spat out the wad.

Now was the moment of decision, action — of ultimate defeat. Where was Jan Stona, who was going to deal with Dawkins? The poor fellow had paid the price of his loyalty for sure. And the boy Kernick? Small enough to tuck himself away, somewhere. The urchin had a genius for concealment, thought Davy, remembering the cliff top at Pencobben an age ago. But not Gurt Jan. And now Davy must do something, to make some gesture. But what? He stepped forward and made to answer the pirate, but his throat was so dry he could scarcely croak. Dawkins perceived his predicament and laughed. Bending back in his gaudy finery and with arms akimbo he laughed and laughed. Scrobbs and Ericson laughed too, holding their sides and pointing at Davy, whose seething anger was generating a physical red mist before his vision. Other laughter assailed his ears, uncertain, sycophantic laughter; he could detect its quality. He was aware that every eye was upon him, the more so when Dawkins bowed and swept his hand across the document.

'Your turn, sir,' he mocked. 'Ye'll not wish to keep us waiting.'

Davy's tormented muscles were under control now, and he must call them to action. He was as a tiger, about to spring at the ring of hunters who hemmed him in. The laughter stopped, abruptly. Dawkins's fist went to his sash; the guns were not there. Davy took a further step, there in the swinging light and shadow. He could hear the surge of the sea at the ship's side, the groaning of the great yards high overhead, the pulse of blood in his ears. A second was like a minute, and time was no longer to be measured by the clock.

But wait. The latter-day Avery stood in a blaze of colour in his stolen garments and he was drawing his sword. A foot of steel below the hilt flashed into the sunlight. Behind, under the poop deck's overhang, all was darkness. But there was movement. Movement that became a shape. A shape as large as a bear. Gurt Jan! He was on Dawkins in a bound, before the pirate, nimble as a cat though he might be, could draw his blade, could even turn to see. Jan seized the back of the sash in his wrestler's grip, with the other hand twisted the lace cravat so tightly at the nape that Dawkins's fingers left the hilt to claw at his neck, and in an outburst of pandemonium hustled him, bounced him almost, to the bulwarks, and with a mighty heave swung him onto the gunnel and tipped him overboard. Again silence, a cry, a splash, the cocking of muskets. Gurt Jan panting, his breath coming in loud gasps; severed cords dangled from his arms. Ericson hurled himself at the giant Cornishman, who side-stepped and with a 'flying mare' smashed him into the scuppers. Scrobbs, slower thinking, presented his pistol at Stona, who picked up the table and hurled it at him. The bullet cracked into the table top; ink spilled like black blood beside the red blood staining the deck. It was a scene to recall, in minutest detail, when extolling the deeds of Gurt Jan Stona.

The Cornishmen were coming up the quarterdeck ladder or over the rail. The two at the swivel on the poop took aim. A Frenchman reeled into the line of fire, clutching a bottle. Davy sprang at him, grabbed the bottle, pushed the fellow aside. 'Up there,' he croaked. '*Là-haut! Le canon!* Blow your bloody head off!' Red hot rage had cooled into a devil-may-care mood.

He placed himself before the deadly little gun, six feet above him, crammed to its gaping muzzle with musket shot and bolts and nails, and pointing straight at his head. He took a swig at

the warm wine. Tilting the bottle till it was a ruby glow against
the blue he drained it dry, and sent it wheeling over the side,
making a weird whistle as it flew. Then he held up his hand,
facing the gun.

'Enough!' Davy's voice, too, could reach the to'gallant yards
in a gale. 'Stand aside — you Jennings, you Brown, stand aside,
I say. The game's over. You've signed nothing. I'll forget the
whole bloody business. Get back to your duties.'

He turned on his heel. Cornishmen and Tynesiders were
mingling. There was shoving and shouting. 'Silence!' roared
Davy. 'What's this about northerners and southerners? You're
all Roscoffs, ain't you? And this is a French ship and if you don't
watch out we'll all end up in King Louis' prisons. As I said,
bygones shall be bygones. You signed no articles but what I gave
you at the shipping office. Now, where's Mr Nankervis?'

'Tendin' to Tim Treloar, 'e is, sorr, and Tim he'm in a bad
way, sorr'.

'Captain, sir.' It was Scrobbs. 'What about us?'

The wind still came in puffs, gusts almost. The ill-trimmed
sails met it with thuds and cracks. The rigging twanged. The
baggy, ship-made trousers of the seamen slapped at their calves.
The scroll of paper with its three thick, smudged signatures
lifted from the planking and floated with sidelong swoops to
flatten itself against the lee shrouds. It was the turn of a card,
the finger of fate. Fifty pairs of eyes watched it; those too of the
French renegades who had not understood a word. The playful
breeze relaxed its grip, the scroll fluttered half way to the deck,
the breeze took it again and whirled it out to sea. Everybody
sighed, even the bewildered Frenchmen.

'You too, you contriving villain,' said Davy.

'Thank you sir. Thank you.' Scrobbs was clasping his hands
like a suppliant. Ericson, bleeding from a gash on his cheek,
spat full in Scrobbs' face, an abject Scrobbs who had no spirit
left for retaliation.

'Not you,' Davy said. He walked up to Stona, took his hand,
squeezed his shoulder.

The boy stood beside him. 'My mate,' grinned the big fellow.

'Gurt Jan,' Davy observed, 'there's work to do.'

*

'Stand up. Show yourself.' Davy sat in the sternsheets of one of *La Reine's* boats, with de Vaucour and his three surviving officers and with a dozen Roscoffs, all but two of them at the oars, bristling with cutlasses and firearms and looking like the pirates the French captain insisted they were. '*Le Corsaire, m'sieur* – pirate, privateer – in my language it is no difference!'

For his part Davy had done nothing to dispel the belief that the schooner was indeed Commodore Jones's *Ranger* of Salem. To inspire Gallic mistrust of her vigorous new ally was to win a victory for Britain when victories were few. The stars and stripes still flapped energetically at *Roscoff's* masthead. The attempt to set sail had only held *Roscoff* hove-to, and she drifted down wind towards them.

'Eyes to the front in the boat! Pull, damn you!' A gunport had opened and now a six-pounder was being sighted on the approaching lifeboat. There would be militiamen among the passengers, better gunners than they were seamen, while that copper-topped harpy still busybodied about the upper deck.

'For God's sake stand up and show yourself, man!' Davy prodded de Vaucour, obstinate and uncooperative to the last, which might be that very instant unless he complied. He got to his feet. There was pointing on deck and waving.

The boat came under the schooner's lee and bowman hooked on to a ringbolt. It was good to be back with the old *Roscoff* again – a reunion Davy had not expected and still could scarcely believe. Unable to bring both ships to anchor in St Ives Bay Davy knew he had made the correct decision in preferring the schooner, built under the noses of her owners solely as a commerce raider, and also for the less manifest tasks she would be called upon to perform, to the ponderous if more valuable merchantman.

The French captain mounted the footholds in the schooner's side first, as an act of courtesy, Davy urged, and because of the unwritten sea-law, soonest aboard in order of seniority; privately because some fool up top might fire at the first head to loom over the bulwarks, and his own was of greater concern to George III than that of the sovereign's foe, and of immense concern to himself! Davy was at his heels, overcoming his predecessor's reluctance to complete the ascent, and vaulting to the deck as de Vaucour's cries of '*Mes amis!*' brought his beleaguered compatriots gesticulating around him. As the three French officers climbed aboard *Roscoff*'s deck, twelve desperadoes, scorning the footholds, appeared over the gunnels simultaneously, a spread of stocking caps and whiskers and glinting blades that roused a howl of alarm from the passengers. Those with cutlasses and firearms Dawkins had overlooked brandished them, but dropped them at their captain's request − twenty dishevelled gentlemen who, hearing of the arrangements concluded between de Vaucour and Davy, were disposed to let bygones be bygones.

Not so the red-head. She stepped from behind the mainmast, no domineering matron, as Davy had supposed, but with every attribute of a fish-wife, but a young woman of his own age and of medium height, seeming taller as she stood like avenging Clytemnestra. Each hand trembled with the weight of a pistol it held, cocked and at the ready, but her deep brown eyes were unwavering as they glared from a face which even at this instant of crisis, and despite the smudges it had acquired that eventful afternoon, Davy had to admit was lovely. Her hair had deserted whatever coiffure it had once supported and flowed, a splendid mane, about her shoulders.

'*Les sales américains! Les corsaires!*' The words hissed from those scornful lips, the under one soft and full − words gratifyingly indicative of a rift between allies. But still—

Davy bowed. 'Does ma'amselle speak English? Parlez-vous—'

'I speak English, American pirate,' she blazed. Welcome news, for what he had to say. But he hoped she had not employed this facility in examining the papers in his cabin.

He bowed again, deeply this time. 'Then, ma'amselle, you will pardon the observation that unless you lower those pistols you will blast to perdition not me, who have the good fortune to be the target of your uncertain aim, but any two of the people on deck, regardless of nationality.'

A long speech, formal but effective. The ghost of a smile lit her face − her hair, he perceived, grew to a 'widow's peak' and when swept back to her ears made her face heart-shaped. She dropped her hands to the woefully torn side panels of her green silk dress.

'Your pistols, ma'amselle; they are cocked. It is yourself whom they will blast now.'

Her little thumbs pushed the hammers down. '*M'sieur,*' she said, 'you are insufferable. But then you are a pirate.'

'A privateer.' About to justify his calling by referring to his commission from King George, he was suddenly conscious that every individual on deck, whether he understood a word of what either was saying or whether he did not, was listening to this conversation as if his life depended on the outcome. Whatever she thought of him, *La Reine de Cornouailles* must arrive at Brest a-bristle with the tale of American treachery. 'A privateer, in service of my country the glorious' − the words half stuck in his throat − 'the glorious Republic of America. The ally of La Belle France.'

'Ally of the devil, not France,' she sneered.

'Tell your friends, ma'amselle, that as I speak the rest of my sailors are leaving *La Reine.*' He and she and all who understood English looked across to the big ship with her contrariwise sails. A second lifeboat had splashed into the deepening swell and men were clambering down her sides. 'Tell your friends, ma'amselle, that when all this ferocious pirate's sailors are on board their own ship you and the other passengers, M. de Vaucour and his officers will be free to return to *La Reine* in the two lifeboats. Tell them that, ma'amselle. I give my word.'

'Word of a pirate!'

'Of a gentleman.'

They gazed at each other as if for the first time, separated by twenty feet of heaving deck golden in a sundown which promised a blow before dawn. I know her like my own life. I knew her before my life. I have known her always, he repeated to himself. It was a revelation which came like a blinding light, excluding all but her.

De Vaucour shouted at her in French; did she tell them or should he? She laid the pistols at her feet − it was a gesture like a curtsey − came up to Davy and touched his face. 'It was a terrible blow, *m'sieur*. You must attend to it.' Her fingers lingered on the contusion from his misadventure earlier that day, and then she rejoined her compatriots.

The boat from the Indiaman was close now, smothers of spray raining upon the crowded thwarts and the waves licking at the thole pins. Stona stood at the tiller and gave an exaggerated thumbs-up to catch Davy's eye. The young woman had vanished presently to reappear with the other ladies. She had rubbed off the more obvious smudges from her cheeks, which glowed apple-red in consequence: and her hair was brushed and tied back in a black ribbon which Davy guessed, with almost uncontainable pleasure, had until then hung beside the mirror in his cabin.

Stona came up over the side. 'Present for 'ee cap'n. 'Eard 'im 'ollerin' by one of the gunports and fished the bugger aboard.' And Dawkins, bound in his turn, was hauled over the gunnel. Davy groaned, as much with a twinge of conscience that he had assumed the mutineer to be dead and had not verified it, as because he must now decide what to do with him. Ericson was pushed up behind him, and then came the remainder of the Roscoffs, shoving and jostling and in high spirits − all but two of them. These had remained to secure the treasure chests to the tackle when they were hauled up. The French officers, about to drop into the boat when the privateersmen had left it, raged helplessly when their captain's chest was swung inboard.

'This is robbery; we are allies!' spluttered de Vaucour.

'For the Glorious Revolution,' grinned Davy. He had come to a decision about Dawkins and Ericson, and felt the better for it. He looked down at the two seamen who were roping the chest of jewels for lifting. 'Leave it'.

'Sir?' queried Gurt Jan.

'We are not pirates,' said Davy.

Captain de Vaucour apportioned his people to the two boats. Every French eye was on the Indiaman, which glistened in the gold-green light; her crew had broken from the hold and were waving. Every eye but two. These held Davy's until diverted by the confusion of thrusting oars into the hands of landsmen and tugging somehow towards *La Reine de Cornouailles*.

'What's to do wi' these here pirates, cap'n?' asked Gurt Jan. 'Do we hang 'em?' It was a task he mentioned with some relish.

'No,' said Davy. 'Call away the jolly boat, provision it with a barricoe of water and a bag of ship's bread − oh, you can add half a keg of rum − cut 'em loose and turn 'em both adrift. And haul down that bloody flag.'

'Aye aye!' said Jan.

The Indiaman had resumed her voyage. Davy watched her fade into the night. There was some satisfaction in the knowledge that if ma'amselle too had yearned across that stretch of darkening sea, and somehow he knew she had, *Roscoff* would still be in sight, limned against the sunset.

And I don't even know her name, he thought, nor she mine!

5

'Your West Indiaman,' said Mr Knill; 'well enough! Lesson for us all, eh? As for this manifest from the brig you took a few days previous—' He prodded the precise caligraphy of the Yankee shipmaster now on his way to the prisoners-of-war fort on Dartmoor. 'It lists amongst other items three hogsheads of 750 pounds apiece and twelve casks of 145 pounds of Virginian tobacco.' Mr Knill bent over his desk in the Custom House at St Ives, neatly ribboned hair — his own — dark and dusty in the morning sunshine that rayed through the window at his back. He rummaged through the papers there and produced another sheet. 'Your report, sir, on the action in which you seized yonder vessel of the so-called United States of America, rebels at war with His Britannic Majesty.'

He jerked his quill, the longest Davy had ever seen, over his shoulder, as if the brig in the harbour, red ensign replacing the star-circle and stripes of Davy's ruse-de-guerre, were the least of his concerns. 'Your report on this prize, *Joshua Clegg* of Baltimore, refers to a hit close above the waterline when you compelled her to heave-to.'

He glared at his young captain, whose 'That is so, sir,' raised a glimmer in that long, gloomy countenance. 'Good, good. Pray be seated. Now, Captain, answer me truthfully as you value your command. I am correct in assuming that seawater could have entered the hold by this shot-hole, and ruined the cargo in all or in part? Come, sir. I am right in so assuming?'

This having been Ned Davy's first voyage as a privateer commander, he was unfamilar with the ways of John Knill Esquire. Mr Knill was a lawyer who combined in his person the diversities of Collector of Customs, Mayor of St Ives, Master of a Masonic Lodge, and — if a secret jealously guarded by the many in his employ and of his acquaintance was indeed worth guarding — smuggler supreme. While to those in the know an almost overriding influence in the privateering enterprise argued not so much persuasiveness as a considerable, if undercover, investment therein. In grudging admiration of the Collector's deviousness, Davy assured him that the cargo could have been contaminated.

'Then you, captain, would have had no hesitation in jettison-ing this — er — damaged tobacco?'

'Had I examined it, and found it to be so, I should not have hesitated to drop every damaged cask overboard.'

'Quite so!' The enormous quill sped busily, its black tip agitating above the stooped shoulder against the sunlit view. 'Now, sir, for your journal.' Davy handed it across the desk, and the Collector laid it unopened among the scattered documents. 'I may take it as a true and correct record?'

Davy stiffened in his chair. 'I should be affronted, sir, an you did not.'

Knill jammed his pen in the pewter ink-pot, and spreading bony fingers in the litter lugubriously met the other's stare. 'It is a question, sir, that the duties of my office require me formally to put to you. I foresee a future in which the commander of a private ship of war must affirm, not by a nod, but on oath, the veracity of his journal and accounts. Not all entertain your scruples, my friend.'

The pen was recovered, scratched, and concluded with a 'John Knill, Collector, 16th May 1782'. The sander sprinkled; and like the dawn of a new day officialdom melted into the expression of a connoisseur sampling some delightful vintage. This delight the rejection of the quill and a grip of the encrusted bottle on the desk indicated was about to be sampled.

'All much to your credit, my boy! Splendid voyage! Squire Stephens, Sir Francis, Mr Trevenning, that new fellow Amor up at Godolphin, and others too, will be pleased, and His Grace shall get his statement by the London mail. Now — a bumper of this rare Madeira, which I'll wager you'll find to your taste.'

They stood together, gazing across the harbour at the *Joshua Clegg*, moored astern of a heavily armed Carter lugger, *The Brothers*, at Smeaton's new pier, past her at the privateer schooner *Roscoff*, which Davy had just brought home and anchored in the Bay, and beyond to Hayle estuary. Thence, in thought, though out of sight, Davy looked towards John Harvey's basin, where lay the corvette he had captured the previous autumn. Her refit had been delayed by an Admiralty tussle anent the apportionment of prize money between the privateers-men and the Royal Navy men of the Revenue brig *Fox*.

Knill was eyeing Davy quizzically. '*Le Faucon Gris*, eh?'

Davy contemplated a far horizon. 'These past six months since we took her I have stepped ashore only in Tenerife, the Azores and Barbados, where Cornwall is unknown and Cornish affairs unheard of, let alone discussed. I should be pleased to know that the refit is satisfactory, and what her destiny is to be. Likely, the navy have bought her. *Fox*'s captain, Tom Lewin, aspired to her command.'

'As did you.'

Davy shrugged the comment off. 'I had no expectation.'

'Young man.' Knill grinned, draining his wine, and beckoning Davy to do likewise thumbed the cork from the bottle and tipped a brimmer into each glass. 'Young man, if the navy had wanted the *Falcon*, as we shall call her henceforth, nothing short of a successful French raid, which heaven forbid' – he touched wood with his free hand – 'could stop 'em. As it is, the navy left her to us. I do not doubt they're persuaded she'll do their work for them, at our cost, and with a good captain.' He looked into the intent face, savouring the suspense that showed in its already crow's-footed young eyes.

'But we lacked the guineas to pay the navy's share.'

Davy leaned against the window frame, his breath expelled in a sigh he had been unable to suppress. But the Collector clapped him on the shoulder. 'Come, my boy! We lacked the funds, then. But she is still on the market, and with Captain de Vaucour's money-box not to mention the prizes you have sent in, we – that is, the Company can pay. And damme we shall, and I'll wager she's yours. But not yet.'

Command of the *Falcon,* enjoyed for the brief hour of bringing her into St Ives last year, had been the daydream of rare moments of hope. But 'not yet' could be never.

'Bassett,' Mr Knill was saying, 'purchased before Christmas eight long-14's off a prize. Four of them he has set up in a battery at Portreath west of the harbour there, with a brace of 6-pounders the other side. Terrified, they tell me, lest another Frog or Yankee privateer should raid his precious port and carry off his tin ingots. And we — the Company — have first refusal for the four remaining 14's.'

Ned Davy was as a man who, having worshipped afar, finds his beloved in his embrace. '*Falcon* could well do with chasers, bow and stern.'

'Outdated, they say.'

'Certainly, for the line of battle. But not for a ship a-roving as the *Falcon* will, often in pursuit and sometimes in flight, as when a big frigate challenges.' Davy was warming to his theme. 'She had to rely over-much on her broadside when engaging *Roscoff.*'

'Precisely. Now be off with you, captain. You shall hear further of this, I promise you. My searcher and his assistants will pay your ship an official visit at noon. No contraband to engage his attentions, I trust?' The grin which accompanied the query was quite out of character, Davy thought as he shook his head. The Collector took his arm and led him to the door. 'By the by, you have well timed your return. Squire Stephens is giving a rout at Tregenna tonight — or rather, Miss Lavinia is. Both will welcome you. And, Ned, continue to deserve Mr Stephens' golden opinions and nothing will stand in your way.'

Davy thudded down the bare stairway of the Custom House. A desire to execute a midshipman's recollection of a Cherokee war-dance almost effaced the decorum proper to the captain elect of a 280-ton corvette, launched two years since from Antoine's yards at Brest. Armed with eighteen 9-pounders and four long-14's, he recollected , with four carronades and a dozen perriers swivelled on the gunnels. A ship, moreover, that properly handled could outsail any vessel in the seven seas. Almost a frigate.

At the comparison the elation dwindled. On what grounds

did the captain of a 12-gun schooner — he stared down the alley to where, framed like a picture between the buildings at the end, *Roscoff* rode at anchor: a sweet, gallant, pretty craft but no *Falcon* — on what grounds did he believe himself competent to command such a ship as the French corvette? Himself, moreover, only now past his twenty-second birthday and, as the Bard of Avon would say, with his mother's milk scarce out of him.

Twenty-two! So by God was young Billy Pitt, nephew of that odd fellow Lord Camelford in North Cornwall! Pitt, Member of Parliament at twenty-one and spoken of as the next Prime Minister! Let Pitt rule the ship of state so he, Ned Davy, ruled the trimmest warship in the West Country! He paused to control his exultation, then stepped out of the alley onto the narrow wharf beneath the Custom House window.

John Knill, looking down on him, tut-tutted. All his world at his feet, hopes realised, yet utterly without emotion! Utterly confident! Young fellows were not like that when I was young, mused Knill, and all the better for a touch of humility and doubt. I do not know what the country is coming to.

Meanwhile the subject of this homily strode through the seagulls squawking and tugging at the offal from the morning fish market, and rising in an angry flurry only when those buckled shoes threatened imminent disaster. Off the water-front and past the granite shopfronts he went, and up the narrow street towards the George and Dragon in the Market Place. And Mr Knill would have refused to credit that Captain Davy's immediate problem was to behave as if his heels did not itch to kick up in a jig, and his tongue to proclaim to the house-tops his glorious news.

The taproom of the George and Dragon was crowded; dangerously so, Davy decided, looking over the open upper section of the 'hep' door before unlatching the more solid portals of the saloon. The Carter lugger at the pier, *The Brothers*, familiar in 'The Trade' at a dozen ports in Cornwall and Ireland, and war or no war in Brittany too, besides half a dozen hideouts in the Scillies, had disgorged her watch ashore into the inn. These sprawled around tables and up-ended tubs already littered with 'dead-men' and tankards. Pewter pots foamed and rattled as servers weaved from tapster to customers. Voices, even this early in the day, raised thick and loud above the general babel, and into the throng were drifting a few of the *Roscoff* men to whom Davy had allowed leave.

Davy entered the saloon, its more genteel hubbub enveloping him and reducing the uproar in the 'public' to a buzz. The saloon was patronised midmorning by the professional and commercial fraternity and such of the gentry as business had brought into town. Davy made his way to a short settle occupied by a solitary stranger, who with an exchange of civilities made room for him. The innkeeper, Ambrose Quick, hurried across the room to greet the borough hero, as he put it, on his triumphant return and departed with his order.

'You'll be the Captain Davy, then, who fought and took the French frigate last autumn?' The stranger's southern Irish accent was familiar to Davy, who like most Cornish seamen of the north coast knew Cork as well as Bristol and better than Plymouth.

It had been his honour to do so, Davy agreed, though it was a corvette and not a frigate. 'And you, sir? I do not recall your being here before I sailed, six months ago, on the voyage from which I am now returned. You would appear to be well informed of the affairs of this small town so far, if I may say so, from your own.'

The warmth and admiration expressed in the Irishman's face abashed the young captain. It was a handsome face, intelligent, with wide-spaced grey eyes and crowned with glossy brown hair that fell free to his shoulders. About thirty years of age, Davy decided. He wore a suit which, though past its bloom, was of an elegance rarely seen west of Truro.

'Sean O'Keenahan, *medicinae baccalaureas* of Trinity, Dublin, and your servant, Captain Davy. My friends call me Keeny, or did when I had friends.' They shook hands. 'I came to Cornwall, as far down the Duchy as I could go and yet lie in a decent inn, soon after Christmas, since when I have had little to do but observe the natives. A diverting occupation, though a mite wearisome: one welcomes the highlights.'

'You are in practice here?'

'Indifferently, sir.' And he sat and mused, and so obviously had no more to add that Davy transferred his attention to

Ambrose's other customers. Old Bart Lemmo, now officially, whatever he might be sub rosa, the Company Captain Superintendent, sipped his brandy with cronies before the smouldering hearth and returned his nod. Nearby Mr Trainer, no longer *Roscoff's* boatswain but employed, as Davy was to find later, as a small craft captain on various ventures in home waters, leaned head to head over a two stooled tub with a weedy individual whose churchwarden issued voluminous clouds. The world beyond the cloud seemed for them scarcely to exist. But Trainer caught his glance and moved hastily apart. A scarlet jacket of military cut enveloped a burly fellow who conjured out of his bosom a turnip of a watch which he tapped significantly. It was the 'Sarcher', the customs officer who would accompany Davy back to his ship at noon to check the cargo before giving *Roscoff* clearance to enter harbour. Angry voices from a private room were becoming distinguishable. Davy hoped tempers were no more heightened in the taproom.

'Interesting, b'Jesus!' O'Keenahan emerged from meditation. 'William Trevenning and John Carter met there half an hour since; I doubt that matters proceed well.'

Davy, out of touch as he was, could yet guess what the argument was about. Trevenning, who notoriously mismanaged Wincarrick Farm on the Trevethoe estate at Lelant, had emerged as the front man of a syndicate which organised 'The Trade' from Zennor to St Agnes and which was suspected of including every great name in West Cornwall. Trevenning was getting richer out of moonshining than ever he did from the land. John Carter, known throughout Cornwall as the King of Prussia, was the senior brother of the family which openly dominated the smuggling business in Mount's Bay, and sought to extend its empire along the Lizard and Land's End peninsulas. They dominated the coasts so openly that Carter had been known to break into the Custom House storeroom at Penzance to repossess confiscated contraband. It was held testimony to his unswerving honesty, as even the robbed Collector admitted in his report to London, that Carter had taken nothing but what he maintained to be his. No doubt he was seeking to spread this dominion into Trevenning territory. And while cargoes were run amicably enough into each other's domain as sea and Revenue surveillance determined, the authority of the principals was hotly supported — not, at times, without blows.

'Trevenning's not the man to handle Carter,' Davy commented.

'Few are; but I know one who is.' The doctor tapped the side of his Grecian nose. 'Two to one he'll be along before the morning's out!'

Davy grinned. 'No takers!' As he spoke the door of the private room burst open, and the doorway framed a figure of dramatic presence that draped a vast boat cloak around it with a heave and a swirl, crammed its tricorn on its head, and roared in tones that cut the talk of the saloon to silence, 'Miserable blasphemer! No God-fearing Christian shall bide to hear you speak thus. Better you should pray on your wretched knees for forgiveness.' And proclaiming that he would have no further commerce with Trevenning or his forsworn associates, be they who they were, John Carter plunged through the gathering in the saloon and out into the market place. At this Captain Lemmo heaved himself from his chair and stepped into the private room, while the weedy individual who had enjoyed such close converse with Mr Trainer snapped his clay pipe and tossing it into the embers followed the King of Prussia through the door.

'Carter's latest jackal, Follick,' O'Keenahan explained. 'Carter can't stand smoking. It's a sin. If th'Almighty had intended man to smoke he'd have created him with a chimney. All part of the Methody belief.'

'He contrives to fetch enough baccy into the country to damn everybody else to hell,' Davy observed bitterly.

'They don't count. They ain't the Elect. It's an everlasting mystery' — the doctor's hands were seconding his theme — 'how some across the water can say "Sweet holy Mother o' God" while chopping up every mother's son, ravishing every mother's daughter, who don't say "Ave Maria" in the Latin. And it's a bigger mystery how Carter's cussing cut-throats smuggle spirits and tobacco by the ton, and his make-believe majesty grows fat on it, yet all the time he abhors swearing, and refuses spirits, while baccy he cannot abide. Who shall reconcile the complexities of homo sapiens?'

Davy ordered an ale for himself and a tot of Jamaica for his new acquaintance. The din from the taproom no longer intruded; it seemed that the luggermen had returned aboard with Carter and Follick. The conversational hum in the saloon subsided, after five minutes' buzz that the imperious exit had generated, to a genteel level. The two young men chatted in obvious enjoyment of one another's company and had fast become friends.

Mr Knill entered, strolled through the saloon with a greeting here, a nod and a bow there. 'I told you!' O'Keenahan exclaimed.

'Captain!' Knill acknowledged Davy with a curt bow; none would have suspected their recent meeting in the Custom House. Doctor O'Keenahan he ignored, passing into the private room where, save in the unlikely event of their having left the inn by the window, Lemmo and Trevenning awaited him.

'Dammed uncivil of His Worship. Why should he snub you like that?' Davy asked.

The doctor shrugged his shoulders. 'It's a long, sad story. Compose yourself and you shall hear all about it.'

But Davy had seen the Searcher rise, again tapping that preposterous watch, and he also stood up. 'Alas, not now, I regret. Duty calls. But I shall be honoured to learn your story and share your sorrow. Do I see you at Tregenna tomorrow?'

'That, I fear, is part of the story. I go nowhere, because no one asks me.'

Davy, concerned, was resuming his seat, but the other shook his head. 'I'll not detain you. We meet again?'

Davy grinned his arm. 'Come aboard with me. The provisions of my table will have become fresher and more various since dawn; let us dine together. Then perhaps you will oblige by visiting with me my parents at Boswyn. They are old, and often lonely, and will welcome you.'

'I doubt it,' mourned the doctor. But there was no doubting his pleasure as they made for the harbour.

*

Miss Lavinia Stephens may have had a welcome for Ned Davy, but this welcome was not remarkable at the Tregenna rout on Wednesday evening. Indeed, for the throng of young army officers in red, and young naval officers in blue and white, and young squires in every hue of the spectrum, not to mention perspiring sons of aspiring farmers and a fair sprinkling of the town's well-to-do, there had been no opportunity for greeting beyond the formal presentation on his arrival. Dinner had of course been held at the customary four bells in the afternoon watch — 2 p.m. as Davy reminded himself now that he was ashore again. And this, despite an invitation despatched to Boswyn by the Squire himself, Davy had been too busy about his ship to attend. Later, the kaleidoscopic whirl that engulfed the younger element around the supper board had posed fewer opportunities, even, of testing Miss Stephens' concern than the preenings and cavortings and changing partnerships of the ballroom floor. Better, thought Davy, feeling himself to be very much the tarpaulin in such dainty company, that he had joined the oldsters at whist in the library.

Davy recollected Lavinia as the fat and frilly infant whose precocity had embarrassed him when, a twelve-year-old splendid in his new midshipman's uniform, he was about to join his first ship at Plymouth. Frilly she still was; fat no more, though perhaps arms, shoulders and bosom, of which prevailing fashion permitted a generous view, promised future amplitude. And pretty; certainly pretty, if your taste was for golden ringlets, rosebud lips and cornflower eyes that disclosed more of planning than of pleading. But all those competing young men — none of the equally competing and numerous young women swam into his ken — engaged her entire attention. Well, they were welcome to the Lavinias of this world! His thoughts flew, as so often since the happy conclusion of the West Indiaman affair, to ma'amselle dominating the dandies on the deck of his ship. There, by God, was a woman! He ached for her.

At the long buffet table beneath the windows he entered into a discussion, over a claret or two, with Nick Toman. Toman had succeeded Lewin in command of the Revenue brig *Fox*, now refitted after her mauling off Pencobben. Naval affairs were a wholesome diversion from the scraping of tired musicians, the shuffle of feet, the chatter and the silly laughter. But Toman's preference, that night at least, was for the flesh-pots.

'Let us eat, drink, and manage a wench or two, my friend! Nation's done for, and tomorrow we die.'

Davy dissented. 'Britannia will find her true self again. I am persuaded, Nick, that the national honour will prove the spur. But enough of high politics. Tell me, what news of Tom Lewin?'

'Oh, he got his post rank all right. Now commanding a '32 and looking for prizes off Finisterre. Strange you didn't meet him. But your pardon!' An opening chord at that moment coinciding with a glint in the eye of Mrs Tregonning's 'purty li'l maid', he left the narrative incomplete.

The tall casements of the ballroom, which was on the first floor and extended along the whole flank of Squire Stephens' Gothic mansion on the hillside, looked out over woodland. However the clearance made for its building nine years before had not overgrown sufficiently to obscure harbour and bay. Davy crossed to the far side of the table and parted the curtains, less for the view than for the cool of the glass and the sea air which, admitted through the fractionally opened frame, dissipated the saturation of perfumes both usual and necessary in the hygienic deficiencies of life ashore.

The great, shielded lantern at the harbour entrance threw the pier behind it into a darkness that a thousand stars, that Venus radiant low above Godrevy Point and Jupiter with his moon specks visible in the clear atmosphere, could hardly illumine. A forest of masts swayed dimly on the paler tide. Davy saw a lamp on the poop of his schooner *Roscoff;* it spilled on an O of deck. A few lit windows marked the sleeping town.

Through the scratch of the fiddles Davy heard the new leaved treetops outside chattering in a puff of wind. It rattled the panes, and fresh with the fragrance of blackthorn blossom set the flames in candelabra and chandeliers dancing in their turn. A footman bustled up to draw the curtains again, shaking a reproachful head that oddly moved independent of its over-large wig. And as the curtain rings clacked along the rail Davy's attentive ear caught the clatter of approaching hooves. Someone in a mighty hurry — at that time of night! About to brave the big-wig's further objections, Davy felt a touch on his sleeve.

'Far away, Captain Davy? The dancing has had to proceed without you.' It was a girl's voice; a youthful, arresting voice with a resonance peculiar to a race whose men and women sing well. He turned abruptly, to meet a shy glance and features which under their high-piled brown hair were vaguely familiar.

A face, handsome rather than pretty and lacking the
pretensions of cosmetics. The girl wore a green dress,
lovingly, no doubt, and patently sewn at home. His thoughts
flew to the green dress, torn but stylish, of ma'amselle of the
ship.

'Faith, ma'am, since I am kin to half those present here you
must be . . . but you have me at a disadvantage; I have been so
much from home since childhood. Ah! Aunt Adeline's girl from
Wendron!'

She lowered her gaze and poked at an erratic curl. 'No
relation o' your'n, sir. Thought twice about intrudin', I did. But
you looked so lonesome.' Her eyes clouded. 'Didn't ought to be
here at all really. Father—' and then the words flowed as if from
a dam — 'he've been doing well lately. Upping himself, like.
Sort of agent for Sir Francis he is now. Squire owed it to him
after what happened that night — with the soldiers, I mean.'
She blushed, then shook her head as if to forbid the thought.
'Father have been huntin' with the Fourbro', and has a mind to
set himself up. He'm losing what he can afford, and not a tup'ny
piece more, in the card room, while ma's sitting yonder with the
ladies and never a word passin' between 'em, and I'm—'

Davy snapped his fingers. 'Miss Porris of Bethlehem Farm!
Bless my soul!' The vision of Jess naked rose teasing like a
succubus, but pleasure at her presence exorcised it. 'Not
dancing, you say? It shall proceed this moment, if you will do
me the honour. No, I don't know the steps well either, but from
what I see we shall be no worse than many.' He led her onto the
floor. And yes, it was good to be home, and young, and with
Jess.

Bow and scrape and prance and bow! There was much to be
said for the setting to partners that the hands favoured on the
foredeck in the last dogwatch, the fiddler squatting on the
capstan head. But here in the Stephens' ballroom 'Sir Roger de
Coverley' and the old country dances were jolly too with Jess to
partner, while the quick-time hornpipe that was replacing the
measured tread of 'The Cornish Squire' was a frolic. The
captain of the *Roscoff* and captain-elect of the *Falcon* caught
himself laughing like a ship's boy, till checked by Mrs Porris,
who had no smile for him as they whirled by, pointedly turning
her back to him. Angling for a better match for her daughter,

Davy decided, that shifting mood of his playing the devil, as always, with any crumb of contentment the gods allotted him. For a fleeting instant the brown hair beneath his gaze became auburn, the face uplifted to his heart-shaped, and then was Jess Porris again.

A troubled Jess Porris. She had sensed his change of mood. 'We did very well, I thought.'

'Famously, and thank you,' he replied. About to escort her to mamma, on impulse he seized her hand. She was a young woman a man could be proud of, desire was there, there was a liking between them, and who was he to hope for his heart's desire? 'I shall not let you go so easily,' he said. 'You have made me happy tonight.'

'I thought—'

'It was your mother. She turned her face from me.' What imp of mischief prompted him to add, 'As you did once?'

Jess snatched her hand from his, and with burning cheeks and blazing eyes met his gaze. 'No more of that, Ned Davy! Shame on 'ee!'

'As if I could forget!'

'Then I'll trouble you next time to remember my face, Cap'n Davy. Oh sir,' she said, relenting and reaching for him, 'let us not—'

The link was broken. 'Until next time, then.' He accompanied her across the room, bowed stiffly to her and her mother, waited despite the dame's frosty stare till Madam bobbed in return, then marched up the temporarily abandoned dance area to where the orchestra were replenishing their tankards. Beside the dais a lively group lapsed into silence as they watched the sailor's approach. He bowed his adieux to Miss Stephens and mumbled his thanks, and made for the door as the band, refreshed, struck up 'The Jolly Tinker'.

There was a cough at his shoulder. It was the footman with the outsized wig. 'Mr Stephens' compliments, sir, and he would be obliged if you would join him right away.'

The Squire himself was standing in the doorway and beckoning. It was a summons not to be ignored. Squire Stephens was chairman of the privateering consortium, the command of the *Falcon* was his to bestow. He guided Davy along a gallery and down the great staircase.

'Deuce of a to-do! I want you to join us in committee. Never been faced with a situation like this before, damme!'

It was serious, all right. A declaration of war. There were two of them waiting in the panelled study, where a log fire flared in an open hearth. 'Rest of the Board in their beds; can't get hold of 'em. Just Mr Trevenning — you know Trevenning? — and me. No need to introduce Smeecher.' It was a bedraggled Smeecher, who had flogged his horse across brake and brea all the way from Helford River, and whose arrival Davy had heard not half an hour since. 'Now, Smeecher — fill the fellow's glass up, Trevenning, there's a good chap — now Smeecher, repeat to Captain Davy what you have told us.'

Smeecher, fluent when so minded, launched into his tale. Hannibal Trainer had sailed the fishing smack *Dorcas* round the land, bound for the Helford River with a dozen casks of tobacco — about three-quarters of a ton in all. Smeecher had as usual ridden to the point of discharge, Gweek, to organise the transport of the contraband to the dispersal point, a cottage which Mr Trevenning had visited himself a fortnight earlier to arrange terms. This run, Mr Trevenning was at haste to explain, would bring the trade far nearer to the Truro markets than was possible on the St Ives coast; moreover there was another reason which would doubtless come to light in the following discussion. Smeecher then described how he had seen the *Dorcas* come in at high water last afternoon and make her way up river by her oars, the wind having dropped before sunset. Smeecher himself saw the tobacco ashore and loaded onto a string of mules; but they had scarcely penetrated the riverside forest when a horde of Carter's villains ambushed them.

'How did you know they were Carter's men?' asked Davy.

'They said as how the king would appreciate the tribute what the St Ives lot was sending him — we took it to mean the King of Prussia and not His Majesty'.

'Quite! Top up your glass, man, and continue.'

Smeecher and the rest of his party did not wait to argue the points of possession, but dispersed among the trees, though Smeecher stayed in the vicinity and watched the mules and their burdens driven away in the direction of Helston. He then ventured to the water's edge, with a view to going aboard the

Dorcas to size up the situation with Mr Trainer, only to see him rowed ashore in a Carter gig and seated beside − of all people − the King of Prussia himself.

Hailing the smack, Smeecher was told that they dared not sail out of the river until ordered by Carter to do so. Smeecher had then spared neither his mount nor himself to bring Mr Trevenning the news.

'Most commendable,' said the Squire. 'You did well.'

'Carter went to a lot of trouble over what for him must have been a modest haul,' Davy surmised.

'It was a trial run,' Trevenning explained. 'That damned King of Prussia aimed to move in on our territory, and I dared him to.'

'Bit of a risk,' opined Mr Stephens.

'Him or us, sir. I had it out with him at the George and Dragon.'

'Half St Ives heard him having it out with you,' Davy commented. 'The man's insufferable.'

'He's got no right to control the river,' Trevenning went on. 'It's any man's province. Always has been.'

'Trevenning's correct,' affirmed the Squire, who was a noted antiquary. 'The Helford district has never been anyone's country. Provided sanctuary from time immemorial for all of us who are, shall we say? not in entire agreement with the law. It's a situation we magistates recognise, and respect. Carter has no claim to the Helford, and his action has been high-handed, devilish high-handed, damme! Haven't heard your opinion yet, Smeecher. And for God's sake sit down. You're fagged out, and no wonder.'

Smeecher perched himself on the edge of a Tudor ham-flattener of a chair.

'Tes all been said, gen'lemen. That there John Carter as do call hisself King of Prussia have been and took what was yours, and he've given me a plaguy hard ride, and the question is, what are 'e going to do about it?'

'What indeed?' said Squire. 'Well, out with it, man.'

'Send a ship,' declared the oracle.

The three of them looked at Davy.

'I can provision, rearm, and get the local hands back aboard by Friday − tomorrow. The other half—'

'I know. John Knill told me. Sent packing. Leaves you about thirty, eh? Enough?'

Davy considered, then nodded. Nothing more was decided than that *Roscoff* should sail for Helford with utmost despatch, and that Davy should act as the situation required. It was a decision which left a load of responsibility, and likely of censure besides, on his shoulders, Davy thought dismally. 'Well, sirs, twenty-four hours leave little leeway. I must be off. Good morning.'

'Egad, so it is!' exclaimed the Squire, quizzing the massive ormolu timepiece above the hearth.

From the ballroom and gallery Miss Lavinia Stephens' laughter still chimed among the same gallants, all redder in face and wilder in gait the longer the revelry endured. Blind Man's Buff, and games invented, it seemed, for the occasion followed the dancing in hilarious succession. Farmer Porris had lost enough, and Mrs Porris had tried enough, and Miss Porris had fretted enough for them to have called their carriage and left. Did he regret not seeing her before she went? Perhaps. But there were matters of immediate import to be resolved. The clock in the church tower struck two as Davy strode down the hill, with the rout still in full blast behind him.

6

The two young men leaned over the poop bulwarks. 'That's Prussia Cove,' Captain Davy explained to his new friend Dr O'Keenahan, who had joined *Roscoff* for the voyage, not as ship's surgeon — Nankervis, at present on leave, was still under contract to tend to such afflictions of the flesh as might occur — but as supernumerary. And indeed it was not only for the pleasure of the Irish doctor's company that Davy had invited him aboard. The schooner sailed a south-easterly course to take her clear of the Lizard, and the Carter haven was a deep shadow in the grey of the cliffs: eight miles distant, but in the clear air visible through the spy-glass the doctor was endeavouring to hold steady against the trembling backstay. A light square against the green of the rolling cliff-top Davy identified as John Carter's house, the thatched building beyond being where he was commonly supposed to store his contraband. A drystone wall, hallmark of the 'King's' strongholds, enclosed both.

'Away to east'rd, that's Breage church tower, and all yonder stretch of coast is famous for wreckers. There's a verse about 'em they call "The seaman's prayer":

> God keep us from rocks or shelving sands
> And save us from Breage and Germoe men's hands.'

'They're the scallyways who lure ships onto the rocks,' the doctor supposed.

'Now look 'ee, Keeny,' said Davy severely, 'rough though they are, and scallywags as they may be, they ain't that bad. Good Methodies, many of 'em, like the Carter brood, and a few Anglicans among 'em too. But they regard a wreck as a gift from above it'ld be sheer blasphemy not to strip; and they ain't over-gentle with misled individuals, even the shipwrecked mariners themselves, who might presume to interfere. But the wreckers don't have it all their own way. The local landowners hold the right to wreck, and deem the Lord's bounty theirs alone. So they summon the military to enforce the law.'

'And the owners?'

Davy rolled his eyes piously. 'The Lord giveth, the Lord taketh away! And heaven preserve us from the wreckers of Germoe and Breage!'

A soldier's wind was blowing steadily over the larboard quarter, the foretopmast curving under pressure of the topsails like a half-drawn bow, a perpetual wave crest bubbling beneath the rising, falling forefoot, the whole ship taut and resonant. Davy took the telescope from O'Keenahan and focussed it on the Lizard Head. A sail beating to windward in the offing was not that of a Revenue cutter, of which he had nothing to fear; nor was it Captain Harry's great lugger *The Brothers,* conclusions with which could prove costly: especially since *Roscoff* had put to sea at dawn that Friday undermanned. Not surprising, for a Friday sailing!

The decision had not been Davy's. Squire, eager to contain the Carters' expansion and uphold ancient rights, was prepared to use his own vessels to that end and had instructed his captain accordingly. But Davy did not doubt that the *Roscoff* was speeding towards the uncertain hazards of Helford primarily because of Trevenning and the nebulous consortium of Free Traders that he represented. I fail, mused Davy suddenly embittered, and Stephens and the Company suffer the loss and I, yet again, the ignominy. I succeed, and Trevenning prospers!

Observing O'Keenahan watching him, he suspected that the doctor, brief though their acquaintance had been, penetrated that shell of reserve underneath which he was at pains to protect his raw sensitivity. The tables must be reversed.

'You know, Keeny, you've not yet told me what misfortunes stranded you so dismally in Penwith.'

The pleasure drained from the doctor's face, so that Davy at once regretted a comment so unworthily inspired. It appeared that the Dr O'Keenahan of half a year since had partnered a fashionable and prosperous practice in Bristol and even attended titled patients at Bath. In that hive of elegance he attracted a bored young Milady of scintillating beauty, elderly spouse and impeccable ancestry who prevailed upon him — so said the doctor — to accompany her to the ends of the earth, this being the far South-West, there to enjoy a new, harmonious and uncomplicated life together.

Taking ship, and the lady's jewels, in a trading ketch, they had found both husband and father awaiting their disembarkation: the Bristol pilot had known where to turn for a guinea or two! It having been the longest and roughest passage the ketch's master could recall, it was obvious from the state of the couple that disenchantment there was, conspiracy there had been, but consummation never. Wherefore, the tongue of ill repute being so remote from Bath as to render disregard the better part of propriety, My Lords and My Lady departed in a hired chaise, while Dr O'Keenahan remained, perforce, to endure the lingering sting of words which had impugned his honour, and the reproaches of a society which, if not unblemished itself, staunchly condemned transgression everywhere else.

Davy suppressed a laugh with such difficulty as impeded speech. For one moment they stood glaring at one another, then burst simultaneously into roars of mirth that set the lookout in the fore-top hailing his opposite number in the main to pass the news, while the officer of the watch, helmsman, and all on quarterdeck and poop joined in for no other reason than that laughter of a sort is infectious.

This would not do. 'Mr Stona,' called Davy, controlling himself, 'I'll trouble you to attend to your duties. The deck is not a bear garden.'

'Aye-aye, sir,' gasped Gurt Jan.

Two bells struck in the first 'dog' − 5 p.m. Smeecher came on deck yawning, having in the past few hours made good some of the sleep recent activities had cost him. Young Pendarves, midshipman of the watch, at a nod from Lieutenant Stona, the second officer, turned the hour glass. Davy had reorganised his command navy fashion, splitting the merchant service's third watch into the navy's two dog watches. Renaming his mates and apprentices lieutenants and midshipmen, with duties corresponding to those of naval officers, he had introduced a tighter discipline which, proving to the whole ship's company more fair and more efficient than under the unpredictable regime of old Captain Lemmo, had ensured the triumphs and rewards of a 'happy ship'. True, Davy meditated, as the topmen leapt into the shrouds at dusk in the last dog to go about off the Men Hyr rock, while the lubbers lay aft with the braces, discipline presented fewer problems when your crew were all volunteers and personally involved in the success of the voyage. How different from the Royal Navy, where most were pressed men and many but lately shanghaied aboard, and where the rule of the 'cat' was enforced by all naval captains save an enlightened few such as Davy's kinsman Edward Pellew. Flogging in a privateer, except in the most exceptional circumstances, would produce only lamentable results. It was as well, thought Davy, that in any event he himself regarded the 'cat' as an instrument of last resort.

An hour's sailing while the rags of daylight dissolved over the Lizard tableland to the north-west, and the look-out's cry of 'Breakers on larboard bow' indicated the dreaded Manacles and the run-in to Falmouth Bay. The first watch, eight to midnight, found Stona back on watch and *Roscoff* close-hauled on a northerly course. The Helford River was by dead reckoning now abeam, but they must proceed further towards Falmouth before they could go about and enter the estuary.

Helford, Davy explained to O'Keenahan, once the medieval haunt of pirates, had long been a haven of sanctuary for vessels of questionable legality. Rather like the thieves' precincts in great cities. No royal fort had ever, as at St Ives, St Michael's Mount or Falmouth, controlled its approaches with cannon. No landlord there had levied more than his just dues, nor been more promptly paid even by those whose preference it was to take. No freebooter or free trader had ever claimed authority over the waterfront there — until now. To restore the status quo was the prime purpose of the expedition.

'And to define boundaries nearer home? What are your plans, Ned?'

'We anchor up-river, where Carter's spies shall find us at dawn.'

'And then?' But Davy had immediate problems in mind.

The schooner was darkened, save for the glimmer of the binnacle. About ship again, when the lights of Falmouth were showing dead ahead, and in past Rosemullion Head with a nor'westerly a couple of points off the starboard bow and becoming fitful as it funnelled down the river valley. Stona had placed a leadsman in the chains. The schooner was reduced to single jib and reefed mainsail, the land was an amorphous mass closing darkly on either side, and the water was shoaling fast. So had many a captain before Davy felt his needfully inconspicuous way to safe moorings and the shield of night.

He took in all canvas and completed the final mile with his great sweeps — back-breaking work for hands, officers and supernumerary too bearing down on the oars, himself balanced on the jib-boom, conning the ship in husky whispers that were grunted along the deck to the coxswain at the helm.

*

'Ahoy! Ahoy!' At the hail the rooks swirled above the treetops like smuts from a bonfire, while the seagulls rose from the schooner's rail and spars, drifting and moaning like the dead men's souls they were. 'Ahoy there!'

Hain, duty petty officer, had ducked into the galley for a mug of tea from the stock the P.O.'s mess had surreptitiously acquired during the recent voyage. He emerged into the grey, dank daylight, mug in hand. Dew dripped from yards and rigging in a slow, irregular patter, and he swore as drops hit him. Midway between the trees that thronged the shore and *Roscoff*, anchored bows upstream against combined current and ebb, he saw a scrawny being waist-deep in a mist which almost concealed the dinghy he stood in and the boatman at the oars.

'Stand off there,' bawled Hain. 'Don't come no nearer now. What do 'ee want?'

'A word with Cap'n Davy, fellow, and be smart about it. 'Tis shivering cold down here.'

'Shiver and be damned!' But before Hain's messenger could scurry down the companion for the captain, Davy appeared rubbing his eyes and flinching in the dew-fall. He had turned in fully dressed against any emergency. 'All right, P.O., I heard. Call him alongside.'

Pinched features in need of a shave surmounted the bulwark beneath a shabby tricorn, and the leg which at the second attempt flung itself over the gunnel preceded a body that matched it in drab and ill-fitting apparel. 'What 'ave we got here?' Hain muttered to the quartermaster of the watch. 'Hind leg of a chicken, is it?'

Davy eyed the sparse figure that had gathered itself together on the desk. 'I've seen you before; George and Dragon, St Ives. You'll be John Carter's—'

'Follick, captain. Ambrose Follick at your service, sir.' The shabby hat tipped in half-hearted greeting as Davy touched his own. 'I have the honour to be Mr Carter's confidential secretary and agent. Mr Carter requires — asks me to —'

Any message from John Carter had better first be received and considered in private. 'Then perhaps you will accompany me to my cabin, Mr Follick. Petty Officer, I'll have a pot of that tea sent below to me right away. From the captain's pantry I don't doubt. Let us consider that this slight return squares the deal!'

Hain, who had been holding the mug behind his back, produced it like a rabbit from a hat, and with his free hand touched his forehead in salute. 'Aye aye, sir. In no time at all.'

Davy led his early caller through the wardroom, whence the
cabins opening onto it were disgorging the first and second
lieutenants Wallace and Stona, Dr O'Keenahan – he occupied
the third's quarters, Richard Trigg being on leave after bringing the *Joshua Clegg* in – besides Gunner, Bos'un and Purser,
all in varying stages of undress but evincing a uniform curiosity.
The captain's cabin extended the whole width of the stern, a
few feet of its starboard extremity being screened off for his cot
and wash-bowl, and its windows closed to the misty waterway up
which the schooner had been propelled with such effort a few
hours previously.

Over the steaming tea, sweetened with molasses, and for
which the 'King of Prussia's' ferret required the addition of a tot
of rum, civilities were exchanged. Then came the message. Mr
John Carter, Captain Henry Carter and their brothers had
purchased all that land which contained the southern shores of
the Helford estuary from the Gew to Bosahan Point; wherefore
they forbade access to and from the Helford river except with
their express authority which they would enforce by seizure and
arrest.

So that was it! Davy held the other's shifty gaze till it dropped.
'They can't do that.'

'They've done it,' snarled the ferret.

'But the freedom of the river is a right British vessels have
enjoyed since time immemorial, and Carter knows it. He has no
jurisdiction here.'

'He has the best of jurisdiction, as presently I'll show you,
captain. Crown and justices can't stop my principals – er –
freetrading: they've tried and they've failed, time and again.
Neither will they loosen the family's grip on the river. West
Cornwall is now Carter country. Look, Mr Davy.'

Follick rose – even on his feet he barely reached the deckhead beams – and reaching across the leatherbound settle
unlatched one of the stern windows behind it. Davy followed his
pointing finger downstream to Bosahan. Mist still wreathed the
surface but lay lower now, vanishing as he watched. The outstretched branches of willow and oak were now clear of the
falling tide; they made a tunnel through the blackness of which
shot an occasional flash of the rising sun. Inshore, above the
trees, a whitewashed cottage shone against the spring verdure,

and round its encircling garden ran a new drystone wall. Davy had once visited the cottage — aptly named La Rochelle by its succession of Duvals, the Huguenot family which had settled there after escaping from Richelieu along with the Bourdeaux, Du Toits, Ruffignacs and others who had settled in West Cornwall a century and a half ago. No one could be friendlier than old Duval. Yet along that new wall, with freshly painted black iron barrels in contrast — in obscene contrast, Davy thought in anger — to the white dwelling and rioting greenery, a battery of cannon was ranged, the gun crews busy about them.

'Pretty, ain't they?' The ferret produced an inch of clay pipe from his pocket and prodded a refill into the sooty dottle. 'Mr Carter bought 'em the other day, all four of 'em, from Sir Francis Bassett. Fourteen-pounders they are, long 14's, sited to command the river mouth.'

His guns! *Falcon*'s guns! 'So I see.' Davy could scarcely bring himself to speak.

Follick fumbled in some deep recess of his attire to produce a flint and steel, clicking away with maddening persistence until a slow match lit and was applied to the nauseous bowl.

'You'd not do that in your master's presence.' The glare with which the ferret received the taunt was a slight emollient to Davy's tortured soul.

'Never fancied snuff,' observed Follick, regaining his composure amid a cloud of smoke while Davy gazed disconsolately at the battery, and beyond into the roadstead, where out of the mist materialised a ship at anchor: *The Brothers*, Captain Harry's armed lugger.

'The odds are against you,' Follick remarked complacently.

'Just let him try coming at me up river,' Davy growled through his teeth.

'He won't. He'll wait. Now you listen to me. Mr John says you're to come ashore with me and discuss the situation with him man to man, not like a thief in the night.'

'Like hell I will, and I'll trouble you to watch your tongue. And you can tell your power-crazed monarch that I've no intention of sharing his dungeons with Hannibal Trainer and the *Dorcas* crew.'

'Very comfortable quarters they've got, I assure you, and very compliant they all are. Now just you come along with me, my friend.'

'Follick,' shouted Davy, shaking the man's hand from his arm, 'it may well be that you are going ashore not only without me, but without your boat besides—'

The ferret was out of the ship and into his dinghy more nimbly than he had clambered aboard. 'Threats, God rot you, will avail you nothing!' he yelled over the water.

That calm exterior he was at pains to preserve erupting beyond control, Davy, who had followed Follick on deck, snatched a potato from within the galley door. Then, propriety reasserting itself, he stood juggling it from hand to hand.

'Allow me, sir,' said Petty Officer Hain, who like everyone else in the *Roscoff* knew his young captain a good deal better than Davy chose to acknowledge. He took the potato and hurled it at the gesticulating ferret. It missed him, but caught the boatman full in the face. The man sprang to his feet in anguish, dropping his oars to hold his nose. The dinghy rocked violently, and over the side went Follick. The boat drifted oarless downstream, fading into the last vestiges of the mist, while the ferret flailed his way to the bank.

'Remind me to stand you a tot, Hain,' said Davy.

*

Davy kept his crew, adequate to sail but not to fight the ship besides, in the two watches normally worked only at sea. Boarding nets were rigged, gunners stood by the swivels on deck and one of the cannon below, a look-out at either masthead ensured against surprise attack, at least by day. And much good that will do! mused Davy bitterly. He should have delayed sailing until a full crew had been mustered and every gun manned, but in deferring to the wishes of his owners he had sacrificed caution to ambition. It ought to have occurred to him that Carter might have placed a battery on the Point; the 'King' had already done so above Prussia Cove. But Squire Stephens's sending him to forestall such an intrusion on rights and custom had closed his mind. But, but, but! One lesson I have learnt, for what it's worth, thought Davy, is never again to let another man's judgement supplant my own.

He called a council of war in the great cabin – Wallace and Stona, James Osborne the gunner and of course Smeecher, Nathan Pendarves as senior midshipman, and Dr O'Keenahan. Sensing some resentment at the doctor's presence, Davy explained that since reconnaissance would be essential, O'Keenahan's being a stranger in the district was a factor worth exploiting.

'Sure, I'll be going as someone from Bodmin—'

'You've no time to learn the language,' interposed Davy.

'From Cork, seeking a peaceful home for my widowed, ageing mother, and for myself that's writing the family history.'

It was decided to take the *Roscoff* higher up the river, out of sight of Duval's cottage, where they could put a party ashore undetected. At the turn of the tide early in the afternoon watch the sweeps were manned again, the anchor catted and dropped half a mile or so up-river in Frenchman's Creek, close in to the eastern bank where the trees almost garlanded the topmasts. A bend in the creek screened the schooner from what scant traffic there was along the river, and the jolly-boat could operate under complete cover. And though, lying as she did barely a pebble's flip from the shore, *Roscoff* was more vulnerable to attack than in the open, it was generally conceded that she was safer there during the few hours preceding inevitable discovery than she would have been anywhere else.

Davy summoned all hands aft, and in the unlikely event that there were some on board ignorant of the purpose of the expedition, its dubious prospects and its certain dangers, he explained the whole position to them.

'Them Carters is ridin' for a fall,' cried one of the thirty seamen he had been able to muster for the voyage.

'Then us'll give 'em a shove,' shouted old Jack Coombes, a leading hand from Barnstaple who had been with Davy the whole of his young captain's time in the ship.

'Three cheers—' But Davy's flapping palms and shaking head contrived to maintain the serenity of the forest. O'Keenahan, Smeecher and Cook's Mate Quinn, briefed to be the Irish gentleman's servant, were first ashore – Smeecher to get them mounts from some undisclosed contact. Then went Gurt Jan, Pendarves and a couple of seamen to spy out the land and assess Carter's defences.

Davy, reluctant to leave the deck lest sudden emergency demand his presence, envied Stona and the doctor their invasion of hostile territory. Envied and feared for them; heard with mixed emotion of welcome and foreboding each noise from enclosing creek and woodland – a pigeon bursting into the sunshine above the trees, a swan working up to take-off speed, the stirrings of a populous undergrowth. As is the custom of sailors not on watch, everybody below slept the long afternoon through. A fisherman, his skiff released from the grip of the mud by the flooding tide, stood among his crab pots sculling single oared over the stern as with a wave and a shout he passed the schooner and rounded the bend for the river and the sea.

The sun sank early into the surrounding foliage, vanishing in a crystalline scatter that lacked any of sundown's embers. The mist stole back upon the water and its wraithes weaved around the spars. The fisherman returned betimes. 'Couldn't stay out there no more, I couldn't. Fog that thick you could lean agin 'un. Ships all about a-ringin' their bells, and the wind puffin' so's there'm clear water and your sails drawin' one minute, and the next flat calm and ye cain't see the foredeck nor I the length o' this little craft. Some collision afore night's out, I shouldn't wonder, or ships runnin' theirselves aground. Plenty o' pickings then. Meanwhile I don't belong to stay out in Falmouth Roads with the fog like 'tis this evening.'

'Fleet out?' Davy, whom Wallace had persuaded to retire to his cabin for a meal and a rest, heard his Number One inquire, his Scots accent necessitating repetition. 'No, all freighters, I reckon. Some do say they'm a convoy out of Plymouth for to relieve Gibraltar.'

'Likely enough. *The Brothers* still out there?'

'Moved in to moorings off the Gew. Lying there like she don't want no one to get in or out, 'cept me. Funny!' And as the fisherman went home up the creek he laughed as if it really were.

'Funny? Yon's sense o' humour is peculiarly his own,' Wallace declared to no one in particular.

Davy surrendered to the comfort of his settee. Wallace! What a relief from the unspeakable Dawkins – even pre-mutinous Dawkins, his unfathomable and in the event rascally associate of half a year, whose treatment of the ship's company as either

cronies or Cornishmen offered a warning which Davy had failed
to observe. Davy wondered if the would-be Avery and his mate
had reached land, and found himself hoping that they had not,
that they were drifting to eternity like the Flying Dutchman.
But the Scotsman, for all his crusty exterior, was a man whom a
captain, even in the isolation to which his command condemned him, might make a true friend of. One of Squire's tried
officers ever since the French war broke out, Wallace had been
second officer in the company's most heavily armed lugger.
Davy, having met him on occasion, had borrowed him for the
Helford venture. He hoped the transfer might be made per-
manent.

But Dawkins . . .! Yet it was not Dawkins he thought of as he
fell asleep in his cabin beneath the poop. It was of the villain's
intended victim. A French girl with red hair and a way with
her . . .

7

It was at Manaccan that O'Keenahan saw it — a notice nailed to the chapel door, in firm if irregular hand which fine weather had spared from obliteration.

OUR PREECHER NEXT SUNDAY
20 APRIL 1782
AT 10 OF THE CLOCK
CAPT'N HENERY CARTER
BLESSED BE THE NAME OF THE LORD

The Irish gentleman thereupon bade a courteous farewell to the Ancient who, uninvited but scenting profit, had escorted him round the village. With slight prompting O'Keenahan had elicited that Manaccan was proper beholden to them Carters these past months, though they was foreigners from Germoe away to the sou-west of Helston. Bought a parcel of land upalong, Mr John had. Had took a cottage up to Bosahan. Captain Harry? That were his lugger in the bay. Gurt cutter there too — biggest in the world. Besides his seafaring he were a Methody preacher on the local circuit. Proper fiery he was with his hellfire and damnation; people do dearly love to be frit by a fiery sermon. No, he belonged to go preaching without his crew; said to Mr Penaluna up to the big house they put him off. Well, if anybody ever had heard as how Captain Harry was in 'The Trade', nobody wasn't saying. Yes. Frenchman's Crick was the next crick up river, and times was hard and the gentleman were lucky to have found a guide as could speak English, though he couldn't speak Irish, ha-ha! he being ostler once at the Angel, because Cornish were the best most of them to Manaccan could get their tongues round. And he thanked the gentleman for the handsome tip and would be brea pleased to see him, and his man, that way again.

'Sooner than you think, maybe.' The gentleman and his man trotted off along the track that twisted through oak, beech, elm,

hazel and sycamore in all the filigree of their young green
leaves, the briery tangle of rioting woodland closing in on every
side, and the pervading fragrance of the upland heath and
pine-coppices borne by the land breeze that heralded quiet
eventide. Presently, turning the shaggy horses loose, as
instructed, to find their own way home, they forsook the path
and struggled down the slope through the undergrowth, discovering between the trunks, at first indistinctly and then,
smudged below them upon the twilit mist, the spars and rigging
of the *Roscoff*.

'Psst!' Quinn laid a hand on O'Keenahan's sleeve. They froze.
A second afterwards other blundering footsteps stopped too.
The doctor drew his sword, slowly to avoid the swish of the
blade, while Quinn fumbled in the belt beneath his jacket for
the butcher's knife which had, on demand, played its part in
repelling boarders.

O'Keenahan put his lips to Quinn's ear. 'Faith now, Paddy,
Captain said no bloodshed. "Dog don't eat dog" — his very
words.'

'Hell, I'll eat rather than be et!' the cook's mate muttered.

'And so, my boy, will I!' They groped through the darkening
tangle.

'Halt, we got 'ee covered!' It was the loudest, most startling
whisper the doctor had ever heard. He span round, catching his
fine black coat in a bramble, while Quinn's step backwards
brought his heel against the root of an elm and himself
sprawling.

'Dr O'Keenahan and Cook's Mate Quinn.' The doctor's
attempt to keep his voice quiet and level failed; his words of
doubt as to the trigger touch of the second lieutenant and his
scouts earned Gurt Jan's reproof for rousing the echoes. It was a
reproof that, following the doctor's answer to the challenge,
had Lieutenant Wallace calling away the gig's crew, so that by
the time the agreed signal — the hoot of an owl — was given at
the bank, the boat was half way to the shore.

Not a glimmer betrayed the silent schooner. The men went
noiselessly about the few duties a vessel moored at night requires
of them. The crew scuttles in the foc's'l and the cabin windows
aft were screened with canvas, and illumination below was
limited to a lamp or two. Frenchman's Creek was as likely a spot

as any up the Helford river for *Roscoff* to be lurking in; but unless some observer — that fisherman, for instance — had already reported her position, a night search would at least have to be conducted with give-away lanterns.

Davy was called to the deck twice that night: once when blurred lights had bobbed like will-o'-the-wisps along the opposite bank of the creek, men's voices loud above the muted ripple of the ebb against *Roscoff*'s anchor cable and her barnacled hull; again when a boat was rowed up-creek almost close enough to pass under the schooner's counter as she merged darkly into her overhanging and leafy background.

With his ship snugged down and screened, Davy had called to the great cabin the first lieutenant, Stona, Dr O'Keenahan, Pendarves and Smeecher, where in the smoky, whale-oil glim he received the landing parties' reports. Stona had made his way to Duval's Cottage, undetected although the neighbourhood teemed with Carter's men. The long-14's were so sited as to command the entire estuary, and constant watch was kept. No slipping out past them! Below, a smack was moored to a newly constructed timber jetty; and though he did not get a clear view of it Jan was almost prepared to take his oath that it was the *Dorcas*. Further up river off Helford a large cutter swung to a buoy, *Carter's Swallow*, while *The Brothers* had moved in out of the haze off the Gew and lay at anchor three cables south of Durgan hamlet. A gig plied between the Carter flagship and the shore, swifter communication being ensured by a semaphore mast of simple design, which rose through the roof of an outhouse within the cottage's defences.

'They seem in no hurry to smoke us out, sir,' the midshipman remarked.

'The night is young,' said Davy.

'If you do want my opinion,' growled Stona, 'we'd best come to terms.'

'There are others to hear before we come to a decision,' Davy observed hopefully, though the ashes of defeat were bitter to his taste.

Smeecher, his sources of information secret but proven, declared that Captain Harry had not put foot ashore all that Saturday. Indeed, the Carter fortifications at Bosahan were mainly the province of the King of Prussia himself. It was John

Carter who, having purchased the land from Helford to the Bay, had evicted old Duval, fobbing him off with a tumbledown shack, part dwelling, part byre at Gweek.

O'Keenahan's report was brief. 'Captain Harry's preaching at Manaccan chapel, ten o'clock tomorrow morning — or should I say — er — four bells tomorrow forenoon?'

Gurt Jan grunted. 'That all? No news of Hannibal Trainer and the *Dorcas* lads?'

The doctor shook his head, but Smeecher had heard that all seven of the crew had been carted off along the Helston road for personal delivery to Godolphin. 'And a rough journey they'll have, gen'l'men, and a rougher reception if I do knaw my man.'

None rougher than I if I don't bring this off, and lose Roscoff as well as *Dorcas,* Davy reminded himself. But perish the thought! Success would be two-phased — to confirm the freedoms of the river; and to retake the plundered contraband.

'So Harry Carter's bible-punching at Manaccan in about eleven hours' time, Keeny.'

'Tomorrow morning — forenoon, and a plague on these nautical terms! Are you thinking what I'm thinking?'

Wallace's eyes grew wide in the lamplight. He thumped the table. 'A kidnap, by God!'

'A hostage,' Davy amended.

'He'll 'ave an escort,' growled Stona.

''Er don't mix sailorin wi' praiching, so I was told,' mimicked the doctor.

'My Aunt Patty lives on one of the family farms on the far side of the river,' remarked Pendarves. No one took any notice except O'Keenahan. 'You must tell me more,' he said. 'But not now.'

*

O'Keenahan sat in the little cob and thatch chapel at Manaccan, ill at ease and not solely from the hard seat and perpendicular back of the pew. A self-confessed freethinker, he yet found his conscience at odds with the needs of the hour that he, raised a catholic, should be attentive to a disciple of Luther, Calvin and Wesley fulminating against the Whore of Babylon. Captain Harry the smuggler might be a less imperious original

thin — out of the duchy Cousin Jacks all. But at home, at each other's throats from first to last.'

Stona span him round and pushed him on. 'Stow your gab, preacher.'

But Carter held his ground. 'I've grown mortal weary of you, Davy, and the company you keep. And keep this hairy ape's paws off of me. I withdraw my parole.' He ducked under Stona's arm, dodged through the ring of captors, and bounded across the clearing, leaping the lower obstacles and swerving as if he held the silver ball at a Feast Day hurling game.

'Don't shoot, get him!'

Nat Pendarves had not awaited orders. He converged on the fugitive, was staggered by a blow to the jaw, grabbed Carter in falling and dragged him to the ground, the queer clerical hat skimming into a bush. Two pistols fired together from the trees. The midshipman yelped and clutched his arm. Davy whipped his own firearm from his belt.

'Halt, Carter, or by God's teeth I shoot.'

Carter hesitated. Past him rushed Stona at the head of the Roscoffs. A petty officer stopped to slip a hitch over Carter's writhing shoulders and hurry him back to Davy, maintaining a firm grip on the lashings as the three of them, deep in the woods again, plunged steeply down to the creek.

'For a man of principle,' panted Carter, nodding at Davy's pistol, 'you change your tune easily.'

'Principle,' Davy retorted, 'is a two-way thing. One-way principles rebound, I find.'

There was the shuffle of footsteps in the undergrowth — steps closing. Then a voice. 'Cap'n Davy, where be to? There, are 'ee? 'Tis me, Tom Polsue.'

Davy halted the petty officer and his tethered charge. 'Show yourself, Tom.'

The man was bloodily bandaged where a cutlass had glanced off his skull. ''Twadn' nothin', sor; nothin' 't all. Doctor tied 'un up proper like.'

'Where are the doctor and Midshipman Pendarves! Mr Pendarves was hit, I believe.'

'Left him being tied up by Doctor. Doctor said as I were to join up wi' you and tell 'ee not to worry. They'll get back all right without being took. Just you look to yourself, sor, he do say.

Mr Pendarves, 'e've got family across the river, and if they don't get back to the ship one way they will another.'

'Very good.' The descent with its slithering and tearing was resumed. But what of Stona and the rest?

As they reached the water's edge, a scuffling among the trees that became a nearby crashing brought Davy's pistol to the ready again and Petty Officer Turner's and Able Seaman Polsue's cutlasses to hand. It was Lieutenant Stona and six others. 'Only six? Where are the rest?'

'Got separated, sir.' Relinquishing his men was hard to admit. ''Twas like this—' Returning to the clearing after driving off *The Brothers'* boat's crew, Stona found that all about him and his squad the woods were alive with men who were certainly no shipmates of theirs. Back in the glade the doctor, the midshipman and Tom Polsue were nowhere to be seen. Moreover Stona had found himself to be short of three of the eleven who had gone into the forest with him. But rather than retrace his steps after them, as he was inclined to do, Stona had decided that his duty lay in assisting his captain to get their hostage back to the ship.

'You did well,' Davy assured him. 'The missing men are all Cornishmen, and will come to no harm in these parts, though to some trouble, I shouldn't wonder, once they are on their own.'

They ran the longboat down the shingly beach, where it now lay high and dry with the tide past half-ebb and dropping fast. Dumping Captain Harry, arms still bound to his body, in the stern sheets they pushed off and emerged from forest gloom into blinding sunshine.

Past the dogleg in the creek they pulled, whilst almost as quickly the outflowing tide was narrowing the navigable part to middle channel, soon itself to become a trickle between mud flats steaming in the mid-day sun. But the view to the river northward was clear to see. Alarmingly clear. Into the mouth of Frenchman's Creek, with huge mainsail and the overlapping sails supported by her far-protecting jibboom drawing enough power from the westerly breeze to maintain a froth of foam at her forefoot, swept the armed cutter. Her crude figurehead depicting the swallow whose name she bore was more like a lectern than a bird, thought Davy, a beautifully carved falcon coming to mind as despair clamped down on him. Her sails came down with a rush and figures appeared on the foc's'l to let go the anchor.

'*Swallow* ahoy!' essayed Captain Harry, struggling to his feet. But Gurt Jan's hand was pressed over his mouth and they bore him to the floorboards.

'Quietly now,' husked Davy. 'Vast pulling. Back water under the trees again. Sun's in their eyes; maybe they won't see us.'

'But we'll be stuck in the mud like a linnet in bird-lime,' Stona growled. 'Jeesus! they'm hoisting the jib again. They've belayed dropping their hook. Now what by Saint Nicholas on the Island do 'ee s'pose they'm about?'

It was incredible. The *Swallow* wore ship, and with the mainsail jerking up her mighty mast was leaving the creek. Harry Carter sighed. 'Cut me loose, do'ee now: I'll not make trouble.' He sat chafing his numbed arms. 'What was my *Swallow* about, deserting me like that? A fine little ship. A fine crew.'

'Little ship, my cap'n?' Stona commented as she slid out of sight round the wooded headland. 'If she be your *Swallow*, which I don't doubt, she'm the biggest cutter in the three kingdoms. Sixteen 3-pounders, they do say, and accommodation for nigh a hundred.'

'Very cramped, I assure you; and I've another just commissioned as big, and better armed.' Pride was at odds with regret in his face.

'Give way,' Davy ordered. 'And I'll trouble you to keep your mind on your duty, Mr Stona.'

'Aye-aye, sir. Sorry, Cap'n Davy. But what they sheered off like that for I shall never know.'

He soon did. As they pulled frantically between the mud flats for the open river, they saw the *Swallow* in chase of a fishing smack which, with the breeze over its larboard counter and tarry lug-sail bulging, was crossing diagonally towards Port Navas creek on the far bank.

'Sink me,' exclaimed Gurt Jan, 'if that aren't young Pendarves at the tiller and him with his arm in a sling too! And there are my missing trio in the waist. And damn my eyes if in the sternsheets that aren't—' His glance shifted to Carter at his side.

'My hat, my confounded hat!' cried their hostage bitterly.

'He's wearing my blessed hat! It's that impudent, damned, perjured Irishman − nothing good never did come from Cork − and they think he's me!'

The longboat had now turned upstream and with a stroke or two would be under *Roscoff*'s guns. Meanwhile it seemed the toss of a coin whether the smack would be overtaken by the cutter. 'Why don't they fire?' fumed Captain Harry. 'God knows they've got cannon enough.'

'Scairt of hittin' you, my cap'n,' laughed Gurt Jan.

'We'll take the pressure off our lads,' cried Davy, restored to good humour and a favourable opinion of human nature. 'They must not catch them. Come along, Harry Carter, on your feet now, so's they recognise you; bear him a hand, Mr Stona. Cutter ahoy! *Swallow* ahoy!' British sailors needing little encouragement for making a hullabaloo, Stona and the others joined in. 'Louder, you dumb-bells. Shout altogether. *Swallow* ahoy!' It was like hailing the Revenue Brig *Fox* those long months ago.

They watched the cutter come up into the wind and beat back towards them. One of *Roscoff*'s stern chasers thundered in a to-do of flame and smoke that set the echoes rumbling, and the gulls screaming, and a ball ricocheting in shortening bounds and splashes to thump into the riverside trees, while the tang of gunpowder quenched the odours of weed and ooze. Of the smack there was no sign. The big cutter wore again, and to cheers and jeers swung an eighth of an acre of mainsail over her beam and retreated to her moorings downstream.

*

Smeecher, who lolled in the riverside cottage of an acquaintance and viewed the scene with apparent equanimity, drained his tankard of the local ale − not to be compared with that of the Sloop or the George and Dragon, but better brew than ever came from over the sea − rose from his chair and conjured a small gold coin from the recesses of his waistcoat. The acquaintance was a farm-hand who, surprisingly to anybody but Smeecher, claimed ownership of a horse; a hand whose protestations of refusal, whose whole bearing, indicated reluctance to accept so much as a half penny let alone a half guinea from a friend, but whose palm, seemingly adopting an independent view of the affair, remained firmly outstretched.

'I'll take good care o' the nag, don't 'ee worry, my 'andsome,' promised Smeecher, pressing the coin into a palm that closed like a mousetrap, 'Bring 'er back in a few days, I shouldn't wonder. And what Collector Jan's going to make o' this,' he asked himself, throwing his leg over the patient beast and jogging off on his long ride across the peninsula, 'God alone do knaw!'

8

'Pray make free of my cabin and consider my berth your own,' invited Davy.

Captain Harry registered slight alarm, the first his captor had observed. 'You reckon I'll be sleeping aboard, then? Time we came to some arrangement, Cap'n. I'd have you know I'm preaching across the river tonight, at Por' Navas.' It was admirable the way the man retained his composure.

'We have much to talk of first, sir, and the sooner we do so the likelier the good people of Porth Navas are to receive the benefit of your ministry.'

'No minister, but a humble servant of the Lord,' Carter said, primly adding that it was a servitude apt to fall hard on whomsoever stood in its way.

Hamlyn, the steward, brought in a decanter of claret and glasses, a set of Venetian ware one would expect to grace the suite of a successful privateer commander. 'A light wine, I imagine, if you are of your brother's persuasion?'

'John's drinking habits are not mine. Like Wesley, he even forswears tea. Moderation is all I ask; and I'll wager this will prove palatable enough. If a captain in our trade don't learn the niceties of the vine in a voyage or two, he never will.' He sampled the rosy liquid, rolling it round his tongue. 'Admirable, and timely. You took this off that *Rochelle* ketch you sank off Quiberon, I'll warrant. I am well-informed, you see.'

'Did you know I sent the crew ashore in my own boat?' Recollection of the sad little incident was not pleasant.

'Indeed? But comforting our enemy is somewhat at variance, my friend, with your letters of marque.'

'Nevertheless a Christian precept.'

Captain Harry's face darkened. 'To comfort *your* enemy, not the king's. Do not presume to teach me the gospels.'

Neutrality was restored over dinner. Davy was now able to keep an estimable table when in reach of supplies, either in port or when the situation of one of His Britannic Majesty's foes enabled him to do so. The exchange value of the hostage was debated over the bread, only three days out of the back oven at Boswyn, and the Cheddar Davy had brought aboard with him. The suggestion that Captain Harry be put ashore in return for a safe passage out of the Helford river was promptly dismissed. 'I've not been sent here just to get out again. There's our smack *Dorcas* and Hannibal Trainer and his crew. There's nigh a ton of tobaccco. All to be restored in good condition. There's those fiendish cannon at Bosahan.'

That was all brother John's concern. Brother John was not 'King of Prussia' for nothing. He was so called if Davy must know because twenty-five years ago when playing at soldiers with his younger brothers, as children will, he as their general insisted on being named after his hero Frederick the Great; and the title stuck. But what had that to do with present problems? One road to victory, Davy replied, was to know your enemy.

'Must we be enemies?' Carter pleaded. 'Look 'ee, Davy, you're employed by a syndicate most of whose names you don't know − an eighth here, a sixty-fourth there − and who don't know yours, save as a mention on a balance sheet they hasten to burn as soon as they've read their portion: while to the whole lot of 'em you're of consequence only so long as you are of use.'

'That's why I'm here,' commented Davy.

'Look at your ships—'

'Fewer than yours, I grant, but better.'

Carter sniffed. 'When in mid-Atlantic, maybe. Not in the Channel or Biscay. Certainly not for a quick passage from Peter Port, Roscoff or Brest. Now we have six ships as can't be beat at that game — two of 'em the largest and swiftest cutters north o' Gibraltar. Both 200 tonners; both carrying letters of marque.'

'Too lightly armed. *Swallow* could not face *Roscoff* this forenoon.'

'Then you don't know my latest, *Shaftesbury;* 6-pounders like *Roscoff's* but more of 'em. Though it ain't a frigate you need in the Channel, but manoeuvrability and speed. *Swallow* and *Shaftesbury* have got both.'

A frigate? Davy pictured the *Falcon:* it served to conceal that he was impressed by these monsters of the Carter fleet, with their immense single masts and massive sail-spread.

'Half a dozen large craft of our own, and a host of smaller ones and those we hire,' Carter went on. 'We muster three hundred men, good seamen all. There's quality up to London to back us. How else do you suppose My Lords of Admiralty are persuaded to issue letters to we Carters!' His laugh was of disdain rather than amusement. Ned Davy, I make you fair offer. Come in with us. You shall have *Swallow* yonder; 'pon my word there's a sailer for a young captain! Built special for me, like *Shaftesbury* after her. Or do you fancy *The Brothers* I'm aboard of now — or shall be when you let me off this shallop of yours.' Noting the glint in Davy's eye he hastened to add that once Davy had joined the Carters the *Roscoff* would be up for sale in a month, and he should have her if he chose.

'You as a preacher,' Davy retorted evenly, 'should know who it was offered all the kingdoms of the world for a change of owner.'

Remarkable indeed was the transition from reasonableness to rage. 'You insult and blaspheme, damn you!' Carter rose as far as the deck-head permitted, and leaned over the table.

'You must find it hard to reconcile your role as preacher with that of predator,' Davy observed coolly but alert for squalls.

The sequel surprised him. Captain Harry, pale eyes glittering and the blood high in his cheeks, crashed down his fist to set the crockery and cutlery jangling. Then as suddenly he sat down and lowered his head into his hands. 'There may be truth in what you say, but it was not for you to say it.'

Davy felt compassion for the man — even friendship, though not on present terms. To be bound, as surely as a carpenter to his maul or a tailor to his shears, to a trade that was always unlawful and often barbarous, accorded ill with a conscience so nice as to need public profession. It must cause Captain Harry much heart-searching and inner torment. I know it would me, Davy decided, believing himself to be a simple soul, as no doubt he was. He rested a hand on Carter's shoulder. 'I shall pass to the shore, should opportunity offer, Captain Carter's apologies for absence from Porth Navas chapel this evening.'

Hamlyn appeared as if summoned to clear away. If it was not second sight that enabled him to assess the moment for his ministrations, Davy had long since acknowledged that it was a deucedly keen pair of ears. Instructing the armed sentry to stay at the door at all times, and keep it clipped open, Davy mounted to the quarterdeck, there to pace five steps forward, five steps aft, avoiding by habit the ringbolts and other obstacles. Much to consider and slight headway made! And anxiety was growing about O'Keenahan and the rest, of whom as the afternoon wore on there was still no news. Meantime he maintained his ship at action readiness, with half her company at quarters.

About to descend at the change of watch for that developing British institution tea, in hope of bringing his discourse with the hostage to a more satisfactory conclusion, Davy was hailed from the foretop. A boat was approaching from Helford under flag of truce. The *Roscoff* lay bows-on to the flooding tide and so to the oncoming gig, which came round in a seamanlike manoeuvre to disembark its passengers at the waist. Davy had supposed his visitor to be 'the King' himself, and had had a section of the bulwark removed for easier entry and the boarding net there lifted. But it was Follick.

'I trust you dealt with the fellow who flung that whatever 'twas this morning,' he growled, stepping to the deck.

'Hanged at the yardarm,' rejoined Davy cheerfully. 'Which reminds me, I owe him a drink.'

'Flippancy won't get you nowhere, Captain. You're trapped, and you know it. Where's Captain Carter?'

'Safe and inaccessible.' No, Davy would not yet release him: matters outstanding must be settled first and a pledge given. Davy would sail when it suited him, neither sooner nor later. No, he was not in the least apprehensive of the guns at Duval's; Captain Carter would be the first to be blown to pieces – Davy would attend to it himself. And Mr John wouldn't care for that to happen, would he? Davy had expected Mr Carter to visit him in person, and not send his − er − associate.

'Fog's still hanging about in Mount's Bay,' remarked the ferret. 'Good daylight cover not to be missed. It's keeping Mr John at Prussia. They are saying,' he went on, 'that two of the relief ships here have collided, and one for sure will have to be beached at Perranuthnoe or she'll founder. That means the Germoe wreckers, with the military called out, I shouldn't wonder. You'll get no help from the troops,' Follick added hurriedly, as if to justify a too free passing of information.

'I never imagined I should.' Davy's further comments as to military involvement were interrupted by a noisy altercation in the cabin flat beneath their feet.

'No you don't sir. Just stay where you was, begging your pardon. I has my orders.'

'All right now, all right!' Captain Harry's voice boomed as from pulpit or quarter-deck. 'D'ye hear me, Follick? No cause to worry. Housed in Cap'n Davy's own cabin, no less. Treated like a monarch.'

Handsome of him, but uncalled for! Davy beckoned to Lieutenant Wallace to check up below.

'Don't you put yourself to no trouble 'count of me,' said Follick, who seemed satisfied to have assured himself of the captain's comfort and well being. 'Should like to have had a word with him, though.'

'And so you have' declared Davy. 'Do not let me detain you. Captain Carter regrets that he is not available to conduct evening service at Porth Navas chapel? Pray be so kind as to convey these regrets to the appropriate quarter. Good day to you.'

To the relief of all before and aft of the mast in *Roscoff* the party adrift − Dr O'Keenahan, Midshipman Pendarves and the three seamen − hailed them at sundown. They came aboard in high spirits that owed not a little to Pendarves' Aunt Patty's hospitality. Her home brewed ale had proved good, her cider better, and her recipes for mead and blackberry wine unparalleled. Indeed the doctor, Mr Pendarves exuberantly recounted, had assured her of fame and fortune in County Cork should she wed a landowner there, himself for instance, and devote her talents to the production of potheen. The dear soul had wished to keep her nephew with her until the wound in his upper arm was well, a desire that Davy noted with approval was not shared by his junior officer. Aunt Patty's proficiency in brewing and the arts of fermentation were equalled, even surpassed, she had claimed, by her expertise in the healing herbs. Davy, hearing in the wardroom the praises of this pearl among women who had dared Carter malevolence to shelter his men, wondered that they had torn themselves away. As O'Keenahan had clambered up the rungs in the tumblehome, he had been wearing the Breton hat which he vowed, as he returned it with Davy's permission to its aggrieved owner, should be the model for every headgear he affected thereafter.

The first alarm came when the schooner was preparing for sea, in the last dog watch.

'Boat approaching off starboard quarter sir;' a husky hail subdued according to Davy's insistence that only necessary talk, and that in whispers, was to be made.

The patter of bare soles indicated that the ship's company stood to action stations, the quarters officers coming to Wallace to report quietly that their divisions were ready. The perriers, mounted on swivels along the gunnels and charged with small shot or half-pound bags of nails, were checked and swung. The rags of daylight filtered down river to outline *Roscoff* against encroaching night and to reveal the closing vessel, lustily propelled with an oar on either side. It was somewhat larger than the schooner's longboat, higher out of the water.

'*Dorcas*, or I'm a Dutchman!' murmured Stona.

'Likely enough. But dangerous still,' Wallace replied.

'*Roscoff*, Cap'n Davy!' The hail was muted but clear.

Davy hurried on deck, leaving Captain Harry pricking his ears. 'Who's there?' A snap of his fingers at the nearest swivel brought the gun to cock and the gunner sighting along the barrel.

'Duval brothers — Joseph, James and Jason, sons of Francis Duval of Bosahan. We bring you your fishing boat.' To Lieutenant Wallace, a red-haired Scot unfamiliar with the family histories of wild Cornwall however versed he might be in the annals of the clans, it was inexplicable that after a hundred and fifty years of settlement the Duvals still spoke with a foreign accent and could be friend rather than foe. But it was no wonder to those who knew the Duvals' origins and their natural preference for French wives, and who understood the racial kinship and continuous communication between Cornwall and the Continent. O'Keenahan's sense of the ridiculous drove him to comment, to nobody in particular, on the mentality of parents who could switch from scriptural to classical nomenclature at the rock of a cradle. Davy handed them aboard, welcoming them with an arm about the broad shoulders of two of them and then a back-slap for the third.

Down in the wardroom they told him that since eviction from their smallholding at Bosahan they had worked for hire at a neighbour's, the hovel John Carter had flung them into on a take-or-leave-it basis being barely large enough for their parents, let alone three sons evenly spread in age from seventeen to twenty-one. With the village buzzing about the arrival in the river of their father's redoubtable friend, it had been a matter of dusk and opportunity for them to cast off the fishing smack moored at the Helford jetty and deliver it where it belonged. Lastly, they hoped that Captain Davy would enrol them as members of his gallant crew.

'What if your father wants you?'

Joseph's face mirrored his disappointment. 'Then I, the eldest, must go. I rode over to my father's early this morning. He approves our action and will send for me if I am needed.'

'Joseph is a prize horse-doctor,' Jason the youngest told them, continuing barely audibly after being hushed by all. 'He'd be wasted on a ship.'

'Would he now? I doubt it.' The doctor in his few days aboard the *Roscoff* had already formed an opinion of ships' surgeons.

It was settled that the three Duvals, with a couple of AB's, Evans and Trembath, a Newlyn man, should crew the smack out of the river under Coxswain 'Billums' Williams, who had fished West Cornwall since childhood and knew the whole coast. So *Dorcas* was watered and victualled and manned. In *Roscoff*, as an afterthought and to the dismay of the gunners, Davy ordered the shot removed from the swivels and only the charges left, tamped with oakum. Deter, not massacre, he explained, and wondered if he would live to regret it. Then, with the capstan pawls lifted so that weighing should not be accompanied by resounding clicks, the anchor was raised, jib and mainsail set, and the *Roscoff* ghosted seawards. *Dorcas* hoisted her stiff, barked lugsail and followed.

Novices on shipboard, the three Duvals saw an ambush in every inlet, in every deeper darkness, in every clearing where winked a cottage candle through horn or sacking-covered window frame. The spars of the ship ahead scraped the stars and were an inducement to attack. The gingerbread gilding on the stern glowed in the starlight as if the poop lanterns were ablaze and dancing on their image in the wake. The water's slap against their hull, the thud of sail against mast or when caught in an eddy of air, drummed up the foe. These perils they perceived, but for pride's sake made no mention of it, either to each other or to their new companions. However Billums, sensing their tension, explained in a hoarse whisper which added to their dread of detection that nothing was not visible nohow from bank to bank against the dark trees, while the tide running through the twigs a-trailing from the trees drowned any ship noises midstream.

'If 'tweren't so I'd ha' been nabbed a score o' times by they Revenue bastards, but I'm still around, an't I?'

Joseph nudged James and pointed. They were abreast the Ferryboat Inn. A slit in the blackness between two amber windows widened. From it a lantern swayed down the slipway and steadied above an orange sliver which fragmented as the wash of the passing schooner caught it. The night was thick with forebodings and the river smells nudged banished fears to mind.

'God's death!' An oath from Trembath, there in the bows with Evans, broke the spell. The coxswain, gripping the tiller tip at arm's length, ducked under the arching foot of the sail to peer ahead and the Duvals crowded beside him, straining to see. *Roscoff* had slowed down. She stopped with a shudder that set every timber groaning and swung broadside to tide and current.

The crew of the smack, bearing down on their stricken leader, stared at one another. 'They've stretched a rope across the river,' Joseph suggested. 'I'll wager that's what it is.'

'A grass,' exclaimed the coxswain. 'A grass line. Grass lines float. Stand by all.'

The smack passed the trapped schooner, hailing her as she swept by the crosswise stern, the Duvals in the eye of the boat to grab the impeding cable and haul it aboard for cutting. Nothing there; and the schooner was dimly receding.

At Williams' command the AB's dropped the sail. 'You for'ad, rouse out the grapnels. Godlemitey save me from green hands! In the forepeak. Grapnels. Hooks. Crisakes laive 'un to me!' He rummaged beneath the half deck and was back with a grapnel triple-hooked at the end and with further hooks branching up its 4-foot shank. It was an implement carried by every inshore moonshiner, to 'creep' or dredge up linked kegs and containers dumped in the shallows by deep sea smugglers and recovered when the Revenue should be looking the other way.

Breathlessly bearing on the oars to propel the *Dorcas* back against the flow of the tide, they saw lights on the shore and the shapes of boats putting out from the Helford bank.

'Ware boarders!' panted Billums, repassing the *Roscoff* and then returning under sail with the grapnel poised for trailing.

They were almost level with the poop when a gig, racing ahead of the attackers, sped out of the gloom to fetch up under the *Roscoff*'s stern windows.

'Cap'n Harry!' Billums put the helm over, steering the smack straight for the gig. 'They'll get the rascal out then blast us all to bits.' The wind plastered the lugsail tight to the mast, a brake when not reset alee, but sheer impetus hurtled the smack into the gig amidships, crushing it like pasteboard against the stout oak of sternpost and rudder, while its crew either splashed overboard or stood with the water rising as their narrow boat sank.

'Boarders, repel boarders!' yelled the coxswain. Fingers, white and portentous, came writhing up out of the inky water to grope and clutch at the smack's gunnels; white faces were staring over the side. 'No rescues, no prisoners,' he ordered. 'They'd heave us over in their place, sod 'em!' He unshipped the tiller, and laying about him assisted by the rest of his crew, the Duvals new to such violence and not caring for it but effective nonetheless, cleared the *Dorcas* of the gig's men. Some swam away into the night, two or three clung forlornly to the rudder pintles.

'Now shove off and let's get goin'.' The two seamen eased down the sail, still tight against the mast, Billums replaced the tiller, and the smack drifted from beneath the overhang of the stern accommodation. The instant it appeared, a shadow in deeper shadows, one of the windows overhead crashed open in a shower of glass and a figure bounded down to the decked-in forepart, in its hand the round hard-wood ruler with which it had felled the guard.

Captain Carter!

Clutching the tiller, now firmly restored to its socket, Billums rose from his seat only to receive Carter's boot full on the jaw. With a grunt he reeled across the transom unconscious and his attacker was down there in the cockpit with him, lifting his legs to tip him overboard. But young Jason in a couple of leaps covered the length of the boat and hurled himself on the fighting-mad captain, his two brothers scarce a blink behind him. They held Captain Harry down while the AB's cocooned him in the ship's painter.

A gun barked overhead; they heard Captain Davy shout 'Stand-to starboard amidships.' One of the seamen took the tiller, the others hoisted the sail again now that they were clear of the schooner, Captain Harry was bundled into the cabin, Billums sat shaking himself like an old dog after a swim and then in a panic of remembrance fumbled with the grapnel, James at once helping him over with it. Abreast of where the boom must lie the tow line became stiff as an iron bar and jerked the smack to a stop, squeaking as it jammed the wooden cleat to which it was secured. They had anchored themselves to a snag in the river bed.

Behind them dinned hoarse cries and the high-pitched pop of the perriers as they spat orange flame into the night. The tin-pan hammering of cutlass on cutlass rang thin but persistent. In the cabin Carter was loudly beseeching them in God's name to tell him what was going on, and to add to the confusion Captain Davy was shouting across the water at them, they could not hear what.

'Out oars,' the coxswain ordered, recovering.

The wind was in the sail; with three men to each oar the blades made whirlpools that flowed ahead with current and tide. Another jerk, and another and a trundling over the ground below their keel, and the *Dorcas* was free. But for seconds only. Again the boat lost way, but this time more gradually. They had hooked the cable. 'Haul 'un in roundly now, lads, roundly,' urged Billums. The heavy hawser, not of grass but of hemp and as thick as your leg, was raised dripping and with desperate haste over the stern and assailed with a clasp knife, which required such a pressure of wrist to bite into the hemp that they worked at it in short and frenzied shifts.

While they were cutting, the uproar from the *Roscoff* had fallen silent. 'She have drove 'em off or been took,' averred Billums. 'Damn your eyes, get a move on!' The hawser was soaked, tough and resistant. 'For God's sake!' A glow like an eruption of daylight flooded the river. It lit the Helford jetty on the one side and made a cameo of the thatch and granite of the Ferryboat Inn on the other, artificially lining the lush banks in every shade from emerald to ebony, like a scene at Drury Lane. It was a naptha flare held high from the schooner's foc's'l-head, above it the highlights and shadows of the useless sails and the silvered filigree of rigging and ratlines. On the green water, out of small arms range, lay four or five boats, the rowers resting on their oars and their faces pale and staring, while reinforcements were putting off from the shore.

'*Dorcas* ahoy!' Gurt Jan's voice. 'Cut that bloody cable, have 'ee? What in hell's keeping you?'

Joseph, taking a turn with the knife, panted that at least they had guessed what he was trying to do. But the coxwain's attention was on the boats, which gave way together and in a long sweep to avoid *Roscoff*'s fire they were too patently making for the smack.

'For God's sake dowse that light,' he bawled.

As he spoke the hawser parted and the ends flopped into the water. Supported by the holed cork discs used to buoy seine nets, but tarred and bunched so that the bight of the rope hung a fathom below the surface, each half of the hawser drifted towards the bank it was moored to.

'Shut your eyes and get your night sight back,' said Billums, anxiously watching the boats. They did not see the flare leap in an arc and vanish, but its shine fell from their eyelids and they heard the hiss as it expired.

They opened their eyes as the tongue of one of the Bosahan cannon licked at the utter dark of the flare's extinction, while its thunder reverberated up the valley, and they ducked as the ball rumbled overhead like a hay wain on gravel to crash into the tree trunks on the far bank and send twigs and splinters pattering into the river.

'Don't they know they might hit Captain Harry?' Jason demanded.

'Imbecile!' James shoved his younger brother impatiently. 'How could they know? They think they've got him safe.'

They were hoisting their lugsail again as *Roscoff* came up on them, all of them sensing the tension there, with screwed-up courage awaiting the whole battery's blast.

The dim shape of the poop was level with *Dorcas*. Davy was calling, only just loud enough for his voice to carry. 'Keep clear of me. They've got Captain Carter, and there's nothing now to stop them opening fire the instant they get a glimpse of us, which they will when we're in the estuary.'

'Begging your pardon, sor,' rejoined Billums gleefully, 'but they haven't got 'im, you know.'

'What do you mean?'

'They 'aven't got him, sor; we has.'

'Good God!' Davy exclaimed, and meant it. 'Pass him aboard. We'll light the poop lantern and bind him beneath it for all the world to see.'

9

'It was a long fuse John Carter lit when he seized *Dorcas*,' Davy remarked wearily to Captain Harry over a mug of coffee in the grey dawn, when the carpenter had left the great cabin with his canvas bag after glazing the broken window.

Carter, to whose cuts Dr O'Keenahan had applied plaster and liniment to his bruises, fixed Davy with his pale, penetrating glare. 'For one who abjures shooting Cousin Jacks you done well enough last night.'

'What choice had I?' The younger man's face, strained and unwontedly unshaven, mirrored his regret.

'Your casualties?' enquired the other with little concern.

'Cuts. Two serious, none fatal or permanently crippling.'

Captain Harry sniffed a dab of snuff from the back of his hairy hand. 'Fewer than in a hurling match, where we've known a death or two, ha?' Hurling was a violent sport of pagan significance which had evolved in prehistoric times and was likely to continue for ever. It was played between parishes with a silvered ball, once symbolising the sun. He yawned. 'I expected more, but you had rigged nets, I'm told. All was over very quickly — five minutes that seemed hours, by heaven!'

'Nought but a dispute over rich men's dividends,' Davy explained, in unpremeditated revelation, studying the table top.

Carter sipped his coffee noisily. 'Now just you leave politics at home, with your theology. You're not to be trusted with either, young fellow.' He sighed unexpectedly, so that Davy glanced up at him. 'Shall know my own butcher's bill when you put me ashore at Porthleven. Those swivels of yourn I heard popping must have murdered my poor lads.'

'Loaded with wads and tow,' said Davy. 'Effect only.'

Carter's expression was either of scorn or of admiration; to Davy it did not signify which. 'I saw you as a Philistine smiting the children of Israel hip and thigh.'

Davy could neither resist a grin nor in his turn conceal a yawn. 'No children of Israel in Cornwall,' he smiled, 'unless you include old Bishopsworden at Praze.'

'Mother's side only,' said Carter, grinning too.

The two privateer captains had talked through the night. It was agreed that the American war could hardly continue another year, wherefore difficulties of employment might arise which would be resolved only by co-operation. Carter had visions of a fleet of free-traders operating from Penzance and so powerful as to discourage any attempt by Revenue or Admiralty to interfere. Davy was non-committal. The respect for navy and law in which he had been bred and which had been fortified by seven years as a midshipman was not to be set aside. True, he had flouted it on occasion, though never with an easy conscience. Smuggling was acceptable, desirable even to a disciple of Adam Smith and Doctor Johnson, so long as it did not bring one into physical contact with the law. Nevertheless, knowing the propensity of British governments to lay up their warships and turn off their crews before the ink on the peace treaty was dry, Davy held a well-armed merchant fleet to be essential.

Trade with the Indies, for instance, or in the Caribbean, with little to fear from pirates while two or three merchantmen drilled for battle and sailing in company could earn rich rewards — he thought of *Falcon* as he made his points. Carter now was not impressed. However, they shook hands on a future if at present nebulous alliance of their combines and pledged mutual assistance. Of greater moment was an agreement that while Davy and his backers would never establish a Helford River *entrepot*, the Carters would reinstate the Duvals, dismount the battery, and sell the cannon with first refusal to the St Ives syndicate. Nor would the Carters extend their operations north of Sennen. But as for the seized tobacco, that was entirely brother John's province; perhaps a payment could be arranged. With so much settled already, Davy was not disposed to press the matter.

But it was much in his mind when the junior midshipman, Harvey, passed the first lieutenant's request for his presence on deck. The three gig's crewmen who, being non-swimmers, had been left clinging to the exposed section of the rudder assembly had climbed into the cabin through the shattered window and been arrested by the sore, worried and over-reacting sentry. When they were brought wet and shivering to Davy he had agreed that once safely at sea they should work their passage to St Ives. Now Wallace, questioning them when the watch turned-to to holystone the deck, had elicited that *Dorcas*'s cargo was stored in Bessie Bussow's kiddleywink down to Bessie's Cove, which being next to Prussia Cove nobody weren't going to get at without Mr John do give he the word. This was news indeed, the alpha and omega of the wretched affair that was so nearly, but not quite, concluded, and he would be glad when the hostage was gone and he could discuss recent developments with Keeny in the great cabin.

Meanwhile *Roscoff* was off Trewavas Head and Davy, taking over, trimmed down to a minimum of sail and conned the schooner between Welloe Rock and the Great Row, heaving to in seven fathoms off Porthleven. It had been a roundabout

route, necessitated in part by the steady sou'westerly wind but
also by a need to evade possible encounter with vengeful
opponents. They had sailed far out to sea past the Lizard,
then after a long tack nor'west to Mousehole Island followed
the curve of the coast to reach Porthleven at the start of the
forenoon watch. They had seen a troop of horses trotting out
of Penzance across the Green on the Marazion road; and there
past St Michael's Mount, in Trevean Cove halfway along the
beaches from Perranuthnoe to Acton Castle, lay the stranded
vessel Follick had mentioned, a bark of about three hundred
tons. She was all that remained in the bay of the Gibraltar
convoy, which according to Captain Harry had scooped up
Davy's former adversary-cum-ally the Revenue cutter *Fox* to
reinforce the escort past Ushant.

'No fear from that old fitcher fox, eh, my lad!' Carter had
exclaimed in a moment of joviality.

Figures were already splashing around the doomed bark
knee deep though at times lifted off their feet by the swell that
rolled up to the pebbly sands and then toppled and creamed.
Others were clambering aboard, while down a dozen tracks
over the hinterland wound columns of people, many of whom
could be recognised through a spyglass as miners, bearing
their picks and tools and with their protective hard-felt hats
rust-red in the morning. Waggons and hand-carts, and strings
of horses and mules, were also on passage to the wreck; but
they must converge at the two or three declivities by which
alone their access to the beach was possible. It was an
organised assault born of generations who, lacking the harvest
of fog or tempest, would hardly have survived. The
Trevelyans, and Squire Stackhouse who had built Acton
Castle seven years previously, would have called in the troops
as the only, if dubious, means of enforcing their cherished
rights to wreck.

After an amiable, almost cordial parting Captain Harry
had been piped over the side — a naval ritual of which he
voiced his disapproval yet appeared to appreciate as an
amende honorable for recent indignities — and his hat
weaving among the onlookers on the quay was the last they
saw of him. Davy then summoned his friend Keeny to join him
over a mulled wine — a Hamlyn speciality reserved for the

Captain's closest acquaintance — and together they discussed developments relevant to the looted contraband.

*

Hand resting on the tiller tucked under his armpit, Coxswain Williams maintained his course by the effortless expedient of sitting still, an immobility which imparted its meditative benison to his young captain sitting beside him. Both wore knitted caps, and the illusion that they were fishing was completed by a line which, hitched to a cleat, trailed astern with the semblance of 'long lining'. But neither hooked nor baited, the line presented no threat to the denizens of depths emerald in the glittering morning. Fish are the last alternative to hunger on messdecks where the smell of cooking lingers, while on plates washed only in sea water the flavour lingers for a week.

The smell of paint, however, passes unnoticed in an atmosphere redolent with tar, turpentine and tallow, damp humanity and the mephitic exhalations of the bilges; wherefore the wet paint with which Davy had taken the precaution of obliterating the letters *Dorcas* on the smack's stern was no obstacle to his enjoyment of the crystal air. The wind swelling the lugsail on the starboard tack was all sweetness, and the sparkling forenoon pure holiday. They were gliding through a shoal of sprats which hissed and bubbled around them as if the Bay effervesced. It pleased Davy to liken the long strip of Praa Sands, with its edge of surf where the waves creamed on the beach, to a gold and silver sash girdling the land: a simile which for no reason that he could think of set him day-dreaming of ma'amselle — a dream that lingered even when he turned his eyes to Mousehole, Newlyn and Penzance bright in the sunshine six miles ahead. At half that distance the mystic Mount, its seaward precipice merging into the fairy-tale castle, gleamed with the warm aura of sun-kissed granite, while high on the topmost turret the ruby speck of St Aubyn's banner flashed in the sapphire bowl of the sky.

'Far, far away, Captain Ned?' O'Keenahan broke the spell. He sat with Jason on the floor boards, so that a simple fishing boat should not appear over-manned, while the other Duvals lurked with Taffy Evans in the cabin. On the half-deck above the other AB, Trembath, leaned comfortably against the mast to tend the sails as required.

'It's spring in the air,' commented Jason, innocently clairvoyant.

Billums jabbed him with his boot. 'You speaks to the cap'n when you'm spoke to, and not afore, *ordinary* seaman.'

Spring indeed! Back to earth Davy's idyll was at once dissolving in discord. He recapitulated a fragment of his all-night discourse. Captain Harry had declared that Davy was lucky to have got out of the river. Lucky?

'Lucky,' Carter had repeated. 'I grant you take your chances when they offer, none better. But there's little forethought to your credit. No, young Ned, luck. The good Lord gives it at birth to a chosen few — and He alone knows how He do choose! 'Tis like the colour of their eyes or an ear for music. He's given it to you. That's why I want you with me, not agin me.' A brittle gift, sighed Davy.

Luck, he could admit to himself if not to Carter, had blessed his venture so far. Now he proposed to despoil the eagle's eyrie, and there it lay, Prussia Cove hard abeam and then Cudden Point, where he planned to disembark. It was not luck he needed, but a miracle.

Activity was brewing up off Prussia. Inshore craft, a couple of them those new-style gigs called galleys, patrolled parallel to the shore in prearranged line of search.

'They'm creepin', sor,' said Billums, 'like we was for the boom.'

'So I can see for myself,' Davy growled. He focussed his glass on the smugglers, his back to the south and so with no fear of watchers ashore catching the sun's reflexion in the lens. He saw one of the galleys hook up a keg to which others, each of them he guessed of about eight gallon capacity, were roped in a line at either end of which was a small anchor. The whole line, kegs, anchors and all, was dragged on board and the boat made for the cove, where blocks and tackle conveyed the cargo to a cave. This, Davy decided, contemplating and then rejecting it as a mode of ingress to the Carter stronghold, was probably an adit, an outflow which before the installation of Jonathan Hornblower's great steam pumps was the prime means of draining the mines.

Time would discover those infernal engines hauling the smuggled goods straight up the cliffs from the holds of Carter's private warships − pirates when the realm was no longer at war − with His Majesty's insignificant peacetime fleet powerless to intervene. It was a picture Davy did not like. The glory of the morning was gone; 'Ichabod!' as that scripture-mouthing freebooter would say. It occurred to Davy that in cap and jersey he looked ridiculous, and would appear more so since O'Keenahan would accompany him ashore normally clad. For two pins he'd leave him on board.

'Take her in.'

They had rounded Cudden and the rocks smothered with mussels and dripping with seaweed at the southern end of the beach. The tide was right out. Davy looked at his watch, irritably tugging up that confounded jersey to get at it. 11.05. Thirteen hours later would be the time for the next move, and heaven grant he would have an hour or two's sleep before then!

He landed with O'Keenahan and Joseph Duval in the smack's dinghy − it would hold only three − curtly rejecting Billums' plea that it weren't proper for him to go ashore in enemy country without a good man, begging the doctor's pardon, as knawed the lie of the land. Then in a wave of self-disgust he pressed the coxswain's nutbrown paw as he helped him into the boat and thanked him for his concern. He prided himself on concealing all outward signs of elation, doubt, indecision, triumph, and yes, fear, as a good commander should; yet he had thought it no shame to give vent to bad temper. Well, he thought it now, and felt the better for it.

They tugged the dinghy well up the beach. Leaving Joseph with the boat Davy led the way up the cliff path, waiting first while half a dozen women scrambled and slithered down the gritty track in a flurry of linen as they hastened to share the spoils in Trewavas cove. Davy, good humour restored, told the doctor that the women would return just as they had come.

'Won't get a look-in yonder?' assumed O'Keenahan, viewing the turmoil round the wreck.

'Loaded. All tucked away under their petticoats. It would be a bold Revenue man or soldier who'd search there!'

From the cliff top they looked along the whole beach. The stricken vessel − she was the *Prince Frederick* of Newhaven −

lay high up the beach. She was already reft of her masts, while
figures milling around and all over her called to mind Gulliver
cast ashore in Lilliput. Horses and oxen strained across the
yielding foreshore dragging carts piled with bales and crates
and timber, tugged immobile in shafts and yoke as men dug
frantically at wheels axle-deep in sand and shingle. Customs
officers would stumble up to halt operations here and there
until, their presence demanded elsewhere, the wreckers could
resume their labours. Mules and ponies filed either way like
caravans of the desert. Groups of people met and swirled and
parted. Davy grinned, imagining the conversation.

'"Tes mine.'

'"Tedn't 't all. How are 'ee so fullish?'

'Shan't 'ave 'n. I seen 'un first.'

'Gissalong with 'ee, damn thy eyes!'

'Findin's keepin's.'

'I'll tak out thy liver an' shaw it to 'ee.'

Then blows and another snatching the prize.

Acton Castle loomed bleakly in the clearing lately created in
hillside forest for its building. It was a mansion certain, like
Tregenna, to become stately as the years mellowed the stone. It
would achieve that aura of Gothic romanticism young Britain
was beginning to discover. But first the trees must grow again,
and exotic shrubs and arboreal rarities planted as fashion and
Capability Brown decreed swell to maturity in the mild Cornish
climate. At present it was an eyesore. So, Davy, himself an un-
confessed romantic, averred; though Keeny, always prepared to
take the opposing view, advanced Dr Johnson's Augustan dis-
paragement of natural scenery.

A squad of redcoats had assembled at the foot of the
castle's access to the beach, down which were being urged a
string of horses, backing and slipping, and surer footed
mules.

'What do you make of that, Ned?'

'I'll wager that Squire Stackhouse has abandoned all hope of
the military driving off the wreckers — they've never done so
yet! — and is grabbing what he can of his 'right to wreck' by
competing with everyone else. 'Tis said the troopers never did
like standing up to crowds.'

'Afraid?'

'Of unpopularity. Now rounding up a few moonshiners is another matter — when they can find 'em.'

Up then, after a wave to Joseph a hundred and fifty feet below, and into a gloom of budding hazel and of May blossom which, being beneath it, they could only smell and identify by the snow-flurry of petals they trod on. A narrow sunken lane where gaps and a gateway revealed pasture, furrowed plough-land and interminable scrub and stunted thickets led them tortuously up and roundabout and down. They maintained direction by the droplets of sunlight which leaked through branches laced with lianas of rose and honeysuckle, and stooped beneath a brambly roof that clawed the unwary. Their hose shielded them little better from the nettles that beset the path, lurking where the brighter gleam of harts'-tongues diverted attention. Yet Davy noticed that it was a well-trodden path, and they emerged unexpectedly from it into a dazzling strip cleared of trees — the highway to Prussia Cove.

This was a road edged opposite with low drystone; little more than a cart-track and no more likely to guide a coach along its rocks and ruts to an inn. But there the inn was, though with slight prospect of conveyance and customers other than hinds and a hay wain: an inn of native stone newly pointed, roof recently thatched and golden in the sunshine, freshly painted windows. An inartistic brush had touched up its crude sign, rendering it more hideous than ever. It depicted a woman's head mob-capped and a very Medusa in ringlets, and beneath it was the legend BETSY BUSSOW'S.

'God forbid it's a likeness,' O'Keenahan implored.

To the women who came to the doorway and stood with folded arms regarding them it mercifully bore no resemblance.

'Mistress Bussow?' enquired the doctor, having whispered to Davy, 'Leave it to me — I'm dressed the part,' an arrangement Davy accepted perforce rather than with enthusiasm. 'Mistress Bussow?' He flipped a thumb sign-wards. 'I shall never believe it.'

'You'm welcome to come in,' she answered agreeably, 'but there's no sleepin!'

Inside, the curtains were of the designs now coming out of the Lancashire mills — Davy's mother had lately in a burst of extravagance bought a few yards for Boswyn. Gay, but nonetheless they robbed the small, west-facing windows of most of the morning light. Upon a peat fire, its dull glow all that at first caught their unadjusted vision, furze materialised from the darkness, in brief but violent blaze illuminating the shadowy figure that had conjured up the flames; a lad of vacant countenance who stood scratching his head while gaping unblinking at the visitors. The room was more prepossessing. Whitened walls above mahogany wainscoting surely stripped from such a wreck as was disintegrating on the nearby beach; polished warming pans hanging there like the pendulums of time. There was a dresser on which paraded, rank above rank, the blue and white Wedgewood crockery that was replacing pewter on the tables of the medium well-to-do, with the martial gleam of a pink-patterned teapot, creamers of the shape and colour of Guernsey cows, and a couple of figures patently from the Wedgewood-Bentley factory at Etruria. Trestle tables ran the length of the room at right angles to the fireplace, on either side of which a high-backed settle condemned the space behind it to perpetual gloom. Their feet crunched on sand that besprinkled the slate floor, as they stooped under beams that only shipboard habits induced by 5-foot deckheads rendered innocuous to anyone above average height. The hearth, granite beneath a mantelshelf ranged with copper pots glowing like embers, jutted into the room. The recesses thus made were on the one side piled with cut furze and logs, on the other neatly stacked with peat turves which concealed, if Betsy Bussow's ran true to form, ready-to-hand jars of Jamaica rum, Dutch geneva and French brandy retailed at less than market price solely to the known and trusted.

'What's your pleasure, sir?' No sirs, Davy noted, with a feeling of being overlooked. 'I got ale and a hogshead o' rough cider shipped special from Devon; we don't belong to make it much down here. Then there's cold pasties, but not a lot else. Don't get much traffic, you do knaw. We'm simple folk wi' simple tastes and ways.'

Over mugs of ale and a pasty apiece, passable but short on meat, O'Keenahan satisfied the proprietress that he was a gentleman tourist and his servant (Davy squirmed) had been hired at Bodmin. 'A very good fellow too,' added the doctor, smiling engagingly at his choking friend. They had left their coach on the Helston highway. 'A coach would hardly reach your establishment with its axles intact, Mistress Betsy.'

'Bessie,' she corrected. 'Wrote the name wrong on the sign, did 'e? Just Bessie. Don't need the missus from the likes o' you, sir.'

While Davy was considering that Bessie Bussow was a women men would admire, but few women, the Irishman slipped an arm round her waist and planted an ample kiss on her lips. His assurance amazed Davy, who would have hesitated and lost — ignominiously — had he had a thought for those ripe lips and that accommodating bosom, which now that the laggard idea occurred seemed a worthwhile notion.

He sought the obvious door into the back yard, discovering there a handcart in which they could trundle to the beach half the confiscated tobacco Davy was determined somehow to recover, but the stables were empty of horse or mule; at Perranuthnoe with the wreckers, probably, but not to be depended on.

Back in the parlour he found O'Keenahan at the dresser, quizzing the plates and pots and complimenting the innkeeper on her taste. 'You'll not be telling me you purchased this west of Exeter?' He fondled a Chinese bowl as though it were her hand.

'Things get give me,' she replied, preening.

'You surely do well enough here — without coaches.'

Caution veiled her face. 'There's the miners and the fishermen and the labourers and I had friends, like I'm telling 'ee.'

'Only one in evidence.' The doctor nodded towards the boy, with whom Davy, one ear alert for whatever information O'Keenahan might wheedle out of the enamoured Bessie, was conducting a difficult conversation.

'Oh, the boy? He's of no account; idn' 'zackly,' if you see what I mean — mazed from birth, poor lad. He earns his keep, and I treats 'un fair. But no, my regulars is down to beach along o' the Prince Frederick, I shouldn' wonder.'

Davy considered it appropriate to recall O'Keenahan to the passage of time and the purpose of their visit. 'Should ha' thought 'ee'd keep a big cellar here, missus,' a venture in the vernacular which provoked her comment that while thinking never hurt nobody, talking did.

'This magnificent creature is the fount of wisdom,' explained O'Keenahan, taking the cue and stepping into the passage with

Bessie anxiously at heel and Davy and the boy behind. The cellar door was opened outward, to reveal in its dark recesses stairs and a pulley. Bessie grabbed his arm and steered him back to the parlour with a 'You too,' to Davy. 'Private, sir, and must remain so.'

'You ain't after telling me,' the doctor persisted, 'that in King o' Prussia country — and who in the West has not heard of the kingdom of the Carters? — that in this enclave of free trade you don't keep a pretty store down there, my dear.'

'There'm a 'ole in cellar,' spluttered the boy, to be cuffed by his mistress.

'I aren't telling nothing. But if you stay a night or two, sir, why, who do knaw but you might find out?'

O'Keenahan reminded her that there was 'no sleeping'.

'No spare room, sir; but there's mine.'

It was time, Davy decided, to be off. High time. O'Keenahan caught his glance, sighed, treated himself to another smacking kiss, and away they went. 'Stap me,' exclaimed the doctor, 'I enjoyed that!'

They returned to Joseph, who after almost an hour's waiting was in a fret of anxiety, particularly since soldiers had looked him over, and thence to Billums aboard the *Dorcas* in a comparable state of furious worry. 'Back to *Roscoff*,' Davy ordered, glad to be in charge again.

*

'Will you fight?' O'Keenahan asked. The stove had been lit in the smack's galley — the size of a sentry box sawn off at eye level — and he sat with Davy under the half-deck, sipping scalding tea with, luxury indeed at sea! milk.

'Fight?' Davy regarded his friend drowsily: it was long since he had slept, and he had been about to snatch half an hour's sleep on the padded bench that served as both seat and bunk. 'I'll fight Frogs and Yankees with a will, as they would me. The lobsters! A capital offence if you so much as draw on 'em, Keeny. And after all they're British — when they ain't our monarch's German subjects. But fight 'em?' He yawned. 'Yes, if I must.'

'You're hedging, Ned. You know I mean, will you fight the Carters?'

Davy brushed a hand across his eyes, a gesture O'Keenahan recognised as defensive as well as weary. 'With fisticuffs, willingly. With the flat of my sword if need be. Pox on't, Keeny, they're my own people!'

'That sort of problem never worries an Irishman, bedad! But what if they stand between you and those damnation casks you're so determined to recover — though why defeats me?'

'Matter of principle, and we'll cross that bridge when we come to it. But mark you me, my Hibernian friend, in robbing my owners those Carters robbed me.'

'Confiscated.'

Davy woke up and jabbed a finger hard into the Irishman's goffered cravat. 'Confiscation which is neither warranted by law nor sanctioned by custom *is* robbery, and mark you me, I intend to get that tobacco, all dozen bloody barrels of it, in any way I must. And what's more,' Davy continued, marking off the points of argument with his finger, 'if you think to deter me on account of you fancying a tavern wench old enough to be your mother, it's a notion you can disabuse yourself of right away, Keeny.'

O'Keenahan opened his mouth and shut it forthwith. He was amazed at Davy's vehemence; but watching him drop asleep on the narrow bench thought none the worse of him because of it.

10

'Back to St Ives for breakfast, shouldn't wonder.' From his leaving-harbour station on the poop Lieutenant 'Gurt Jan' Stona addressed an undistinguished minion of the port authority, who disengaged the singled-up mooring line from its bollard and flopped it into the water, the last link with the shore severed again. It was information Davy had required should be implanted in the local mind, and so inevitably in local chat, and Wallace had said much the same to the youngster casting loose the head rope.

While Davy and his friend like Joshua's young men spied out the land, the first lieutenant had awaited them as prearranged just over the horizon south of the Lizard. A return to port, to ship supplies ordered by way of the chandler's launch that morning, and on the evening tide the schooner was slipping out of Porthleven to sea. A week of clear skies and nothing worse than a lop in the Channel had been weather too perfect, the fog apart, to last much longer; an opinion confirmed by the barometer when Davy left the deck on clearing the land. But he judged there to be no cause weather-wise for abandoning the final phase of the mission on which his owners had so hastily sent him.

He lingered in his cabin over the meal Hamlyn had prepared with customary skill from ingredients fresh from the farm, and propped his notes for the night's expedition against the solid silver cruet he had acquired, on some occasion that escaped him, during his privateering rampage in the winter. These notes were a novelty inspired by Captain Harry's criticisms, which Davy was coming to believe he had taken too much to heart — a belief already discussed in that chapter house of shipboard opinion the petty officers' mess.

On re-reading the notes, penned with care to prevent his volatile brain from concerning itself with the next stage of the plan before the one in mind had been digested, Davy felt that they presented a picture of success so infallible as to be suspect. But at least it was a picture that surely took care of every foreseeable eventuality.

Davy leaned back in his chair rubbing his eyes. They burned and his back ached. A night begun in action had continued in debate till dawn. The daylight hours had been busy and the watches of the next night would be busier still. What was it those farming johnnies said? Cut a couple of straws to prop your eyelids open!

A less pig-headed fellow than himself would have rested on valuable achievements. He, the captain, could still go about and make for Land's End. Give the word and he would hear the call 'Lee-ho!' from the deck above his head and bare feet padding to the braces as *Roscoff* turned for home. The loss of the twelve casks of tobacco would be nothing compared with the advantages he had won. The Carter monopoly was frustrated. His owners were secure now, perhaps for ever, from domination by the historic and immensely powerful Arundels who, he had heard whispered, religious differences or not stood behind the evangelistic moon-shiners. There was more to 'The Trade' than bringing the goods ashore. He yawned, and yawned again. God, he was tired!

Stooping by habit below the deckhead he flung wide a stern window. The ship not quite keeping pace with the following wind, night air breathed softly upon his cheek. Sea spangle tumbled in the murmuring wake. The cabin had been stuffy, but he felt better, and thought more clearly now. Abandon what he had come for in the first place? Let the Carters take the last trick? Catch snatches of slipped-off commentary on deck— 'Cap'n's slung his hand in . . . All this corant and nought to come of it . . .'? Davy took the notes to his desk, flicked the tip of his quill across his teeth a time or two, suppressing the yawn that this stimulated, then wrote carefully across the top of the page, 'Night Orders − Officers read and initial.'

The notes seemed comprehensive enough; it was hard to imagine that the project could go adrift.

Objective: Recovery of 12 casks of Virginian leaf tobacco 1740 lb in all from cellar of B. Bussow's inn.
Plan: Pose as Captain HM Sloop *Osprey* on Revenue Service (Self)
Ditto Commissioner of Customs London Division (Dr O'Keenahan)
Ditto Collector of Jersey (Jo Duval).
Revenue raid to recover contraband.

Landing party — equipment — longboat — instructions . . .
Was he asking for trouble, detailing it all in black and white?
God forbid I should rewrite it! yawned Davy. Let 'em know what
to do in given circumstances and improvise the rest.

Davy took a few turns across the deck, head hunched to his
shoulders and his thick hair brushing the beams. A party of a
dozen was about right. More could hardly approach the inn undetected, fewer could not handle the load they must bring back.
It would be a long pull to shore; but *Roscoff* must be out of sight
of look-outs on Cudden Point. Come in slowly for the last five
cables, to escape detection. Ground as far up the beach as
possible without entangling with wreckers, some of whom would
be busy till dawn and all next day. Davy wondered if the soldiers
would still be there, and felt his stomach gripe. But no, not a
chance! Useless at night, these cavalrymen. A strange, rough
and hostile countryside in the dark was not to their liking at all,
much less the cliff top and tides no landsman ever got the hang
of.

Keeny had remarked, on scanning the document earlier, that
Davy had plumbed unexpected depths of imagination. Did the
Captain detect a sour note there! It was the doctor who had
originated the plan, but he had not met Bessie Bussow then.
Raiding the Carters was one thing, tricking and perhaps
trussing up a buxom doxy quite another. Well, Bessie's faith in
human nature, in so far as publicans ever do retain such faith,
was due for a jolt, while Keeny's hope of dalliance must fix on a
remoter future and another partner. Faith and hope were
common casualties when Greek met Greek!

As for the parts to be played, the near naval uniform Davy,
Gurt Jan and the petty officers wore would fool a better
instructed observer than Bessie, especially since uniformity was
by no means invariable even in the Service itself. Keeny's rig as
the Irish gentleman was impeccable. No doubt a respectable
civilian outfit could be contrived for Joseph.

'Sblood, I'll be set fair for Drury Lane on this tack!' grumbled
Davy.

He returned to the table littered with the notes and the
scatter of crockery, which Hamlyn had not dared to interrupt
his master's promenading to clear away. 'Gone to his hammock,'
assumed Davy, deciding not to call him.

'1.50 a.m. − Arrive at inn,' Davy read, blear-eyed and blinking. 'PO and 4 to rear. Prevent escape. Bring handcart to yard door. Prepare horses for packs (if available). Otherwise load cart and stack remainder tobacco for burning.'

And burn it he would! Davy scowled at the lantern, steady in its slowly swaying gimbals. What he couldn't shift he would destroy. John Carter should no way benefit from his high-handed expropriation, not if Ned Davy knew it. Then there was the boy. He might be needed to reveal the 'hole' in the cellar he had mentioned. Otherwise they must get the information from Bessie, somehow. It was not a pretty thought. But the boy would be amenable. And having told all, he would be exposed to reprisal after the raiders had left. That, with the Carters' methods in mind, was even less pretty a thought. Davy added to the instructions, 'Hold boy for question and bring back to ship.' Withdrawal, signals, and 'Embark 2.55 a.m.'

It was Mr Wallace's watch. Davy ordered a replacement and summoning him down to the cabin hurried through the plan with him. No council of war this time. He would resolve the problems himself; provide that forethought for which Harry Carter said he substituted luck.

'In my twenty years' experience of anything to do with seamen and operations on terra firma, sir,' Wallace averred in his clipped Scots tone and with some emphasis, Davy detected, on the advantages of an older head over a young one, 'I have obsairved that time tables bear scant resemblance to reality. They habitually underestimate the time our tarry friend takes in this unaccustomed element.'

Davy nodded, replying that fixing a time limit might speed him up.

'Perhaps, sir. There is another point. There may be an emergency ashore, when I must embark you in a hurry. I suggest you take a red rocket with you, sir, to fire if things go adrift and you need me to land a party to assist. I would send Mr Pendarves with it. Otherwise, show me a light from the beach when you want the longboat to take you off.'

Davy approved, and indicated that the interview was concluded by moving towards his curtained-off berth, where he hoped − and how desperately he hoped! − to snatch an hour's sleep.

'There's one more suggestion I would put to you, sir. That you blacken your faces. It's going to be as dark as a pig's belly when you go ashore, and you'll become almost invisible.'

Davy sighed and returned to the table, picking up his pen and addressing himself again to his notes. 'You ought to be going yourself, Number One, instead of me, you're that brimful of ideas. Very well, black faces — all except me and my two Revenue officials.' He pushed the notes across the table. 'Treat these as operation orders, and I shall be obliged if you will see that they are promulgated and studied.' He yawned. 'Kindly tell Hamlyn to shake me at one bell in the middle.'

But if Davy slept at all in his gently swaying cot, it was only fitfully. Long before the patter on the planking above announced the change of watch he was back in his chair, where though an infrequent smoker he lit a pipe. He would have preferred to go on deck, but had he done so his men would have concluded that 'the old man' — traditional nickname of even the youngest of captains — was losing his nerve. So he sat in his chair and smoked, and so contrariwise is nature that half an hour into Tuesday, 22nd May, he emerged from deepest slumber at his steward's insistent shaking. He never ought to have lit a pipe if he weren't going to stay awake to finish it, he was told. Not that Hamlyn considered smoking as aught but a thilfy habit, and if he had had his best jacket on he would have burnt a hole right through it he would, and set hisself afire, instead of ruining his old weskit which would have to go and not afore its time.

'That's the sort of tirade men go to sea to escape from, damn your eyes!' groaned Davy, sleepily picking at the charred and still smelling worsted.

Meanwhile in the second lieutenant's cabin, the petty officers' mess, and on the seamen's messdeck faces were being daubed with lampblack. All right for Jimmy the One, pox rot him, they growled in the foc's'l, who did not have to make hisself look like a blackamoor, and even if he did would not have to swab it off with lard and salt water. Yet it was a cheerful septet who sat before their ditty box mirrors of burnished copper or steel, heads even then little below the transverse beams which supported the upper deck, and in the glim of a slush lamp smeared on the soot. While not one of their mates but would have swapped places given the chance.

Thirty minutes to go! It was another starry night that met Davy's upturned face as he mounted the companion to the quarterdeck. There Midshipman Pendarves who as senior member of the gunroom took the middle watch on account of the unavailability of the ship's quota of lieutenants, shifted to give Davy his captain's right to the weather side of the deck. In the zenith Leo's mighty question mark, against which the star-silhouetted maintopmast gyrated to the schooner's dip and roll and lift, seemed aptly to symbolise the night's work. Jupiter, low in the south-west, illumined a pale pathway which invited Davy to travel home, satisfied with what was already achieved and abandoning an enterprise which hazarded the whole. To larboard the Newlyn harbour light stabbed a bloody reflexion into the bay. Otherwise the one glimmer ashore was the glow of the furnace at Gwavas battery, in wartime manned night and day for heating the red hot shot so dreaded by attacking wooden warships. History could hardly record all the centuries in which this region of the British Isles has been assailed and ravaged and burnt, and the Cornwall of this year of grace 1782 was taking no chances. Yet he himself, mused Davy, was tonight an invader.

The young captain shuddered as the omens closed in around him, but it was no more than the shudder one gives when someone walks over one's grave, as they say, and he quickly regained his composure. He must appear calm and confident at all times. Moreover unlike most people he knew, and not just the mystic and piscey-haunted Cornish either, he chose to appear amused rather than moved by superstition. Which was not to say, Davy grinned to himself, that he did not at times touch wood, or that having sailed on this present venture of a Friday he had not been disposed from the start to expect difficulties. Well, they had come his way a-plenty!

'Dowse all lights,' he ordered, then strode up and down on his quarterdeck, becoming aware of the chill that even Maytime in Cornwall prepares for the unwary when the sun is down, and of the fact that he was still in his shirt-sleeves. There was nothing more to be done now, except to receive the reports of subordinates that all was ready, to resist the urge to check in person as undermining the authority of his officers, and to equip himself as befitted the commander of His Britannic Majesty's schooner *Osprey*. Why the deuce had he thought up that name? And then its affinity with *Falcon* brought a flush to his cheeks. Dammit, how should a fellow be besotted with a ship! Lastly he must pay yet another call at the captain's heads — a need Davy was not alone in anticipating on the threshold of action.

Wallace, who had had no more sleep than Davy since leaving Helford, came on deck rubbing his eyes and took over from the midshipman. 'A couple more cables and that will do enough, Mr Wallace, thank you.' The glittering constellations provided a contrasting background to the black mass of the land, but shed little light. For a watcher on the cliff there would be no background to the schooner but the sea, while the matching darkness of sea and ship would let never a shadow stray to view. Davy went below to the great cabin two steps at a time, and with Hamlyn bustling about him like a hen with one chick heaved himself into his jacket with the bullion epaulettes, buckled on his sword, eased a pistol into his waistband with a prayer that he would not have to use it, and clapped on his newest hat.

'Decked out like a Christmas tree!' he muttered to nobody in particular, as he mounted to the stars and the bustle on deck while fore and headsails crumpled and *Roscoff* came right round into wind. 'Kismet, as the corsairs say. And here's to luck!'

The anchor rumbled through the hawsehole and found bottom in twenty-five fathoms; not Davy trusted, among the trunks of the ancient drowned forest said to have covered Mount's Bay when the lost land of Lyonesse stretched to the Scillies and a hundred churches tolled vespers there. The seamen remaining on board manned the falls. The davits took the weight of the longboat and were swung outboard.

'Roundly, for 'ad. Handsomely aft. Hold it. Marry the falls. Lower away together.' Stona launched the boat neatly on the crest of a wave, the crew slid down the ropes to their places on the thwarts and brought it to the entry port, special duty men bundled aboard. A more frightening gang of rascals, thought O'Keenahan morosely, clumsily following them down, never scared the wits out of an honest woman, and a pretty one at that, even if a trifle matronly. Gurt Jan sprang lightly, for all his bulk, to the stern sheets, and then Davy paused, raised his hat as

Wallace saluted, both actions being barely perceived yet acknowledged as a matter of course, and jumped down beside the coxswain at the tiller. The excitement within him was like wine; Davy even felt a little drunk.

'Give way together.' The schooner was black and towering, was a shadow, was nothing. Night smothered the sea surface, stifling the grunts of men straining at oars almost noiseless in greased rowlocks. It shrouded the boat with a thin exhalation that absorbed the starlight, apportioning a tiny quota of luminosity to each frothing eddy round the oar blades, to each anonymous blob that was a white face, but nothing at all to the landing party, sitting like shades on the thwarts between the rowers.

The night, where it pressed like a film on the water, was chilly, eerie. Davy felt O'Keenahan, seated beside him, shiver' and spoke loudly to break the spell. An involuntary 'Ssh!' from for 'ad, certainly not addressed to the captain, decided Davy that to dissipate the mood might well replace it with a worse. In the longboat with him were moonshiners who were neither pressed men nor prisoners. They pursued their trade behind the shield of silence and the night, and knew the rules of the dangerous game they played.

Presently moving out of the shallow mist, they were overtaken by the crest of a breaker surging past them, to tumble noisily in the glinting smother Davy now perceived ahead. Above it, the gap in the trees and a roof and chimney stacks edged in star-glow showed the boat to be on course. Another breaker curled past, and another. Action exorcised visions, phantoms became men again. They caught the next wave as it curved over, rode in on it pitching and in a flurry of spray, and glided to a stop as the backwash swished down the beach. Bowmen jumped out, a phosphorescent spattter around their ankles, and held the boat steady, easing it further up the sand as a following breaker renewed its buoyancy.

While the raiders clambered from the longboat and squelched ashore, Stona, black as the rest and looming even larger than usual, checked off the equipment: each seaman a cutlass in his belt, four grasping pick handles which the captain himself had purchased with a plausible excuse in Porthleven. (Like those martial monks of the Middle Ages, thought the doctor, but kept it to himself, who to avoid bloodshed battled with maces rather than swords.) Chippie Boyce carried five feet of 4 by 1-inch oak plank, drilled for the nails which filled his pocket, and a hammer. One rating, heaving lines coiled across his torso like bandoliers, carrried a red rocket sewn into a canvas sheath and flint, steel and tinder in an oilskin pouch. Another was laden with a sledgehammer and a crowbar of which after a dig in the ribs, Joseph Duval relieved him. Duval, dressed for his part in garments borrowed from the doctor, had been handed only a lantern, for the time being unlit.

Down the beach a lamp glowed in what remained of the *Prince Frederick*, a far-away hammering persisted above the rumble and hiss of the surf. As the party strained and scuffled up the cliff path behind their captain, the petty officers in abusive whispers enjoined silence of the younger hands. The older men were too well seasoned to need telling. Groping cautiously up the narrow trail was routine to them, though it was normally with a load to carry, as at Cobben Cove last autumn. Starlight exaggerates darkness, but in the tunnel of trees into which the track led them darkness without starlight was near absolute. Their eyes became adjusted even to this, however, since the leaves were not everywhere thick on the twigs and in spaces admitted a little light towards which a man could stumble. But there was tripping and shoving and clutching, and even the old hands were constrained to snarl.

Davy halted and had one of the heaving lines uncoiled and passed down the column, for each man to put a hand on it and so maintain contact and distance. With his portion of the line he took a turn round his waist, then brought the end up over his shoulder for holding, forgetful of gold epaulettes and Hamlyn's fastidious pressing. It seemed as if all the other eleven members of the party were in tow; but better progress was made, and sooner than he had anticipated Davy found himself at the verge of the open road.

He stopped, staggered as Stona bumped into him; a succession of bumps and swallowed expletives sounded alarming to his over-sensitised hearing.

'Pass down the line,' he whispered, 'we're there. Pipe down!' He beckoned Stona to his side. A lamp hung over the inn door, the swinging sign yellow in its glow. A man leaned against the doorpost. A hemisphere of pallid light illuminated a circle of the façade, and in the diametric centre, standing in the cone of shadow cast by the lamp's base, dark yet unmistakable, a man — with brass helmet and a red coat!

Stona whistled through his teeth. 'The lobsters!'

O'Keenahan, Duval and Petty Officer Boyce were brought to the fore of the Roscoffs now grouped beneath the trees and staring at the inn. 'We proceed as planned.' Those around Davy leaned with ears cupped to catch his orders. 'Follow my lead; we must take things as we find them. Keeny, if the need arise and not unless, you draw Bessie aside and say what we're about. Don't arouse suspicion — again you must act as if on the boards. Get her help against the soldiers. To them you're the Commissioner and you, Duval, the Channel Islander. As such, Duval, speak only the French your mother taught you. Lieutenant, you and seven men surround the building. Watch out for other sentries. You yourself work round with us to the sentry yonder, keeping out of sight; he may need attention. Don't hurt him. Report as soon as you can on the situation outside — that is, unless you hear an unholy to-do going on inside, in which case break in. Understand?'

'Aye-aye,' growled Gurt Jan, looping the guide line into a coil.

'Duval, hand that confounded crowbar to Jenkins there. Noall, take his lantern.'

Meanwhile the sentry, conscious of some indefinable intrusion into the quiet of his beat, ambled to the gate in the low boundary wall between inn property and road. There, as Davy and his three companions the doctor, Duval and the ship's carpenter stepped into the starlight, the sentry presented his carbine and challenged.

'Friend. And for God's sake keep your voice down, man. You'll rouse the neighbourhood.' It was in the carrying whisper that leaders develop in surprise operations ashore and afloat.

'I've got me orders,' husked the sentry, steering a hazardous course between army regulations and this brassbound naval officer who had bobbed up out of the night like a jack-in-the-box. 'Advance, friend, and be recognised.'

'Captain Edwards of His Majesty's Ship *Osprey*. These gentlemen are custom officers.'

'Good 'evvings, who's that?' The sentry had just spotted Chippie Boyce's blackened face. ''Ere, you stays where you are; I mislikes the looks of he.' The muzzle of his gun was a few inches from Davy's chest, and the man was scared. Dangerously so. A nervous glance round to the inn, where his officer would be, a nod from Davy, and a shadow materialising behind the soldier swung the gun barrel away from the captain and out of the sentry's hand, mercifully without its discharging. Then Gurt Jan pressed a hand over his face, holding him a-tiptoe by the head.

'That's better,' said Davy reasonably. 'Put him down, lieutenant, if you please. Now, trooper, just you lead us to your commander. He's indoors there, ain't he!'

The man nodded, clutching his neck and running his fingers inside his tight stock. 'Yes, sir. Ensign Jocelyn is. Not the captain.'

Davy looked about him apprehensively. Was there some sort of a guard maintained out there in the dark? 'Where's he?'

''E's took the main party off to attack the pirates' stronghold, sir.'

'Has he now? Pirates!'

'Sort of, sir. The Carter gang. New Collector's leading.'

The conversation was interesting. 'Keep your voice down, trooper. Now won't the — pirates — hear the horses a mile off?'

'Detour, sir, on foot.'

'Very wise. How many of your troop in the inn?'

'Four, sir. Not counting me, sir, and Bevins with the 'orses.'

'And in the main party?'

'Look, sir,' said the man, alarm evident again, 'I dunno as I ought to—'

'Quite right, trooper. Can't be too careful. Give him his gun.' Davy had seen Stona shake out the bullet and charge. 'Now just you introduce us to your ensign. The captain of HMS *Osprey* and custom officers.'

Davy hitched his pistol to easier reach, a new-fangled firearm, spoils of war, double-barrelled and with a copper cap beneath each hammer to fire the powder. Noticing that O'Keenahan did the same he followed the sentry, who burst through the door, an instant's hesitation being resolved by a shove in the small of the back. Within, the lamp rayed down on the fireside and the two settles there, leaving the rest of the inn parlour in gloom.

Bessie sat crumpled, somehow smaller than yester-morning, in the corner of one settle. Over her knitted shawl two long plaits hung from a frilly night-cap.

At a querulous 'I say, damn your eyes, what the devil's the meaning of this?' Davy's attention shifted to a young man who had half risen from his seat opposite Bessie, and glass in hand remained in that 'twixt and 'tween posture while Davy strutted cautiously into the lamplight. The young man, whose uniform proclaimed him the ensign in charge, was disfigured by a pink scar that ran from the hairline of a barber's white masterpiece to between black eyebrows, and imparted a saturnine quality to a face otherwise undistinguished.

Davy heard O'Keenahan behind him assuring a sergeant that violence among friends and allies would be regretted. Then the terrified sentry stammered the required introduction.

'Never heard of you.' Jocelyn completed the movement to the perpendicular.

'So yet again,' said Davy pleasantly, 'the High Command have made a cock-up! Whitehall and Admiralty still ain't on speaking terms. They continue to leave it to His Majesty's officers on the ground, as it were, to complete the formalities. Captain David Edwards, of His Majesty's schooner *Osprey* seconded for Revenue duties, sir.'

'You call me My Lord, captain; and bless my soul if I know what you're doing here.' He reluctantly returned the nod Davy had vouchsafed him.

Davy drew himself to full height, hat among the oak beams, and subjected his junior to a head to foot scrutiny. 'You, sir, are an ensign and I am a captain. You will therefore treat me, His Majesty's commission, and His Majesty's uniform with respect. Now, Ensign Jocelyn, allow me to present Mr Kelly, London Deputy Commissioner of Custom and Excise.'

'My lord!' O'Keenahan advanced and bowed.

'And Monsieur Duval, Jersey collector of Custom and Excise.'

'*Enchanté.*' Duval bowed to the ground.

The ensign grabbed his sword hilt. 'A bloody frog!'

'A Channel Islander. No doubt you've heard of the Channel Islands.' Davy observed Bessie's despondency had turned to scorn, and he deemed it time to act. 'Mr Kelly, sir, this good woman here may well assist us to expedite our task. You are?'

'That you do knaw well 'nough,' she began. But the doctor had her ear, and those expressive features that the sign artist had so ill depicted underwent further change. To keep the ensign's mental powers fully diverted, Davy informed him that M. Duval would expound the purpose of the raid, and was then able to scan the now visible corners of the room.

The most puzzled sergeant Davy had ever met stood at the edge of the light, obviously unsettled by events that were moving too fast for his comprehension. 'It's not for me, sir, to overstep the bounds of military ekitek, and speak when I ain't spoke to—'

'It ain't indeed,' Davy agreed.

'But begging your pardon, captain — if y'are what you says y'are, me being unfamiliar with naval faldelals — there's too much being took for granted, if you was to arst me.'

'I was not intending to, sergeant,' said Davy, noting not for the first time what perspicacity was wasted in the forces of the crown by rigid distinction between us and them. A couple of armed troopers took up position by the sergeant and the sentry, while of the marine detachment only Petty Officer Boyce was to hand, and he with no more than a cutlass. To establish himself en rapport with the superior force, Davy nodded towards the hearth, where the strain of translation and impatience with the garrulous Channel Island Collector was turning the ensign's forehead crimson and the scar blood-red. 'Some men achieve rank by family connection.'

'You're dead right there, sir. There's some of the nobs — I hopes you're not a nob sir.' The sergeant was thawing.

'I wouldn't say so.'

'Well, there's some nobs I've served under as needed wet-nursing from cradle to grave, sir. Our ensign, sir — Mr Jocelyn's — my lord's uncle have just died and his father's now a earl, but I dunno which one.'

'Your ensign is a courtesy title, then.'

'If that's how you calls it, captain, that's what it is. Well, he's due for promotion any day, 'count o' that, and my chances of making sar'-major will be the better for him not being round me neck. So I wishes him luck,' the sergeant went on, warming to this theme, 'which he's never had none of up to now. Dead unlucky, Mr Jocelyn − my lord − is. Did he get 'is only wound at Yorktown? Not he − his daddy wouldn't let 'im go. No, sir, walloped by a slip of a girl he was, with a piss-pot.'

'Ain't you going a bit far, sergeant?' Davy asked severely.

The sergeant's face fell. 'Maybe I got carried away, sir, and I'm sorry. Wouldn't have fired off like that wi' the army, sir.'

'I'm sure you wouldn't. And now had you not better see to your duties?' A roar from Boyce at the door sent two whey-faced characters, whom the military had held sitting bolt upright at a trestle and who had seen a chance to escape, cringing back to their benches.

His nibs won't get much help from his squad beyond the call of duty, thought Davy − and detected a stirring in the dark behind the settle from which, patience exhausted, Jocelyn flounced to his feet, flung his glass to the floor with a crash and the tinkle of fragments skittering upon the sand, and bawled, 'Sergeant, damn you, get rid of these kippered herrings!'

In the silence sudden upon this outburst the figure behind the settle rose. 'My lord, listen to me—' It was Hannibal Trainer, to whom Davy was as familiar as he to Davy. Trainer the turncoat.

'Your pardon,' shouted Davy, drowning whatever Trainer might be saying. 'Petty Officer!' Chippie had also seen who it was − doubtless the fellow had sat shielding his face till then − and grabbing the renegade by arm and neck swung him towards the door, the sergeant standing aside with a 'What's all this, then?'

'Hannibal Trainer; deserted my ship last Christmas with the petty officers' mess funds. Warrant for his arrest.' Davy rushed to the aid of Boyce, who seemed to be losing his grip of the struggling fellow; and at that moment Gurt Jan came in, took in the situation at a glance like the good officer he was, the pick of the lower deck, and spun Trainer into the hands of the seamen outside. 'Keep him for questioning,' Davy said quickly: smugglers had a way with informers.

The ensign had relaxed again on his seat, amusement replacing ill temper as he remarked upon the internal dissensions of the Royal Navy. Ignoring this, Davy quietly demanded what it was he had said as the Trainer incident started.

'I gave an order to my sergeant, damn you.'

Davy stiffened like a ramrod. 'Ensign, stand when you are addressed by a senior officer.'

Jocelyn slouched insolently eye to eye with Davy. Again stillness, and the clink of his spurs touching. Stona and the seaman Jenkins, he with the crowbar, stood side by side with the soldiers. My lord's eyes shifted from Davy to the sailors, and back again. 'Tell me, do you recruit all your men from the plantations?'

The flat of Davy's hand caught him hard on the cheek. Recoiling, the back of his knee struck the edge of the high-backed bench, and over they crashed, settle and ensign together. A squeal from Bessie, long and penetrating. Stona was at the flank of the soldiers, pistol in hand. Jenkins' crowbar and Boyce's cutlass were raised. The cavalrymen's carbines pointed at Davy.

Jocelyn slowly got up, staring down at the tumbled settle, wig awry on cropped head. Then with feline speed he was facing Davy, knees slightly bent, sword at Davy's throat. Davy stood motionless. Stona's voice filled the room. 'I shoot the first redcoat as moves.'

O'Keenahan in one stride was behind Jocelyn, pressing his pistol into the ensign's neck. 'Enough,' he cried, 'Lay down your carbines. Put up your cutlasses. And sheath your accursed sword, my lord. We're all in this together for a common cause, and in my capacity as Commissioner I order the arrest of the first man who breaks the peace.'

Davy swallowed and bowed. Losing his temper he had jeopardised the whole venture and must pay the price. 'I apologise.'

'Not accepted.' My lord remarked, sheathing his sword, that at some more suitable time and place he would require satisfaction.

'Quite so,' said Davy. 'Presently I shall explain why my men indeed look as if recruited from the plantations. First, my lieutenant came in with a report, and I must speak to him.' At the far end of the inn parlour Davy learnt that there were twenty-two army mounts in the yard, that a trooper put to guard them had been seized and bound, and that none other than Carter's agent Follick had been taken climbing from a bedroom window. He instructed Stona to prepare what horses were needed for packwork and turn the rest loose. They would find their own way back to barracks as, later than intended, would the troopers. It seemed that all twelve casks would be recovered. One problem solved satisfactorily, provided that they could get them away, and that the main body of dragoons had not abandoned the attack and would return prematurely! Davy's desire to avoid open conflict was causing the whole operation to drag; maybe it would have been policy to have carried the confrontation with the stupid ensign to a conclusion there and then.

'Rig the horses', he told Stona, 'post a sound man to watch the prisoners — Trainer, Follick and the trooper. Above all Trainer. Another on the roof if he can get there, as a lookout, and a third to mind the twelve packhorses. Then bring all the rest of our men to the doors. Enter when I call. Nine of us — it should be enough. And Jan, every minute's precious.'

Naval orders given sotto voice did not impress Jocelyn, nor did Bessie's conversion to co-operation, which his lordship would have enforced by his own methods, without the tars.

'Now I suggest,' concluded the ensign, 'that you and your darkies stop wasting time in this benighted kiddleywink and support me.' He took out a flat, bejewelled watch. 'Twenty minutes, and Captain Smith and sixteen dragoons mount a surprise assault on Carter's place. I take the smugglers in the flank and prevent escape.'

'Why the delay? A blind man could walk there in that time.'

'New Penzance Searcher — now there's a damned interfering fellow for you — is guiding them across country.'

'If Carter's been warned and his men stand to, you'll never get in without cannon, and he's got a few rigged too, they say.'

Jocelyn laughed. 'If he's been warned! Those two shivering rats yonder, and your precious deserter, were look-outs. We caught two of them on the road, the third was half seas over in the public here. Well, do you join me?'

'My duty is here,' Davy replied.

'Nicely remote from the fighting.' It was an added insult which Davy could swallow with equanimity, in view of what he had decided for the redcoats; an insult, too, to be repaid with others in good time. Sufficient unto the day! A rating entered with the boy, his simple features bright with welcome, so Davy sent him out again. He addressed himself to Bessie, who unlocked the cellar, and explained that the block and tackle just within the door were not wholly for cellar use, but to open up the smugglers' hole. Under her direction the sailors lifted out a section of the wooden stairway, to reveal a dry well with iron rungs descending into darkness. Davy took a lantern and climbed down a dozen rungs, through a rocky ceiling to a stone floor the extent of which the jumping flame was inadequate to disclose. And there were the familiar casks, each stamped VIRGINIA LEAF 145 lb Carvill Brothers, Exporters, Newport News,' and labelled 'Lardinière et fils, Camaret, France, for passage in the Union Ship *Joshua Clegg*.'

A net handy in the cellar, and the casks were swayed out of the hole by practised hands, one of the troopers trundling them to the yard door with the comparable expertise of an ex-publican. 'Plenty o'liquor, sir.' Noall held the lantern high. 'Do we bring it up?'

Davy shook his head, not to be outdone in fair dealing by John Carter's famous raid on the Penzance Custom House.

Jocelyn was putting on his gloves, fitting them carefully, finger by finger. 'Must be off, captain. Do you, or do you not, accompany me to the sound of the guns?'

'I hear none.' What Davy did hear was Gurt Jan coughing the sort of cough that attracts attention.

'Nor will you, for seven more minutes. We six shall ride down the road. You are advised to leave first, when the cavalry will cover you. Come, let us forget differences until we meet on the field of honour, and together strike a blow for King and Exchequer.' My lord seemed at last to be all good humour.

'I'll consult my lieutenant.' The time for action has come, thought Davy morosely, as he faced Stona. 'What is it?'

'Game's up if you let him out, sir.'

'I know that, confound it! Are the men handy?'

'At the doors fore and aft. Only got cutlasses and pick-handles, though.'

'Enough. Your pistols primed?'

'Both of 'em ready. So are the horses. Half turned loose, the rest laden like camels of the desert. All linked together like a moonshine drop and rarin' to go.'

'How will you summon the men?'

Gurt Jan produced a bos'un's whistle. 'Three blasts, sir.'

Jocelyn was shouting. 'Get to it, navy, get to it. Don't stand around gossiping like a bevy of old women. I must be off.'

'My task here is completed, ensign, and I shall return to my ship.'

'As you please, and damn you!' His lordship adjusted his hat on his splendid wig. 'I shall of course report your lack of cooperation.'

'One moment—' But as Davy's hand closed upon the butt of the pistol in his sash a hand was laid on his arm, and O'Keenahan stepped between the two officers. 'The proprietress here, my lord, informs me, and I have verified it, that there is direct access from the smugglers' hole to Prussia Cove and the storeroom there. You would of course expect such access in a country where every smuggler is a miner and every miner a smuggler. I intend to make my way along that passage, and I shall be obliged if you will escort me.'

'You've got your precious sailors.'

'The sailors!' The doctor's tone was so redolent of scorn that the blood mounted to Davy's cheeks and Stona across the room swore obscenely.

'The sailors,' commiserated the ensign, shaking his head. 'Commissioner, you shall have my sergeant and a trooper.'

The doctor shrugged his shoulders. 'Good men. But you do not begin to imagine what opposition we must face.' From the sergeant's expression it was apparent that he did. 'My lord, I implore you to come with me. I am a man of parchment and ink, and my parchment and ink will do for your reputation what heritage will do for your rank. For me, promotion. For you, the man of action and decision, the command befitting your station.'

'Damme, I'll come! Sergeant, follow me. Leave Bevins with the nags. Good night to you, Edmunds or whatever 'tis, and no thanks. We shall meet again, depend upon it. Depend upon it.' And with a glare the more ferocious for the mark of the pot on his brow, young milord stalked into the passage, sergeant and three troopers at heel, and O'Keenahan well to the rear.

'Bring in the lobster who was with the horses,' Davy ordered when the inn parlour was clear of all but the beaming Bessie. 'Stand by, Chippie.' At the cellar door the jingle of spurs rang from the well, a lantern below cast writhing shadows on the whitewashed ceiling above the stairs. Petty Officer Hain hustled in a terrified trooper and pushed him to the hole. 'Down and join your mates, mate.' The man hesitated, peering over the edge and obviously fearful that the tales he had heard of the fiendish Cornish smugglers were to be proved true. But on his officer's voice calling sepulchrally, 'Get back to the horses Bevins and make way for the Commissioner,' Stona had him over the edge and down as the sailors began to lower the lid onto the hole. It dropped, a section of treads and rises, fitting snugly into place. Davy heard the ensign's muffled voice demanding to know what was going on, and spurs ringing on the ascent. Bessie's great key turned in the lock and two great bolts thudded home, and the carpenter's hammering as he secured the heavy door with his 4-foot plank was echoed by the smashing of gun butts against the stairway.

'Was there a passage through to the cove?' Davy inquired.

'How should I know?' O'Keenahan grinned. 'Ask Bessie.'

Bessie's laughter as she shook her head was of the explosive, even hysterical type peculiar to West Cornwall. And it was infectious. 'What a Thespian was lost to the stage!' choked Davy.

'I have thought of it,' O'Keenahan spluttered through his tears.

'Well, they'll be above ground in five minutes, and out of the cellar in thirty, if the rest of the cavalry don't turn up before then. So we must away. But stay,' Davy added. 'The rocket. Our martial allies must not catch the kingdom of Prussia unawares.'

The rocket soared from the deserted yard to burst over Prussia Cove with a tremendous scatter of crimson stars and an explosion which shook every regal window and surely interrupted Captain Harry's nightly tussle, if report be true, with the devil. The horses, preceded and succeeded by lanterns, were strung out along the nutwood trail to the beach, Trainer walking roped to the saddle of the last. The two men in the parlour were nowhere to be seen, and Follick was freed to join them, wherever that might be. Bessie was to go to a neighbour's, where there was no chance that a vengeful but steedless cavalry would discover her. There were the Carters.

'I couldn' do nothin' to stop 'ee, my 'andsome, could I now?

They can't hold nothing against me, nor shall they. I'll tell they a pretty tale.' She grinned. 'But I shan't mean a word of it, really.'

And there was the boy, about whom Davy had decided long before.

'I'll take him with me, if I may,' he said, 'and make a seaman of him. And now, Bessie my dear, farewell!' He kissed her. So did Keeny, but longer.

11

Dr O'Keenahan sat at the table in the great cabin, reading *The Ship-Master's Assistant and Owner's Manual*. Or attempting to. For the cabin was rising and sinking like Gossip Janie Jarvis last month on the ducking stool, her antics when undergoing punishment affording such merry diversion to the otherwise dour little seaport. Like Gossip Jarvis, the doctor clutched the seat and held his breath as the stern plummeted and green water rushed up to the scuttles. Unlike her, he was subjected also to a roll and a corkscrewing lurch, for which a stoical resolve to ignore *Roscoff's* endeavour to stand on her tail was proving no match whatever.

Davy, astraddle with practised ease and balancing a steaming mug in one hand while biting a leg of chicken in the other, was snatching a hasty repast. Captain's place in a gale was by the helm. Freshly towelled hair hung in a tangled tail between his shoulder blades and his eyes shone. Bless my soul, the man actually enjoys the weather, the doctor realised incredulously.

'Listen to this, Ned.' With gulps and pauses O'Keenahan read, '"Persons opposing, obstructing, or assaulting, officers of His Majesty's forces, or in the service of the customs or excise, in the execution of their duty" − don't this bloody ship ever stay still a moment? − "may be carried before a justice, who may commit them for trial; and upon conviction, shall be sentenced to hard labour on the river Thames, or to the house of correction." A bit ominous, ain't it! Have you seen those hulks?'

'No, but I've heard all about 'em. Have you?'

'I've heard − enough. What do we do! Flee the country − not, I trust, by sea?'

Davy laughed, finished the leg and chucked the bone into a tub that was sliding back and forth between the bulwark and the carriage of a 9-pounder chaser. 'It's like this, Keeny − law's one thing and enforcing it's another. You're Irish and ought to know. Because a parcel of big wigs up at Westminster make an act of parliament, it don't follow that there are men to catch the offender, or lawyers to accuse him, or juries to condemn him, or justices to pass sentence.'

'They hang thieves and deport poachers by the score,' Kenny panted.

Davy downed the hot toddy and summoned Hamlyn. 'That's because everyone's hand's against 'em. The watch, the military, the jury, the bench. And even so, far more get away than are nabbed. Now what'll happen when news of our little expedition leaks out − if for shame either the Carters or the lobsters have a word to say about it? The navy will laugh their brass buttons off, that the army have made such a sorry showing. The Carters will say, the St Ives lot have got their own back, and what's worse, we're in their debt for disorganising the lobster's attack—'

'They'll admit that?'

'Deed they will. You don't imagine either John, or Harry, will forget it even if they never mention it. Got a reputation to maintain as the most honest and incorruptible Methody moonshiners this side o'Tamar. And damme, Keeny, that's what they are too!' Hamlyn, with a dexterity O'Keenahan could only marvel at, was helping his captain into monkey jacket and then oilers, without grabbing at or missing Davy's back-stretched arm as the deck dropped beneath them, then soared sea-sawing to heights the doctor's bowels magnified in torture and revulsion.

'And have you considered,' Davy went on, turning to face his friend while the steward followed the movement like an orbiting moon, 'what magistrate is going to issue a warrant, or listen to a word against us in court? Maybe he is and maybe he ain't personally involved in free trading and moonshine, but brother William and uncle Tom and cousin George are up to their necks in it. And if he puts you in the dock, or me, he can't abide to think what's coming to light in the examination. So he dismisses the case for lack of evidence. Wouldn't you, Keeny, in his boots? Lastly, the jury — should it get that far. What Cornish jury do you suppose will convict an accused who's added a taste of pleasure, of prosperity, even, to the damnedest hardest, poorest life you ever did hear of? Why should they uphold a London law, when they've got their own stannary parliament to churn out all the legislation they're minded to observe? What's there to do about a fellow who stands up to foreign redcoats and the Revenue but pat him on the back and drink his health?'

O'Keenahan's handkerchief was to his lips and his face no pinker than the tips of the waves which leapt at the stern windows. 'Why then,' he managed to ask, 'at such pains to avoid capture?'

Davy's expression darkened. 'Depends who you are. If you're the sort they'd sell their mothers to make an example of, stay at large, and they can do no more than slap a charge against you which will fail and make'em look foolish. At least in Cornwall. Get took, particularly with the stuff on you, and given half a chance you're bundled into England, saddled with every unsolved shooting that's baffled 'em the past year or two, and—' With hand and jaw he indicated all too dramatically the jerk of the noose. 'Moral — don't let 'em get you! And now duty calls.'

Accoutred in sou'wester, a dry oilskin all stiff about him, with a towel tucked between neck and collar to keep trickles at bay, and cumbersome in the sea-boots he had worn ever since weighing anchor twelve hours ago, Davy paused at the door, the hinges of which added one more creak to the working of the schooner's timbers. 'Now don't you worry, Keeny. Just watch out lest one of the lobsters recognises you and goes into action. Stay over on the north coast awhile. And if I were you, I'd stop trying to be a hero, and lie flat in your bunk with a bucket.'

'You didn't say as much — to that silly boy o' Bessie's — you sent back to the galley.'

'Because he'd a job to do and must learn to do it in all weathers. With you, 'tis different. Besides, Keeny, at any time now on you ain't going to be quick enough for that Kashmir carpet of mine — 'tain't every day you can relieve Johnny

Crapaud of carpets like that in his saloon.' And with a grin and a wave Davy clumped up the companion and onto the streaming deck.

The end of the afternoon watch found *Roscoff* no further west of her starting point off Cudden, but far south of it, with the Lizard glimpsed occasionally through squalls and scud low on the north-east skyline. The *Dorcas*, name painted in again now she was clear of Carter waters, would be safe in the snug little harbour at St Michael's Mount, whither Davy had sent her when the twelve casks had been stowed in the schooner's hold and the raid was over. James and Jason Duval, not being known that side of the Lizard peninsula, had been instructed to keep alert in Marazion for comment about the night's work. Joseph, to whom O'Keenahan had made a present of the coat and hat loaned to the collector of Jersey, was given a purse and ordered to travel by hired horse or carrier's waggon − a common mode of cheap conveyance − to St Ives. Smeecher would have informed Squire Stephens of events up to Captain Harry Carter's capture. Joseph must make his way to Tregenna Castle and report final success. Then he would be made welcome at Boswyn where Mrs Davy would feed him pies and pasties without equal in Penwith, and Mr Davy would ply him with questions, mainly about his son.

During the first 'dog', with the first lieutenant on watch, the blow began to abate. Not that O'Keenahan, supine in his bunk, noticed it. But the seamen detected quieter intervals between gusts blowing sometimes harder than ever, but less frequently. Storm trysail was set, a reef shaken out of the mainsail, and into combers built up hugely by Atlantic rollers congesting between Land's End and Ushant, and steepened by the continental shelf, Davy set about the long haul to weather the land.

As *Roscoff*, hove to and drifting, sprang to life and turned away from the wind on the starboard tack, a sea surged over her bow and heeled her so far further as to tumble O'Keenahan to the deck and send cargo crashing in the largely empty hold. Davy sent Wallace to investigate, and he shortly returned.

'I suggest, sir, that I resume the watch and you have a look-see below yourself. It's those bloody casks; four have broken loose. No, I judged not to call the hands until you should see for yourself. There's no immediate danger to the ship.'

It was dark down there after the daylight and the brightening sky, dark and in the glimmer of a solitary lantern dangerous, if not to the ship, then certainly to Davy as he stood on the bare floorboards above the bilges, with four casks of over a hundred-weight apiece trundling up and down and across with every movement of the ship. Three casks of over a hundredweight. The lid of the fourth had burst open, spilling a wad of tobaccco leaf and — what the devil was it? Two or three chair legs? Davy, as near as dammit looking three ways at once and with a special focus on a fourth, risked crushing to grab one and carried it to the lantern. Being the last object he would expect to find in a cask of Virginian tobacco, Davy turned it this way and that until he placed it. A musket butt! Of unusual yet unmistakeable design, still — a musket butt! A cask full of butts, and for all he knew eleven more casks similarly packed.

The steadier progress of the *Roscoff*, while keeping the casks rolling, gave slight risk of a stove plank in the schooner's side. But if they were not secured further disclosure was inevitable. And Davy was now quite certain that before the astonishing contents of the 'tobacco' casks became common knowledge in St Ives the views of his owners should be sought. Watching his opportunity, he upended the damaged one on its base, and dragging it to where the foot of the mainmast dropped to its step in the keelson lashed it firmly. Then, shoving the musket butts back and levelling the spilled leaf on top, he called Chippie and his mates to the hold and had the loose casks secured and the broken cover replaced.

Then up and down on his captain's walk along the weather side of the quarterdeck! Why should America send military stores to her ally, France, in the guise of tobacco? And what earthly use, other than as firewood, were gun butts without gun barrels? But hold it! Davy told himself, stopping in his tracks. The *Joshua Clegg* had carried three great hogsheads besides the casks, each five times their weight and also addressed to Lardinière et Fils. Three hogsheads for musket barrels to match every butt in the casks. That must be it. Davy snapped his fingers to the astonishment of his number one on the lee side and resumed his walk. Had the customs people by now disposed of them as bonded tobacco? And what could Lardinière et Fils, Tobacco Importers, possibly want with guns?

At four bells, Davy invited Wallace on being relieved by Lieutenant Stona to join him at supper. When Hamlyn had gone for'ad, all unsuspecting of missing a unique 'buzz', for his 'last dog' stand-easy in the petty officers' mess, Wallace agreed that the mystery of the butts should for the time being remain a mystery, even from Dr O'Keenahan. Davy found it difficult to accept that Keeny should be kept in ignorance of this intriguing development. His knowledge of affairs was wider than that of a young captain continuously at sea and denied the Admiralty information that his Royal Navy counterpart would receive. But Davy realised that although his friend was as popular with the officers as he was everywhere else, there was some resentment at his involvement in shipboard problems, however admirable and indeed indispensable his contribution to their solution. Not without a sense of betrayal, therefore, did Davy confine conversation to trivialities when later he coaxed Keeny from his bunk to enjoy, or endure, a light meal in the great cabin. Meanwhile *Roscoff*, with lessening pitch and roll, weathered Land's End and taking the wind over her stern spread wings of sail to a boom on either beam, and flew for home.

*

The stone bench beneath the library window was warm in the sunshine. It was one of several on the narrow terrace that skirted the west wing and thence, in an L-turn, the granite façade of the ancient house. Boswyn seemed to be as native a product of the timbered and bouldered hillside as the ivy, bright with new leaf, that each year must be trimmed back from mullioned windows and the pillared porch. The porch, which knew only the wind and the northern sky, bore on its flat relieving-arch the arms of Boswidden, but when the Great Queen reigned, the manor house and its immediate environment had passed in marriage to the Davys. The two latest of this line, father and son, sat round the corner on the warm stone bench.

Davy gazed with deep affection at the old man, who had fallen asleep. Franklin Davy, whom his son could never visualise as having once been young, had been thirty-six when he wed Thamsyn, the seventeen-year-old youngest of Penhallow of

Carwin. She gave him one son and, to the regret of both, no more. An impoverished inheritance, the unavoidable sale of his mine Wheal Gavin shortly before the American War had revived the demand for copper, disappointment at this and helpless anger at the shame that had beset his undeserving son, had taken toll of his middle years. Under sixty, he looked seventy.

Ned Davy understood his father's troubles, his efforts to keep the property intact, the privations which his parents had uncomplainingly endured. In the past six months he had been able to pay off the overdraft at Molesworth and Eliot's bank. On his first whole day at home since the Helford river expedition, Davy had been as eager as his father to discuss affairs in general and family in particular. They had ambled through the garden together, Davy mentally stretching himself to appreciate the plants and shrubs on which the old gentleman lavished such care; to learn their names, a process repeated at each return from sea, and each time a lesson starting at page one on the hornbook.

'Og's wounds!' old Davy would exclaim, tipping back what remained of the straw hat his son had brought him from Jamaica before that dreadful surrender. 'I've told thee time and again that yon's an *aquilegia glandulosa*, and this a *primula auricula*, yet still you confuse them. The good Lord surely sent thee with one side of thy brain addled, for with t'other you remember all those outlandish ship-names, spars and rigging and all.'

'An I did not,' Davy would reply, 'I'd long since have broken my neck or lost my ship.' Then they would catch one another's eye and grin, and father would seek to touch his son's hand yet not let him know he did it. And on that bench two tall, straight figures, the black head and the white head at either end of it, would relax in the sunshine until sleep claimed the one, while the other would plan the days ahead until recollections of those past won the hour.

On leaving the ship, Dr Keenahan had nailed up his board in Market Place with prospects of a fruitful practice now that a full, and no doubt embellished, report of his exploits on the Helford had gone the rounds. Keeny and Joseph Duval entertained a high regard for each other, and Joseph was learning the mysteries of Aesculapius at the doctor's feet. James, and not Joseph as originally agreed, had returned to Bosahan to help his father.

Davy had watched a frigate, upside down in the lens of a spyglass cherished by his great-grandfather, sail out of St Ives Bay with Hannibal Trainer reverted to the tyrannies and indignities of the lower deck in the navy. Squire had had him impressed. Trainer, it transpired, had a family to support in both St Ives and Plymouth, and finances had been strained.

And those casks labelled 'Tobacco'? Ten of the twelve, broached in *Roscoff*'s hold in Mr Knill's presence, were found to have been packed with musket butts. The three great hogsheads, warehoused under seal, contained as Davy had guessed the barrels to match the butts. Moreover these were the newly invented rifled barrels of an accuracy proved all too often by the rebels against the British Generals Howe, Burgoyne, Clinton and Cornwallis in America. Why they were to have been smuggled into France Davy could only suspect; Mr Knill had nothing to add. There had been talk in West Cornwall of disaffection yet again in Haute-Bretagne. With the West Cornish finding rumour from Britanny nearer truth than most news that crossed the Tamar into the Duchy, likely enough the purpose of a clandestine shipment to Camaret was for terrorism, war even, against King Louis XVI. There were better ways of waging that war, though, mused Davy, in his mind *Falcon* with her long-14 chasers, and Cornish sharpshooters behind her bulwarks aiming rifled muskets as the lovely ship closed with the foe.

In France the lady he longed for but would never meet again! In Harvey's yard a ship refitting; not the *Falcon*. The girl – married for sure, by paternal arrangement, to some pompous frog whom she loathed. Davy was convinced she had given her shipboard acquaintance of a few fleeting minutes a thought at the altar. Well, he must fret no longer. He had not known even her name before, and was the less likely to know it in the future.

And the corvette, that other unrequited love of his twenty-two years? She lay in the Hayle river, moored fore and aft, afloat at high tide, at the ebb careened on mud. Slimy green weed coated her lower hull for all its copper sheathing. Blocks and rope ends swung adrift, knocking as the wind shook the rotting rigging, while rust from fittings and the bower anchors on the foredeck streaked the grey falcon's outspread pinions like a wound. Temporary repairs where *Roscoff*'s guns had blasted her stern were still unsightly patches, incapable of staying the decay of weather and neglect. Davy had ridden round to see her and could scarcely withhold a tear. He ached for that ship as grievously as any one of the many mothers in Cornwall who watched her child dying of the wasting disease, but could only pray.

But Davy had been assured by Mr Stephens, who as an honoured magistrate must mean what he said, that the syndicate would get the *Falcon* into Harvey's dock as soon as the present incumbent was off the stocks, that the Collector was negotiating with the Carters for the long-14s at Bosahan Point, and that all agreed the command was to go to Captain Davy. He must stand by to supervise the refit.

Roscoff was at sea again, under Wallace and with most of her old ship's company. But without Davy. He had watched her departure in the ancestral telescope, had nurtured a dog-in-the-manger resentment, and been angry with himself because of it. About to turn his gaze from ageing ship to ancient home, the glass which showed sea above and sky below, and sails filling below deck level, revealed Dr Nankervis looming from the hatchway. His eyes, Davy guessed, would be bloodshot, his cheeks white as the new topsail. When he commissioned *Falcon*, her captain-elect resolved, he would have O'Keenahan in Nankervis's place if he had to drag the doctor from satisfied patients and shanghai him aboard, for all that he got seasick in a capful of wind. And Gurt Jan Stona and Pendarves — a voyage would be unthinkable without them too. The decision cheered him up.

It looked, though, as if he were in for a longer spell at home than he had known since schooldays with the famous Dr Cardew of Truro. It was a spell he could only with difficulty persuade himself to accept, let alone welcome. Here he was at Boswyn, no more the monarch of the quarterdeck, arbiter of lives and fortunes, but the lad whose parents could never realise how the years had passed; who alternately scolded and coddled. Now they expected that the son who would one day inherit the property — and God forbid it should be nearer the present

than the twenty years which are eternity to anyone under thirty!
– would prove himself caring of his inheritance, however
truncated and overburdened it might be. And there was
another family duty to which they, or at any rate his mother,
required his prompt attention. Marriage.

To whom? Davy asked himself. There was neither pleasure
nor anticipation in the notion. Lavinia Stephens? Davy doubted
if he were match enough to win Squire's approval; and even if
he should, he had no desire to compete with the popinjays he
had watched at Tregenna. Amelia Pentilly of Polvalgan Farm
past Hellesveor? The only girl among seven sons, she and her
mamma had taken tea at Boswyn twice since Davy's return;
rather pointedly, he considered, and doubtless at his mother's
invitation. His mother was the dearest, sweetest, most
managing female of her generation in the world. But even she
was not going to manage him into Amelia's plump embrace.
Amelia was an agreeable enough wench, if of apple-cheeked
simplicity and spoilt by her brothers. But no! The prospect of
Amelia's ample bosom spilling out upon him in the suffocating
environment of drawn bed-curtains and feather bed appalled
him.

But somewhere, someone . . .! Davy discovered that he had
forsaken the bench with his father asleep on it and was
automatically pacing five up, five down, on the gravel terrace.
He pictured himself back aboard his ship, the mutiny having
been settled, to find himself confronted by – Marie, Louise,
Madelaine, Jeanne? There was no name he could think of for
ma'amselle with the sunset in her hair, and in her eyes the
amazing revelation that he and she belonged to one another and
would find one another, if not in this world, then in the next.
'Oh stuff!' he said, waking his father up.

Stuff maybe. But the ache of it, the pain at heart, was real.
God, it was real! Next you'll be snivelling like a lovesick wench,
he scolded himself. It's all this idling. 'That fencing in the
meadow – I'll fix it right away,' he told his delighted parent.
And tomorrow, he told himself, it's away to Bethlehem Farm
near Camborne town. A couple of hours' ride on old Hector, his
father's hunter and in need of exercise, would shake his own
liver up too. He would see how Farmer and Mrs Porris were
faring in their new-found gentility; and even if madam still

harboured such ambitions for her daughter as put a half-pay sea captain out of count, Jess would welcome him.

Tomorrow? There were six hours of daylight left, so why not now? Jess tousleheaded in the dairy that night of the 'run'. Jess in scruffed-up nightdress with legs and thighs all light and shadow in the candleflame, his tenderness rather than his passions aroused by the shameless behaviour of her father. But it was not all tenderness now, Davy realised, stopping in his tracks. Then there was Jess in the green dress, very fetching with evasive ringlets and her hair piled high, merry glances turning to puzzlement and then to distress. It occurred to Davy that a handsome *amende* was due, and that he should have made it sooner.

'The fence must wait after all, father,' he said. He was on his way to the stables when a clatter of hooves brought the old man to his feet and alerted Davy as surely as ever did the cry 'Sail ho!' from topmast crosstrees.

It was Mr Knill, and all notion of visiting Bethlehem Farm that day went by the board. The Collector was leaving St Ives, and would resume his former profession of attorney at Gray's Inn. An additional appointment was that of Inspector of Customs for the ports of South and East England. Far, far away! Davy's expectations turned to ashes. Without John Knill to back him, what prospects had he? Other captains stood closer to Squire Stephens, all of them senior and ambitious, several with as considerable and certainly more profitable achievements than his.

Tea, conducted by Mrs Davy with proper formality and polite small-talk, was a misery to all, however nicely partaken, however genteel their deportment; and to none was it a greater misery than to the disappointed young sailor. Farewells at the porch choked in his throat. John Knill kissed a tearful Thamsyn Davy, exchanged a significant grip with his old friend Franklyn Davy, and clapped Ned Davy on the shoulder.

'Ride part-way with me, Captain. We have unfinished business.'

12

Old Hector's grey rotundity and the chestnut's sleek flanks brushed brambles, brier and woodbine a-tangle either side of the sunken lane as Davy and John Knill walked their mounts uphill towards Hellesveor. The Collector, leading, had proposed this roundabout route for longer conversation and for a view of which, he confessed to realising now as seldom before, he would never tire.

'I side with the lately lamented Thomas Gray, as against Pope and the venerable Sam, in preferring the natural to the artificial and antique,' he admitted to Davy, who was a little surprised at first to find his mentor atune with wakening opinion; a student of life as well as of dusty law. Davy had been on the point of forthright questioning, but then deemed it politic to let Mr Knill come to the future in his own good time. How should romantic notions be far from a man for whom the custom house ledgers were a blind for moonshine, and who both warred and trafficked with his country's enemies at sea?

So they ambled along the lane, ducking as overhanging boughs threatened their hats and the tie wig Mr Knill sported when on a visit, the horses evading from long practice rocks tumbled from the hedge, and striking noisy fire where drying ruts gave place to the exposed surface of a buried boulder.

Davy fanned his way through a swarm of gnats and spat out an unfortunate. 'Cornwall,' he commented, for no better reason than wanting something to say that was not all ships and their command. 'Cornwall is all trees and stone and under-growth.'

'And holes,' Knill added, as they entered upon the moorland above the hamlet. He turned in his saddle, and stared past Davy to where a spurt of steam from Trenwith engine house puffed up round the stack and merged with smoke pluming into the still air. 'And hills, and valleys, and the sea.'

They reined up their horses and sat side by side, looking down to the town, to Tregenna Castle's mock battlements surmounting the treetops above Porthminster, further round to the gleam of new-cut granite — Knill's own mausoleum stabbing into the greening sky on Worvas Hill. 'I go, in hope to return — yonder.' Then John Knill shivered, though the evening was warm. 'Somebody walks there already! But to the present!'

At last! said Davy to himself.

They flipped a leg over their saddles, and hat in hand led their horses, the chestnut and the grey, white wig and black hair, across a sea of heath. The Bristol Channel dreamed to the north, and old Atlantic reached up cloudy arms to ease a dying day into the reviving mists of Newfoundland three thousand miles westwards.

Mr Knill filled his lungs with the sweet air. 'The *Falcon*, Captain Ned, is yours. You knew?'

'Squire Stephens told me. But I feared that with your departure—'

'Fiddlesticks! Then nothing remains but your articles of commission.'

Davy shook his head. 'Begging your pardon, sir, that is the least of what remains to do. The ship is rotting in Harvey's mud. There are letters of marque to apply for. There is provisioning, and the crew.'

'Formalities!' The Collector's attitude to such problems appeared to be that so long as he chose to ignore them they did not exist. 'But 'twill take time,' he conceded.

Davy remarked that he had been ordered to stand by until the *Falcon* was ready to sail. 'And much more of kicking my heels ashore and I'll live aboard — in the mud.'

Knill chuckled. 'Ninety-five per cent of your time as autocrat of your own quarter-deck, the residuary five per cent the dutiful son at home. 'Twould tear a young sea-captain apart, eh? Your mother has a rod in pickle for you, I'll be bound, with all that wasted effort to get you a wife instead of a ship. D'ye know, Ned, that when we met at the custom house a week or so ago—'

'An age ago,' Davy interrupted.

'Aye, indeed! Well at our meeting then, the first since you were a snottie off to sea, bless my soul if I did not assess you over-confident and too self-assured by half.'

And now?' Davy was unsure whether to applaud or deplore this revelation.

'I know you better. You present a bold front but you are human, and I like you for it. Now look'ee, Ned, I've a task for you will fill time till your ship's on the stocks. Lardinière and son—' John Knill has ascertained, through his devious cross-Channel connections, that the consignees of the musket parts were leaders of yet another Breton rising to win autonomy within the French kingdom. 'Now let us suppose that your prize, the *Joshua Clegg*,' he went on, 'the cargo still in her hold — guns, the rest of the tobacco, cotton et cetera all presently stored in my warehouses — just suppose she's been delayed a fortnight en route, storms and a calm, say, then sails into Camaret.'

Davy perceived what was coming and recoiled, as though from an infamous suggestion, but as was his wont he preserved outward aplomb. 'You will have Captain Venables released from the Moor,' he surmised, well knowing Knill would do nothing of the sort.

'I would have *you* as the worthy captain. Your talent for histrionics rivals young Kemble's Hamlet they're raving about in Dublin. Captain Edwards, wasn't it? Revenue schooner *Osprey*!' There was a hint of steel in his laugh.

'But I have scarce a word of French.'

'No more, I'll warrant, had Venables of Baltimore.'

'I'm not familiar with the approaches to Brest—'

'And was Venables? He would use his charts, and we have 'em. Look'ee, captain, this job must be done. Delivery of those weapons will comfort England's friends — God knows there's precious few of those! — and confound their foes, or at least some of them. It will also pay us well — the rest of the cargo too, the British market being so depressed. It will put money into our pockets — principally mine, if you want the truth of it — for final payment and fitting out the *Falcon*.'

Davy objected that the sale of the brig was said to have completed the purchase. They would have to buy her back.

'Not sold,' said Knill. 'At Portreath, with first refusal to Sir Francis, who is looking her over.'

'You had first refusal of his cannon,' Davy remarked, 'yet they went elsewhere.'

'Precisely,' said Mr Knill, setting foot in stirrup and

mounting the chestnut with a grunt. 'Now we shall repossess the vessel. Call at my house when you see the *Clegg* alongside Smeaton's pier again in a day or two. And do not fret, my good friend.' He reached down from the saddle and patted the young man on the shoulder. 'All will be settled and done with when I get to London. It must be and I intend that it shall — the guns, the *Falcon*, the records of the custom house.' He stared down at Ned Davy, silent for several creeping seconds and considering. Then, 'I'll wager it is news to you that I own, in entirety for the most part, a whole fleet of ships.'

Davy nodded. News indeed, though he had guessed something of the Collector's maritime investments.

'I tell you this, Ned Davy, here on this lonely moor where none but you can hear—'

'To demand my confidence,' Davy interrupted, 'to consider that otherwise I should betray your trust, impugns my honour.'

'No, no, of course not, my high-minded irascible young friend; though the years will teach you that interest and honour are rare bedfellows. But think of these things I have told you. You have in me a patron worthy of your loyal support.'

'You need never doubt my loyalty, Mr Knill, nor my devotion to your affairs.'

'As much is proved already.' John Knill leaned forward, patting the chestnut neck. 'Bear in mind, Captain, that for many years my customs duties have not been performed for the salary they confer. Further, that my standing in the Revenue service, my forthcoming entrée to every port that feeds the metropolis, are golden assets few shipowners possess. Your hand, Captain Davy, in earnest of an association of profit, and yes, of honour to us both. To you, wealth and the revival of your family's fortunes; the times of glory you men of action crave; sometimes the peril; you have the youth, the courage, and above all the foresight and intellect to face. To me, blessings that make even the latter years better than those which went before.'

Now why all this? Davy wondered, as they solemnly shook hands. Then Mr Knill grinned and touched his hat with his crop. 'Thank 'ee for accompanying me thus far, and for our talk. See me when the *Clegg*'s in. And tell your mother it is I she must blame for parting you so early from the fair, if a trifle fat, Amelia.'

Davy watched him canter down over the moor towards the

town, where the lights matched the stars in sudden appearance as one gazed, and the ships in the harbour were fading into the shadows.

*

A disgruntled Ned Davy rode from Bethlehem Farm into a drizzle that became a downpour, gushing from his hat brim as from the gargoyles on St Eia tower. Drenching the brine-impregnated boat-cloak he had strapped behind Hector's saddle against such a turn in the weather, trickling into his riding boots from soaked thighs. The relic of a medieval farm-house overlooking Gwithian village offered shelter. He spurred to it over the upper moorland, hooves squelching in the heather and mossy turf. The combined instinct of horse and rider picked the easiest passages between boulders and bushes, while evading bogs and half-hidden rocks which would have trapped or tripped a stranger.

Davy swung himself down into the puddled yard, the sudden weight of his sword on its baldric — it was a weapon three generations of Davys had kept keen and bright — squeezing the wet from his shirt to such parts of his torso as had hitherto stayed dry. Brushing through tall nettles that filled the entrance to what must have been the kitchen, he huddled with the old horse in a corner, the steam from them both hazing to a strip of slates which remarkably withstood pressures to which the rest of the roof had long since succumbed, beams and all. There, with the spatter of raindrops overhead obscuring every sound from the world outside, he hung his cloak on a nail, shook his dripping hat, retied his sodden hair ribbon, and marvelled that he should be wetter and far, far more miserable ashore than on his quarterdeck in a squall. It had been the devil of a day!

Yet it had begun well enough. Sunshine all the way to the low-water ford across the estuary at Lelant, early June merry in the air and heart; and hastening him on the lure of a nubile lass, long of limb and lovely, in a green dress with rebellious hair piled high. Then some obstacle, probably wreckage he should have noticed in the sand under the swift, shallow current, had not a more intimate image intruded, on which Hector had stumbled and almost thrown him.

It had been a near-mishap recalling Davy to a present which from that moment went sour. First, grit from the copper-smelting chimney-stacks of Angarrack and Copperhouse got in his eye. He had reined up to see the intruder still on Harvey's stocks, and observed with distaste the smoke rolling down to the foreshore from the whole deep valley, to dissipate over a sea that was blooded by the waste outpour of the mines.

From the Towans, the sandhills above the estuary, like Moses on the mountain he surveyed the impact of new ideas upon an accustomed view which he now saw as if for the first time. The locusts of this ageing century were busy around the green hills, and the new nineteenth would find them devouring the hills too. Plumes of smoke writhed about the Norman keep on distant Carn Brea, white plumes signalling the proliferation of engine houses upon abandoned farmlands. Nearer, haphazard clusters of hamlets and mine-workings were linked by chewed-up rusty earth, criss-crossed with tracks and tramroads. Along these the patient beasts plodded. Their packloads and the burdens they hauled, mused Davy, had never known light other than the flickering tallow in the miner's hats in all the recorded millenia since Genesis.

That was when, descending from the Towans to the salt-flats, his eyelid had trapped an atom that felt like a hot rock. Pity the ore had not been left where it was, or at best dug, as they dug tin, in the Phoenician golden age, from quickly overgrown trenches! He worsened his eye by rubbing it. Thought and pain veered by association to the copper plates fitted to the *Falcon*'s bottom against the auger-like depredations of sea-worms. The thought, while disproving his thesis that the ore was best undug, did nothing to alleviate the pain, now aggravated by the image of that noble, neglected hull, green with oxidisation and stinking weed, keeled over on an ebb-tide mudbank.

With Bethlehem Farm in sight both eyes, the one apparently in sympathy with the other, were still as red as the stream, gurgling from tin-stamps in the hinterland, which he had crossed beyond Gwithian. Feeling himself singularly repulsive, he was dissuaded from turning back only by the notion that if French cannon or piratical pulpit thumper had never daunted him, why should a wench in a green dress? At the farm he was confronted by an unwelcoming Mrs Porris. Jess was wisht and seeing nobody, being in bed with the doctor. Since usage did not require him to take this candid statement literally, and admitting to himself that he was not at his best with the sick, Davy made a discreet enquiry as to her ailment, and was minded to leave with a word for her swift recovery, a clear conscience, and a preference for ships.

'Poor maid have had a nasty fall from her horse and have broke her leg. She've been bled by the leech, though why cupping and bleeding should mend a leg any better than a dish of senna tay is beyond me, Mr Davy.' And she had glared at him as if, from first to last, her daughter's accident were all his fault.

It was beyond him too; and Davy resolved as he retreated to send Dr. O'Keenahan to the rescue as soon as might be. But farmer – or was it gentleman? – Porris had heard voices. Shunned by his own sort and avoided by those to whose fellowship he aspired, Porris bore Davy off to an empty hearth under the antique blunderbuss. There his guest supped, perforce, an admirable claret and listened with less relish to Redruth market gossip. Only after attacking a rabbit pie, a sirloin of an indifferent syllabub had Davy's excuses for leaving been accepted; whereupon a relenting Mrs Porris suggested he might poke his head round her little maid's door and give she a smile. The grit having ceased to trouble him, Davy trusted that he no longer seemed presently emerged from inconsolable grief, and complied.

Jess's welcome had been sincere. She had been so obviously at pains to make herself as attractive as a pallid invalid in a hugely frilled night-cap could be, that the young sailor again felt shame at his first approach to her bedside and his abrupt treatment of her at the Tregenna rout. Such a shrunk, beaten little figure on her pillows, face pale as the sheets – damned leech and his thirst for blood! – but with the roses flushing there in startling contrast as their glances met and she held out her hand towards him.

'No, no visitors,' the ogre had ordained. A few stinted phrases, then out into the drizzle and the long ride home.

The rainfall was easing: surely he heard movement in the yard! He went to the doorway, to stare across the weed-tufted paving straight into the face of a soldier – a corporal of dragoons, brass helmet bold against the interior of an open-sided barn opposite. Davy withdrew hurriedly, an instinctive but suspicious move which he endeavoured to correct by reappearing with a friendly wave. The man stared, motionless. Two troopers stood behind him, and all three held their horses, a fragment of thatch providing like cover to the roof above Davy. Time to be off, and the confounded rain bucketing down again! Clasping soggy cloak about his throat and jamming soggier tricorn over his ears, he led the steaming Hector into the yard — and recognised the corporal. The fellow had been a sergeant when they met, at Bessie Bussow's. Davy had no doubts where, in the line of duty, he had lost a stripe and would be none the sweeter for it.

'Now 'aven't I seed you afore, sir?' the corporal enquired, squinting as a flurry of rain swirled beneath the peak of his helmet.

'I think not, my friend.' Davy attempted to behave as if casual conversation, in torrential rain, when one stood with one foot in the stirrup of a restive steed, were the most natural thing in the world. 'And what brings His Majesty's horse to these parts?'

'If you don't know, sir, I'd be mortal surprised,' the warrior replied. Whereupon some sequence of memories chased in phases across his features, a chase which started as puzzlement and ended in an explosion. 'That bloody smuggler — got 'im, by God!' Agilely, for a man bulky and not so young, he snatched a pistol of intimidating size from his charger's saddle holster, and stepped from cover. 'Halt, Edwards, or I fire.'

'I'm sure I don't know—' Davy began, hopping and failing to mount as the old horse, perturbed and misliking the turn of events, shuffled and snuffled.

'Crap!' bawled the corporal. 'Stay where you are. Trooper Smith, ain't this the moonshining bastard as done us at Prussia Cove?'

'The very one,' Smith agreed, 'as busted 'Is blooming Lordship and docked you a stripe.'

'And here's where I gets it back!' The ci-devant sergeant spat through the raindrops that dripped before his face. 'No you don't!' He pointed his great pistol as Davy made a last, frantic effort to leap into the saddle. But the grey, sensing his master's tension, chose that instant to rear. Davy somehow avoided falling flat on his back. He disengaged his foot from the stirrup;

and as click of hammerlock pierced hiss of rain he dodged, shoulder blades rigid for the shot, to the far side of his mount. There was no shot, nor likely to be with the flash-pan exposed to such a downpour. The corporal barked an order, then hurled his pistol at Hector, who bucked in agony and backed, snorting, to the length of his rein. Davy and corporal glared at one another. Trooper Smith was advancing with drawn sabre. His mate, dry under the thatch, aimed his carbine. Davy saw the three cavalry horses huddled at the far end of the barn.

Twenty seconds for the lobsters to mount up, Davy reckoned. Desperately trusting the old horse to stay within distance, he flung the cloak clear of his shoulders to free his right arm and twirled its end round his left as a buckler. He slipped the reins, with a heave at his baldrick drew the cavalier sword, and as in battle on a hard fought deck kept shifting position to confuse a marksman's aim.

Smith attacked. He yelled as he pounded over the slippery flagstones. His curved blade streaked through the rain as he slashed downwards in a cut that, had not Davy taken it high up on his ringing steel with an impact that jarred like a wound, would have severed an arm. Davy riposted with a thrust that the trooper evaded by springing backwards. A slip, a grotesque attempt to keep his feet, and the man was sprawling with clank of spurs in the puddles. He rolled over onto his back, striving with arms bent across his body to shield himself from the coup de grace.

But Davy stood his ground; and anyway the corporal, sabre in hand, was thudding across the yard to get at him, rage blinding him to the fact that he was depriving the carbineer of the first fair shot offered. The young captain had glimpsed Hector standing between the ancient gateposts, head lowered to the torrent and reins dangling. As the corporal bounded over the prostrate trooper he fled, swerving as some sixth sense warned of a finger squeezing the trigger. The discharge cracked into his eardrums; his flesh, tensed, felt — nothing. Momentarily deafened, he wheeled and turned, and the corporal was at him, right arm drawn back for the slash, left flung forward. Davy lunged, but as inhibited as ever from striking home at a fellow countryman checked, and merely pricked his assailant. The corporal had no inhibitions. A howl, and curved steel flashed before Davy's face.

Davy sprang back a bare foot or so to the yard wall but with space enough to parry the blow and then counter. His sword pierced the length of the corporal's forearm like a needle in a ball of wool, and was wrenched from Davy's grasp to clatter upon the flags a few paces away. The sabre cart-wheeled and stuck, quivering and chiming like a bell, in the drystone walling where Davy had leant.

A scene rooted, tick by tick, in remembered time − the corporal clutching his wound and cursing. The floored trooper rising to his knees and staring stupidly. The carbineer racing through his reloading drill. Hector for no known reason other than providential fiat clumping a pace forward and whinnying at Davy's elbow. And there, three or four strides off through nigh liquid air, the family sword gleaming among the drops that splashed and sizzled on the paving.

It was a moment for priorities: to horse, or to sword? Home without honour, or honour − and with luck home too? Davy dived for the sword, so close to the trooper, who was getting off his knees, as to bob up under his sabre and fell him anew with a rap of the retrieved sword's hilt. The carbine exploded again, and now Davy felt that a white hot poker had been drawn along his scalp from front to back. The corporal, red smudges spreading on his white woollen breeches as the wound dripped blood between his gripping fingers, was shouting, 'You've hit him, by God! You've hit him!' Davy shoved him aside, and in a bound gained the wall and heaved himself up to its tottering top. Hector waited in the gateway. Sword in hand Davy vaulted into the saddle and was away.

There was no pursuit. It was as well; for Davy, with holes fore and aft in his hat, and blood both dribbling down his forehead and seeping stickily into his wet queue, was hard put to retain his seat. It was the devil, the very devil, of a day!

Nor was that the end of it.

Hector homed, his rider swaying in the saddle and eventually dropping his head to the old fellow's mane, bleeding into the white fur and no rain falling, now, to wash it off. Someone checked the horse, not a redcoat, led them on and over ground spatchy with leaf shadow, got him into a chair before a hearth spitting with the blaze of fresh furze, and tied up his head. Of all these happenings Davy was aware, as if they occurred to some wretched individual he was dreaming about. Then a measure of good Jamaica was tipped down his gullet, and his body received him again. A face which he could not tell whether to love or to hate, gnarled and nebulous at one and the same time, closed and withdrew before his gaze, and dwindled and grew, and steadied into the familiar features of Smeecher.

Smeecher grinned and squeezed his shoulder. 'Been pokin' thy nose where thee never ought to, my cap'n, have 'ee?'

Davy sat up. His head ached, but not so badly that he must deny himself the relief of sharing his story, and his fears, with someone he could trust. Over a slice of hot potato cake, and a mug of tea sweetened with honey and liberally laced with rum, he told his tale. Smeecher listened in silence, and whistled when it was done.'

'Bloody lobsters, eh? Best keep shot o' they, for when they do put their claws out − But you done bravely, my cap'n, bravely. Though 'tis just so well you'm off to t'other side in a day or two. Give 'un time to blow over, like. Word or two up to Lunnon, and the unit's relieved. 'Bout time too! Fit to go, are 'ee? But if you ain't, they'll have to wait, and that's all there is for it.'

'You know about − you know—?'

Smeecher's smile absorbed the lower half of his ferocious visage, and pressed his watchful eyes into slits. 'I do, Mr Davy, and I don't, if you see what I mean.'

'I don't see,' said Davy. The effort of trying to hurt abominably.

'Then ye'll find out, all in good time, won't 'ee?' This was a remark which the man, for some obscure reason, found amusing. 'I'll tell 'ee this much, my old dear. I'm as at home over to Brittany as backalong here, almost, an't I? Mates everywhere, that's me! And harken, Mr Davy,' he went on, 'if ever ye do find yourself or your lads at Brest, say, and gets in a fix, like, just ask for the Coq d'Or. Near the church and under the north ramparts. Got a swinging sign of a bloody gurt old rooster. Landlord's a mate o' mine.'

A tall, angular woman, who in a room crammed with bits and pieces yet contrived to remain unobtrusive, with an extraordinary succession of motions and facial contortions prompted Smeecher to explain that while it didn't do no harm to chat away the cap'n was not to be upset. Not nohow. 'And who be she? you ask.' Davy hadn't. 'She's Honor. Proper little 'oman. Deaf and dumb, as a 'oman should be. A man couldn't find a better in a month o' Sundays. So good as a bull mastiff. Villagers frit of her. Think she'm not 'zackly, as they say. Touched.' He chuckled, slapping his knee and then tapping his head. 'Got more up aloft, that 'oman, than the whole blasted lot on 'em. And guards the 'ouse like a lion, she do. You do know how I got to be away days, weeks at a time, cap'n, sleeping rough often as not, but never a care with Honor to watch over all this here.'

A casual wave of the hand in no way concealed his pride in what, looking round the room, Davy saw to be a veritable jackdaw collection. In the corners — and with a staircase along one side, a windowed alcove in another, and a projecting fireplace there were many corners — against the walls, on the table, were ranged as varied an assembly of this and that as in any cottage parlour west of Taunton. Ropes and brooms and a besom, blocks and sheaves, a peat stack. Unexpectedly, a tattered pile of London magazines. A sampler and a ship tawdrily painted on the bottom of a barrel. On a battered dresser scratched and sanded pewter shone dully. There were a cabinet, a cupboard, a rug, chairs and even a Chinese screen obviously from that common provider of Cornish comfort, wreck. A ship's lantern hung from centre ceiling. But by what moonlit escapades came that inlaid pistol, those glass decanters, that exquisite miniature of a girl's head, those little Dresden figures, and the tortoiseshell and silver snuff box from which Smeecher took a pinch before handing it nonchalantly to his guest?

'You'm startin' to wonder, Mr Davy. Now that there 'oman says you wasn't to wonder, and what Honor says, you does.' Smeecher ambled about the room, his thick fingers touching his treasures. 'All proper come by, an't it? I does this sir a favour, and "Smeecher" he says, "here's golden guinea for thy pains."' Smeecher paused now to act out his scenario. 'Then I shakes me head and says as 'tedn' nothin at all. Wouldn' take a brass fardin', I wouldn', your honour. Tell 'ee what, just you give me some li'l token, yon li'l pot, now, to remember you by. 'Twould shine like a beacon in my humble 'ome, while you'd never miss it, great man that you are.' Smeecher roared with laughter.

'Gurt fool! But me? I an't no fool when it come to trinkaments, an'I? A guinea!'

Davy put his hand to his head, which was throbbing. Smeecher, concerned, began to unwind the strip of linen that bound it, but Honor stopped him. Following further extraordinary gestures Davy was informed that he must have medical attention, and that Smeecher would ride to St Ives for Dr O'Keenahan. 'Back in two-three hours, cap'n, sir, and Honor'll look to 'ee here like thy own ma.'

Davy got up and took a turn or two. He felt the better for it. 'I'm fit to ride home, thanks to you and Honor. I'll give Keeny a call on the way. And maybe, my friend, you'll allow me to add to your collection if you will be my guest at Boswyn before we sail.'

'When I do want somethin', I shan't be afeared to ask. And I'm comin' with 'ee. Honor do say so.'

They rode quietly through the moonlight, at first across unfamiliar country, then over the medieval packbridge at St Erth and so by dark ways to Boswyn. Not, as Smeecher surmised, that the redcoats had cause to believe Davy were other than a Carter man from Helston district. But they'd be out searching, for sure; and Davy's old horse showed up a bit, didn't he! besides, being careful was the reason Smeecher was at large that night, and not lying on dirty straw to sleep off twelve hours on the treadmill.

'Do I have to call you Smeecher?' Davy asked. They were jogging side by side, and Davy, ill and dependent upon this unexpectedly kind man, warmed to him. 'Ain't there a Jack, or a Jim, or a Joe? What's your real name?'

'Aven't got one, 'ave I? And how should I, ah?' A name, Smeecher explained, was useless to the likes of him. A millstone round the neck. A handle people could hold you by, when you wished to be up and off. Like when he was a gunner in the militia. Signed as William Brown. Had to have a name, you know, in the army. Had enough of it at manoeuvres on the Moor. Quit. Warrant out for arrest of William Brown for desertion. 'Never caught him, though, 'cause William Brown weren't me, was 'e?'

'But you are William Brown,' Davy persisted.

'My life, no! How are 'e so dense, cap'n? Must be that crack on

thy nuddick. 'Twas like this here.' Smeecher explained that he
had been a nameless infant, left as was and always would be the
fashion in the church porch, and taken to Madron workhouse.
He had been left over-long, by all accounts, and when they took
him in he was a proper little stinker. The name stuck. And if
Smeecher did not object, how should anyone else? He was
Monsieur Smeechere across the Channel, he concluded, not
irrelevantly, indicating the *Joshua Clegg* moored to the pier in
St Ives harbour.

But Davy's concern for anything other than his own splitting
head had evaporated. Smeecher handed him over to his calm
and tut-tutting mother, and to his father who bustled hither
and thither with a warming pan until little Lizzie, the
maidservant, with a remarkable show of independence took it
from him and warmed the sheets. Dr O'Keenahan, Joseph
Duval a-pillion behind him, was along within the hour. Matted
hair was sheared away and the stubble excruciatingly shaved,
and lotions were applied while Mrs Davy prepared prescribed
possets in the kitchen.

'Ye'll live to breed thirty youngsters bigger, better-looking
and even dafter than yourself, me boy,' Keeny prophesied,
washing his hands. 'Oh, and ye'll be needing a wig. There's a
perukier in Redruth—'

Davy reached for his friend's hand. 'Bethlehem Farm. Half a
mile inland of Pencobbben hamlet. There's a girl there. Jess
Porris. Daughter of the house. Broke her leg. Bloodsucking
leech running riot.'

'You talk too much,' said O'Keenahan. 'Leave it all to your
Irish uncle.'

In the stable Tim Chiddick was sucking his teeth over the
graze on Hector's flank where the corporal's pistol had struck
him, with as much to-do as was Davy's portion in the house. The
lore of generations of grooms and ostlers evoked a concoction
which was slapped onto the wound with soothing phrases and
not a little agitation on the part of the patient.

And when the lamps and candles at Boswyn were extinguished the east windows were pearly grey. It was another day.'

13

There was a lop in the Channel approaches. It rode the even-spaced combers, a cable's length from crest to crest, rolling in across two thousand miles of ocean. Now and then a wave lifted above the *Joshua Clegg's* blunt bow and slopped inboard. The *Joshua Clegg* was seaworthy, but built for capacity rather than for speed. And at present she was decidedly uncomfortable; though having tested her only in the prevailing conditions, Davy was disposed to attribute her jerky motion to the choppy sea. It was apparent, after he had rounded St Ives head, that she sailed a full point further off the wind than the *Roscoff*. Thus, the breeze blowing steady and promising to stay so, with glass and weather-lore agreed, Davy had sailed a long west-nor'west traverse before going clumsily about onto the equally long sou'-sou'-east course for Brest roads. A shorter route would have taken time, manoeuvring the brig among hostile coastal islands, that was better spent in mid-ocean.

The ship's company whom Davy had signed on for the short voyage included most of *Dorcas*'s crew, with Billums Williams as first mate and officer of the starboard watch, and under him the two AB's, Taffy Evans and Samson Trembath, with Jason Duval. Joseph Duval had lacked enthusiasm for the trip, being reluctant to forego one hour of his surgeon's apprenticeship. But Davy needed him as an interpreter and relied on his calm support and judgement; his medical skills might well be called upon, and with his brother he constituted that proportion of 'Frenchmen' who might be expected in an American vessel bound for France. Non-watchkeepers besides Joseph Duval were Chippie Boyce, who had hoped for a voyage off, and Brian Quinn, cook. They, with the watch below, were passing off-duty hours in the only way an afternoon watch below ever considers appropriate — asleep. Some after the excesses of leave ashore needed it.

Barnabas Polurrian was acting Second. A Sennen man, he had moonshined between West Cornwall and Brittany in peace and in war, under the noses of British and French authority alike, for the past twenty of his thirty-five years; his seamanship amd pilotage were first class. Far beyond his comprehension, though, were the navigational books and tables in the charthouse where Davy had just completed his reckoning of the noonday position. The captain was now standing at the door, hands on hips, hailing Tom Pritchard. Pritchard balanced nonchalantly on the foreto'gallant yard, forearm shielding his eyes while the other arm embraced a mast flexing with the pressure of the sails. 'Tennessee' Tom claimed to have fought Iroquois Indians, and had sunk many a tankard on tales of escape from redskins and Yankee rebels, tales that improved at each telling.

'What d'ye see?' Davy hailed.

'Nothing sir,' floated down the lookout's reply.

'Very well. Keep looking.' It was disappointing that the dead reckoning, after so short a time at sea, should be wide of the mark even by a little. The new 1781 second edition of *Maskelyne's Almanac*, that John Knill had thrust into his protégé's fist before catching the London mail coach, was surely reliable, so Davy's calculations must be adrift. And Davy, rightly priding himself on his navigation, would never allow himself error beyond the margins of the system. As he pored again over his figures, Tennessee's voice was again audible above the sighing of taut cordage and the crack of canvas.

'Land ho'? Three points off larboard bow. More land four points. The Scillies, I reckon, sir. Now I see Bishop Rock a point off the bow.'

'Very good.' And to Polurrian at the helm, 'Steady as she goes.' Davy returned to the charthouse to shut his almanac reverently and tuck it into its oilskin case. Pride was satisfied.

The other members of the starboard watch were Noah Berryman and Paul Hockan. These two, palm and needle in hand, squatted on the deck amidships patching a sail, the shadows of the square rig on the foremast coming and going as the brig, heeled over to larboard by the steady wind, climbed and descended the combers. Berryman was the son of *Roscoff*'s gunner killed in the *Falcon* battle. Hockan's father farmed

Fairlea, east of Zennor; but Paul, not inheriting a love of the land, was proving himself a born seaman. Davy was minded to sound him on becoming a midshipman, which now he came to think of it was not the worst of reasons for a call later on at Fairlea. Paul Hockan had two promising sisters, Lyn and Alice; pity Mrs Hockan was on bad terms with the Pentillys, and so was not of his mother's circle! Yet, he had to wed some day; the family must endure.

This led Davy to consider his own appearance, which was certainly not what he would wish to present before a handsome young woman, let alone two, even though unlike the daughters of the gentry they would be well enough inured to life's indelicacies. The only sign of his wound was the red handkerchief, knotted above his ear, that concealed a plastered and tonsured scalp. Not of itself too repellent! But with Solomon Venables, the *Joseph Clegg*'s Yankee skipper, in mind, Davy had not shaved since that ill-starred visit to Bethlehem Farm. With the stubble he presented a piratical appearance on which his crew had remarked with nudges and chuckles that became coughs when they caught his eye. Davy was sure he could never accommodate himself to being a Solomon Venables, though he was satisfied he could be taken for such a man.

It was in John Knill's own handwriting, in style as universal amongst British lawyers and scriveners as was Latin amongst academics, that the crew list had been rendered as if in the shipping office at Baltimore. Knill had thought to include the original list, but Davy had persuaded him that to require a seaman to assume a name as well as a role was to ensure trouble at the first enquiry. Some flustered innocent would let slip his own name, or someone else's, and the cat would be among the pigeons. As it might well be in any case, Davy had complained miserably. Besides, there were hundreds of families of Tre-, Pol- and Pen- settled on the eastern seaboards of America, and likely enough rebels or sympathisers among them. Cornish names would not read amiss.

'It matters little,' Knill had concluded. 'Since when has Authority had an ear for a common sailor?'

These matters had been argued out in the library at Boswyn, two days after Smeecher had brought him home. Dr O'Keenahan had come and gone earlier that morning, declaring that the dragoons had made perfunctory enquiries in the town the previous forenoon, but found out nothing because nobody knew anything and would not blab to a lobster if he did; secondly that Davy would be fit for duty by the end of the week; thirdly that having visited Miss Porris as requested, he would be returning frequently to restore that lovely limb to the appearance and efficiency of its partner. And no more stupid blood-letting; rather port wine and red beef, and a herbal specific to his own devising, warranted to restore the circulation of an Egyptian mummy.

Davy was relieved that the young lady was in the good hands of his friend, but regretted that he could neither disclose nor discuss with him the deeper significance of the forthcoming voyage. Moreover he would have welcomed Keeny's company then. Keeny's French too, although of the Irish, was passable. However, he would not wish to deprive Jess of such expert attention. In any case, even though Joseph Duval could probably continue the doctor's ministrations satisfactorily for the week or two O'Keenahan would be away, there were other reasons than the medical for taking Joseph with him.

So Dr O'Keenahan had left, after a surreptitious cup of tea in the kitchen with little Lizzie, who had scalded her hand. The maid, maybe older than she looked, had took quite a fancy to the Irish gentleman, which she never done to no other gentleman she knawed, apart, perhaps from the old man and young Mr Edward. Then Mr Knill turned up, his valise stuffed with papers to thumb through and documents to sign, and a half-hour's pleasantry declined to business and doubts, and that confounded headache again.

There was a point to consider, additional to carrying the war into the enemy's homeland as King Louis sought to do in Ireland, and to reaping a golden profit. The war, however it ended, could not endure much longer. Arrangements for free trading between France and England must then include reciprocal banking agreements, and co-ordinated measures to defeat the Revenue forces of two countries in alliance. Now it transpired, from Mr Knill's urgent and impeccable enquiries, that a partnership of two such trading companies, either side of the Channel, as his own incipient enterprise and the established

Lardinières, was well worth setting up. For this reason alone the delivery of the *Joshua Clegg*'s cargo was a necessary preliminary. The Breton firm had wide banking and commercial interests in maintaining this free trade.

'Smuggling,' Davy had interposed, wearied of lawyer's jargon.

'Call it what you will, it involves the entire coastline from Yarmouth to Bristol − I retain my West-country connection, you see—'

'Your prospects expand, Mr Knill,' said Davy sourly, coming to the point. 'Mine, as regards ever taking the *Falcon* to sea under letters of marque, or in truth under no letters at all, dwindle.'

Knill leaned forward and tapped the invalid on the knee. 'So! "He that is not with me—"', he quoted. And have not you yourself told me of fighting off pirates and competitors in the opening markets of the Southern Ocean? And in the West Indies, where by all report present upheavals offer enormous scope for the astute and the daring? Come, Captain Davy, a Ministry certificate to trade or an Admiralty letter to fight − where's the difference?'

'You'll see me through; get me my ship and her warranty?'

'I can. I will. So have I undertaken,' sniffed Mr Knill. 'I can be as touchy on matters of honour as you, young Davy. But—'

Davy smiled ruefully. 'Touché; and I apologise! Though that "but"—'

'These Breton connections are necessary to my plans and to your future. And now,' Knill had risen and gazed down on the bandaged head and disconsolate countenance, 'I must depart. I take ship for Bristol tomorrow− had you heard that Harvey's have inaugurated a new interport service? − and thence by turnpike to London. Mr Stephens accompanies me. He has a mind to challenge the Trevethoe Praeds for one of the two St Ives Parliamentary seats, and with the likelihood of the Camelford lad heading the nation after the next General election, he would exchange pledges − either on his own or his son's behalf − with William Pitt.'

At mention of the Tory leader, whose father the great Earl had so dramatically bowed out in the Lords four years since, and with whom Davy felt his own fortunes to be bound, the outlook somehow brightened.

This the keen eye of the Collector not missing, he had gripped Davy's hand a moment. 'There will be other matters Sam and I must discuss on our journey, and they concern you. Trust me, Ned.'

*

Dawn, and the *Joshua Clegg* trimmed to jib, topsail and mainsail stole through a melting haze that dimmed only the far distances. Barney Polurrian was perched like a crow on the foremast crosstrees, conning the ship past the rocky southern shores of Trielen and Beniguet islands.

'Larb'd, Larb'd your hellum. Larb'd, damn your eyes! Hold it. That's the job, my boo-ey! Keep your bloody hellum up, ye son of a whore! You'm worse'n a cow handlin' a musket. 'Ods teeth, that were a close 'n! 'Midships. 'Midships your hellum. Pretty, me handsome, pretty! Steady as she goes. Damme, ye're falling away—'

At the wheel Tennessee's sole reply was to spin the spokes, leaning on them at the extremity of each turn, ears alert and gaze intent on the leech of the mainsail, and with faultless aim to squirt a jet of tobacco juice into the spitkid beside him. Around him the off-duty watch busied about the age-honoured dawn chore of swabbing the decks, Jason brooming down, the first mate everywhere about the deck pointing and chivvying, while Taffy Evans hosed to his shrinking feet the foamy gushes that Trembath pumped up from the territorial waters of France.

In the chains Berryman called out the depth of those waters. 'By the mark, six. And a half, five.' The lead line, marked in fathoms and fractions thereof with knots and leather and rag markers, ran through his practised fingers as the lead, swung ahead of the bow wave, curved to the seabed immediately beneath him.

Davy moved between the poop rail, right aft under the lantern, and the chartroom just behind the binnacle on the flush deck. Here he checked off his course on the chart, taking bearings of the landmarks to establish, by comparison with estimated positions, the strength and direction of the currents. One day, thought Davy, some self-respecting navigator would draw a reliable map of these rocky approaches to a great seaport, like Tovey and Ginver's recent chart of the Scillies. Meanwhile he must do the best he could with what France and America had provided. Back at the rail, he eyed the formidable coastlines of islands he was too close to for comfort, stifling a desire to take over the pilotage himself, from Polurrian whose experience he could not equal and whose professional skill in these circumstances he could not better.

An undeviating run-in well to the sou' west of Ushant had brought him under the lee of a French *stationnaire*, which had made him heave-to while a naval lieutenant cursorily examined the ship's papers handed down to him in the boat. The examination had been conducted within a ball of orange lamplight in the darkest hour, and with Davy's stomach griping, however nonchalantly he leant over the rail, at the prospect of sudden discovery.

'*M'sieur Venables, n'est ce pas?*'

Then a cheerful and prolonged conversation, Joseph engaged in the time-doubling process of translation, about weather in the Atlantic and British warships in the Channel and the triumphs of La France and her glorious ally. Meanwhile the set of the tide changed, and daybreak smouldered behind the islands, and the *Joshua Clegg* had drifted closer than Davy cared to the rocks and islets which clutter the northern limit of Brest roads.

As they got under way, it had been a time for decisions that outweighed the satisfaction of passing the first barrier unscathed. First, whether to go about to win sea room for the run-in Davy had planned for. This he had rejected on the ground that approaching for the second time he would probably encounter a relief guard boat inclined, in the light of day, to board and search. Davy could not imagine what could be found, save in the unlikely event of opening up the staves of the tobacco casks. And these were clearly entered in the manifest as what they were supposed to be; there was no attempt at concealment or smuggling. But Davy decided not to try his luck again. Better to skirt the islands, luffing to the sou'westerly wind as closely as the old tub could. A lee shore was the natural mightmare of a ship's master, but with this fair breeze and a seaman aboard who knew every inch of these waters even a tyro might reasonably expect a safe passage. And Davy knew himself to be anything but that.

Then there was the pilot cutter. This came up from among the islands the instant the *stationnaire* had moved off. The pilot, of even more villainous appearance than Captain Davy-Venables himself, and twice his age, tendered his services – nay, demanded their employment at a rate which Joseph's horrified expression was reason enough for rejecting. The man's eruption into English gave Davy some satisfaction. 'Dairty Yonkees wizz mooch monaie it come out of your stinkin' ears, but mean!' The pilot flung up disgusted hands and spat into the sea. Then with her great sail reefed and singled up to a solitary jib, to allow her to keep station on the slow-moving brig, the cutter followed, agog for salvage or call for assistance. It was this that, despite the added insurance of placing hands wherever emergency might require them, decided Davy on continuing normal sea routine. He'd show 'em!

With Le Conquet three miles off his larboard beam and Camaret due east, Davy changed course for the headland which, as at St Ives, shielded the town from Atlantic gales. As the *Joshua Clegg* nosed briskly round, as if scenting home, a yawl ran alongside. Without loss of way it hooked on below the 'mid-ships gangport and disgorged a man with wild hair and drooping moustache, who vaulted over the gunnel and ambled up to Davy.

'Captain!'

'*Oui, M'sieur*,' Davy replied

'From Lardinières. I'm to pilot you in to Brest.' The man's English was colonial, and awkward questions were to be expected.

'I'm bound for Camaret,' said Davy.

'Brest,' the other corrected. 'Company orders. What in hell took you so long? Been hanging around here, off and on, a fortnight.'

'Weather.' The brusque phrases were catching. 'Blown off course by gales, becalmed before I could get back on.'

'Blasted Atlantic! Where you from?'

'Baltimore.'

'Not the ship. You. Venables, ain't it?'

Davy thought fast. This was no occasion for disclosing his identity for all that the newcomer was – or said he was – a Company pilot. But preserving it might prove difficult. He had already worked out a plausible background, and now was the time to put it to test. 'I lodge in the General Wolfe — the Washington as it now is — on the waterfront.' His mind ranged over the letters, and the terse entries in the diary, taken from the American captain on his surrender. 'Handy for the ship.'

'I know it. Bit of a dive. Weren't born thereabouts, I'll be bound!'

'Jamaican trader. Lost my ship after a dispute with My Lords as to who took Brazil coffee to Boston. Great, great, great-grandfather Venables settled in the Indies way back,' Davy went on, warming to his theme. 'But family records lost in the Port Royal Earthquake. No great loss, I guess.'

The American eyed him from his thicket of hair. 'I suppose not.' He was standing beside Williams, who had himself taken the wheel, and extended his hand. 'David Rogers. Who'll you be?'

'My mate, Mr Williams,' Davy interposed, perceiving that in the current situation, Billums, who in his own environment was the coolest of men, was not sure even of his own name. 'Captured from HM Frigate *Heracles*.'

Rogers nodded. 'Heard all about it. Disgraceful affair.' Davy turned away, unable because of his own involvement those years ago to look straight at him, however the circumstances of then and now might absolve him.

'Joined the rebels — the true Americans — for shame of his own officers, did you not, Mr Williams?'

'Aye,' confirmed Williams gravely, shifting his quid from one cheek to the other, and spinning the wheel violently as Rogers ordered 'Ten of starboard helm.'

'Pleased to meet you,' said the American when the manoeuvre was completed. Not lifting his eyes from the channel ahead, he addressed Davy from the corner of his mouth. 'Small stuff at Camaret now. Big business Brest. New wharf down-town. Nearer th' warehouses. Get rid of the cargo quicker.'

'Why the hurry?' Davy must play his part to the full.

'Thought maybe you'd like to know.' Rogers was achieving the facial contortions of an amateur ventriloquist.

'Thank you,' said Davy.

'You're welcome,' the other replied.

A flotilla of small naval vessels, fifth and sixth rates, swept past, racing rather than keeping station. A sloop veered off course close enough for its jaunty young captain to recognise the pilot and return his wave, with a friendly if indelicate gesture, as the *Joshua Clegg* dipped the odd American ensign on its jackstaff in salute. 'Off to escort allied merchantmen from Bilbao,' Rogers vouchsafed. 'Take 'em a week if the weather holds. Come tomorrow, dockyard's empty. Spaniards too busy at Gib to do their own dirty work. Big attack on British garrison brewing there.'

It was a point to pass on when he got home, thought Davy, watching the pilot produce from his breeches pocket a dark, squalid and putty-like roll and regard it, turning it this way and that. It was not until Rogers gnawed through a half-inch from the end that Davy regonised it as a plug of tobacco. After an expression which left one doubting whether the taste were really to his liking, he directed a jet of amber saliva expertly into the spitkid beside the wheel.

'Down with your hellum a mite, Mr Mate. Steady now. Hold it.'

The topmasts of several large ships appeared above a huddle of buildings and fortifications away on the larboard bow. 'Masthead,' hailed Davy, 'what d'ye make of 'em?'

'Battlewaggons, sir, First or second rates. Four – no, five on 'em. Yards crossed and trimmed for sea, I'd reckon.'

'The dockyard's empty, didn't you say, Mr Rogers?'

'Nope; tomorrow.' The bulge of his quid shifted from one cheek to the other. 'You heard what the man said, cap'n. Two transports and three ships o' the line. Reinforcements for Admiral de Grasse and th'Army.'

It was time for Davy to maintain the illusion of a Yankee fresh from the States, as the rebel colonies were calling themselves. 'Little enough fighting yonder on land or sea, now.'

Rogers hit the spitkid with a ringing plonk. 'Well, y'know how 'tis, cap'n. Set the juggernaut a-rolling and y'caint stop the goddam thing. Sailing tomorrow, at a guess, and by the day after for certain. Then damn-all but the admiral's staff o' desk and arm-chair lubbers, the Gendarmerie – all four of 'em – the customs officers, round dozen of them, third-rate garrison, under-strength, disaffected, and pop goes the weasel, as the kids say.'

He bit off another quid. 'Thought you'd like to know,' he said again.

14

M. le Capitaine Venables, du vaisseau americain le *Joshua Clegg*.

Monsieur,
   Kindly visit me at my château where you shall dine if it please you an hour after noon. My carriage shall fetch you.
                              I remain,
                                   Yr Obedt servt.,
                                        Jean Lardinière.

The letter lay opened in the captain's narrow cabin, its signature in different handwriting. So the invitation had been left to a clerk to pen, Davy deduced, stropping his razor; a clerk who, judging from the formal and abbreviated ending, had sought guidance from American commercial correspondence in the company files. As it was not a personal letter, for two pins Davy would have declined the invitation and hurried off to sea and security. Discharge of the cargo, which had begun immediately on making fast alongside the Lardinière wharf just upstream from the Quai de la Douane, was proceeding with a vigour Davy had yet to witness in Cornish ports. There, he supposed, energy was expended under the moon rather than the sun. And it could even be that the cheerful activity at Brest was the expression of a nation elated by victory rather than, as at home, alas! weighed down by retreat and surrender, with Britain's Atlantic forces dissipated and ineffectual, and De Grasse's naval triumph over Graves still rankling.

How could one be other than uneasy, Davy asked himself, slicing a strip of leather from the side of his strop as the razor skidded, and cursing loud enough to be heard above the bustle on deck? He was in the midst of a people whom he had met only in midnight encounters, to shift kegs and casks from some *bateau de pêche* or *chasse-marée* to his own decks in exchange for a dozen bales of Cornish wool or a few ingots of tin; whom otherwise he knew only behind gun-smoke or the flash of steel. A people who, once they had discovered the deception in which he was so reluctantly engaged, would have no longer shrift for him than three fathoms of hemp.

This was defeatist and not to be thought of! Here was an opportunity for a contact Mr Knill was anxious to establish, and of which he himself could expect much advantage. The Lardinière messenger was waiting at the quayside for his answer. Davy penned a reply under his assumed signature. Then deciding that the less he committed to paper the better, he tore it up and through Joseph instructed the man that he would present himself with pleasure at the given hour.

On receiving the invitation, Davy had at first endeavoured to preserve an appearance untypical of himself by merely trimming his stubble with the sailmaker's shears. It was a sort of mask to hide behind. But the result has been too great an affront to the young man's sense of *amour propre*. A quarter-inch growth of black whiskers, which before shearing had suggested no more than a disinclination to wash, now presented the spectacle of some patchy disease of the skin. So unrolling the 'hus'if' of his naval days Davy conjured up brush, soap and the 'cut-throat' that Wilkinsons, who had fashioned his sword, were now manufacturing for 'gentlemen of taste and professionals of discernment'. Accustomed, ever since regular shaving had needs become a habit, to the ministrations of his steward Thomas Thomas, the barber-surgeon whom Dr O'Keenahan had half-driven out of business, Davy scraped away inexpertly, the pain of the operation far outweighed by the pleasure of watching himself emerge to view in the mirror. This was eight by six inches of polished steel, within whose limits he manoeuvred to frame his lathered cheeks. It hung between the corner washstand and the aftermost of the two cabin portholes, opened in harbour to odours that bespeak seaports the world over. But oh, to be seeing the wave-tops leaping up at them now!

Yet of course he had chosen aright. Not that there was a real alternative to leaving the ship at the hour of dining. What had posed an impossible choice was revulsion at finding himself as vulnerable as a hare at hay-harvesting. For by the time the cargo was piled on wharf or in warehouse, the brig would be trapped in the river mud, and must remain so until the flood tide lifted her off in the first watch. Through the porthole Davy saw the flotsam of the river Elorn, and the scourings of the ebb, rippling past into the estuary so aptly named Le Goulet. Not long and the keel, touching bottom, would release a cloud of stinking bubbles. This, did not, however, appear to be a prospect which daunted Able Seamen Berryman and Hockan. They stood side by side in the dinghy, immediately beneath their jaundiced captain, caulking a weeping plank under the ship's counter, and whistling unharmoniously as if for a breeze in the doldrums. Davy envied them their ignorance and gaiety. Not least of the burdens of command was too much knowing what was and what might be.

The philosopher dabbed a couple of cuts into insignificance. His face was vastly improved. What of his head? Damme, he would step ashore as himself, whatever his stupid *nom de guerre!* From the shallow wardrobe he extracted the maroon coat and fawn breeches that had seemed as sorry as their wearer that disastrous night, but which his mother and the kitchen maid had sponged, and pressed, and brushed to pristine splendour. He would need money. He unlocked the safe and took from it a purse his mother had stitched for him years before. In it were forty Louis d'Or, changed for him by his acquaintance Mr Praed of Lelant, a partner in Molesworth's Bank. He took out a handful of gold coins and then, in a reckless gesture, trickled them back and thrust the whole lot into an inner pocket. It was a pleasure to produce from the drawer under his cot a clean shirt and white cotton stockings, and the cravat of Honiton lace he had sported at Lavinia's ball. Here were the silver buckled shoes with the rather high heels a gentleman wore about town. And a sword? It might be needed. Lighter than the family broadsword, it swung on its blue poplin baldrick from a hook in the cupboard. His hat? Not the one with the shot holes fore and aft, but the new one with white fur trimmings. And of course the wig, the brown wig of real human hair that the Truro perukier had travelled to his bedside to fit him with — in the circumstances a painful process — and charged him thirty guineas for. Davy wondered how much of the thirty guineas had gone to the wench whom destitution, or needy or greedy parents, had induced to sacrifice her rippling tresses to make it. As yet he had never worn it. 'Sdeath, he would show these Froggies how a Cornish – no, dammit, what was he thinking of? – an American gentleman bore himself.

'Joseph! Pass the word for Joseph.

The work on board halted, the slinging and heaving in the hold, the painting and splicing and the clatter in the galley, as Joseph Duval was summoned. His gentle fingers dressed his captain's fast healing scalp and eased the wig into place. 'Good to see you looking decent again, sir, begging your pardon,' he admired.

Davy clapped him on the shoulder. 'Good to feel so, Joseph. Now look ye, you and your brother Jason are to shift into clean clothing and pass yourself off as French colonials. Here's a gold Louis spending money. Don't have too much to say, and don't try to make up a lot. Just describe Helford and call it Louisiana. No one will know the difference. Say if you're hard-pressed that it's a settlement called – Nouvelle Camaret or however you'd put it. But don't make a spectacle of yourselves; stick to wine and not much of that. I just want the news spread around that the old *Clegg* has come straight from America, and that there's Frenchmen aboard. Understand?'

'Aye, aye, sir.'

'*Oui, oui,* Joseph. French from now on. Oh,' – he put his hand to his head, to wring from memory the name Smeecher had given him – 'locate the Coq d'Or inn, somewhere round the ramparts to north'ard. Be back by eight bells. That'll give you four hours. *En avant!*'

Davy mounted the companion and surveyed the scene. Billums Williams walked up, touching his hat, and they stood side by side staring up at the great sheerlegs that supported the lifting gear. 'Primitive, effective,' Davy commented, 'but too much of a fixture. You ought to be able to move the apparatus, not the ship, when you must empty a second hold. I cannot see why the whole structure ain't mounted on wheels.'

'Don't affect us none; and they couldn't never do it.' Consideration of a novel idea was far beyond the worthy fellow's scope. 'But I'll say this, cap'n; 'tis mortal glad I am to see 'ee looking thyself again, so to speak.'

'Not you too, Mr Mate!' But the compliment pleased him, as

all the hands within sight and hearing observed, pausing to regard their young captain with an approving eye.

'Haven't you enough to do,' Davy roared, 'without gawping like a gaggle of starlings! Mr Williams, keep 'em busy.'

The Mate turned the hour glass. 'Noon, sor.' It was more of a request than a statement.

'Oh very well, Mister. Make it so.' Davy's reply was in the tradition of the sea. 'And you may as well pipe the hands to dinner. And take note, Mr Williams,' he added in a low tone, 'that those — that tobaccco ain't to be shifted till I return. I have my reasons for being around when it goes. After all,' he grinned, deliberately misleading, 'we had enough ado getting it.'

'I'd say, sor! But I seen 'un aboard myself, cap'n, when you was upalong with your scat nuddick. First in the 'old, they casks was, and last out. And that won't be till the end of the watch. Shore leaf, sor?'

Davy shook his head. 'I wouldn't dare let the men ashore. You don't think they would all, every man of 'em, be back in time to sail on the next tide? Sure enough some silly drunk or other wouldn't turn up—'

'Sail without 'un, cap'n. Serve the sod right.'

'And leave him in custody, making it plain to everybody in earshot, if not in actual words, that he's a simple Cousin Jack of a Cornishman? Sending King Louis' revenue men to turn Lardinière's storehouses upside down because something that smells damned queer has been going on.'

'I can't think why that should be, sor.'

'Then for God's sake don't think, Mr Williams! Just listen, and obey my orders, as I know you will. I am letting Joe and Jason Duval ashore to prove we're Yankees with our fair share of frogs in the ship's company. They'll report back at eight bells. And hark 'ee, Billums my friend, if anything should go wrong — It won't, of course,' Davy added, as Williams showed every symptom of alarm. 'How should it? But when you are in command, you have to consider every eventuality. That's something you will need to remember, if your acting rank is to be confirmed. It is not enough, you know, to be able to take a sight, plot a course, furl a to'gans'l or shout like a blast out of hell. You must look ahead, all the time; but there, I am sure you understand all this without my preaching. Another Captain Harry, eh?'

The jest did nothing to lessen the gloom. 'But if anything happens — and I'll wager the *Joshua Clegg* to a cocked hat it will not! — don't try to fight. You haven't a chance. Get ashore and split up. Find your way to the Coq d'Or, the Golden Cock — there will be a sign. It's a tavern, due nor' nor' east of here, the far side of town. Near the church — you'll spot the tower if you climb half way up the shrouds — under the Vauban ramparts.'

'The what, sor?' Billums was plainly upset.

'The city wall to the nor'east. Tell the landlord — or get one of the Duvals to tell him — that Smeecher sent you.'

'Smeecher?'

'The very same. Smeecher! I am reaching the conclusion that there is no place between Bristol and Bordeaux where that remarkable man is not known. Now do not forget, from this moment on, that you and the hands are Yankee Doodles and that you hate the English.'

'Hardly that, sor; being Cornish I don't 'zackly love 'em. But I couldn't pretend I hate 'em?'

'Damn your eyes, man! You're American; and well, you don't exactly love the English, and that will suffice.'

'Sor,' said Williams, 'have you got to go?'

'I asked myself that very question, Billums, and you know what I replied?'

'What?'

'Yes,' Davy concluded. 'That's what I told myself, dammit! Bloody yes.'

The noon gun thundered from the castle on the western side of the Customs quay. Both men started, then grinned sheepishly at each other. 'Trouble is,' said Davy, 'that we are both getting old.'

The church of St Michel beyond the northern ramparts struck the hour. The stevedores and dockers disappeared into the narrowest of side-streets, and the first mate cried, 'Hands to dinner.'

Davy sat in the charthouse, planning his way out past the rocks and islands of the Brest approaches. It was a cramped charthouse, and his sword got in the way. Also, he was hungry.

Everybody else was feeding, but he must wait an hour or more. 'Od's teeth, he'd make up for it; that he would!'

*

It was one bell in the afternoon watch, or would have been had sea routine prevailed and the foc's'l lookout struck it; thirty minutes before the Lardinière conveyance was due. The ebb had lowered the brig a fathom below the level of the wharf. At half tide Davy's sole view of the town was the weedy wall of the quay with its two iron ladders cemented into the granite, and though but lately installed already rusting. He stared without pleasure across the river, the distant rivage a broader replica of the Helford's. An overloaded barge drifted slowly downstream with decks almost awash, a barked mizzen sail keeping it head to wind and the current doing the rest. Wooden jetties partitioned the company wharf from the customs quay astern, and ahead from the fish wharves. These while of even more recent construction than Lardinière's were as noisome as if of a century's impregnation. Here scavenging seagulls, where earlier they had plunged and squabbled for offal, still wheeled hopefully, although the fish market was now as inactive as a Cornish quay on a Sunday. Others were white bundles on the criss-crossing timbers that supported the jetties, watching the dirty tide beneath them and launching themselves with raucous cries at sight of a tit-bit.

Davy's shave and general smartening-up had brought relief, but it proved fleeting, and he viewed the riverside the more disagreeably as the minutes passed. He had misliked the voyage. The present situation worried him more than he cared to admit, even to himself. He had shifted into the rig appropriate to his station for nobody's benefit, it seemed, but his own; and in May at mid-day the wig was damnably hot. And he had missed his dinner, a deprivation the promise of a better did nothing to alleviate.

Mr Williams who had chosen to dine with his friend Quinn in the galley, presumably to remain within reach of stew and dumplings still steaming in the bottom of the iron saucepan, waved at him through the hooked-back door. Davy smirked and turned away to brood in his cabin, but thought better of it. He hitched his sword to the back, under his coat, where it stuck through the slit in the skirts like a yawl's spanker-boom, and in doubled-up posture to keep the rust from his clothes began to climb one of the iron ladders. A stroll topsides to stretch his legs would ease the tension; and he brightened at a prospect which would dispel, if only until the carriage arrived, those nagging doubts and fears. Here was an opportunity to estimate the practicality of his notion that dockside sheerlegs could be made as mobile as those erected on a sheer hulk.

But there was a further, mercifully brief, setback to Davy's restoration to the gaiety and curiosity proper to a young man of twenty-two, even if he be a captain and master. Peeping down under his armpit as he scaled the ladder, rather like a monkey as he confessed to himself, stopping to ease away those full skirts of his coat from contamination, he observed Williams standing in the galley doorway, face registering horror.

"How do 'ee come to choose that road upalong, cap'n?' he called. 'Stand easy or no, we'd ha' rigged a decent ladder for'ee. 'Tis a shame to ruin a good suit.'

Davy smothered an expletive. It was odious that his every movement should be observed and commented on, even in the levelling proximities of small-ship life, and particularly in so ridiculous a situation as the present. It was not to be endured, that his subordinates should treat him like a younger brother. But what could one say? They meant well, and extraordinarily enough they were fond and even proud of him. Evading that basilisk stare, he shouted that he would take care and was not going far from the ship, and bounded to the top of the ladder. Hand-grips had been let into the paving at the edge. He grabbed them, swung his feet up, straightened, his scabbard caught between his knees, and only Providence saved him from hurtling among the mounds of horse dung that befouled the wharf. It was a mishap mercifully out of sight of Billums, and Davy's curses became a snigger. He had been lucky; perhaps fortune began to smile on him again.

It is natural for a sailor to lock into his mind, against emergencies, the easiest egress from any part of his ship below decks. By the same instinct Davy's first inspection was of the accessibility of the streets leading away from the wharf. Of a width that, standing with arms outspread, one could touch the walls on either side, they ran between tall warehouses. Two, Lardinière's, the name painted large across cream stucco that emphasised the derelict appearance of their neighbours, were a storey higher than any of the other buildings across the way. A dozen strides took Davy over the granite-paved wharf. The ground floor windows of the company's warehouses were shuttered and protected by tall iron spikes; the double gates of heavy ironwork which led to the yards and unloading bays were padlocked. The building could withstand a siege! The only unguarded aperture was a floor-to-lintel window in the third storey, above it a beam extending outwards rigged with a pulley, the hauling line hanging in a slack loop halfway to the *pavé*. And nowhere was a soul to be seen.

The street most nearly opposite the brig finished, Davy discovered, in a dead-end of ancient hovels which the new buildings had consigned to gloom. But the next along, Rue Rivière, ran straight into a thoroughfare wide enough to admit the sunshine. Staring into the dazzle a hundred yards on, one could distinguish in the tunnel-like darkness the signs and portals of bistros, which had doubtless absorbed many of the local workers during their dinner break. An outburst of laughter echoed distantly, and Davy pictured the dockers engulfing their bread and cheese and *vin ordinaire*, and perhaps celebrating the triumphant return of neighbours from the war across the ocean. For an instant the silhouette of a female appeared in the middle of the long passage, and as suddenly vanished. The odds against his crew's resisting both bottles and ma'am'selles confirmed his refusal to grant leave. On the other hand, here was a means of escape if, which heaven forbid! the brig and her cargo should be revealed in their true colours and with her ship's company placed under arrest. Though what they should do once they had filed into the Coq d'Or he could not contemplate.

Four foot of pavement skirted the warehouses, and against it stood a few canvas covered booths, as empty of display as of stallholders, who would arrive, Davy supposed, with wares and customers after the long dinner break. Despite these intrusions there was a spacious roadway the whole length of the new wharf, except where the mechanism of the sheerlegs protruded, to narrow it at that point only to about four paces. Now what sort of a contraption was this?

Meanwhile Billums Williams had interrupted his meal to satisfy himself that all was well in that unknown territory above the sea wall. The cook being of like mind, they mounted high enough up the main shrouds to observe, at ground level, their captain sauntering from the buildings opposite to where the sheerlegs soared into a zenith liquid with sunshine, in which floated powder puff clouds and a heavier cluster to westward — a phenomenon the mate had interpreted, when they commenced their brief climb, as 'Ye can put your dhobeying out, Quinn, but bring it in in the third watch.' Davy's left hand was resting on the pommel of his sword, now properly at his side but still projecting astern. His hat he was spinning in his right hand — a casual action which ceased abruptly, as if it had aroused comment.

'Cap'n don't allow hisself no relief from what do bother 'im or draw 'im out tight-like, Quinn,' the Mate murmured, shaking his head sorrowfully. 'See that just now, did 'ee? Nothin' to ease 'off with, like you and I might, such as a good spit, or stanking—'

'Or what?'

'Banging with 'is foot, ye Irish heathen. Or shaking his fists. Or cussin' — leastway, not when nobody's about, he don't.'

'He'll be always keeping up the style,' Quinn ponderously agreed. 'But that's what a cap'n gets paid for, b'Jaisus, and so he ought to!'

'Few do. And if you are criticising, Quinn, that I won't have.'

'Be gob, no!'

'All right, then, Cap'n Davy may be young for the job, but there aren't nobody as I do know as could do better, or for that matter one half so well. And if we don't lower our tops'ls pretty damn quick we'm due for dismasting, for here he do come.'

The object of these observations was circling the sheerlegs. There was nothing novel about the principle, which was as familiar to the Phoenician and Greek adventurers who had visited Cornwall as to any modern sailor with King George and King

Louis on their respective thrones. You lashed a couple of masts together at the top, spread them to make an angle of about 30 degrees, made fast a block and tackle there, attached a couple of stays for alternate holding and heaving, and it poised over the hold on its spread ends for all the world like a colossal crane, or grue, as the French call the bird. And indeed crane, or grue, was the word coming into use in both tongues for this antique device. You hauled your load as close to the top as necessary, the hands on deck tailed on to the holding line, the dockers ashore or on board the hulk pulled the dangling load towards them, through the vertical, till it swung over where it was to be lowered, and this done the process was reversed. It was a simple matter of seamanship.

The French improvement was to replace the two manned stays with a beam hinged at the top, thirty feet overhead, to the mastheads which were bolted together within an iron rim, and at the bottom to an iron plate. Through a hole in the plate ran a thick screw on Davy's reckoning quite twenty feet long. It was coupled by cogs to a handled wheel like that of a mangle at home, which when turned, two men doing the work of half a dozen, drew the beam nearer or further. This positioned the crane to lift, and deposit on the wharf ten feet in, loads of the greatest bulk; certainly the three hogsheads which were the source of so much of Davy's anxiety. Each sheerleg was affixed to a ringbolt in the paving along the wharf edge, while the gutter-like box in which the screw worked was bolted to the cobbles. It was a well-constructed outfit. But suppose you mounted it all on a sufficiently strong carriage, wide enough and heavy enough not to tip over when legs and load were past the perpendicular, and running parallel to the edge! How to keep it on course? Perhaps along plates flanged at the sides, such as were laid down at Portreath for the trucks discharging coal and loading tin ore at Basset's new harbour there.

It was a problem another would undoubtedly solve, thought Davy, transferring his attention to a one-horse vehicle clattering into view from the fish-market.

'*M'sieur Venàbles, n'est ce pas?*'

Venables? Allowing for the misplaced accent, and recollecting that this was for the time being his identity, Davy climbed into the shaky contraption. The Lardinière equippage, indeed?

It was scarcely better than a cab. What the hell was he going to? He waved to the head of the mate that appeared at the top of the ladder.

'Back within three hours,' he hailed. Williams saluted and enemy country gobbled his captain up.

15

The wharf road led into the thoroughfare Davy had glimpsed down the narrow street, an evenly cobbled surface between shops, most of them closed and with blinds drawn, and taverns, the pavement tables of which were sparsely occupied considering the June sunshine. Occasional passers-by stared, somewhat longer than seemed necessary or polite, at the stylish figure in the common cabriolet. 'Sdeath! What was expected of him? Davy thought irritably. That he should doff his hat or toss a coin? The city of Brest was almost as empty, it seemed, as the morrow's dockyard. Seemed; that was the operative word. The bistros and estaminets looked full enough, when you glimpsed their interiors. Someone would slink from one into another as though traversing the streets were the most perilous of hazards.

Davy sensed himself to be under scrutiny from behind curtained window-panes. There was an air of furtiveness, of waiting. Nonsense! The young captain snapped his fingers, subconsciously averting morbid fancies, at which the coachman looked round. He stuck his whip between his knees, thus freeing a hand the grubby forefinger of which he laid alongside his nose. This prominent feature he then wrinkled with a wink that involved his entire cheek. Something was brewing for sure. Davy was glad he had brought his sword. He tugged it across his knees and flipped the tasselled thong round its hilt from one palm to the other. Why must he always be fiddling before he could sort things out? he scolded himself. He plunged his hands into his deep pockets, and finding a coin in one fiddled with that, unobtrusively.

At the Vauban ramparts, their generally dilapidated state highlighting recent renovations, the carriage turned left into a lesser highway that eventually curved round a squat, cone-surmounted tower. Thence it debouched unexpectedly − so closely the houses huddled − under the great north gatehouse, a twin turret at its further end. Between the turrets loomed a Gothic archway through which they clip-clopped beneath the spikes of a portcullis which, Davy surmised, could not have been dropped in a hundred years. Larboard, starboard, larboard again and through the gate, he memorised. Probably not the shortest route afoot, but the surest.

Cramped as the lower side of the gate had been, Davy was astonished to find himself borne beyond the fortifications into a spacious square flanked by dignified buildings, with a fountain splashing somewhat reluctantly in the centre, and an entire side occupied by a palatial edifice splendid with regal emblems. 'L'Hôtel de Ville!' the *cocher* announced above the clatter of his nag's hooves on the cobbles, pointing it out with his whip.

Past the square the road degenerated into a hotch-potch of *pavés* interspersed with the rutted roadway of the countryside. The streets were wider, rows of terraced houses ending at spaces ripe for development and then beginning again further on. Davy saw a town bursting haphazardly beyond its mediaeval confines, and with his orderly seaman's mind disliked what he saw. But not so the coachman.

'*La nouvelle ville,*' he called over his shoulder with evident pride. '*Elle est bonne, n'est ce pas?*' And then, as he reined in his horse. '*Ici, M'sieur!*'

They were before massive and ornate iron gates, set in a high wall that was certainly there long before Brest expanded round it. The gateposts were crowned by heraldic monsters supporting identical coats of arms; and Davy, never having heard that the Lardinières were armigers, concluded that this was a property acquired by plebian affluence from aristocratic poverty doomed to an attic at Versailles.

The coachman shouted, '*Pierre!*' and again, '*Pierre, ouvrez!*' Awaiting the gatekeeper's appearance to admit them — the Lardinières favoured locks, it seemed — Davy studied what he could see of the château through the intricately patterned ironwork. It was four storeys high and half as long again, with a steeply angled roof through which peeped the dormer windows of the servants' attics. At its eastern end a round tower, kin to those guardians of the old town they had recently left behind and like them crowned with what Davy could liken only to a gargantuan candle-snuffer, gave to the Louis Quatorze façade an archaic, even sinister, cast. The main entrance was by way of a terrace, reached by an east-west stone staircase, each newel pedestalling a statue. All eight of the lower windows led onto the terrace, those of the floor above being scarcely less lofty − in incongruous contrast to the slits in the tower.

The forecourt was paved overall, a formal design of miniature flower beds among the slabs evidently existing for the propagation of weeds. Davy was coming to realise the strictly utilitarian outlook of the Lardinières, *père et fils*. The structure within the soaring walls of the forecourt was the *portier's* lodge, whence presently emerged, not the doddering retainer Davy had anticipated, but an ogre of a man in his prime, massively proportioned yet astonishingly light of foot, who put to the test would have made mincemeat of Gurt Jan. The ogre wiped his mouth, belched, unhooked from his belt a key that worthily companioned his bulk, and jabbed it into the lock.

'*Sacré bleu, Henri!*' he rumbled, complaining that a fellow could not sit down to his dinner without an *anier imbécile* ruining his digestion.

Henri's terse reply was drowned by the groaning of the gate as it swung open. The *cocher's* whip cracked so close to Pierre's ear as to evoke a curse and the shaking of a leg of mutton fist. The horse, conceivably in resentment at being termed an ass, cavorted in a futile attempt to overthrow the carriage. The gatekeeper, aware for the first time of the quality of the passenger, muttered '*M'sieur!*' gave a hurried bow, and slammed the gates to. And Lardinière's château received the Cornish captain within its ponderous defences.

M. Lardinière regarded Davy, resplendent in the maroon coat with the blue sash across his sprigged waistcoat and a foam of lace in its V, and standing there in the vaulted hall as though he owned the whole place from its probable dungeon to its certain turret, as if beholding an apparition. He returned the bow with the addition of an unmistakable genuflexion.

'*Je vous demande pardon, m'sieur,*' he spluttered. The man was flushed to the nape of his neck. 'To 'ave sent you so miserable a conveyance! I thought—' His shoulders were up and his palms extended.

'M'sieur,' Davy entered into the spirit of the interlude and bowed again, this time making a leg. 'It is excusable. *C'est* − um

– *pardonnable*. A common American ship-master does not expect the courtesies due to a lord. *Il ne compte pas*, damme! – *M'sieur, parlez vous anglais?*'

Lardinière waved a large hand. 'Of course. For business it is necessary.'

'Thank God!' Davy muttered. Now that the preliminaries were completed they could stand eye to eye, though to be acccurate the Frenchman's was inches below the Cornishman's. Lardinière was presumably the *père* of the firm, unless the senior member were of a considerably advanced age. His white bob wig gave nothing away except, maybe, an aversion to personal extravagance, but seamed features and a stoop bespoke the passage of three score years at least, many of them at his desk. Nevertheless there was a power in the man that impressed Ned Davy as, after a courteous invitation, he was led into a study which more resembled a counthouse than a private den. Lardinière's step was firm and brisk. The face above the neat piles of papers and books on the table indicated decision and command; dark-complexioned, wide nostrils over ample, pepper-and-salt moustachios, square jaw with a dimple, broad forehead, eyes which although set about with wrinkles were neither faded nor rheumy. It was, Davy recognised, a face of a type he had often looked into at home. A Celtic face.

Davy appreciated that his host's embarrassment at underestimating the quality of his guest had disadvantaged the man from the start; though how this could be used he had yet to discover. Lardinière would be one of those rising entrepreneurs on both sides of the Channel who, having attained wealth and authority, secured their position, and their family's, by cultivating the high-born and privileged and aspiring to their ranks. This must involve a nice assessment of breeding, Davy imagined – the ability to know a fighting cock – as against those attributes other than dress, manners and speech which he was of the opinion were far more worthwhile. It was an opinion he had formed early in his young life, and not infrequently defended.

These metaphysics were terminated by Lardinière's conjuring from one of the stacks a letter which Davy recognised with a start as in familiar handwriting. 'From M'sieur Knill, my good friend, whom I have not yet met in person. He writes of a

young man who will go far.' M. Lardinière readjusted the
goldrimmed spectacles he had put on when he opened the
letter. 'Will go far? What does that mean? Have success?' He
continued to read. '"A man I can trust in every way." But he
does not say you are a gentleman. *Ma foi*, why does he not say it?
I thought of you as of Le Capitaine Salomon Venàbles.' He
shook his head in disgust.

Davy suggested that he ought to continue in the role, however
he disliked it, until he was well out to sea, and that he would be
sailing as soon as possible after discharging his cargo early in the
evening.

Lardinière's nose was in another document, but his eye was
on the captain rather than the script as he recited. '*Douze* –
twelve casks and three hogsheads, of *tabac*.'

'Virginian,' Davy added. 'Two of them. The rest—' A Gallic
shrug.

'They were still in your ship when you left? My man says they
are not in the *entrepôt* – the warehouse.'

'Have no fear. M. Lardinière; they are in my ship. And there
they shall remain until I am myself present to watch them
unloaded.'

Lardinière nodded approvingly. 'And they are?'

'Tobacco. All cleared with the customs.'

'Aha. *Tabac*.' He raised his eyebrows as if expecting the
answer he did not get. 'I myself shall visit your ship with you if
you permit.' He rang a bell, and gave the horsey servant who
answered it a few concise instructions. '*Allons, M'sieur le
Capitaine.*'

Davy was ushered into a large room, its three windows
leading onto the terrace but, judging by the arrangement of the
furniture, no longer used as doors. Curtains and coverings were
of yellow and green silk, faded and in places threadbare. There
were chairs and tables proper to this epoch of Gallic elegance,
also newer furnishings of more practical durability and design.
The salon, indeed the entire château, appeared to deploy the
resources of the present to fortify the past. Did this characterise,
too, the people he was meeting there?

'The family, *m'sieur*,' declared Lardinière, introducing him
simply as 'the young gentleman' – the emphasis was noticeable
– whom they had expected. An order to a footman at the door,

which Davy interpreted as laying an extra place at the table,
sent the fellow away, while Davy was led up the room to a group
who sat before a projecting fireplace. Here, exuding the
fragrance of resin rather than heat, a couple of tree trunks
smouldered beneath an emblazoned canopy which reached to
the high, painted ceiling. Two ladies sat rigidly on chairs they
almost concealed by panniered dresses. Davy had supposed,
listening to his mother and Mrs Pentilly, that this fashion had
disappeared when Queen Marie Antoinette decided at court no
longer to dress up as lamb. Doubtless Brittany, like Cornwall,
lagged a little in such matters. Two gentlemen rose as he
approached. The family were four in all. No − five. The
towering, floured, beribboned, out of date coiffure of one of the
ladies obscured a younger person who stood behind her chair,
Davy glimpsing a snowy headpiece, mercifully plain, as he was
presented to Lardinière fils. Paul was a tall, thin man in early
middle age who probably resembled his mother, whoever she
might be, since there was nothing of his father about him except
that dimpled jaw.

'Captain D'Arvi,' Paul greeted, bowing slightly and looking
puzzled, though no more puzzled than Davy at mention and
mispronunciation of his name.

'Madame Lardinière, *ma belle-fille.*' This was the lady with
the lofty hair style; the wife of Paul, then, and not his mother
though old enough to be, so far as one could tell for the wig and
padding and cosmetics.

'M'sieur le Baron de Treverreau, *mon gendre*." And what
relationship is that? wondered Davy, checking his bow on
perceiving himself to be favoured by no more than a nod.

Madame la Baronne was Lardinière's daughter, and all was
explained. So the man of trade had already made his alliances,
through son and daughter, with the ruling, if impoverished
aristocracy of Brittany who dominated the *parlement* and
claimed independence of Versailles! The baroness, too,
addressed him as M. D'Arvi, extending beringed fingers for his
salute.

'*Et Ma'amselle Geneviève Lardinière.*' Ma'amselle was
curtseying prettily as he put his lips to her hand. Next for
the sacrificial altar! he thought as her thickly powdered
'head' caught his eye again. But he hardly saw her face as,

introductions completed, an urgent question needed answering.

'M'sieur Lardinière, they know my name?'

Lardinière inclined his head. 'I know from your Mr Knill, and it is good they know also, do you not agree? This is an affair for us all. I read to them the letter immediately it came. We discussed it together.'

'Even your youngest daughter, Ma'amselle—?'

'Geneviève. She above all. She is my — what you call in English, I think — private secretary. Her English is perfect, like my son and me. She reads my letters. She writes. She write to you.'

'I must protest, *m'sieur*, that I am no further implicated in this — this conspiracy than in bringing the cargo into Brest.'

'I regret, captain, that you are.' Paul's English was indeed fluent. 'You are of a nation at war with France; at war, *m'sieur*, whatever our common ties. You know of our plans far more than the Yonquis who bring us so much — tobacco. We thought you and your men to be Cornish *contrebandiers*, smugglers, and have agreed what we shall do with you.'

Davy's eyes narrowed. 'What *you* shall do with *us*!'

Paul inclined his head gracefully. 'Until we may safely let you go.'

Davy's left hand was steadying his scabbard. 'I desire to know nothing of your plans. But to suggest that what I do know I may compromise is an insult I'll not take.'

'*Non, non!*' M. Lardinière grasped the young man's elbow. 'We expect not you, but one tough matelot — *un corsaire*.'

'A corsair?'

'The captain of a privateer, *m'sieur*.'

''Odsoons, I *am* captain of a privateer!' Davy's patience would not hold out much longer.

The old man turned to the others. 'We did not know he is—'

'One of us.' The words came, unexpectedly, from Ma'amselle Geneviève, and all turned to her. She was petite, compared with her sister. There was a dab of powder at mid-hairline of the coiffure — was ever flour plastered so thick? — that set the echoes flying, somehow, in Davy's brain. A pretty face, were it not for that hair style. A deucedly pretty face on any count! But there were other matters to preoccupy the captain in a situation which, although he had believed himself to possess an advantage, he found no advantage at all. Paul Lardinière must retract.

'One of us,' the baroness repeated.

'One of us, as now we know you to be,' said Paul. 'It makes the difference. I am satisfied—' and he adorned his apology with such eloquence of hands and shoulders that Davy could not but be mollified.

'My honour would not permit me to utter one word—'

'Of course not. And Arnaud say dinner awaits. *Allons*,' said M'sieur.

One of its several doors led from the salon into the dining room. This was so darkly panelled that the candelabra were lit although it was but an hour or two from mid-day. The very setting for a gunpowder plot, Davy decided, appalled at what he might find himself committed to. John Knill with his − what was it? − his 'blessing of the latter years' and 'glory his men of action craved'! He sent them on tasks he could not dare to tackle himself, and would disown them and leave them to their fate if they failed: as must surely befall the captain of the *Joshua Clegg* unless he sailed on the next tide.

Eight modern and utilitarian chairs were ranged closely along an antique dining table. A huge buffet left just enough room for the butler, Arnaud the footman and a maidservant to serve the meal.

The attendance of these three prompted the baron to question the advisability of proceeding with the discussion in such company. 'But Annibal, *mon fils*,' cried the head of the family, Davy picking up what he could from this uninterpreted interlude,' these are my friends, picked and pledged to our cause. Tell Madame and Messieurs, Clément − in English, for our friend.' The butler replied that Arnaud was his son, Clementine ('named after me, your excellencies') his niece, the cook his wife, the housemaids the daughters of cousins, and the groom his nephew.

'*Et grand Pierre, le concierge?*' Davy could not resist interposing.

Lardinière smiled, Clément chuckled, and Clementine's blushes were in vivid contrast to the freshly starched cap, collar and apron that she wore in the Breton style.

'You are a lucky girl − *une fille heureuse!*' Davy endeavoured to expiate his gaffe.

'Holy Virgin!' Treverreau loudly questioned, so far as Davy could make out, whether there were not other matters to discuss than a wench's sweetheart. At this the butler went on to explain that it was he, Clément, who thirty years ago as a humble footman had dared to mention Brittany's subjection to the young m'sieur, and finding in him admiration for the lords of the Breton parlement persuaded him to adopt the cause. The four Lardinières murmuring agreement the baron nodded acceptance.

'That was in my father's house at Rennes,' Lardinière explained; and the meal proceeded. He of course sat at the head of his table, the unmarried daughter at its foot. The baron was on his right, then madame, and then Davy. Opposite were the baroness on her father's left, and next to her her brother Paul. Paul explained, between constant sips of an admirable muscadet and mouthfuls of a dinner Davy's mistrust at the turn of events quite spoiled for him, that the Bretons were as loyal to their King Louis XVI as the Cornish to George III. This both had proved in battle, on land and at sea. But in Brittany traditional rights had been taken from them. And now that France and her allies needed the might of Brittany less − 'No respect, M. D'Arvi, but the war is almost won—' Davy shrugged his shoulders. It was! And the great fleets based at Brest were still either in Indian or Caribbean waters. The naval dockyard was practically empty.

'Now that our country's need is past, we can without disloyalty press those rights, fight for them, *m'sieur*, take up arms.' And those arms had been arriving, in regular shipments, for the past six months − ever since Cornwallis's surrender at Yorktown. 'Many of them British, *m'sieur*.' The *Joshua Clegg*'s delivery, a consignment of the latest weapons, had been the last. All was now prepared.

A hundred and seven years ago, Paul lectured, the oppressions of Minister Colbert had prompted the 'Revolt of the Stamped Paper,' a popular uprising in Brittany that had been savagely suppressed. But the duchy was still governed by its own *parlement* or 'estates' of nobles. 'And here, while there are many nobles, *m'sieur*, our duke, our marquis, our counts and viscounts are concerned only with life at court. They leave their lands at the mercy of stewards and lawyers, and the people look for rescue to the lesser landlords.'

'Like our squires in England,' Davy commented, trying to generate in himself concern for plebian Brittany.

The orator went on to recount how twelve years after the 1675 revolt Intendants − governors, M'sieur D'Arvi − were installed by Louis XIV, Brittany being the last province in France to be degraded. The Intendant collaborated with the military commandant in this tyrannical intrusion, but the leader of the Breton parlement, the Procurer General − Paul Lardinière intoned the words as if referring to the Holy Ghost − defied them. He had defied them ever since.

Davy stole a glance at his watch. Nearly three o'clock. Courses had come and gone. Accustomed to plain Cornish cooking, he was not certain what he had eaten. But it was good. And now that the servants had left and the wine was flowing he wished for nothing but to doze in his cabin until the evening tide. Paul's instruction into the causes of Breton discontent had developed into a lecture. He was now speaking up-table and expounding the more explicit points of his thesis in the vernacular, far beyond Davy's comprehension.

The concentration of the speaker on M'sieur at the head of the table, and of everyone else on him, permitted Davy the relief of a yawn. As he indulged it, it suddenly occurred to him that his gaping profile was in full view of the youngest Lardinière, that he was being infernally rude to her, particularly as he had scarcely vouchsafed her a glance since taking his seat, and that she was watching him. All he knew of her were her silly coiffure, her hands, her voice quietly addressing the servants − oh, and that unforgettable 'One of us now'. What a bore she must think him, not knowing how desperately he had had to attend, to follow the life and death conversation of the conspirators, and their tedious explanation. He turned to her and their eyes met.

Good God, her eyes were full of tears! How should he have neglected her so? He was moved to touch her, but he kept his hands in his lap. There were things to be said, regrets he must express. But no words came.

'*A tort ou à droit*' declaimed Paul . . .

Her eyes held his. He saw the candlelight in the tears there, and he saw deeper. What he saw was familiar, precious, beyond description. It was some basic truth about their two selves, borne in an emotion that had become over-powering, painful even. A single instant that was changing his whole life. It was witchcraft. It was − Ma'amselle!

'Ma'amselle.' Had he said it aloud? Not a day but he had thought of her, wondered, despaired, time and time again.

'So it is with me.' She read his mind.

Paul droned on.

'*M. le corsaire!*' she smiled.

'I have loved you,' he whispered, half out of his chair, 'ever since—'

'Sssh!' Her restraining hand was white against his maroon sleeve.

He would have fingered her hair, probing like a prospector for the red gold beneath. She answered his glance with a gesture of resignation. Even her name was right − the name that had eluded him. Geneviève, Guenever, Jennifer, Jenny. Pure Cornish. But of course Cornish and Breton were one people.

Their whole attention focussed upon one another. Nothing was real but they. They shone for each other, crystal clear in a world of shadows. Yet that world obtruded. Paul had stopped speaking, the queries and comments evoked from Treverreau, M'sieur, Paul's lady and the Baroness ceasing too. Every gaze fell on Davy, and the spell was broken.

'*Pardon, M'sieur.*' Davy addressed himself to the scowling Paul. What more could he say? He felt like a boy in class caught cheating; rot it, even his neck was afire! A fine spectacle the gallant Cornish captain was making of himself! He could now turn dispassionately to Geneviève, who was smiling up the table at her father.

'Papa, we have just discovered' − cool as a cucumber! admired Davy − 'M. D'Arvi and I, that we are old friends.' She continued in French, Davy making of it what he could, that he was the gentleman she had spoken about, who has seized the Indiaman but sent it home. There had been the mutiny.

'*Oui, oui!*' M. Lardinière raised his glass to the young gentleman who has so strangely interrupted his son's discourse. '*Mon ami*, we owe you much.'

Talk was resumed. Davy consulted his watch. Just after three. It had seemed an hour since that last furtive glance, or a second. Oh, time had lost its meaning! He surrendered himself again to her nearness. His right hand beneath the table sought her hand and their fingers locked – a gesture, he felt, of everlasting union. Her eyes were on her brother now, and Davy's too, with an expression of complete absorption which must have gratified the orator.

'. . . and the new Procurer-Général,' Paul concluded in triumph, 'certain to be elected by the Estates tomorrow, will be our son and brother M'sieur le Baron de Treverreau. Annibal will demand the withdrawal of the Intendant and *parlement* will agree. All is arranged. But the Intendant will not resign. He will call upon his infamous ally M'sieur le Commandant.'

'Mais le commandant est corrompu—' began the baron.

'Bribed,' said Geneviève, rapt and gripping Davy's hand as if she would never let go. The halves of a broken coin lost in the treasury of time had come together. This was a miracle compared with which Breton politics were but a game, played by the barons with the people as pawns; a game she knew for the first time for what it was.

'We shall have to fight. There is no other way,' continued the baron. He fixed his gaze on Davy. 'Because of his men, M'sieur le Capitaine D'Arvi must stay. We have a place for them where they will be happy but can tell nothing. Only until the fighting. Then they fight too, *M'sieur le Capitaine,* eh? The English fight good. They love the fight. Our plan is to hold Brest while Haute-Bretagne, Basse-Bretagne, march. I, Annibal, march, Jean et Paul, they hold. M'sieur D'Arvi must stay.'

Davy thought so too. Then he was aware that just as every corner in this dark, lustreless room had become strangely bright, and that in every face before him he could somehow see behind the mask it wore, so could he see into himself. In self-revulsion that an officer's first thought had not been for his men, Davy decided that at all costs he must catch the first tide. He would return as soon as they were safely home. As though following his thoughts Geneviève pressed her little hand into his own. At this stage an image of the *Falcon* recurred, and the press of hands contracted. But the corvette had not been ready after six months, and could not be so after six days. Even if she were – well, he would return. Desperately he returned Geneviève's grip. He and she – they must never let go.

'Eh Bien!' M. Lardinière rose, and the others with him, Davy

and Geneviève after a disentanglement that must be effected with lingering care. 'I think M'sieur must leave and not stay. It is best. If his ship can get to sea without being stopped by the marine, l'Atlantique will spread no tales.'

Davy contrived, or maybe Geneviève contrived it, that he should make his adieux apart from the rest. 'It was not last month we met,' he said. 'It was five hundred years ago.'

'It was a thousand, or it was fifty; but we met. When do we meet again?'

'Soon, very soon. Not today, nor tomorrow, but before summer is out, *chérie*.'

'The next minute would not be soon enough, *bien-aimé*,' she whispered.

The Lardinières were watching, wherefore he kissed her hand and ached that it were not her lips. When he left with her father, all the family at the château door to watch them go, he saw her press that hand to her cheek.

'She is to marry a great lord,' said Lardinière, conversationally.

'Who?' Davy asked hoarsely.

'That shall be settled when all Bretagne is at our feet. Perhaps M. Le Vicomte de Jarnac. A great name in Haute-Bretagne.'

They drove through crowds which now thronged the streets. 'Are you not well, M'sieur D'Arvi?' asked Lardinière, returning one of the many greetings that came from either side of his splendid carrriage, the florid 'L' adorning its glossy panel where soon the crest was to be, and boys keeping pace in expectation of largesse. He tossed a handful of small coins onto the pavé. 'One must please *la canaille*, and I keep a bag of sous under my seat. But you do not look good, captain. My doctor shall see you, if you honour me by staying and fighting at our side. But I think it is best you go, *mon ami*.' He squeezed the young man's arm. 'The sea — it soon make well, no!'

First seen of the brig as they rounded the bend to the wharves were her two mastheads, high above the spars of the fishing fleet moored at the nearer quay. Seamen were busied aloft on her fore top-gallant yard, and Davy yearned for the last dog watch, when the ship would be afloat again and he could have them shaking out the sails for urgent departure. The apex of the sheerlegs was now visible. A bale rose beyond the new roofs that flanked the fish-wharf, swung inward, and disappeared in measured descent. Here was the orderly life of the sea. You loaded, you sailed, you discharged. You fought the eternal foe — the French, or the sea itself. But there was a proven, practical solution to every problem, even to an emergency. There was no situation you did not understand, the course of which you were unable to follow, let alone control, nor its conclusion to foresee. There was no Jenny of the dark, absorbing eyes and soft touch, whom you had known at first glance to be your soul's own twin, as she knew you were hers — and who was to marry a great French lord.

Onto the wharf road then where a merciful disturbance distracted Davy for a moment. From an open shed a clerk chipping at a tally stick raved in familiar sounding Breton at a carter who tossed empty crates and baskets into a wagon. The fellow's misdirected energy — the vino had clearly preoccupied him well into mid-afternoon — was unsettling his two huge percherons. Hooves plunging, they backed the wagon into the road. The Lardinière equipage pulled up, bouncing on its leather springs like a Mevagissey hooker in a squall, an exchange of incivilities between coachman and carter augmenting the din. M. Lardinière stood up, rapping the woodwork with the handle of his cane. At sight of the great man the drunken fellow touched his forehead and led his horses forward to clear the way, whereupon the coachman with a parting comment shook up his pair into a jingling trot.

'Handsomely there, ye bastards, handsomely!' Davy was roaring ten minutes later, to the no-concern of dockers manning the lifting tackle, but expressive of his anxiety for the first of the hogsheads labelled 'Tobacco', now head high as he stood at the quayside. He had watched Williams and his party slip the slings round the massive barrel they had eased onto its side, held his breath as the new hemp took the strain, observed with relief the rope which ran through the six sheaves of the massive block sway its burden up from the hold. Four smaller casks — Davy had not allowed more at a time — had already been transferred by net to the Lardinière dray, a stout-timbered cart waiting beside the sheerlegs. They were ranged in a tier against the head-board. It was Davy's plan next to lower the upended hundred-and-forty-five pounders preventing the hogsheads from rolling. These must be kept on their side lest lowering them upright should burst the hidden ironware through their bottom. And never would master mariner shift cargo ashore with greater satisfaction than when discharging those barrels of trouble he had unwittingly captured in the Channel approaches. Had he the gift of foresight, Davy thought bitterly, he would there and then have sunk the *Joshua Clegg*, freight and all, sooner than bring her in. Yet even as the thought occurred he wondered, would he? Would he have foregone meeting Jenny, even knowing that he must lose her at once?

Shoppers at the wayside booths, who had cheered as the ponderous load soared to view, fell silent as over-energetic dockers hauling it up set it swinging like a pendulum and threatening to strike the sheerlegs. They heard the scowling young Yankee patron bawl an order in his barbaric tongue, and watched the load steady against the many-stranded pulleys. At his warehouse gates, now wide open, M. Lardinière chatted amicably with a knot of officials whose uniform and insignia established them as customs officers. Lardinière gave no sign of nerves, Davy noticed. The hogshead was now creeping past the bulwarks towards the wharf as a pair of muscular individuals cranked the mechanism. The dray backed into position, and the hogshead was deposited 'so gentle', commented Billums, up the ladder to eye level once more, 'as a cluck hen on her eggs.'

Now the second hogshead swung up and across with scarcely a quiver. The dockyard mateys tailing on the rope, a well drilled team, held it firmly to the lifting tackle; the stay-beam was nearing the limit of the screw; the half-loaded cart was moving into place, the haunches of the horses pressing back upon the harness. All went well. But there was a sudden shouting from the fish wharf, and the thunder of hooves. Davy saw the men at the rope gape past him, and turned to look. It was the percherons, charging along the wharf with reins flying and the driverless dray bouncing after them, shedding crates and baskets in every direction. They pounded into the Lardinière section. A wheel span off and bounced into the water under the brig's bows. Iron rims and shoes struck fire from the cobbles. Women shoppers screamed, and the horses under the sheerlegs reared.

The runaways were abreast the ship. Davy sprang to grab the

bridle about the nearer flaming nostrils, but a toss of the great head sent him sprawling on his back. There he watched, in a few expanding seconds, the weaving wagon strike the staybeam and snap it; the sheerlegs twist, one breaking away from its ring-bolt in the pavé; the dockers jump over the edge onto the *Joshua Clegg*'s deck below; the hogshead drop from the squealing block and crash down on the cart, which collapsed on one side; the driver dive clear and the frightened beasts stampede into the road in the runaways' wake.

As in a nightmare Davy saw the whole load, the two hogsheads and the four casks, spill a jumble of staves and musket butts, firing locks, tobacco leaves and rifle barrels at the feet of Lardinière and the *douaniers*.

16

A silence froze the wharf, deadening even thundering hooves. Then a gasp and every sense was alert. Crystal-clear came each anvil clash of ironshod cart-horses, as they stampeded over the paving stones and cobbles. The thud and scraping of what remained of the two wagons they drew provided a mad accompaniment, the debris of disintegration marking their trail. From the fishwharf at the opposite end of the quay came the clamour of a swelling crowd. Davy scrambled to his feet and sprang towards the edge of the wharf, colliding with Williams who had swung up over the ladder. He looked down onto the deck of the brig, now aground in the ebb, and hailed Polurrian, who stood up staring above the open hatch, yellow teeth bared in a snarl.

'Bring 'em all ashore, double quick, Barney.'

His mind registered the dinghy, half hidden under the ship's counter and with its painter secured to a cleat on the poop. The dockers who had leapt down to avoid the tottering sheerlegs were clambering back again.

Over at the warehouse half a dozen customs officers prowled among the strewn firearms, prodding with their feet and stooping to handle specimens. One with more gold braid than the rest pointed to Davy and screamed a command. Two detached themselves, drawing their swords, and one presented a pistol. They moved cautiously to the middle of the road. Old Lardinière still stood as if petrified. Jason Duval came running from one of the alleys. Now the dockers were clustered clear of the shambles on the quay, all talking at once. The foreman, shouting unintelligibly above the babel, turned towards Lardinière, who snapped into life and strode purposefully up to the halting *douaniers*. Amazingly, he appeared to be urging them on. Davy drew his sword with a hiss of steel. His ten seamen from the *Joshua Clegg* were ranged behind him. Jason

Duval rejoined the crew, covering the cobbles in great strides. Only Joseph Duval was adrift.

'Find the Coq d'Or?' snapped Davy.

'Aye, sir. Safe enough,' said Jason.

'Get the ship's company there, split up if possible.'

Duval hesitated, considering. So, after a further step or two, did the *douaniers*, confronted by a British phalanx as astonished as the customs officers to find themselves gun-runners, but resolved to stand by their captain.

Lardinière came up to Davy, loudly proclaiming 'Capitaine Venàbles, you have betrayed my trust. *Rendez les armes* — give yourself up!'

Davy stood appalled, but at a step from one of the officers thrust the old man aside. The other officer, the one with the pistol, levelled it and called on Davy to surrender. Surely he could not have anticipated its use, and would have no opportunity to load it! Davy maintained his defiant posture, though feeling his flesh shrink beneath his fine maroon coat. Billums Williams, unarmed, stepped to his side.

Lardinière grabbed the captain's arm, croaked into his ear. '*M'sieur*, you do not understand. We are not ready. *Rendezvous*. Two days. Two day only. *Parbleu*, they must not know! You are in no danger; I shall get you free.'

The man with the pistol flung it to the ground, and with a yell both officers charged. Lardinière stumbled clear. Billums caught a flashing blade in his leathery hand, following it down to dull the cut, and jerked it from his assailant's grip. Then with a blow that had felled British seamen in its time he proved French jaws to be as brittle. The other officer hurled himself desperately at Davy.

Engage, swords ringing. Parry thrusts at the chest, one, two, three: fellow must have learnt his sword play from a groom. Riposte, slitting the *douanier*'s right sleeve from elbow to shoulder and evoking a howl of pain. No use spitting the man; in trouble enough as it is! Meet a half-hearted counter, adversary's eyes changed from glaring to staring. Then to the cheers and jeers of the little band of Cornishmen the officer lowered his sword, turned and fled to the protection of his colleagues, clutching his slit sleeve where doubtless a scratch had persuaded him that honour was satisfied. Davy jumped at him and welted him across the rump with the flat of his sword, an act which delighted his men but of which he was at once ashamed. Meanwhile the disarmed man struggled to his feet, his unnecessary riding boots skidding on the cobbles, and clasping his jaw fled too.

Lardinière was at Davy's elbow again, noisily demanding surrender and as guardedly renewing his plea. He must give himself up. They would treat him well − he, Jean Lardinière, guaranteed it. It would be for two days, no more. Then the fleet would be gone. Now it was not gone. They would all be captured, Davy then if not now.

'*Geneviève aussi,*' he concluded.

Geneviève! The lull continued, but it would not be for long. Reinforcements from the Custom House were doubling along the wharf. Military headgear became conspicuous among the heads of converging spectators, whose excited uproar seemed directed as much against the officials as against the crew of the American ship.

'Two days?' Davy asked.

'*Oui, m'sieur.*' And the other's voice dropped to a whisper. 'Then the rebellion. Then you are free. Word of honour.'

There was too much to consider in the swifting seconds. Davy's own attire not only made it impossible for him to mingle undetected with the crowd, but presented a threat to his unarmed men, some of whom would certainly be arrested with him. He had few doubts that were he to cry '*Vive la Bretagne, à bas le roi!*' he would win precious minutes, though it was hours and not minutes that must determine the brig's sailing, alas! For the Lardinières and their revolution he cared little. But as the old man has so craftily said, there was Geneviève.

Yet he'd be damned if he put himself at the mercy of the enemy. Little use then to her, or his men, or himself. And he was damned if he trusted the old man.

'Mr. Williams, you know where to make for. James Duval will guide you, and for God's sake wrap this kerchief round that bloody fist!'

'Shan't laive 'ee, cap'n.' Billums accepted the handkerchief and gripped it in a ball to staunch the blood.

'You'll do as I say,' snapped Davy. He flipped out of his pocket a handful of French coins. 'You'll need these. Lose yourselves in the crowd but keep an eye on Duval. Hear that, men?'

'But you, sor?'

'God's death, go! They'll not take me. I'll meet you at the Coq. Mr Williams, Jacob, off with the lot of you.'

The ten men dashed across the road, a venturesome customs officer springing out of range as Quinn, the one man among them who carried some sort of weapon, swiped at him with his butcher's knife. Davy sighed with relief as the crowd engulfed them.

Now the *douaniers'* target was isolated. They paused a moment as though drawing strength from the heinous evidence amid which they stood, then charged at Davy with a roar of triumph. Davy shoved the bewildered old merchant into their path and sword in hand leapt down onto the deck of his ship, a long drop that tumbled him to his knees, vaulted into the dinghy moored beneath the counter, by the mercy of heaven neither upsetting the boat not plunging his foot through the floorboards, and with a couple of slashes severed the painter. A black-suited figure slithered over the poop bulwarks and groped with his feet for the dinghy's gunnels. Joseph Duval. By all the Powers of God, it was good to have a friend! Davy jerked him onto the thwarts. They pushed themselves clear of the ship and into the muddy current. Then they slammed the oars into the rowlocks, and as pistol shots kicked up the bubbling water astern they pulled out into the stream.

Overhead the late afternoon sky was duck-egg blue, but away to westward cumuli were groping for the sun, their towering summits darkening as they moved across it. 'Mid-channel, downstream,' Davy panted, staring at the eddies round his straining oar. 'Pull lad, put your back in it.'

'Never get through the Goulet, sir,' Duval gasped. He watched uniformed men bustling along the wooden jetty between the Lardinière and Customs wharves.

'Brest — wettest town in France, they say. Weather's breaking. Rain on the way — don't look, pull. Then up-river hidden in the rain.'

The men on the jetty were taking aim.

Duval licked dry lips. 'Saved by the weather, sir, like at Helford!' His laugh was more of a croak. To be fired at by a solitary cannon ball in the dark was one thing, to be singled out as the target of a line of muskets quite another. '*Ma foi*, what a time that was in the old *Dorcas*!'

'Keep your French for the Frogs, Joe, and your breath for the oar.'

'Muskets!' Duval blurted out.

There was a ripple of flame from the quayside. 'I know,' said Davy. It was like seeing a broadside from an enemy warship, only infinitely smaller.

A shower of bullets hissed round the boat, the crack of the volley almost simultaneous. One lodged in the top of the transom, hot enough from the friction of its flight to conjure a feather of smoke that curled to leeward with the tang of burning. Davy, at stroke, scooped a bailer of the water that sloshed half an inch over the floorboards, and extinguished it. Duval sighed deeply.

'Not much fun, being shot at,' Davy said, understanding. 'But you get used to it.'

The diversion had cost them ground, while the loading drill of the marksmen proceeded mechanically. They rowed desperately across wind and tide, helped a little by the semblance of a current which still contested the invasion of its confining banks by the sea. A second volley sizzled about them.

'Pull, damn you, pull!' Davy's stronger stroke was edging the dinghy up-stream. His ankles were confoundedly wet. 'S'death, the bilge water was over his shoes! But there was no leak aft that he could see. The boat being lower at the stern than at the stem, the water would only now be apparent to Duval, whose discovery of the leak coincided with Davy's order to seek it for 'ad.

'Shot-hole in the boards behind me, sir.'

'Then think of the boy at the dyke and stick your finger in it. Pass me your oar.'

Distance now foreshortened the jetty, and the *Joshua Clegg* was less conspicuous against the granite quay than were her masts stabbing above the warehouses into the blue. The sight made Davy uneasy. He had never abandoned a ship before; and although the Yankee brig had no place in his heart he felt regret, even guilt. But what else could he have done?

'I've jammed a thole pin in it,' cried Duval triumphantly. 'And put on your sou-wester, sir; squall's coming.' The squall was racing in before the storm-clouds, pushing a cool wind ahead of it and flattening the ripples. The water in the bottom of the boat was several inches deep now, and the rainstorm would add to it.

'Take over while I bail.' Davy shipped oars and pushed them behind him to Duval. Then the rain thrashed down on them; and the last view they had of Brest, before they were enclosed in a cascade which obliterated every urgency save that of seeking cover and finding none, was a flickering row of sparks from the quayside. Davy's knees were wide apart as he stooped to grasp the bailer. Then he gave a yelp, while a shower of spent bullets fell with the raindrops from the sky. Face contorted in agony he tipped the bailer over a tear in his breeches above the knee. Duval leapt up, rocking the little boat violently, and leant over his captain's shoulder, but Davy shook him off.

'Keep going!' he muttered between clenched teeth. 'Not out of the wood yet.'

He rolled down his left stocking, started to ease his small-clothes up about the wound, swore mightily. Hat and wig dropped into the bilge water, no wetter then than before. He ripped up the oppressive garment to mid thigh. The top of the ball protruded red-rimmed from bruised skin − a sort of devil's poached egg, he told himself, trying not to shout as he touched it. With a string of whispered oaths he began to squeeze it out like a boil.

Duval the doctor spoke. 'Don't touch it.' He shipped his oars. 'They won't see us now.' And indeed they were an island beyond all horizons − the dinghy, themselves, and a ten fathom radius of tideway where the rain poured down and every inch of surface vented a dancing waterspout. He knelt at Davy's feet and produced a scalpel from his pocket case.

'We'll let the tide work for us, sir, just as you said.'

One dexterous, excruciating flick, 'like removing a stone from a horse's hoof,' Duval said, and Davy held the ball in his hand. It was still warm. 'Wound cauterised by the heat,' Duval continued, peering professionally into the fleshy, almost bloodless cavity. 'Now for a bandage. This, I think is the cleanest. Dr O'Keenahan has impressed upon me the necessity for cleanliness about a wound.'

He laid hold of Davy's lace stock. Davy clutched it to his chest. 'Vast there! 'Tis the best I've got.'

''Tis the only one you've got, sir, and we must make good use of it.'

The storm was deluging Brest, which with the easing of the downpour around the boat they saw as a strip of darker mist. Of the south bank of the Elorn estuary where they must seek shelter little could be distinguished but the shape of trees, a hamlet and the blur of a few riverside buildings. Davy shifted himself painfully to the stern seat and sculled with a single oar, leaving the flooding tide to take them up-river at three or four knots and exerting himself only sufficiently to keep on course. Duval bailed the boat dry, then shook out Davy's thirty-guinea wig and the soggy felt that had once been a hat. Next, he examined the scar left by the trooper's carbine.

'You'll do again, sir!' The expression, typically Cornish, was reassuring; Davy had been in a mood to consider himself a battered relic. 'Now what are we going to cover it with?'

'Shove that damned wig back on again; I can't get any wetter.'

It was eased into place, Duval then sitting on the thwarts Davy had vacated and aping the ecstatic motions of a fashionable perukier. The two young men looked into each other's face and laughed, there on the river in the rain, one of them injured, and with the armed forces of a naval base after their blood. Davy's laughter was brief, but his eyes stayed bright.

'Now, Joseph — shipmate, give me your hand. You're a gentleman.'

It appeared to have been the wrong thing to say, for all the merriment went out of Duval. 'My people were once,' he murmured, accepting his captain's handshake, 'and in this very land. But I — I have no hopes to be.'

Davy leaned forward, the effort making him wince, and slapped Duval on the shoulder. 'Cock!' he said.

They kept to mid-stream, where in that narrowing, though still broad, stretch of water they would with luck avoid identification, if not sighting, from either bank. They agreed, however, to risk approaching whatever part of the southern rivage promised cover. Shelter too, perhaps, though this was not of prime consequence. But maybe it was, Davy realised. Ten years almost continuously at sea had accustomed him to wet clothes; indeed he had already forgotten them until reminded by Duval's condition. Joseph was shivering so that his teeth chattered. Evening found them nosing through rushes, to tie up under a roof of trees.

'Jump ashore, Joe,' said Davy, 'and look around. There may be some deserted spot or other where we could even light a fire without being spotted. No, I'm all right, the exercise will stop you from being the patient and me the doctor, and all I know of curing the ague could be scratched on a button. Just remember where we've moored the boat, eh?'

Duval reported back to his captain an hour later. Following the bank a few hundred yards up, through woods that became denser as he struggled on, he had come upon the mouldering remains of a small wooden pier, the ribs of a skiff lying alongside in the river reeds. He reckoned that this betokened a dwelling, so forced his way inland for a short distance, to find himself in a clearing which was reverting to forest with saplings and a riot of bracken and bramble. In the midst the glow of a green, clearing sky illumined the burnt out ruin of a cottage. A slated lean-to, which Duval had entered with face in arms to shield himself from the nettles that crowded the doorway, still offered shelter. The dim interior preserved the familiar, if mildewed, harness of an ox, and a manger that might even now prove sturdy enough to support his wounded captain. And the stall was dry.

'You could light a fire there, quite invisible even at night,' Duval enthused.

Davy had all the seaman's mistrust of fire in a closed space. 'Complete the conflagration, eh Joe?'

'Oh, I can contain it all right, sir. And there are gaps in the roof slates that will let out the smoke.'

'Flint and tinder?' Davy sounded anxious.

'I am supplied like a pedlar,' laughed Duval, slapping his voluminous pockets.

'Then why the hell the delay?'

They cast loose and worked their way beneath the overhanging branches except where projecting trunks forced them out into the reeds. Duval leapt onto the pier, and the rotting planks giving way, fell through to stand waist-deep among reeds and rushes.

'This bit of Brittany cannot have been visited for twenty years, and won't be again for a further twenty,' Duval exclaimed cheerfully, head and shoulders projecting through the hole.

Davy meanwhile heaved himself to the dinghy's bows, and making fast the painter struggled to sitting position on the edge of the pier, whence he had swung and wriggled himself to the bank by the time his companion had clambered dripping out of the hole. 'Do you not want your sword, sir?' asked Duval. 'It is still in the boat.'

'I'd get more use from an oar.'

Duval handed him one of the sculls, then slung the blue baldrick with its scabbard and sword round his own shoulder. 'If you do not object, captain,' he said.

'Why the deuce should I?' Davy was hauling himself erect, clinging to the oar with one leg bent and foot dangling, and punctuating his remarks with curses as he hobbled into the trees. 'And for God's sake, Joe, belay that sir and captain nonsense — at least,' he added, 'when we are not on board ship.'

With Duval to larboard and the oar to starboard he reached the cottage. In the dusk it looked secretive and sullen, resentful even of some remote evil which had stamped it into ruin. It was Davy now who shivered. But he limped into the lean-to and let himself be hoisted onto the manger, where he sat juggling with his souvenir of a musketeer's aim while Duval foraged for firewood inside and then beyond the door, soon to return with an armful of furze. As the flint sparks started to fly Davy, who had come to a decision and dropped the ball into his pocket, stopped him.

'Sorry, Joe, but there's other work for you to do while daylight lasts, and the fire would leave you blind as a bat down by the water. D'ye think you can shove our dinghy out into the river?'

Duval got up off his knees. 'Why? We shall need it.'

Davy shook his head. 'We cannot always reckon to hide in a cloud, like Venues hid Hector before the walls of Troy or was it Athene hid Achilles! No, Joe, with us aboard that boat would be our death. It ain't even as though we'd find a British blockading squadron waiting of us if we did contrive to get through the Goulet. But we'll use the dinghy to throw the hounds off the scent. Take out the thole pin so she'll sink to the gunnels — she won't submerge — and get her clear of the reeds so that the tide can take her. It will have turned by this time, and with luck some frog — begging your pardon, some ancestral countryman of yours — will report our certain demise. Afraid you'll get damned wet again, but it won't be for the first time today — I'm scuppered or I would go myself.'

'I know you would,' Duval replied cheerfully.

'And Joe, if you can part with it, what about leaving that sword etcetera in the bottom of the boat?'

'A pretty touch I had already decided on myself.' And Duval was gone, leaving Davy in pain, damnably hungry, and helplessly alone. Every whisper of nightfall, when the off-shore breeze began to stir and the night creatures in the undergrowth woke to their day, warned of imminent discovery.

Then came the conviction that Geneviève was with him in this crisis. They had met only a few hours ago, and it was a reunion. Somewhere they had known each other before — even lived out a life together, a concept not beyond Celtic wit to accept; though he doubted whether the phlegmatic Joseph would assess it as anything more mystical than the yearning of the child-in-man for its mother's comfort in the dark. The Rochellais were notable rather for common sense than for imagination, and Huguenot Rochellais more so. No, he'd send Joe for her; she would want that. But only with the sketchiest account of their mutual concern. Certainly not that love at first sight, when shared, is of the ages.

Now there was a marvel to think about, with neither embarrassment nor need for subterfuge, alone and reaching for memories that beckoned at the rim of consciousness. Troubles receded, the wound in his thigh ceased to throb, the tension eased.

Duval returned to find him stretched out in the manger as peacefully as in his bunk. What an iron nerve the man had! No fretting, no worrying! He had made best use of the hand Fortune had dealt him, and like Malbrouck after one battle and on the eve of the next yielded to untroubled sleep. Quietly

Duval coaxed a little blaze in the middle of the floor and sat by it, steaming while the shadows danced and nodded, until only the ashes flowed and he, too, slept.

17

They came up from Landereau, Geneviève and Joseph, where the Lardinières reared their percherons and hacks and coach-horses and hunters. Joseph Duval, who among his many accomplishments had the aptitude of a columnist in the *Gentleman's Magazine* for ferreting out trivia in minimal time, had ascertained the existence of the stud farm; more, that ma'amselle was the only member of the family who rode to hounds. The next move, after Ned Davy had sketched out a plan of campaign, was to present himself at the château in Brest as an applicant for the post of veterinary surgeon. Thence it had taken none of the persuasion he had prepared himself to employ to get her to accompany him to her farm, where Joseph's way with horses, and the Parisian accent he had imbibed at his mother's knee at Helford (the Duvals consistently importing their spouses from across the channel), impressed the staff and got him the job. But first he must escort his new mistress ostensibly back to Brest, actually along the left bank of the Elorn, where he would have to guide her unnoticed to the hideout. Ma'amselle must have formed a high opinion of his friend and captain, Joseph decided, to be willing — insistent, even — to help him in his plight.

Geneviève, when she had found herself alone in the château office with Joseph and learnt of Edouard Davy's survival, although unable to check a trickle of tears which she concealed by the expedient of looking out onto the terrace, had first to satisfy herself that this scholarly young Parisian who claimed to be a horse doctor was indeed Edouard's friend; like him, from *le Cornouailles*, and not an agent of the *Intendant*. For the better part of a week since finding the flooded dinghy, empty of everything save a British sword and a pulped hat, a search for the two escapers had revealed nothing. Local opinion presumed them shot or drowned. Eye-witnesses at Portzic Point, where the

boat had come ashore a mile or so below Brest, even reported
the end of the two *déspérés* as they sprang overboard in a final
bid to evade their deserts. Nevertheless Government inquiries
were by no means concluded.

The disaster on the wharf had enmeshed the Lardinières in a
net of suspicion and examination, which the head of the firm's
accusation of his Yankee shipmaster had done little to ease,
though doubtless saving him from arrest. A warehouse messenger
had ensured the hasty dissolution of the house party, while a word
to old Clément had ensured a thorough briefing of all below
stairs. So Geneviève had been left to face alone the Gendarme and
his retinue who arrived on the heels of the departed family. All
they got out of her was a statement that le Capitaine Venâbles had
been brought to the château for no purpose other than to report
and to receive instruction for his return. There had of course been
an emotional outburst or two, which Geneviève had been quite
unable to contain. But, *pardieu*, had she behaved as the English
were supposed to do the inquisitors would not have considered
themselves to be doing their duty!

All this she told Joseph as they jogged along lanes which
reminded him of home, after satisfying herself of his identity
before leaving Brest by demanding of him a description in
detail, which he had been made to repeat, of Captain Davy's
appearance. Such an observant young woman, to have perceived so much in the casual contact of a dinner table and yet
briefer contact in mid-Atlantic Davy had spoken of.

Later she learnt that Edouard had confided to his friend,
while they hid together in the ruin in the clearing, the true
purport of the *Joshua Clegg*'s mission.

Joseph wanted to know why, three days after the time
planned for the insurrection, no church bells called to arms.
Where were the rebels in the streets and the oppressors in the
goals? Although the transports had sailed, she told him, one of
their convoy of great battleships had remained in the dockyard,
while only the day before a detachment of *cuirassiers* had
arrived from Rennes. No signal could be given for the rising,
and all that was left of the great, national movement of the
Bretons was suspicion and a ferment which, when it boiled over,
could result in a mob eruption which was anything but what the
planners had intended.

Now Joseph must relate the events of the past few days — so far as they concerned Davy, for in himself, for all that she had just thought fit to employ him, she showed little interest. The hideout had been secure. Casual inquiry in nearby St Erne as to the fishing down by the river had elicited that he might fish there if he chose, but alone. *Nom de Dieu!* no one of the village would venture there. The devil rode the forest night and day. Joseph, whose scientific mind rejected such myths, had found this superstition most comforting but he had told Davy only that the woods were never entered. To your Cornishman of immemorial ancestry on both sides the supernatural was as much a fact of life as earth, air and water and the humours that rose in a man's body to determine his character; and Joseph was as yet unaware of how his new friend stood in such matters.

Davy, it transpired, was well furnished with French gold. With it Joseph had bought food and also the horse on which he was now mounted. *Oui, ma'amselle,* and from the local apothecary such herbs as the captain's wound required and in the use of which he, Joseph Duval, had been trained by the best physician in the world.

Oui, the wound was healing well. Davy hobbled about on a branch he had torn from a tree — a strong one — that Joseph had trimmed into a crutch. Soon he would be fit to ride, and in a week or two fit to fight.

Clothes? Geneviève had asked, her long red hair a-flutter as they trotted.

Clothes were a problem. A traveller could reasonably buy a horse to replace one he had left lame at the coach depot. He could buy provisions for his journey — there were inns where one must starve rather than eat the rubbish provided — and medicaments for anything from saddle sores to stomach disorders. But clothes, when the gendarmerie are seeking a man who would wish to change his maroon coat and fawn breeches for less conspicuous attire—

Geneviève's reply had been to collect from a tailor at Landereau the suit he had just finished for her brother Paul, together with sword and pistol he had ordered at the local gunsmith's with more than self-preservation in mind. These were bundled on the saddle of a hunter from the Lardinière stables which Joseph was now leading.

He asked for news of the ship's company; the tribulations of the Lardinières had been sufficiently reviewed, he felt, while Ned Davy's affairs were as far forward as they could be for the time being. Moreover this was a point Davy had impressed on him to resolve, while there was the additional circumstance that his brother was a member of the crew. Indeed, once the captain was safe in other hands he must rejoin him, and the sooner La Manche separated them from these Breton lanes the better. Geneviève had heard nothing. Her father would have mentioned it had the Cornishmen been taken; he was as avid now to support the Government as he had been to destroy it. Her North French accent was well adapted to express her scorn at this turnabout.

His brother, Jason, was among them, he added.

She looked into his tired eyes, into his youthful face already seamed a little.

'Poor Joseph!' she said softly.

All they had spoken had been of herself and Edouard, and there had been never a thought for their good friend. No, she knew nothing about the Coq d'Or, though of course she had passed it many times. It was not the place for a young lady; none of her friends would speak to her again if she entered those wicked portals. And she laughed.

Joseph and Davy believed it to be a haunt of smugglers. They might well be right, she agreed. There were many bands of *contrebandiers*, but this one she did not know.

They worked in collaboration with the Cornish smugglers, he explained.

Mais oui – of course! The men of La Bretagne and Le Cornouailles were the same people. And if his brother Jason had half the courage and resource of her good Joseph, there was nothing to worry about. She leant across and touched his hand with the tips of her gloved fingers. But she would visit that shocking old tavern and find out everything.

The path through the woods had been trodden by his new horse. It was remarkable, Joseph thought, how a single horseman could leave such a trail in a couple of rides. Perhaps these redskins in the colonies you heard so little about nowadays found tracking easier than one had imagined! The path began behind a bush and meandered through trees so closely packed in their thrust towards the sun that each stirrup touched a tree as one wound through. The afternoon's glory gave place to a green gloom; the air was dank and chill, with a whiff of fungi. Small wonder the local villagers feared the woods as a haunt of demons and hobgoblins! He remarked on this to ma'amselle, who followed at the tail of the horse he was leading. To his consternation she seemed as apprehensive as they. There was nothing for it but to comment on peasant ignorance and assure her that there was not far to go.

In the clearing smoke was wriggling through the lean-to roof. They approached, Joseph hailing Davy and Geneviève shaking up her mount to pass him. A figure appeared at the doorway — and another; large men in uniform. They held pistols and cocked them, the two clicks filling the silence.

'*Démontez!*'

Nothing for it but to dismount. One of them saluted. Ma'amselle, he said, he had not expected. She was a gratifying addition to his bag. He pushed her and Duval into the ox stall. Davy was sitting on the floor, back to the manger. His hands were bound behind his back, and his spread legs almost reached the ashes of the fire that burned dully in the centre. The bandage round his knee had been stripped off, the scab with it, and blood had dried over his thigh. When he saw them an expression of misery masked his face.

'Edouard!' Geneviève went to him but the gendarme pulled her back.

'Good God, that they should get you too!' Davy groaned, struggling violently.

One of the officers laid his pistol on the manger and producing a length of cord attempted to tie Duval's hands, the other covering him with his pistol. On Joseph's resisting, he pressed the muzzle of the gun into Geneviève's neck. She sank to her knees, defeated, her little hands in their riding gauntlets limp in her lap, her head bowed and her hat with its great feather hiding her face.

'Bloody savage! Woman beater!' roared Davy, his words ending in a yell as the man with the cord back-heeled at his knee. The fellow with the pistol turned it again on Joseph. Davy watched, as in a trance, Geneviève reach towards the embers as if to warm her hands. She held them there while another loop loosely encircled Joseph's wrists. And then she was on her feet in a whirl of skirts and ashes. The pistol the gendarme was holding clattered to the floor and went off, the explosion in that confined space like the thunder of a cannon; the man, hands to his face, screamed as the hot ashes seared his eyes. Joseph slipped the cord and grabbed the gun on the manger. His erstwhile captor lunged at him, but a flick of Davy's injured leg tripped him into the fire, further scattering the ashes. The stall was a chaos of coughing and shouting and groaning, stench of burnt gunpowder and smouldering clothing, and unseen movement in the pervading smoke.

The fellow in the fire hurled himself desperately into the open and rolled in the greenery outside. Joseph bounded after him, impeded by the blinded man who had groped to the doorway and now sprawled in the nettles. The other gendarme got up and ran erratically towards the horses, weaving and stumbling, hardly able to see for smoke-induced tears. No more could Duval, nor Geneviève and Davy, whom she was helping out into the fresh air, his hands still bound behind him.

Duval called on the running man to halt, and fired. A miss! His food was in the stirrup of Duval's horse. Duval tugged him to the ground, and though the gendarme was bigger and stronger hit him with the side of his hand in the neck; O'Keenahan's elementary instruction in anatomy had not been wasted. But the blow lacked strength, and the two wrestled together, rolling and clawing in the bracken. The gendarme's fingers closed round Duval's neck, and his thumbs pressed into his windpipe.

But Davy, his hands free now, was charging through the ferns and saplings with a shuffle and a hop. In the rage of the moment he felt neither pain nor restraint. He seized the fellow by the collar, twisted him off Joseph, and felled him with a hook to the jaw. The man lay still in the flattened foliage.

The lean-to was ablaze. Joseph dashed in shortly before the roof fell in to snatch from its hook the bag containing his selections from the St Erne apothecary. Likely enough it was the apothecary who had betrayed them, he thought: his eyes behind the steel spectacles had looked sideways too often. First for Duval's attentions was Ma'amselle Geneviève, the palms of whose hands were blistered: the pain when untying the captain's bonds must have been exquisite. Then there was Davy's wound,

not much the worse for its ill treatment. Lastly came the victim
of Geneviève's hot ash attack. He would not lose his sight, Duval
told him, and would in fact see as well as ever. But he must keep
the bandage round his eyes for a week. These ministrations
would be remembered in Duval's favour, the gendarme
murmured, when he was brought to trial. It would mean the
difference between the gallows and the galleys. Duval shivered.
If the inscrutable laws of chance allowed him to return to
Cornwall, he promised himself, he would qualify as a doctor
and never go to sea again. But it was a big 'if'! He left the two
officers and walked across to Captain Davy and ma'amselle.
They sat in a ring on the trodden bracken.

Davy had lashed their wretched prisoners back to back, and
what to do with them was a problem they must now debate. The
best solution, almost the only solution, was to shoot them. All
three agreed on this. But could you do it? they had asked one
another, and each had declined, horrified at the very notion. So
the gendarmes must be left, securely bound, in the hope of
discovery by any St Erne folk who had remarked their non-
return to the village and could summon up enough courage to
search for them. What more could one do?

'I tell you,' Geneviève said, in English for Davy's benefit. 'We
must look for their horses. These men, they do not walk here,
no? The horses will go home and help will come. If not—' She
shrugged her shoulders.

'I reckon they'll get themselves free by daybreak.' Davy had
tied the knots and should know. 'But oh, Jenny, Jenny my dear,
what is to become of you?' He covered one bandaged hand with
his own, then flung himself away from her. 'God's death! The
demons of this cursed wood must have possessed me, that I
should have brought you into their trap.'

'I think it was not demons, Edouard,' She lowered her eyes, to
raise them, with a swirl of her splendid hair, so that he must face
her again. 'It was love. You called; why should you not? I came;
how could I not; Tell him, Joseph, there was nothing else to do.'

'Better for you, my dear,' said Davy, 'that we had never met.'

'*Fi donc*, Edouard D'Arvi! Why do you say that? We did
meet. We meet again, again and again. *Le bon Dieu* wills it. It
is for always.'

He took her hand, roughly. She winced but held it steady.

'Let us plan our return to Cornwall, then, and you with us, Geneviève D'Arvi née Lardinière.'

'First we must plan our way out of this *corant*,' Joseph said, practical as ever and relieved that an embarrassing interlude was past.

'Well then, Joseph' — it was the captain speaking now — 'let us consider where our present safety lies. At home, ma'amselle will be safe only until the gendarmerie arrive tomorrow morning. You, Joseph, can depend on twelve hours, longer if you return to the stud farm at Landereau. They have cause to forget you, and may do so. For me, if I can find my way to the Coq d'Or — you know the place, *chérie?*' She nodded. 'I'll join my men there or get news of them. But Jenny, where will you go before they knock at your door tomorrow?'

'*Mon père* thinks to marry me to M'sieur le Vicomte de Jarnac. M'sieur will protect me. He is — *puissant.*'

Davy felt his stomach contract at the bare idea. Nevertheless to seek refuge with the Vicomte was the rational solution. 'With me there is nothing but danger,' he made himself say.

'I go with you, Edouard,' she said decisively. 'Perhaps my father will not want me now. He will kick me out.' She laughed as if it were a tremendous joke.

'But M'sieur le Vicomte?'

'I think he will want me still.'

Davy swallowed. 'Then you must go to him..'

'But I do not want the Vicomte. He is fat, and so old.' She laughed again.

Davy was in no mood for jesting. 'You are too precious to me to risk your life.'

That delicious little shrug again, and then she squeezed his hand — and gave a little cry as her blisters hurt, so that he must take her finger tips and press them severally to his lips.

She looked at Duval, who had turned away. 'We shall wait and see what is good for me to do, no! Edouard shall come with me to the château dressed in your clothes — yes, it is too tight, *mais n'importe!* People on the road will think I come back as I go, with my horse man. Clément will take care of everything. You, Joseph, put on Paul's new suit and report to my patron at Landereau. Say you have orders to come to me tomorrow at mid-day. You shall ride through the lanes, not by the road, and enter Brest to the north-west. At the gate there is your only danger, *mon ami*. If stopped, say you are *l'espagnol*. You will wear Paul's sword and look down your nose *comme ça*.' Her mimicry earned a laugh. 'You Cornish are like *les espagnols* sometimes. Le Coq d'Or is round the corner by the tower on the right. *C'est bon, n'est ce pas?* It is a very good plan, no?'

'*C'est bon, chérie*,' Davy agreed. 'And Joseph, at the Coq d'Or tell 'em Smeecher sent you.'

The girl and Ned were holding hands now, she seemingly impervious to the pain that the sailor's grip must cause to her burns. They were lost in each other's gaze. Joseph got up and walked away. 'He is cold, *cher Joseph*,' Geneviève commented, the spell broken.

'Joseph, put on Paul's new suit, you lucky dog,' called Davy. He nodded but said nothing.

'He is jealous. I don't wonder,' Davy said, as Duval went off.

And in fact Joseph was strangely disturbed. Such quick courtship was beyond his experience. Oh, there had been dalliance a-plenty. But this was not dalliance. If it were — he clenched his fists, then shook his head. No, it was altogether different. His father would arrange his marriage, as the eldest son, through French contacts. That had been the lot of all his progenitors. It was a good arrangement; but perhaps they had missed something of value. Perhaps he would miss — but no, there could never be anyone like ma'amselle.

A crash and a smother of smoke. The wall common to cottage and lean-to had collapsed. Buttoning a splendid waistcoat, he strolled across to the ruin, where the dust was settling and the smoke rising, though the flames were gone.

'Captain, sir!' Davy saw him beckoning and joined him there, leaning on Geneviève and she apparently happy that he should do so. 'I wish this day may never end,' she whispered.

Through the parlour floor of the ruin a thicket of bramble and bush had grown a fathom high against the wall that had just fallen into the ox stall. Now the leafless interior of the thicket was exposed. A crumble of mortar trickled and stopped; away over the clearing the blinded man was groaning, but the other was silent. Dust and ashes were a carpet under foot as they stood beside Duval, staring where he stared.

'Good God!' Davy muttered.

There was a shallow pile of rubble from the roof. The hilt of a rusty sword rose from it and the stems of the bramble writhed up through the rubble. Through the rubble and through shreds of clothing and through the skeleton that the sword transfixed.

'Now we know what emptied the woods,' said Duval. 'Mother Nature buried him — no, her — as best she could.'

Geneviève had not moved. Davy turned her away. 'Edouard!' She resisted a moment, to cross herself hurriedly. Then with a convulsive shudder she pressed her face to his chest. He hugged her to him — at last. Arms around her he limped slowly to the further end of the ruin, comforting, uttering endearments he had imbibed at his mother's breast and stored unknowing for twenty-two years against that moment. Now she was responding with like endearments, though in another tongue. Looking up at him. Stroking his hair.

Duval approached the bound men, who in fearful agitation were calling to him. They would die of thirst and starvation if not of exposure. Felix could not get at his eyes, though they were driving him mad. No one would venture to help them; the apothecary had made that plain.

So it was he! thought Duval. But then, was it betrayal to inform on one's country's enemies? Moreover, had not these wretches done their duty too, as they saw it? He would discuss the prisoners with his captain. But no; Davy and ma'amselle were so engrossed, there by the wall that had survived the former burning, that he made his own decision. He moved out of their sight and opened the medicine bag.

They would need to drink before they were left, he told the gendarmes presently, proffering his saddle flask. The blinded man sipped and spat it out. *Nom de diable*, what was this? Piddle or poison? Duval explained that he was a doctor, his purpose to heal and not harm. On his oath the draught would fortify them both through the night, and in the morning succour would come. Ten minutes later he untied their bonds and propped them back to wall.

'Hi, Joe, what's afoot?' Davy had returned to earth.

'They're asleep,' he replied.

Geneviève came up to him while Davy squeezed himself into Duval's discarded coat and breeches — which had once belonged to O'Keenahan, he recalled. She gazed down at the recumbent forms. Noting the empty flask she crossed herself again and remarked, as the officer had, '*Le poison!*' She shivered. 'Three now to walk the woods by night.' The shadows of the western trees stretched long into the clearing, and the rooks were circling the tree tops. She squared her shoulders and lifted her chin. It was for the best, she told Duval. Had they lived, they would have hunted Edouard and her and Joseph too, or set their comrades to do so.

Duval shook his head. The hunt would still be on, he told her. They would wake up eight hours or so later. If they did not wake up, it would be — murder. He spoke in English for Davy's benefit as the captain hobbled up, wincing at every step. He approved. 'Drop this over them,' he said, tossing across his maroon coat

'Their mounts — they are not yet set loose.'

Davy looked at the darkening woods, then to the newly fallen wall, and lastly to the gendarmes, where they sat side by side still and pale as though dead. 'No matter,' he said, and tensing his shoulders clapped his hands together spasmodically, startling the horses and bringing the eyes of his companions on him. 'It's cold,' he said. 'Let's be off.'

They helped him on his horse, and they crouched low in their saddles and rode away.

18

'M'sieur, there is a clergyman demands to see you after dinner,' said the goaler in his academic English. 'Like many of his Order he is a skilled doctor, and will attend to your spiritual and physical needs both.'

'Needs which have another twenty-four hours to run.' Davy's mouth was full; he was still able to savour the roll and fresh wine the French called breakfast. 'A Catholic?'

'Mais oui!'

'Then I won't see him. He will be that Jesuit fellow Doctor Poltaire told me about. Just arrived from Ireland and hasn't stopped stirring up hatred against the English ever since.'

The goaler humped his shoulders. "O − Who 'as better cause than an *Irlandais?* But there, I shall refuse him. I do not like these fanatics. Nor does the Bishop. The curé of St Mullion's had been ill of a most strange flux, and the Bishop had appointed Father Patrice to undertake his duties tomorrow. The Jesuit is a forceful man, and his desire to − to—'

'Gloat?'

'Ah non, m'sieur. But he persuades the bishop that all must see Church and State to be in accord. And it gives the bishop better control, you know, to have him under his command. We do not want a harangue from the − um, ah − from *la tribune*, do we? We want no disorder in Jarnac.'

'My − execution − must proceed peacefully?' Even after a fortnight of accepting the inevitable the word was not easy to frame, less easy still to utter without a tremor, his whole being recoiling. But Davy was not going to let these Frenchmen see him rattled.

'Now, now!' The gaoler of Jarnac was a kindly individual; there were those who said that to be a prisoner in his care was a privilege beyond the deserts of a criminal. 'Let us not − how you say it? − cross our bridges before we come to them.' The key grated in the lock, the bolts were shot, and Davy was alone, that is if one discounted the face of the sentry that continually scowled through the grill. He flung himself on his bed and stared at the cobwebs on the ceiling.

What was it Doctor Sam Johnson had written? 'When a man knows he is to be hanged in a fortnight it concentrates his mind wonderfully.' Davy supposed it did; whenever had the great man been mistaken! But all the rememberings and longings of his own last fortnight were nearer day-dreaming than concentration. Maybe the concentration came in the final hours. He reviewed, as so often these past two weeks, all that had gone before, and could not feel much at fault about anything to do with his being there, in the death cell of the otherwise empty little prison at Jarnac. Since evading capture at St Erne it had all been so orderly; without fuss, as the governor of the goal liked it to be!

Back from the fracas among the ruins, Jenny had herself handed him over to Georges, landlord of the Coq d'Or, with a passing of coins Davy was not supposed to notice. M'sieur Edouard must be given a good bedroom to himself, rather than be hidden in the tunnels as his ship's company had been. A discreet physician must attend to his wounds, and she would visit daily to satisfy herself as to his treatment. Indeed, Davy had arrived in poor shape, with his knee swollen and recovery in the damp underground a doubtful prospect. Georges was a granite-featured ex-matelot lacking an arm which had been shot off by the British, he said, at Lagos Bay. Their commander had been the Cornish Admiral Boscawen, on which account Georges had no liking for the British, be they Saxon or Celt. This he made plain to his guest; also that his membership of a smuggling ring that extended from Brest to St Malo, and dealt exclusively with the Cornish, was maintained solely to provide compensation for the loss of so necessary a limb.

For whatever reason, in the days of the great King Charles V a plague of tunnelling had reduced a considerable proportion of the population of Brest to the condition of moles. After the foundations of dockyard extensions, the Vauban ramparts and recent wharves had been dug, what remained of these tunnels served for the passage of goods and people better not taken openly across the town. They had provided route and shelter for the *Joshua Clegg*'s crew until all, with the exception of the Duvals, were safely at home. This had been information of the greatest relief to Captain Davy. Five English guineas, Georges explained on being pressed, were later paid per head by Mr Trevenning. And how had payment been guaranteed, Davy had wanted to know. No cash, no contraband said Georges. The money had arrived by the next free trader. It was a fair and common arrangement which worked both ways.

Jason Duval, French being literally his mother tongue, had offered to work at the Coq without pay, an offer Georges had no qualms in accepting. Jason would stay until brother Joseph turned up — a likelihood which sadly faded until almost a week later, working in the cellar, he heard his *'M'sieur Smeechère m'envoyait'* above. A few minutes afterwards Joseph was dressing Davy's wound, first pouring down the privy the dubious concoction prescribed by the nearest back-street doctor.

Thereupon Davy surrendered himself to bitter-sweet thoughts of Geneviève, whom he was not, after all, to see since she had left him with Georges those twenty nights ago. Her courage, her concern, her beauty, her love, her conviction that they were for ever one another's — he revelled in them, and mourned them. The massive porter Pierre had roused him on the second night at the Coq to drive him, in twelve hours and with a change of horses, to the small town of Jarnac, three or four miles south of the north coast and west of Treguie. There Davy was lodged in a cottage on the Jarnac estates, whose lord Jenny was to wed, and waited in patience and resignation — until the gendarmes came and arrested him. He was promptly brought to trial, at first as Salomon Venables but afterwards, with all the evidence submitted, as Edouard Davy, and charged as a spy. It had all been quite fair. He had been condemned to death by hanging, and the hour of retribution drew near.

The thought brought him from his bed pacing his cell; five steps up, turn, five steps back as in his daily walk on *Roscoff*'s quarterdeck, but in circumstance no pretence could hide. His knee hurt; but he was shortly to receive that final, infallible remedy for pain, a while more of which could be equably — thankfully — endured. He regretted losing the sea, and the sun, Boswyn and Jenny. How he regretted losing Jenny! And yet he observed in himself, now, what he had so often remarked in battle, that the young with all their days before them were readier to die than the aged with their full quota of years to count over time, time and again like a rosary.

For that last meeting with Lardinière which had introduced the final act of the drama there were no regrets. On his first morning at the Coq d'Or Lardinière himself had been ushered into the room. No, Geneviève had not given him away; it was Clément, whom she had begged to look after Davy should she no longer be there to do so herself, and whose concern for his mistress had outweighed his concern for her friends. By the time Geneviève had determined her course of action, her father already knew where the Cornishman was. She, trusting to the old servant's silence, had refused to reveal Davy's whereabouts, but had otherwise told M. Lardinière the whole story. She had offered to marry the vicomte willingly, on her father and de Jarnac's using their influence to call off the chase and guarantee Davy's safe return to England.

The arrival at the château, sooner than she had expected, of a cavalcade of *gendarmerie, douaniers* and *cuirassiers* had terminated the conference without the deal being clinched. While M'sieur had denied knowledge of either his daughter's or Captain Venables' recent movements, he had struck a different bargain with the officers. He would give them him, or her, within two days, provided they dropped the charge against the other. It was for Davy to decide. Davy had of course insisted that it was he who must be surrendered to justice. It was in keeping with the deviousness of the old man that he should have presented Davy with a choice that was no choice at all. Still, Geneviève was now under no obligation to marry someone she disliked and despised, while there was comfort in this feeling they shared that their love was an enduring presence not to be measured in lifetimes.

That part of the agreement which had really depended on Davy's compliance was his transfer to Jarnac, in his rival's domain. Otherwise not Lardinière, but the *gendarmerie*, would have stood at his bedside. The old man had explained that the trial of the gun-running Captain, as a friend of the rebellion which its leaders had abandoned, could well set it off after all in Brest. But it would not then have been the aristocratic uprising planned − the restoration of power to the *parlement* of nobles.

The common, commercial and professional classes had been well primed; light the fuse now, and in the explosion a lifetime's preparation would be destroyed. But Jarnac though remote was within the sphere of Lardinière's interests, and there the whole affair could be concluded without fuss. It was an expression Davy had come to hate.

The prisoner produced from his pocket two crumpled sheets of paper, both in her handwriting. One was that fateful invitation to dine at the château. The other had been smuggled in four days ago.

> *Bien-aimé,*
> I only now hear where you are. I too am shut up. I am in Treverreau's castle but Pierre will get me out. He has been sent because *mon père* does not trust the gendarmes. I will never marry old Jarnac. I will marry you. Never despair.
> I love you — before, now and always.
>   Gen.

He kissed it, misty-eyed, and prayed that she would not be there to witness his end. It would haunt her all her days.

There were letters to write — to his father and mother; to Dr O'Keenahan; to Mr Knill, the author of his downfall who had yet meant well. Knill must be urged to sell the *Falcon* rather than let her rot. Davy's mind dwelt on the ship he had fought and captured seven months ago — her lines, the falcon on her stem, his plans for her. He thought of Jess, for whom there would be an ample choice of young men to lead her to the altar when she was minded to go. And Jenny! What joy to have taken Jenny to his father and mother as their daughter — the daughter they had always desired! But it was foolish to think of it. And how would she, a Catholic, have got over marrying a Protestant? Well, san-fairy-ann, as sailors used to say who had picked up a smattering of French in their wanderings.

He found himself on his knees. It seemed shabby to pray now when he had prayed so seldom before; litanies indifferently led and indifferently repeated could not count, Still, he felt that God understood; would stand by him in his ordeal.'

Mostly, he walked. But he was growing confused, and a single notion began to persist. He must cease this tramping up and down; they must find him dreamlessly asleep when they came for him in the morning, even though he had not slept all night.

A British captain must at all times appear calm and in control, particularly before his enemies. To this end he lay down, though he would not sleep. Yet sleep he did. He could not bring himself to swallow the travesty of a last breakfast they brought him, but he accepted a bumper of cognac; not enough to make him falter on the steps up, but enough to ensure that what-the-hell-anyway feeling which the comparable excitement of battle stimulated. With some care he donned his captain's jacket that they had released, at his request, from the sequestered brig.

They tied his hands behind him and pushed him into a cart, alone in it except for the driver and a soldier with a musket. Not in quiet, law-abiding Jarnac did several wretches take their last ride together. The populace had not turned out in force to enjoy the spectacle as they did at home. But he must not take it amiss, he gathered from the driver's comments. There was the hell of a fire at the château — all the barns and outbuildings ablaze. Some maniac at large, for certain! And all the country round, being tenants of the vicomte, had to help. M'sieur himself, always good for a laugh with his stays and his plum of a nose, would be missing too, *tant pis!*'

But as they neared the square, trundling over the uneven cobbles, they entered a sea of faces, silent as he appeared, then stirring like the wind on the water with chatter and some shouting. There would be spectators there from the whole region, he supposed. The only execution he had witnessed was at Bodmin, when a notorious highwayman was topped. It had been a triumphant procession to the gallows, with the fellow bowing and exchanging pleasantries with the crowd; a jolly affair altogether, though Davy knew how the victim felt beneath it all. But that was not the way for a British sea captain to go, in the land of his country's enemies. Though perhaps a compassionate glance or a smile from some onlooker might dispel this friendless hopelessness that so chilled him that he feared he would shiver.

He kept his gaze to the fore and his chin high, just as his men had seen him on his quarterdeck in the crisis of battle. Nevertheless some concept about the hundreds of upturned faces registered. How like their Cornish cousins were these Bretons! The dark hair and eyes, the distinctive round faces or the long, swarthy ones from another strain that some people took for Spanish and pointed to as earnest of Armada landings.

There were faces at the edge of vision he could pretend were friends at home; Smeecher, for instance, or Gurt Jan and Barney Polurrian. But he must not let imagination run loose, lest it unman him.

He mounted to the scaffold with sufficient dignity, though it proved far from easy to climb the steep steps when your hands were bound behind you and you limped. But the guard was understanding enough not to give him a shove. There stood the hangman, a horror in black from head to foot, all but his eyes hidden in a mask, and beside him that fanatical priest with his hat tight down over his tonsure; the sort of hat, Davy recalled in an irrelevant flash of memory, Captain Harry was wearing when they kidnapped him. And between them hung the rope, with its obscene knotted throat by which it differed from all other bights in a seaman's world. Davy averted his glance to the edge of the platform. The shako plumes and bayonet tips of a widely spaced ring of soldiers were all he saw in the immediate vicinity. He looked up at the Hôtel de Ville balcony, where sat the Mayor of Jarnac and several worthies, one of whom must be the Intendant of the Province. Davy nodded to them with as much pride as his situation allowed.

The space between town hall and scaffold was occupied by a company whose irregular formation, and individualistic adjustment of hats and crossbelts, proclaimed them to be local labourers and apprentices on parade as militiamen. Davy gazed back over the heads of the crowd as the Mayor got to his feet and read a lengthy rigmarole from a scroll. In front of the buildings surrounding the square were several stalls. He saw the death cart there, while as he looked a farm cart, driven by a large bumpkin with a bonneted wench at his side, moved in closer on the flank of the martial ranks, its clatter winning a glare from His Worship before he recommenced his proclamation.

The troops presented arms with a ragged shuffle. A drum began to roll. 'The hangman slipped the noose over Davy's head and tightened it when his victim speechlessly refused the hood. There was still a patch of blue sky to yearn for. The fanatical Jesuit was close to his side, mumbling and flipping the leaves of his prayer book.

"That scar on your top-knot is mending nicely, Ned me boy-O," he thought in mounting delirium he heard the priest say.

Then he saw, or imagined he saw, a boot appear from beneath the clerical habit and with the flat of its sole shove the executioner in the back, toppling him onto the soldiers. These scuffled round to face the disturbance on the platform only to be overwhelmed by a surge of spectators.

A roar filled the square, a roar that separated into such manifestations of fervour as 'Carter and Cornwall!' 'Roscoffs, Roscoffs!' – a familiar war cry, that. And 'Cap'n Davy, Cap'n Davy, don't 'ee worry, my handsome, we'm come to fetch 'ee home.' 'Davy, Davy, huzzah for Cap'n Davy!'

There were cries in French and Breton and screams, and an uproar that raged like the sea.

The bumpkin stood up in the cart and with a howl lashed his horses into the militia, drawing up alongside the scaffold. The militiamen turned this way and that, and threw down their arms as ruffians with clubs and cutlasses hurtled into them. Grappling irons fastened onto the stonework of the balcony balustrade, and seamen were swarming up the ropes. O'Keenahan deftly sent an empty noose swinging like a pendulum, then skimmed his Breton hat over the seething crowd. Davy caught himself giggling, and suddenly found tears filling his eyes he could not dash away before they were spotted. But now he could; a severed strand hung from each wrist as he clapped his hands to his face. A French officer, more professional that the rest, bounded up the steps with drawn sword.

Big Pierre leapt nimbly across the platform like the champion wrestler he was; kicking the blade out of the man's hand he thrust him backwards, into the arms of Gurt Jan Stona who was attacking from the rear. Gurt Jan swung him to a knot of the Roscoffs below, and with a hand clasp and a grin the giants parted, Pierre to steady the horses, Jan to lift his captain bodily and dump him in the cart with the wench. Pierre cracked his whip, and the cart backed and was away.

Davy's cheeks suffused with shame. This was a fantastic dream. He had swooned on the scaffold, poltroon that he was, and they were bringing him round before carrying out the sentence. Daylight burned through a reddish, perfumed screen. Warm drops splashed on his face. Tears! Not, heaven forbid, his own! Lips were pressing upon his. They brought Davy back to reality and his arms around Jenny, the grip of a drowning man who is saved and cannot let go.

"I shall reform you. You drink too much," said Geneviève. 'You taste of brandy, *mais je t'aime!'*

'It or me?' Davy managed to ask.

'Guess!' she said, sealing off all further irrelevancies.

Pierre stopped the cart as they were about to leave the square, while their escort of smugglers and privateersmen, many of them Davy's shipmates, looked back to see what the huge fellow was shouting and shaking his fist about. Captain Harry Carter had strutted onto the balcony, and was receiving the Mayor's surrender like Morgan at Panama.

'*Voyez!*' Pierre yelled, and in a surprisingly tenor voice uttered a torrent of vituperation that made Davy now sitting against the side of the cart with Geneviève in his embrace – and who cared if half his ship's company could see him then? – ask what he was saying.

'He says he is not joining this – this "deliverance" to give *les anglais* the victory. But what do we care, we *Cornouailles?* I do take my husband's nationality, no?' she added anxiously.

'It's we Cornish, and you do, Cousin Jenny.'

She drew back. 'Cousin?'

'All Cornish girls are Cousin Jennies. We are Cousin Jacks.'

'You are very funny people,' she declared, kissing him.

*

Davy was riding alone along the high road through Tregenna Woods, this second escape being from the wedding preparations at Boswyn and an overwhelming impression that he was in the way. As he jogged in and out of the patterned shadows of the leaves he saw again, as if but yesterday and not a whole month gone, Captain Harry on the poop of his *Shaftesbury* cutter, high sea boots rumpled round his thighs, sash stuck with two pistols and a cutlass, for all the world as if new from buccaneering in the Caribbean. Carter stood with gargantuan boots astraddle and indicated his fleet with a sweep of his arm. From horizon to horizon the Cornish squadron, trimmed to the pace of the slowest, was crossing the Channel on a soldier's

breeze for a Lizard landfall. *Roscoff* was close also, the other
out-sized Carter cutter, *Swallow*, in the van. Half a dozen
luggers and a few smacks, *Dorcas* among them, heeled to the
wind within the horizon's circle.

'I told thee we could do it, Ned lad! Been done afore, and
could be done again, and so, by God's help, it was — as by that
same help we seized you from the altar of Baal.'

'I am eternally grateful that you bore the Lord a hand,' Davy
had said.

'I say again you're weak on theology,' Carter replied, and
laughed. 'You must see he reads a portion of the scriptures
morning and night, ma'am,' he advised Geneviève, who hugged
Davy's arm as though she would never let go. And though this
was for the most part sheer love, Davy joyfully admitted to
himself, he sensed in it a need for protection from the vastness of
ocean and the unaccustomed motion of the ship.

A navy frigate had just sailed through the midst of the
armada, gunports closed, and on hailing *Shaftesbury* as to her
cargo had been answered, 'Captain Davy'. Now she was
receding astern, having passed close enough for her crew to
cheer the hero of the hour, and for her captain to see Davy and
Geneviève together at the break of the poop. He had thereupon
swung into the mizzen shrouds to greet Davy as 'One old Fox
from another,' and demanded an invitation to the wedding. It
had been his former adversary-cum-ally Tom Lewin.

'Yon's the King's ship as stood off when we put to sea,' Carter
declared. '*Daring* is her name. "Dare not", my lads called her.'

Davy had suggested that she knew wherefore and why the
squadron had weighed.

'Couldn't have been kept more secret,' the buccaneer had
growled. 'But you never know—'

To Davy, now ambling past Trecobben Hill on Hector's
comfortable back, every word and every instant of that passage
home remained as fresh as the hours before it were confused —
a period in his life which nature seemed intent on expunging
from memory. Carter had gone on to explain how he had
marshalled his force from the moonshine and letters of marque
men then in port between Falmouth and Portreath. 'You, my
lad, were the bait.' That Smeecher fellow had been of use there.
'"Land in force," I told 'em. "Plenty along the coast t'other side

o' the Channel to welcome you and stuff your holds with everything you belong to sneak in for when the moon's high." Then sparing a thought and a prayer for young Cap'n Ned, who's got himself in a right mess he can't wriggle out of for once, to up all peaceful like to that little town off the coast where they don't know how to treat a Cousin Jack proper.'

On the eve of departure Carter had assembled his captains at the Dolphin in Penzance and briefed them from a plan received that day from Joseph Duval at Jarnac.

'You have a gift for arousing loyalty, captain,' Carter had commented when telling the tale to Davy, there on the poop. 'Duval yonder — he was the king-pin of arrangements t'other side o' the Channel.'

'First he hid in le Coq d'Or,' Jenny interposed. 'He could not help if he were at your trial.' She could hardly bring herself to frame the word. 'Hippolyte — *le Vicomte* — he told me everything. I think he liked telling. How they questioned you. The things they said. Horrible!' She had clung more tightly and pressed her face to his shoulder.

Davy had said that the Lardinière horse-doctor would have been recognised as Joseph and brought to witness, and they would never have let him go.

'He stayed alive to help you, Edouard.'

'I know.' Davy put his arm around her, abandoning the restraint he had built around himself for so long.

"Tis a good yarn about that curé of St Mullion's,' boomed Captain Harry. It was his story and he was going to tell it. After the trial was over, ma'amselle sent for Joseph to work at Jarnac's stables. The curé's anxiety about his own health was a parish joke, and Duval had seen this as a means of gaining a foothold on the scaffold. He established a friendship with the old priest, and at the appropriate hour had got him to take a purge that would shift a mule! Carter's laughter had diverted the helmsman's attention from the great sail and earned a reproof.

From Davy, ambling today down Lelant Church Lane on old Hector, the occasion had been too recent for him to appreciate its humour. A month later it still impressed only as a monumental triumph of planning, and the dearness of friends.

Back in Penzance, on that fateful eve, the privateer and smuggling captains had studied Joseph's sketch of the square at

Jarnac. It detailed how arrangements had been made for the last execution held there, in '79. The Cornishmen for the most part retained enough of the Celtic tongue to mingle with the inhabitants as strangers from Tregastel or Paimpol, come to enjoy the spectacle — 'begging your pardon, my young turtle doves'. Each ship's company had preselected a position in the square, and would reveal themselves only at a signal from the scaffold.

'Left it a little late!' Davy had observed.

Well, he must not blame the lads for that. Dr O'Whatsisname over there in the waist with Joseph had explained that the general attack must start when everyone's attention was on the performance; like them conjurors who do their tricks when they've got all eyes fixed somewhere else. Then there would be no opposition a couple of hundred privateersmen couldn't deal with.

The doctor had come over with Smeecher in *Dorcas* to a mate of that old rascal's on the coast, and with Joseph had finalised the Breton arrangements while Captain Harry organised his campaign at home. 'I was on my knees day and night that the wind should blow fair, cap'n. And the good Lord heard me and I took the town and got a thousand gold pieces out of the deal.'

'All for chapels and distribution?' Davy could not resist asking.

Carter grinned. 'Some of it!'

'That blaze at the château?' Davy had wanted to know.

'Your Smeecher again. Diversionary tactic. Got the loyal musclemen otherwise engaged. Set the outbuildings afire as pretty as if he were burning the gorse at Goonhilly. We saw the smoke before we sighted the town.'

Then Carter had put an arm round Davy's shoulders, pulling him aside a little from Geneviève. 'You may think we Carters have paid our debts now. Proper fools we made o' them lobsters after you'd fired that warning rocket, though we'd have been caught napping otherwise. Even brother John agreed, though he aren't exactly your friend for life. But you can count on me, Ned.' The two men's hands clasped firmly, while Davy yet again had sought words to express his gratitude. Carter turned him round and pointed to the *Swallow*, riding easily ahead along the swell which steepens between Ushant and Land's End as it rolls in from the Atlantic.

'Now to business. Yours, captain, whenever you say. Plenty of profit, short trips to sea, long nights ashore between runs, and she's swift and beautiful. What about it for a newly wed young sea-captain?'

Davy, doffing his hat as the Trewinnard coach bumped past in a progress of dust and affluence, reflected on that nightmare in which only Geneviève, and his good friends and countrymen, had seemed real; one of those nightmares where you wake up or you are dead. He shuddered, and then the morning brightened again. There back at Boswyn was Jenny, happy as a sandboy among her new family. His father adored her. She and his mother were so inseparable in their women's world of domesticity and visiting and church work — the Catholic Jenny's marriage to a Protestant making her, Davy thought, a little desperate at times — that there were moments when he felt excluded and even resentful. Sensing this, Jenny would contrive to squeeze his hand wordlessly to assure him that nothing mattered to her but himself. Even Lizzie in the kitchen, who never had no use for they furriners, was yet her devoted slave. And Jenny was proving, in the sweetest possible manner, more than a match for Mrs Pentilly, the frustration of whose earlier aspirations had been forgotten in a resolve to run the whole wedding her way.

Jenny was overjoyed, too, that her father would attend the wedding — for all the world as though a Davy-Lardinière alliance had been from the start a cherished aim. It had something to do, Davy would wager a guinea to a groat, with a deal his prospective father-in-law had in mind between himself and Mr Knill, who was returning to St Ives for the happy event. Well, old Lardinière had squared his daughter's nuptials with his archbishop and was now already at sea with Captain Carter, both transactions doubtless at an exorbitant fee. Overt transit was difficult to arrange in wartime, and impossible after a recent enemy raid. Ancient Tim Chiddick had chased the chickens out of the Davy landau and cleaned it up in readiness to drive Jenny and himself to meet the old man at Marazion. It would be a quid pro quo, Davy grinned, for the contraption sent for Captain Venables at Brest.

If only, Davy mused, jogging through St Erth and touching crop to brim as folk in their doorways greeted him — if only

Jenny and he could have gone off together, as O'Keenahan had proposed, to the doctor's relations in Ballycotton Bay. Captain Harry would have cleared the way for them. As they talked, the two captains, on *Shaftesbury*'s poop at a time when the ocean swell had sent Geneviève below, Harry had offered to marry them there and then, by common law licence, on the deck of his own ship. An attractive, an almost irresistible, proposition. But for Jenny marriage without her church's dispensation would have been a grievous burden growing more intolerable every year, and was not to be thought of. While if he robbed Jenny of the great occasion of her life his mother would never forgive him. The occasion was as much hers as Jenny's. But once the hoo-ha of ceremony and reception was over, a few weeks with the O'Keenahans would be both a relief and an enchantment.

Davy still found it amusing to contrast the doctor's characteristic aplomb with his sheepish confession that during professional calls on his friend's erstwhile amorata, as he chose to express it, he had dallied, and proposed, and even formally requested of her father his daughter's hand. But Mr Porris was still considering the prospect of a medico in the family. It was not what he had in mind for Jess. Perhaps the farmer, or more likely Mrs Porris, was right to weigh the odds, mused Davy. He doubted whether O'Keenahan was yet ready to settle down, as he himself was.

And now his own future must concern him. To run Boswyn while his father still held the reins was unthinkable, though it must remain Jenny's home so long as she was happy there. And what would he do! Those voyages he had planned for *Falcon* — the Caribbean, in a ship sturdy enough to beat off the pirates who still menaced the Main if not as in the days of Morgan and Teach. The Spice Islands; Van Diemens Land — the new Continent Captain Cook claimed to have discovered. There was much reading, much study of commerce and charts to be done.

But what nonsense was this? The *Falcon* lay on a sandbank in the Hayle estuary, soon to disintegrate into a sad relic of no consequence to any but himself. Even if she were still seaworthy the voyages for which she had been built and of which he had dreamed would keep him too long from Jenny. His day was clouding fast. Besides, with peace in the offing there would be no more privateering under letters of marque, no salvation, no prospect of employment for the lovely ship designed for a nobler destiny than trade. Despite the certainty of that further conflict with authority to which he was now so much less inclined, he would have to consider Carter's offer of the *Swallow*.

Indeed, what point was there in proceeding a step further? He would turn about and visit Keeny in his surgery. He would time his homecoming for when the daylight was too dim for threading needles, when Mrs Pentilly must depart to queen it at her husband's and his farm-hands' supper, and when he might have Jenny to himself awhile. He checked, and from the high ground at Mellanear looked down upon the estuary — and looked again. The tide was high and small boats were manoeuvring round the *Falcon*. They had secured ropes from yard to ship. They were heaving up the anchors that held her fore and aft. They were warping her in. Her ribs were not to lie, preserved in the sands, for a future generation to wonder at. He spurred Hector, snorting indignation, downhill to the yard.

John Harvey was in his shack of an office there, a letter before him among the scrolls and diagrams and chippings and instruments on his desk. 'From Mr Knill,' he declared, flipping the letter with grimy fingers. 'Shouldn't wonder if there an't one for you, too.'

Davy's foot was back in its stirrup before Mr Harvey could follow him out. 'Hold hard, cap'n. The post messenger's still in the Hart, I shouldn't wonder. Dry as a wooden god, he said he were, after his hot ride. I give him a shilling to wet his whistle.'

There was indeed a letter, addressed to Captain Ed Davy, MM, of Boswyn, St Ives in the County of Cornwall. With fumbling fingers he broke the wafer that sealed it. It too was from Mr Knill.

Dear Captain Davy,
    Thanks to God etc . . . Your Fortunate Escape . . . your impending Nuptials . . . M. Lardinière and the prospective Conduct of our Business etc. etc. And now to that Mutually Advantageous Association of which I spoke to you.
    Through Influential connexions I have obtained a Commission to continue, in the Southern Ocean, those Remarkable Explorations and Observations inaugurated in recent years by the lately lamented Captain James Cook and Mr now Sir Joseph Banks.

You will appreciate that with the Abandonment of America the Government are now contemplating the Development of New Colonies on the Far Side of the world. To this End I have instructed Mr John Harvey to Overhaul and Out-fit my ship Falcon of Hayle, with as much Dispatch as the Proper Completion of the work will permit. I confide that this will proceed under your close Supervision and Scrutiny.

Wherefore, Sir, I have herewith the Honour to offer you, as from this date and time of writing, and subject to your Immediate Acceptance, Command of my Ship *Falcon* as Captain and Master.

Harvey watched him reading, observed impatience, interest, incredulity moving across features upon which events that had stirred Cornwall had stamped their mark. A woebegone shaking of the head worried him into taking an involuntary step forward. He endured a dragging half minute of mounting anxiety as the set of Davy's mouth and brow hardened into grim resolve. Then every tension snapped in a flash of sheer delight. Harvey relaxed, propping himself against the tall desk and stuffing tobacco into the blackened, broken clay he favoured. Davy was re-reading the final paragraph, his face completely blank.

Suddenly the pioneer shipbuilder found himself seized in a painful grip by the young man – this phlegmatic Captain Davy who even up to the moment of execution had, they said, held his emotions rigidly in check. And this young man had taken leave of his senses and was whirling him around like a dervish, which was no way to treat an honest tradesman, and a master crafts-man at that.

'Gadsoons, cap'n, lay off, do 'ee now! Thou'lt scat my pipe. Gone mad, 'ave 'ee?'

'Listen to this,' crowed Davy, vaulting up onto the desk and perching himself among the scatter there to swing his legs in the bursting exuberance of a fellow of twenty-two. ''The eminent Botanist, the Honourable Sir Walter Raymont, Baronet' (never heard of the chap, Harvey. Did you? Well, the Hon. So-and-So) 'in Association with the Royal Society, of which his friend Sir Joseph is now President, will Finance the aforesaid Expedition, which he estimates as of a Year's duration.' (Two years at least, Mr Harvey.) 'He will require Accommodation for himself and his Staff, and also' (just you hear this, Harvey) 'for his Sister, the Honourable Mistress Amelia Raymont, who will be taking

Passage to Bombay for her Marrriage to an Officer of the East
India Company's Army of the Deccan. This Lady' (and you can
stop looking so damned disapproving, for here it comes, old
lad!) would welcome the companionship during the Voyage of a
Lady of like Youth and Quality.'

Mr Harvey beamed and caught Davy a mighty swipe on the
thigh. 'Gaw 'strewth, Cap'n Davy, if that don't beat all! Your
intended, eh? What do 'ee know!'

'What do 'ee know indeed?' Davy thumped the ship builder
equally mightily between the shoulder blades. 'Now, Mr
Harvey, when do we sail?'